"HELP!" LEE SHOUTED. "SOMEONE HELP ME!"

She pounded the door with her fist and in doing so dropped the key. Panic gripped her. She felt tears streaming down her cheeks.

Suddenly a key scraped in the vault door from the other side. The door opened and Burr called to her. "Lee? Lee...."

Then she was in his arms, pressing her cheek high against his shoulder, her breasts against his chest. Her body was molded to his.

"The lights went out," Lee muttered. "Trapped. Dropped the key. Fire." She couldn't control her shaking.

"Everything's all right," Burr said, his voice calm. "There is no fire."

Embarrassment flooded through her, and she tried to ease away from him. But his hands slowly began to move over the hollows and curves of her body. And then his lips found hers....

AND NOW...

SUPERROMANCES

Worldwide Library is proud to present a
sensational new series of modern love stories—
SUPERROMANCES

Written by masters of the genre, these longer,
sensuous and dramatic novels are truly in keeping
with today's changing life-styles. Full of intriguing
conflicts, the heartaches and delights of true love,
SUPERROMANCES are absorbing stories—
satisfying and sophisticated reading that lovers
of romance fiction have long been waiting for.

SUPERROMANCES

Contemporary love stories for the woman of today!

TREASURE
OF THE
PAT LOUIS HEART

A SUPERROMANCE FROM
WORLDWIDE

TORONTO · LONDON · NEW YORK · SYDNEY

Published March 1982

First printing October 1981
Second printing January 1982

ISBN 0-373-70014-8

CHAPTER ONE

LEE CAMERON WANTED TO IGNORE the knock on her motel-room door. It could be nobody but Raul. All the distant aunts, uncles and cousins had left right after the funeral, hoping to cover many of the miles between Miami and their homes in Atlanta before dark. And what more did she have to say to Raul? She ran her fingers through her golden pixie-cut hair in a nervous mannerism she was barely aware of.

At age twenty-one her brother knew he could do exactly as he pleased and she could do nothing about his activities except pick up the pieces—when there were pieces to pick up. It had been that way all their lives, and Raul's activities usually left plenty of shattered pieces. Yet she had not minded picking them up. She was devoted to her family, and Raul and her mother had been the only family she had.

Her father had been dead for years, and now that her mother was gone, too, Lee was head of the family. To be sure there were only two of them left and she was only four years older than Raul, but her mother had made it clear from her deathbed that Lee was to be in charge. "Promise me, Lee. Promise me you'll look after Raul until he can take care of him-

self.'' How could she refuse? She loved her mother
and she loved Raul. She had promised, and that
promise had given her a new sense of importance, a
sense of being needed at the same time she fought a
pervading loneliness. Perhaps she had been hiding
behind her mother's illness, using it as an excuse to
avoid men. Ever since Ben jilted her three years ago
she had erected a barrier between herself and all men
who might have the power to hurt her.

"Hey, sis, you in there? Open up."

Raul's muted-cello voice matched the soft April
afternoon, and Lee marveled at his ability to get his
way without ever shouting or creating a scene. Sotto
voce, that was Raul—a soldier of fortune trading on
a ready smile and a smooth line. Following the traffic
pattern that had flattened a path in the shag carpeting, Lee crossed the room and opened the door. She
had to look up to Raul. At six foot four he towered
over her by a foot, and where their mother's death
had made her feel diminished, it seemed to have
given Raul a new sense of strength and freedom. Perhaps it was because she was the only person now
standing between him and what he wanted to do.
Was she going to be able to direct that newfound
freedom, to look after Raul as she had promised?

"Aren't you going to invite me in?" Raul asked as
Lee just stood in the doorway eyeing his bare chest
and feet, his frayed cutoffs.

"Of course." She stepped back so he could enter,
squelching her disapproval of his appearance by concentrating on the gasping wheeze of the air conditioner. "Come in."

Raul entered and immediately slumped his muscular frame into a plastic chair as if his backbone were made of boiled spaghetti. He lolled his leonine head against the chair's back, giving Lee a full view of his face—the well-trimmed hair and carefully shaped mustache and beard.

"You don't seem very glad to see me. Were you going out?" He noted her tailored skirt and blouse, her high-heeled sandals, and gave a low wolf whistle of approval. "You'll knock 'em dead, sis. Did anyone ever tell you that honey-colored hair is sexy? Of course it would be sexier if you'd let it grow. But don't worry...you may find a guy who goes for the sea-sprite type."

"I'm not hunting for a guy," Lee sighed, Raul's words making her very conscious of herself. She had a trim well-rounded figure that rated enough male stares and whistles to let her know she appealed to men, yet she knew Raul was merely flattering her in a way that was second nature to him. He traded on his maleness, winning female favors wherever he could. Lee sighed again, feeling a protectiveness toward Raul in spite of her resolution to make him stand on his own two feet.

"No. I'm not going out. But I wasn't expecting company. What more do we have to talk about, Raul? We've covered it all."

"I just want to make one more plea, sis." Raul turned on his melt-a-banker's-heart smile. "Don't tag after me to Key West tomorrow. I've got this neat job with Burrton Adburee II. Don't mess it up for me. Please."

"I don't intend to mess things up for you." Lee perched on the edge of the bed. "But I made a promise to mother. I can't let you go off on this wildest of chases alone. Burrton Adburee II! Treasure diving! He's nothing but a playboy seeking the limelight by destroying the underwater heritage of the citizens of this state." Lee stood and paced. "Besides, you haven't had enough diving experience. It just isn't safe."

Raul let his lids half cover his coffee-colored eyes as he shrugged and gazed at her in an affectionate way calculated to melt her resolve. "I'm a certified diver, Lee."

"As of only last week."

"That was enough for Burr."

"So now it's Burr, is it?" Lee snorted and folded her arms just above her waist, clamping them tightly against her body in a way that made her feel in charge. "He's asking you to risk your life for three dollars an hour. Can't you see the man's trying to exploit you? A sunken galleon! Spanish gold! He baits a hook with sea-chantey glamour and you go for it like a shark scenting blood."

"Would you rather I continued my magic act? I could probably book a one-nighter at the Tropicana and maybe a week's play at the Copario. I was doing all right as an entertainer, you know. But you and mom didn't like that. What do you expect of me?"

Lee scowled, but she had to say what she felt. "I've made my expectations quite clear, Raul. I'd be pleased if you'd earn your business degree at university. I'd like to see you headed for a steady job, a job with a future, not a pie-in-the-sky sort of thing like entertaining or treasure-diving for a person like Burrton Adburee. You can't drift through life forever."

"If you think Burr's such a playboy how come you're willing to work for him? Not that he'll give you a job, of course. Of the two of us, you're the biggest dreamer, Lee."

"I feel confident of getting a job," Lee said.

"Burr isn't going to hire you. Why are you wasting your time going clear down there to beg for a job? Why don't you find a guy and get married? You're a family-type person, and ever since Ben split you've cut yourself off from men, from any chance of a romance that might lead to marriage."

Lee felt her hackles rise. "My personal life is none of your affair."

"It is if it'll distract you from *my* affairs. Dad's been gone five years, Lee. You can't live his dream. I have a feeling his death in that diving accident is the only reason you went into marine archaeology."

"Perhaps you're right in a way. I intend to carry on his crusade to protect our underwater environment. Dad believed that all undersea excavation should be recorded by systematic and scientific methods. I've learned to make such recordings and I intend to use my knowledge and my skill."

"Fine. In the meantime, just leave me alone, okay?"

"I'm going to see Mr. Adburee in the hope of getting a position in a place where I can at least know if you're alive or dead. And I'd like to get a position that will enable me to help protect our environment from greedy moneygrubbers like him. It's high time I left the protective atmosphere of the university and found a position in my chosen career. I realize that jobs in marine archaeology are hard to find."

"Oh, to aspire to such lofty purpose!" Raul clapped his hand over his heart and rolled his eyes toward the ceiling. Then he frowned directly at Lee. "Stay here, sis. I know it must be dullsville just typing up notes for some professor who's having all the fun of treasure diving. And on a wreck that's already been salvaged at that, but—"

"Oh, come off it, Raul." Lee walked to the door and leaned against it. "You know I'm diving, too, but marine archaeology involves more than mere salvage. That's what you don't seem to understand. An underwater wreckage site should be studied carefully so the special relationships between found artifacts can be observed and carefully evaluated."

"I still say Burrton Adburee isn't going to go for the marine archaeology bit. Granted, he has an eye for the ladies and you're one attractive lady." Using both hands Raul shaped a figure eight in the air. "Your model figure, that perfect oval of a face, those high cheekbones accenting your sea-gray eyes—wow! And that subtle plumeria scent you wear can really turn a guy around. You may get to Burr all right, but not in the way you want to. He may ask you to dinner and invite you for some fun and games afterward, but he's not going to let you upset his diving operation with your plumb lines and charts and grids and all that other underwater stuff you work with."

Lee opened the door and stood by it tapping her toe. "Out, Raul. I'm leaving promptly at ten in the morning. If you want to ride down to the keys with me you're welcome. Please be on time."

"Don't hold your breath waiting. I'll hitchhike before I'll ride with you. And if you come nosing around Burr's operation I'll pretend I don't know you. Give me a break, Lee. Leave me alone."

"Have you got enough money to pay your motel bill?" Lee asked. "I think it was a dirty deal for the real-estate agency to make us get out of the house right before the funeral."

"You had the house on the market for six months. You're lucky you sold it when you did. If the lawyer's fees aren't too high we may have some money left over after all the bills are paid."

"That won't be anytime soon," Lee said. "I'll pick up your motel bill this one last time. Then you're on your own."

"There won't be any bill. I'm not staying here."

"There are laws against sleeping on the beach, you know."

"So I've heard. Don't worry, sis. I'm a big boy now. Sometimes I have quite a choice of beds." Raul gave Lee a knowing look as he rose, sauntered from the room, and closed the door quietly behind him.

Lee slept fitfully that night, tossing and turning, dreaming then starting into wakefulness. She had given Professor Hoskin notice that she was quitting two weeks ago. When their mother's condition had worsened and Raul first broke the news that he was going to the keys she had made her decision. Professor Hoskin had taken the news well, telling her that anytime things didn't work out for her she was welcome to return to her old job. He had been impressed with her work as well as her deep interest in the wreckage of the 1739 galleon they had been excavating.

Now alone in the soft darkness Lee felt totally bereft. She had been prepared for her mother's death for weeks, yet the final parting had been a shock. She had faced leaving her job with Professor Hoskin with much reluctance, but with the knowledge that she must find a full-time job. And then there was the promise. A promise was a promise. And a promise to her mother was the most solemn promise of all, wasn't it? Sometimes she was afraid she was using the promise as a crutch, that she was trying to use Raul as a substitute for the husband and children she had always dreamed of caring for.

It was Raul's attitude toward life that completely bothered her. Although he had enrolled as a business major at the university only to please their mother, he had done well. Then one day he had come home and announced he was quitting. Dropping out. The end. Lee couldn't bear seeing him drift his life away. Raul needed direction in his life and someway she must help give it to him. "Promise me, Lee. Promise me."

The next morning Lee dressed in the white slacks and shirt, the brown sandals and belt that set off her golden tan, then she waited until 10:15 before she loaded her few possessions that she hadn't placed in storage into her blue Chevette. She had hoped Raul might appear at the last moment, yet she knew in her heart he wouldn't. To have appeared and accepted a ride would have been to approve of her presence in Key West. He definitely hated her tagging after him.

Lee had only been to the keys on brief vacations, and now she relaxed and enjoyed the drive through the balmy tropical morning. The overseas highway was like a lifeline stretching into the glittering sea southwest of Miami and all the keys clung to it for safety and sustenance. She watched sea gulls soaring and diving like dark kites against a gossamer drift of clouds. There was no traffic this morning and she set the cruise control and relaxed, watching the sea and feeling pleasantly adrift as she left Miami behind her.

She sensed the slower pace of the keys the farther she drove. Lobstermen in skiffs motored leisurely from trap to trap, the sun burning on their bronze skins. Here and there sailboats bobbed on the waves, their sails billowed by the gentle trade wind like sheets on a vertical line. On the catwalks along the bridges fishermen nursed poles and lines as if more interested in basking in the sun than in catching fish.

Lee stopped at Islamorada for coffee and at Marathon for a Coke, half hoping she might see Raul somewhere waiting for a ride. But she didn't. She drove on more slowly, inhaling the salt tang in the breeze that wafted through the car windows and watching the sun glaze silver tips on the endlessly rolling waves.

Sugarloaf Key. Stock Island. Key West, or *Cayo Hueso*, as she had read the early Spanish sailors called it. Lee tried to imagine the island as it must have been when only the Calusa Indians inhabited it, but establishments like Holiday Inn and McDonald's kept intruding on her mental image of the old island.

Where to stay? She would have to settle in somewhere until she obtained an interview with Burrton Adburee. Turning onto Roosevelt Avenue she followed the highway that circled the tiny island like a necklace. Ignoring the shopping centers on her left she gazed at the bay where coral rocks protruded through the surface like gray cushions, attracting gulls and cormorants that used the perches to dry their feathers after a dive into the sea. Farther out Lee saw a maze of waterways studded with mangrove islets. The hue of sun and clouds changed constantly, as if artists were adding and subtracting colors on a watery palette. One moment the sea was blue, then the next moment it was lime green.

As she neared the downtown area traffic increased and Lee gave full attention to cars, mopeds, pedestrians. She knew from a glance that she couldn't afford the posh elegance of the Pier House or the Casa Marina with their uniformed doormen guarding the palm-shaded entryways.

On her second time around the island she turned onto Eaton Street and drove slowly until she saw a sign in the tall window on the first story of a square frame house. Rooms for Rent. Why not? Why not enjoy the exotic setting of an old-island home rather than the commercial sameness of a motel?

Lee parked the Chevette under an almond tree at the curb in front of the house and strolled up a bricked path to the door. By craning her neck she could see a small widow's walk on the roof; then the gleaming white gingerbread decorating the upper and lower porches caught her gaze. So intent was she on studying the old house that she wandered from the path, tripping over a heavy cable and almost falling before she could regain her balance.

"Careful, miss." A slender, dark-haired woman hurried down the porch steps, concern painted on her face like a mask. "The cable, it is a hazard. But it helps hold the house down when the bad winds come."

"Really?" Lee asked, peering at the offending wire. Then she noticed a similar cable leading from the other side of the porch to a stake in the ground.

"Really." The woman nodded. "This house was built in another century, yet it still stands."

"I guess that's proof all right." Lee smiled again at the woman who was not much older than herself, noting her cotton dress and her scarlet apron smudged with flour. "I see I'm interrupting your work."

"Not at all, miss. Can I be of help to you?"

Lee nodded toward the sign in the window. "I

need a room. Just for a night or two, I think. I'm job hunting and my plans are uncertain. Do you rent by the night?"

"During the season I rent only by the month." The woman shrugged. "But the tourists have gone now. I rent whenever I can find a renter. Please come in. I'll show you an upstairs room. Very cool. Catch the sea breeze all day long."

Lee followed the woman to the side of the house where an outdoor stairway led to an upper porch that ringed the second story of the house like a stiff collar. From the porch they stepped into a narrow hallway, then the woman showed her into an airy room with windows on two sides. Lee inhaled the fresh clean smell of the house. Fiber matting covered the pine flooring, rattan chairs with jewel-tone cushions sat on either side of twin-size beds, and a watercolor seascape hung on one pine-paneled wall.

"It's lovely, Mrs.—"

"Gomez. Maria Gomez. Just call me Maria. Let me show you the closet space." Maria hurried to the closet, opened the door and pulled a chain that lighted a bulb dangling from a black cord.

"I'm Lee Cameron, Maria. This room will be fine. May I bring my things up now?"

"Five dollars a night?" Maria said.

"Would you like your money in advance?"

"No. No." Maria shook her head. "Just want you to know the price."

"Five dollars a night is fine, Maria."

Maria took a slim skeleton key from a nail behind

the door and handed it to Lee. "Your key, please."

Lee pocketed the black key and smiled.

"You need help with your things?" Maria asked.

"No, thank you. I'll be fine."

They walked back down the stairs together and Maria smiled as she returned to her kitchen. Lee ran her fingers through her hair, suddenly feeling uneasy at taking a room in a private home, yet liking Maria with all her Spanish friendliness. She carried her two bags upstairs, unpacked slacks, skirts and blouses.

No telephone. She should have thought of that. A motel room would have had a phone. No doubt Maria had one downstairs, but Lee felt a need for privacy. If Burrton Adburee flatly refused to grant her an interview she would be embarrassed to have the Gomez family know all about it.

Lee found the bathroom down the hall from her room, took a bath, then returned to her quarters to freshen up in clean clothes. Yet what did it matter what she wore? Burrton Adburee couldn't see her over the telephone. But she felt better once she was dressed in a blue sheath that not only fitted her like a glove, but also brought out the blue tones in her eyes. Then after slipping on walking sandals she slung her purse over her shoulder, tucked the skeleton key inside it and headed toward Front Street.

Touristy. There was no other word for it. Souvenir shops lined one side of Front Street. Shells...scented candles...T-shirts. And across the street was a sidewalk café where girls in bikinis and boys in swim trunks ate key-lime pie and sipped lemonade. Lee jumped as a miniature tour train tooted its whistle, the driver pointing out the Spanish architecture of the bank as she lectured over her hand-held microphone.

The afternoon sun turned the tiny phone booth near Mallory Dock into a broiling oven. Lee's fingers were slippery with perspiration as she deposited her quarter then pushed the buttons that rang the number listed in the telephone book for Burrton Adburee II. Lee tried to picture him looking up at the sound of her ring, reaching for the phone.

"Dive Boys, Inc.," a silvery voice answered. "Margo King speaking. May I help you?"

Lee gulped. But of course Burrton Adburee would have a secretary. What had she expected! "This is Lee Cameron speaking. I would like to talk with Mr. Adburee, please."

"What is the nature of your business with Mr. Adburee?"

"I'm a marine archaeologist from Miami and I wish to speak to him on business." Lee swallowed with difficulty. Why was she letting a silvery voice unnerve her?

"Hold on a minute and I'll connect you."

Had there been relief in the silvery voice once Lee had stated her business? She could only guess. Surely Burrton Adburee's secretary would have a crush on him, probably was having an affair with him. And certainly she would make it hard for any other female to get through to him. Lee wiped sweat from her forehead and tried to laugh at her wild imaginings. This secretary was probably sixty, having been

selected by Burrton Adburee's current live-in girl
friend. And what did she care? She was not going to
let the glamour that surrounded his name blot out the
fact that this man was a moneygrubber, only interested in the monetary value of ancient Spanish treasure.

"Burr Adburee here, Miss Cameron. May I help
you?"

Burrton Adburee's voice was throaty and sensual.
It reminded Lee of velvet smoking jackets and red
wine and.... Lee found herself leaning closer to the
telephone as if to hear him better. She cleared her
throat, which didn't need clearing.

"Miss Cameron? Do we still have a connection?"
The voice flowed lazily, seductively.

Lee tried for a businesslike tone. "Yes, Mr. Adburee. We do. I am an experienced marine archaeologist and I would like to talk with you in person about
the possibility of working for your treasure salvage
operation."

The line hummed for a moment and Lee felt the
receiver warm and slippery against her ear. What if
he said no? One brief word and her trip would have
been for nothing.

"What sort of work do you have in mind, Miss
Cameron?"

Lee felt her face flushing. Was there a note of suggestiveness in his tone? But no. She was imagining
things. She forced an even brisker tone. "I had in
mind gathering scientific data from the wreck site of
the galleon you claim to have discovered and perhaps
writing a monograph on the subject."

"I'm afraid you'll be disappointed, Miss Cameron. We have failed to discover the galleon hull as yet, and my divers have brought up only a few gold coins and pieces of eight so far."

"Then I've arrived in time." The thought of Burrton Adburee tearing the remains of a galleon from its resting place all but sickened her.

"In time?"

"In time to save the wreck site from oblivion. You see...."

Now the wine-and-velvet vanished from his tone and it was abrasive as sea salt and coral. "Miss Cameron, if you've come here to deter me in my search...."

"I assure you that is not my intention. If you will be so kind as to talk with me in person I'll explain exactly what I think I can do for you."

"Oh, will you now?" The soft sensuous tone returned. "Your offer sounds most intriguing. If you'll be at the dock at Whitehead and Front Street tomorrow morning at eight I'll arrange to speak with you. Is that time okay?"

"Fine. I'll look forward to seeing you."

"Goodbye, Miss Cameron, until tomorrow."

Burrton Adburee's soft seductive voice lingered in Lee's mind long after the click that told her their connection had been broken. "I will explain exactly what I think I can do for you." Why had she chosen such suggestive words? Had it been a reaction to his own sexy voice? She had intended no double meanings. Lee turned from the booth, feeling her small chin rise with her determination and her anger. Consciously she lowered her chin. Raul always said he could tell when he was getting her goat by the tilt of her chin. She did not intend to let Burrton Adburee get her goat—or anything else.

What did it matter what he might have read into her words? She had secured an interview and she would make her position clear enough when the time came. Lee was tempted to walk to the dock right that minute for a glimpse of Adburee's office, but she quashed the temptation although their meeting place was only a block or so away. He might see her. He might guess who she was. And he might remember her when they met the next day and realize his voice had drawn her to him. Tomorrow was quite soon enough to meet this man who had mesmerized Raul and who might hold her own future in his hands. Perhaps his operation would offer her the toehold she needed to start establishing herself in her chosen career.

ALTHOUGH LEE WONDERED about Raul's whereabouts she spent a restful night, but the following morning as she walked through the steamy air to the dock she felt as if someone were tightening a steel band around her chest. Although sleeveless, her avocado-green shirt felt hot and her matching skirt clung to her legs. She wished she could shed her panty hose and sandals and go barefoot, but she knew she must look businesslike at this interview. The wind whispering through the palms seemed to carry warning signals. She was so nervous she could hardly breathe. Why was she letting Burrton Adburee do this to her before she even met him? She inhaled deeply, trying to relax.

An early-morning sleepiness hovered over the dock and Lee thought at first it was deserted, except for the brown pelicans perched on every piling watching her with their wise-grandfather expressions. Strange, there were no offices in the vicinity. None at all. She listened to the lonely sound of waves lapping against the dock, the mocking cry of the gulls. She clamped her jaws shut on her anger. Was this Burrton Adburee's cruel way of telling her he didn't grant interviews to strange women over the telephone? Was he ensconced in some seaside mansion laughing at the thought of her believing she had an interview scheduled with him?

"Miss Cameron?" A bearded man in jeans and T-shirt waved and called to her from a speedboat anchored at the far end of the dock. Barrel-chested... legs like pilings. He walked with a rolling seaman's gait.

"Yes?" Lee studied the man, but she knew immediately he wasn't Mr. Adburee. She had seen Adburee's picture often enough in the society pages to recognize him on sight.

Now the man was walking toward her. Hairy. That was the only word Lee could think of to describe him. Black hair all but covered his face: bangs, sideburns, beard and mustache. His mouth looked like a pink hole in a black fuzzy blanket. He wore a sailfish tattooed on his left forearm.

"I'm Harry Dahm," the man said.

Lee swallowed a smile. A different kind of hairy,

but the connotation was apropos. "But I have an appointment with Mr. Adburee. He was to meet me here at eight o'clock." Who was this man? Would he believe her? Why did she feel so inadequate?

"Perhaps you misunderstood," Harry said. "Miss King and I have instructions to take you in the speedboat to Mr. Adburee's office."

Lee felt that even from a distance Burr Adburee had managed to throw her off-balance. Had he done it perhaps intentionally? "But where is his office? I thought it would be here at the dock."

"Yesterday Mr. Adburee was working from his home office, but today he's at his office aboard the diving boat at the wreck site," Harry said. "It's a little over an hour from here in the *Buccaneer*." He nodded to the speedboat where a sleek young woman with platinum blond hair sat thumbing through a copy of *Vogue*. *Who is this*, Lee wondered. The woman looked perfectly at home in the speedboat and she wore an expression of near boredom.

"If I go out there, how will I get back?"

"I make return trips. Or maybe Mr. Adburee will fly the heli in later. Coming along?"

"Of course." Lee forced bravado into her voice. Why hadn't Burrton Adburee told her the location of his so-called office? She felt uneasy. She was not dressed for a boat ride, but there was no time to change now. She was determined to keep this appointment.

Harry helped Lee into the Chris-Craft and glanced at his other passenger. "Miss Cameron, I'd like you to meet Margo King. Margo's the business manager for Dive Boys, Inc.''

"Glad to know you, Miss Cameron." Margo King scrutinized her as she spoke. "Do sit down." Her voice exuded a salute-and-obey authority as she patted the stern seat beside her, giving Lee little choice in the seating arrangements. "We talked on the phone yesterday, Miss Cameron."

"Call me Lee, please." Hastily Lee destroyed her mental image of Margo King as a senior citizen chosen by Mr. Adburee's girl friend. Her first impression had probably been the correct one—a glamour girl madly in love with her boss.

Margo appeared to be in her early twenties and her figure would have enhanced any garment shown in the fashion magazine she carried. Her lemon-colored shell snugged over her breasts provocatively and she wore a slate gray wraparound skirt that fluttered in the breeze, revealing a shapely knee and thigh. Lee eyed Margo's yellow platform sandals, which had neither backs or straps, and her chunky gold earrings and bracelet. Glamour with a big *G*. Only Margo's stentorian voice seemed at odds with her appearance.

"Mr. Adburee doesn't receive many callers at his shipboard office, Lee. He must consider your business very special." Margo looked Lee over in a way that made her feel exposed and vulnerable, and as if she were intruding into an area Margo had staked as her private territory.

Lee was relieved when Harry started the engine and its roar prevented further talk. For a moment she smelled diesel exhaust, then as Harry eased the craft across the harbor the sea breeze hit her nostrils with its sweetish Gulf-Stream aroma and she felt revived.

The *Buccaneer* hugged the water, and Harry handled it expertly. The hull banged hard against waves only when other boats raised a wake. Margo had covered her sleek pageboy hairdo with a Kelly-green scarf that brought out the green in her eyes, but Lee had come totally unprepared for a boat ride. She felt her short hair slick back against her head like a helmet as she faced into the wind, peering at distant islets almost lost in the blue mist of the morning.

After an hour of feeling the stinging wind against her cheeks, Lee smiled when Harry turned and shouted over his shoulder, "We're almost there." He nodded to his right. "There are the Marquesas Keys in the far distance to the east."

With amazement Lee studied the deep blue channel in which they were traveling. How narrow it must be. Only a few yards to their right a silvery gull swooped gracefully as it searched the water for food. Except for the lone bird and the Marquesas Keys mounding from the sea like low green cushions there was nothing in sight for miles and miles except the cloudless azure sky and shimmering water. Lee felt mesmerized by nature. Then Harry shouted again.

"There she is!"

Lee followed Harry's gaze. At first the diving boat looked like a child's silver bathtub toy bobbing on the waves. Then as they drew closer the aluminum

boat loomed above them, dwarfing them until Lee
herself felt like a toy. She guessed the vessel to be at
least a hundred and fifty feet long and she was surprised to see a silver-colored helicopter perched like a
giant water bug on the topmost deck.

As Harry eased the *Buccaneer* alongside the big
boat Lee saw Burrton Adburee himself, tanned and
rangy, his brooding features darkened by a scowl.
Mid-thirties, she guessed. He wore tight-fitting jeans
that emphasized his flat stomach and narrow hips,
and Lee knew without looking that designer Calvin
Klein's name was stitched on his hip pocket. Unbuttoned to the waist, his white sport shirt revealed an
expanse of virile dark hair as it stretched across his
muscled shoulders. Sexy. No wonder Burr Adburee's
name made the gossip columns so often. No doubt
women vied to see their names linked with his. Lee
turned to look at him, trying not to appear to be staring.

Burrton Adburee was standing on the main deck,
in deep conversation with a boy who could have
passed for Raul had his hair been lighter. Bare chest
and feet...cutoffs...rubber flippers in hand. Clearly the boy was a diver. And clearly he and Burrton
Adburee were at odds. Lee couldn't help overhearing
their words, nor did she try to.

"If you can't follow orders, then you're through."
Adburee's voice grated like sand against slate, hiding the sensual quality Lee knew was there. Surely
this man was aware of the power of his voice to intrigue women. Did he turn its sensuality on and off at
will?

"If I'm through you owe me back pay in cash,"
the boy said. "I can't spend pieces of eight."

"Take it or leave it." Adburee held the coin
toward the boy and reluctantly he pocketed it and
strode into the enclosed cabin that comprised most of
the boat's main deck. Lee felt anger and indignation
clump into a lump in her throat. How unfair! How
dare this man run roughshod over both people and
the environment!

Now moving with a pantherlike grace, Adburee
lowered a boarding ladder to Harry without ac-
knowledging Lee or Margo. He disappeared into the
cabin, leaving Harry to help the women aboard the
big boat. *Sea Deuced.* Lee read the name painted in
bold black script on the boat's stern. Who but Burrton Adburee would have thought of such a name for
his boat!

Once Margo was aboard she hurried to the cabin,
passing Burrton who returned to the deck to watch
Lee come aboard. Lee felt her hands grow damp and
she blushed under his gaze as the wind whipped her
green skirt, revealing calf, knee and thigh. To hold
the skirt down would be to lose her grip on the ladder. Now she felt the wind blowing into the V of her
blouse until it flapped the fabric, first pasting it to
her breasts, then releasing it, only to repeat the former action. Lee felt Burrton Adburee's gaze like a
hot invading touch.

"Welcome aboard, Miss Cameron." A sardonic
smile played on his lips.

"Thank you." Lee awkwardly stepped aboard
ship, aware that Burrton Adburee had deliberately

refrained from touching her, although a steadying hand would have been welcome. Lee tried not to stare, yet she knew she was staring. Burrton Adburee's dark hair lay in crisp waves and his sideburns extended just below his earlobes. Heavy brows hooded his eyes so Lee couldn't see them clearly. Deep lines ran from his blade-straight nose to the corners of his mouth and his broad forehead was furrowed, making Lee want to touch it, to smooth the creases away.

She scowled, trying to banish the last thought. She wanted nothing to do with this man other than to work for him.

"I said I'll see you now in my office." Burrton Adburee spoke in a tone that warned Lee he was repeating his words, yet the sexy, deeply provocative quality was there. Deliberately there?

"Of course, Mr. Adburee. I didn't mean to keep you waiting."

"I assure you I never mind waiting for lovely ladies like yourself. But I know you're a busy person, so let's get on with whatever it is that's brought you here to see me."

Burrton Adburee looked directly at Lee and she felt his animal magnetism as she followed him from the open deck into the large cabin, then on to a smaller cubicle that served as his office.

Now she could see that Burrton's eyes were like black velvet sponges, absorbing much but revealing little. His strong square chin balanced his broad forehead and although his nose was thin and straight, his lips were full and sensuous. If he had been wearing a bandana headband and a gold hoop in his earlobe he could have passed for a pirate, ruthless and demanding yet with a touch of elegance. Had this office smelled like sandalwood before he entered or had he carried the scent inside on his person?

"Miss Cameron? You did have *business* to discuss with me, did you not?"

Lee felt herself flushing. Burr Adburee's eyes were like warm hands touching her face, her throat, her breasts, then roving all over her body. Her heart pounded. Why was she behaving like a schoolgirl under a spell? She cleared her throat. "I've come here to offer Dive Boys my services as a marine archaeologist."

CHAPTER TWO

LEE WAS SURPRISED at the decor of Burrton Adburee's private office, yet she realized that she shouldn't have been. It matched the man who worked in it. Instead of being as utilitarian as the *Sea Deuced* itself seemed to be, the office bore its owner's mark of casual elegance: polished walnut desk, leather-bound chairs, sea-green carpeting. Lee basked in air-conditioned comfort as she noted the gold-framed photographs of a man who looked surprisingly like Burrton Adburee himself. A brother, she wondered. The series of photos was mounted on a tall privacy screen that hid part of the room. And there were more photos of the same man on the desk and on the bulkhead to her right. For a moment Lee had the eerie feeling that she was in some sort of a shrine.

Burrton Adburee piqued her curiosity, and although she told herself her only interest in him concerned business, she wanted to know more about him. His gaze had followed hers to the collection of photographs and now as she looked back at him his gaze suddenly seemed somber and thoughtful and he blinked rapidly as he glanced away. Had his eyes misted? She felt sure they had.

"Do have a chair, Miss Cameron." With eyelids still lowered, Burrton Adburee nodded to the seat across from his desk and Lee sat down. "Please tell me exactly what you think you as a marine archaeologist can do for Dive Boys."

Lee felt more at ease as Mr. Adburee's eyes cleared and his manner became totally businesslike. "I can give scholarly credibility to your search, Mr. Adburee. I can help make sure the artifacts your divers bring up are of historic and educational value."

"In what way?" With elbows on his desk Burrton Adburee placed his fingertips together in a steeple formation that Lee found overbearing and disconcerting, yet he was still all business.

"Archaeology embodies more than a mere salvage operation, Mr. Adburee. Once divers excavate any site, that site is destroyed forever as far as historians are concerned. But if an archaeologist excavates a site scientifically the world not only can enjoy the artifacts that are found, but it also benefits from the archaeological records and from the monographs that may be published. In future years other scientists can judge the archaeologist's interpretations and conclusions. Only by this means can the results of your salvage operation become a new paragraph or page in history."

Burrton Adburee leaned forward, and although his penetrating gaze never left Lee's face, she saw the sardonic smile that curled his lips. Was he going to laugh at her? If he made fun of the ideals and goals her father had lived for, the ideals and goals she her-

self held dear. . . . Lee forced herself to wait until he
spoke.

"I'm impressed with your ideas, Miss Cameron.
Do tell me more. I'm caught up in this search for the
Santa Isabella. Fascinated by it. It would please me
to share the romance of the quest with other interested persons."

Lee exhaled slowly, feeling a mingling of relief and
hope. She had expected derision from this man. Perhaps she had misjudged him. "I could help you keep
an accurate record of each artifact your divers salvage. There are charts and forms for recording such
information. I could issue scientific memos to envi-
ronmentalists concerning this underwater heritage."

Again Adburee leaned forward. "That interests
me. Surely such scholarly memos might spark more
investor interest, generate more money to be used in
continuing the search for the *Isabella*."

Lee forced herself to hold back words she might
regret. She felt disappointed and angry because her
first assessment of this man had been right. He was
only concerned with the rising price of gold and silver
and with the riches his divers might find. If he hired
her it would only be to aggrandize his own fortune.
Her thoughts churned with hostility.

"Where did you get your original information on
this wreck?" Lee asked when she was able to smooth
the anger from her voice.

"An old college buddy found some lines scratched
in a diary that belonged to one of his ancestral great-
grandmothers. The diary was written in 1640 and in
ancient Spanish, of course. My pal knew little other

than the name of the galleon, the year of its sinking and the approximate location."

"Three very important things to know, I'd say." Lee fought to keep sarcasm and anger from her voice.

"He sent me the information a couple years ago rather as a joke, yet demanding half-interest in anything I might find."

"Why did you wait two years before starting your quest?" Lee asked.

Burrton Adburee looked at her sharply and scowled. "I had my reasons, Miss Cameron. Personal reasons."

Lee squirmed, sensing that she had accidentally pried into a private matter. Hastily she changed the subject. "You've had previous salvaging experience?"

"My great-great-grandfather was a wrecking captain both in the Bahamas and Key West back in the 1800s, so the idea of salvaging wrecked ships isn't new to the Adburee family."

"You're sure the wreck you've found is the *Santa Isabella*?" Lee tried to puncture his complacency to salve her own anger, yet she felt helpless in the face of his evident self-assurance.

"How can one be positive about an event that happened centuries ago?" Adburee shrugged as if to say only a fool would expect such knowledge from him, and his voice took on a slow sensuous quality that hinted that he would rather be discussing other matters.

"If you had a copy of the galleon's manifest it

would help." Lee snapped the words, feeling a need to keep her voice in sharp contrast with his.

"Are you serious?" Again the sardonic smile played on his lips. "Where would I get such a document? You're forgetting that the galleon went down over three hundred years ago."

"And perhaps you're forgetting that the treasure ships were big business in Spain at that time." Lee could not resist displaying some of her hard-earned knowledge for this dilettante. "Spain's House of Trade kept accurate records of everything that was loaded aboard her galleons. Then, as now, money was king. At Cartagena the galleons gorged on treasure that they carried back to Spain. Wealth flowed to Madrid in seemingly endless amounts."

"I'm impressed with your knowledge, Miss Cameron, but where are these records—these ships' manifests—today? I can't believe they still exist."

Lee felt herself blushing as she realized Burrton Adburee knew she was trying to impress him. But he had posed another question and she had at least a partial answer. Yes, she wanted to impress him.

"It's my guess that the *Santa Isabella*'s registry is lying in a bundle of papers on some almost forgotten shelf in the Archive of the Indies in Seville. At the time the *Santa Isabella* sailed, it was the custom of the House of Trade to order four copies made of a ship's registry. The ship itself would have carried one copy. The fleet's flagship and vice-flagship would have carried copies two and three. And the fourth copy would have been sent out the following year on the next fleet. Those Spanish officials knew that ten percent of their galleons would be lost at sea, but they tried to make sure at least one copy of each ship's registry would survive."

"You seem to know your subject well, Miss Cameron. But I'm interested in gold bars and pieces of eight, not in musty documents rotting away in Seville."

Again Adburee's voice grew low and slow, and such a sensuous quality crept into it that Lee could imagine his slim tanned fingers caressing doubloons, his strong hands cupping ancient pieces of eight. She felt his disdain for anyone interested in 'musty documents'. Again she tried to puncture his complacency.

"I don't understand how you were able to locate the *Santa Isabella*, if the galleon you've found *is* the *Isabella*. You have no proof, you know."

"If I hired you, then it would be up to you to find the proof, right?" A taunting quality tinged the sensual tones.

"Possibly." Lee found Burr Adburee's voice hypnotic. She had to fight a temptation to let her own voice go as low and throaty as his. "But since you have nothing more than diary information to go on, scholarly proof might have to come from Seville. I do speak Spanish, and I've had some experience in reading documents from ancient Spain. Professor Hoskin let me study a copy of the manifest from the 1739 ship we were excavating last summer. Of course, regardless of whether or not you have the *Isabella*'s manifest, any artifacts you uncover can be, and should be, recorded. But tell me, how did you locate this wreckage?"

"Margo and I used a portable magnetometer, dragging it persistently behind the *Buccaneer* as she traveled back and forth across miles and miles of these waters."

Lee felt sure that anything Burrton Adburee did would have been done persistently, everything including impressing any female companions. "I see. The magnetometer detected metal objects beneath the sea and recorded readings on graph paper, right?"

"Right. Margo operated the boat at high speed to keep the mag head from hitting bottom. The water depths in this area vary greatly from very deep to very shallow. Have you ever worked with a magnetometer?"

"No, I haven't." Again Lee kept her voice crisp in contrast to his. "But I have dived on a sunken galleon. My work was under the direction of Professor Hoskin at the university. He's still recording findings on this wreck—the *Santa Catalina*. But that galleon sank in very shallow water. Some fishermen located it when they were checking their lobster traps. Parts had been salvaged earlier, probably by the Spaniards themselves. Professor Hoskin was making a scholarly study of the ship's hull, its fittings."

"Margo King helped me with the magging for the *Santa Isabella*," Burr continued smoothly, seemingly uninterested in Professor Hoskin's endeavors. "Margo guided the *Buccaneer* on course. I watched the tape threading from the magnetometer box. Whenever the instrument recorded an anomaly I tossed a buoy over the side to mark the spot. Margo would stop the boat and I would strip and free-dive on the site.''

Lee felt herself flush as she imagined Burr diving nude into the sea, his slim taut body gliding into the cool depths. And what of Margo? Lee could not imagine Margo shyly turning her head on the scene. "Such diving must have been fascinating.''

"Right. It was exciting work. But sometimes it was very disappointing. We would find we were diving on discarded oil drums, lead pipe, even pieces of downed aircraft. Then one afternoon all our search paid off. The mag gave a strong reading and I went over the side.''

Lee leaned forward. She didn't know if it was Adburee's voice or whether it was the tale he was revealing, but she was as caught up in listening to his story as he was caught up in the telling. And now his dark eyes captivated her, burning with amber lights like fire against smoke. He spoke slowly, as if he could sense her desire for him to hurry and was deliberately making her wait, deliberately teasing her sensibilities.

"The sun was shining and the water was clear at the surface. But as I went deeper the light diminished to a murky green. I was about to surface, thinking that whatever the mag had reacted to must be buried deep under the sand. Then I saw it.'' Burr paused dramatically. "At first it looked like an encrusted log. Or a piece of pipe. Then I realized I was looking at an iron cannon.''

"Where is it now?'' Lee wished she could concentrate on Adburee's words without being distracted by his eyes.

"The cannon's still down there. I wasn't sure what would happen to it if we hauled it up. I was afraid it might disintegrate."

"That's doubtful. But sometimes it's good to keep artifacts awash in seawater for a time." She was glad Adburee had shown some concern over the safety of the cannon.

"Well, it's still there. We use it to mark the wreck site. As soon as we made the discovery I bought this old fishing boat, outfitted it as a diving boat and anchored it above that site."

"I'm glad the cannon's still submerged," Lee said. "If you hire me I'll use it as a marker when I project coordinates and elevations."

"I'm not eager to have anyone on the dive scene who might slow down the work of my men." Burr's voice grew businesslike and the grating sandy quality he had used with the diver returned to it.

Lee vowed to meet his grittiness with a grittiness of her own. "I would try not to slow down your operation, but time must be allowed for careful work. Archaeological excavation is a painstaking and difficult job."

Slowly Adburee tilted back in his chair and studied Lee from under hooded lids. "It has been my experience that all professionals tend to overestimate the difficulty of the work they perform. Perhaps they do this to justify mistakes, perhaps to frighten away competition."

What arrogance! Lee felt anger flood through her

body like a surge of heat at Burrton Adburee's implied insult. She refused to let him put her or her profession down. "Nobody is immune to mistakes, Mr. Adburee. And I doubt that you've had too many marine archaeologists seeking out your operation."

"I like a lady with spunk, Miss Cameron." Again the sardonic smile played on his lips and now he looked Lee up and down, his smoky eyes resting on the V of her neckline, her waist, her legs in a way that told her he was admiring more than her spunk. "Tell me, why does my operation and the salvaging of the *Santa Isabella* interest you? Why are you willing to leave a documented wreck and the opportunity to work with a scholar for the dubious chance to work on an undocumented wreck with a person who is interested mainly in the monetary value of the galleon's cargo and the physical adventure of the search?"

Lee stared at Adburee until his eyes stopped exploring and his gaze met hers, but she hesitated before answering. She certainly couldn't reveal her need to keep her deathbed promise to her mother. Adburee seemed like the type who would be unimpressed by promises of any sort. Nor could she bring herself to reveal her relationship to her father and his work, or to Raul. She would disturb Raul's life as little as possible. Again she tried to sound brisk and scholarly.

"I'm a scientist eager to find a career opportunity, Mr. Adburee. I don't believe anyone has the right to destroy sites of historical importance. The underwater wrecks in the keys belong to the people of Florida. It is their heritage and I want to see it protected.''

"Your wreck up the coast may belong to the people of Florida, but my wreck site is in international waters. It's a finders-keepers situation.''

"If the wreck is in international waters it is the heritage of mankind and I still want to see it protected. I certainly haven't come here to take anything from you. I merely want to establish myself in my field and to give scholarly credibility to your endeavor.'' Lee inhaled deeply, seeking the strength and courage to deliver her next line. "I would like to go to work for Dive Boys tomorrow.''

Burrton Adburee grinned at her in a maddening way. "That's laying it on the line, Miss Cameron. I like a woman who knows what she wants. I'll consider your application and give you my decision tomorrow. Will that be satisfactory?''

Lee felt the buildup of hope inside her dissipate like frost in the sunshine. She had hoped for an immediate affirmative decision, but in spite of his slow soft voice there was a hardness in Adburee, like the hardness in a coral reef. Perhaps that hardness protected his ego. She knew she dared not pressure him. The next move was his; she must wait for his decision.

"Would you like a tour of the diving boat, Miss Cameron?''

"Thank you, sir. I would.'' Lee's heart pounded at her temples. Surely Adburee wouldn't take the time to show her the boat if he didn't intend to hire her.

Or would he? The amber fire flickered in his eyes again.

"Then come with me." He held her gaze an instant longer, giving special emphasis to the four words, then he led the way to the boat's large enclosed cabin. In one end there was a galley with stove, refrigerator, freezer and a bar with high stools. She guessed this was where the crew and the divers ate. Lee felt irritated with herself for admiring Burrton Adburee's graceful walk, the pantherlike way he moved and carried himself.

"This is the general-purpose area," Burrton explained. "We eat here. The divers take turns cooking. Sometimes I cook them a gourmet meal if they bring up lobster. This is also my men's recreation area. Sometimes they live on this boat for a week or ten days at a time before they go ashore and a relief crew arrives."

Lee noticed books and playing cards and poker chips lying like a child's discarded toys on one table while copies of girlie magazines lay scattered on another table. Her heels clicked against aluminum as she followed Adburee down a companionway leading into the hull. Here the air was rank and smelled slightly fishy and it had a hot stuffiness that made sweat ooze on her upper lip.

"Please watch your step, Miss Cameron. Please hold the handrail. These are the divers' living quarters down here." He eased through a maze of unmade canvas cots, the sheets gray with grime. Foot lockers. . . duffel bags. They stepped over the squalid clutter until they reached a small doorway. Opening the door Burrton stood back so Lee could look inside.

"These are Margo's quarters when she stays aboard overnight."

"Oh?" Lee spoke without trying to keep the surprise from her voice. Was Burrton Adburee weighing her reaction to this information? She bit back quick questions. How often did Margo spend the night here? And why? The roll of the boat seemed more pronounced down here and Lee clutched at a bulkhead as a wave of dizziness made her unsteady. Would she be expected to sleep in similar quarters? How often? Burr cupped his hand under her elbow to steady her and she felt as if an electric current shot up her arm. She wanted to pull away, but the current held her.

"It isn't always possible to go back to Key West every night," Burr said, as if reading her mind and silently laughing at her. "Sometimes the work or the weather holds us out here at the site. I have a cot and a wardrobe in my office."

Lee remembered the privacy screen she had noticed earlier, but she carefully avoided imagining Burr Adburee in bed. "You seem to have thought of everything."

"I hope so." He guided her back to the companionway. "The sea allows man a few errors, but no mistakes."

Playboy...wastrel...manipulator, Lee described Burr Adburee in her mind. But why? He was nothing to her...yet. And even if he became her employer she must not allow herself to....

As they climbed back to the deck cabin Lee was startled to see Raul at the galley bar drinking coffee.

"Miss Cameron, I'd like you to meet a new diver, Raul Johnson. Raul joined us just yesterday."

For the first time Lee noted a cruel curve in Adburee's upper lip as he performed the introduction. She held her face in a firm mask of politeness as she nodded to her brother as if he were a stranger. "I'm pleased to know you, Raul."

"Pleased to meet you, ma'am."

An alias. For a moment Lee felt hurt, but she forced a smile. So this was the way Raul had chosen to keep their relationship a secret. Inwardly she fumed at Burrton Adburee, not at Raul. This showed her exactly how shallow Adburee was. This showed her just how little he valued his dive boys—not even enough to ask for their credentials or to check thoroughly into their backgrounds. Raul could be working with a gang of murderers for all Burr Adburee knew or cared. She would have to guard Raul against his boss.

"Now if you'll come to the stern, I'd like to show you the deflectors, Miss Cameron." Adburee strolled to the stern and pointed out the huge metal ducts that had been snugged over the boat's propellers. "They fit like sleeves in a shirt, don't they?"

Lee smiled in spite of herself, noting Burr's little-boy pride in the strange deflectors. "Yes. But what is their function?"

"I'm sure your Professor Hoskin didn't need such equipment to find his shallow-water wreck. But I use these deflectors to blast a column of clear water to the sea bottom and to dig away the sand in a manner that helps my divers discover any buried treasure. Thanks to this invention the divers can see clearly at great depths. Perhaps someday you can come aboard as my guest and watch our operation. You do dive in deep water, right?''

''Of course. I'm a certified diver and I find the ocean depths fascinating.'' Again Lee felt sharp dismay. She didn't want to come aboard as a ''sometime'' guest. She wanted to come aboard tomorrow as an employee.

''Diving doesn't frighten you?'' Burr looked at Lee in a way that made her feel as if he were looking directly into her soul. Diving with Burr Adburee could frighten any girl, she thought, trying not to picture herself gliding through the satin-smooth depths with this man at her side. She looked away. ''As a diver I have a healthy respect for the sea and for the creatures in it, but I'm not afraid.'' She shied away from the intimacy of his eyes as he touched her with his gaze.

''Spunky.'' Burr whispered the word. ''I told you I like my women spunky.''

''I am not your woman, Mr. Adburee.'' Lee sensed that Raul had followed them and was grinning at her discomfort. She felt like stamping her foot and she knew she was blushing. ''I've only come here to apply for a job.''

Burrton looked at her knowingly. ''You mean you've come here to *create* a job for yourself. Very innovative of you, I must say, but I didn't advertise for help.''

Was this man hinting that she was chasing him? Had he been trying to lead her on with his come-hither voice? Her anger flared and she controlled it only with great effort. "You've granted me a job interview, so you must have a feeling that archaeological assistance might be in the best interest of everyone concerned with the salvaging of the *Santa Isabella.*"

Burr Adburee turned from the duct-covered props and ignored Lee's last comment. "Would you like to see the loot we've hauled up so far?"

"If you're referring to the artifacts from the *Isabella*, yes. I'd be delighted to have a look at them." Lee clipped her words, pretending her voice was a pair of scissors neatly snipping one word from the next.

"The artifacts." Burr winked at her. "I'll try to remember the term, Miss Cameron. We've only found bits and scraps of treasure so far, but when we locate the big heap, the sight of all that loot may make even you forget scientific terms."

Lee's heart leaped. He was assuming she would be present for the big discovery, wasn't he? Or did he have something else in mind? Surely he meant to offer her a job. It required great restraint to keep her voice calm.

"By the 'big heap' I presume you mean the primary cultural deposit."

Adburee chuckled. "Have it your way, ma'am. The big heap. . . the primary cultural deposit. It's all the same thing—gold."

"It may be silver, you know. The mines at Potosi

in Bolivia produced considerable amounts of silver at one time and the Spaniards took over those mines when they conquered the New World.''

"We've found a little of each at this point.'' Now Adburee led the way into a small cubicle next to his own office where Margo King was bent over ledgers. Margo stood as they entered her domain and when she spoke her voice was low and soft. Gone was the stentorian bossiness Lee had noted earlier.

"Can I be of help, Burr?'' Margo looked up at her boss, deliberately easing herself to his side so that her supple, rounded figure contrasted with his lean tautness.

"I don't want to disturb your work, Margo. I'm just going to open the safe and show Miss Cameron some of the. . . loot.''

"Do you think that wise?'' Margo gave Lee a disparaging glance. "The fewer people who know exactly what we have salvaged. . . .''

"Miss Cameron is a scholar, Margo. I'm sure she has only a scholarly interest in the. . . artifacts.''

Lee felt like an intruder as she sensed Margo's possessiveness where her boss was concerned. Margo used the word "we" like a string tying the two of them together. Surely Margo King was Burr's current girl friend. Live-in? Lee shelved that question. King was as old and respected a name in the keys as Adburee, and Margo flaunted the glamour that Burr Adburee was rumored to seek.

Now Burr pulled two chairs near the safe that crouched like a black monster in the corner, and motioning to Lee to take one, he took the other. For a

moment he looked at her in a way that made her feel
that she was the only woman in his world. But how
crazy! Margo was only a few feet away. Burr's
tanned fingers turned the safe's dial quickly and surely and he seemed to pay no attention to whether or
not Lee was watching. When he opened the heavy
steel door she inhaled the metallic smell that wafted
from the safe—a smell so strong it left a bitter taste
on the back of her tongue.

Lee was surprised to see so many artifacts lying on
the green felt of the safe's interior. News stories had
carried pictures of certain finds by other treasure
hunters, but surely Adburee had kept much of his
salvage operation a secret. Lee could only wonder
why he was showing the things to her. Was he trying
to impress her? He knew she was eager to work for
him. Was he trying to impress her for other reasons?
For a moment Lee felt flattered, then she quashed
those feelings. Burr Adburee might be physically attractive, but his thoughts and ideals were sordid to
her thinking.

"Have you ever held a gold bar from ancient
Spain?" Burr picked up a thin gold rectangle and
hefted it on his palm.

Lee shook her head. "No, I haven't." She felt a
pulse pound at her temple.

"Then do." He dropped the gold finger bar into
her hand and pointed to the indentations on it. "You
can see on this side the mark of the conquistadores
and the tax indentation that shows that the king of
Spain had received his fifth of the total value." Burrton turned the bar over and Lee was careful that their

fingers didn't touch. "On this side of the bar you see the cross of Christianity." Burr outlined the cross with his slim finger. "These gold bars were as two-faced as Spain herself as she proclaimed a religion of love at the same time as she sent conquistadores such as the crew of the *Santa Isabella* to loot and murder in the New World."

Lee felt awestruck. The touch of the gold and the virile vibrancy of Burr Adburee's voice held her transfixed. Yet, she was aware that much of the Spanish riches had been bought with human blood. Much of it came to the crown in payment for slaves, and the Spaniards had literally worked the native Indians to death in the Colombian silver mines, digging riches for the king back in Spain. But she mentioned none of this. Clearly this man was totally uninterested in the human tragedy that lay behind the wreckage of any of the galleons. Could she enjoy working for a man like this?

"Those silver coins." Lee pointed. "Pieces of eight?"

"Right." Burr picked up an irregularly shaped coin. "Can't explain its strange shape. But I've checked it out. It's a piece of eight."

"Its shape is irregular because silver was measured by the troy ounce in ancient times—as it still is today—and a person buying something might cut his coin or shave off the correct amount of silver needed for payment." Lee welcomed the chance to play scholar again. It helped conquer the sense of awe Burr Adburee had aroused in her. "Many coins salvaged from the sea bear no dates because the date was usually stamped around the outer rim, which was the first part of the coin to be shaved off.''

A half smile curled Adburee's lips. ''Miss Cameron, you needn't continue to try to impress me with your knowledge. You made your point in my office. Right now I'd like you to enjoy my artifacts.''

Lee squelched her anger at this man's ability to see through her motives. She had been trying to impress him again. But why? To get a job? Yes. But down deep she had to admit that Burr Adburee attracted her physically, if not mentally. Then suddenly Lee saw him in a new light. He was no longer a treasure seeker, or a moneygrubber. He was a small boy showing off his toys, wanting her to enjoy them, to be impressed. ''Fine, Mr. Adburee. I will enjoy your artifacts. Is that a gold chain I see there in the corner?'' Lee leaned forward to peer into the dark recesses of the safe. She saw that it was, and realized that Burr had not previously mentioned having discovered it. Did he not trust her as completely as he pretended to?

Burr picked up the heavy linked chain and dropped it into her hand. Lee gasped at its beauty, its weight, its ability to pull her back across the centuries to old Spain.

''It's exquisite, isn't it? It....'' She bit back the words that rushed to her lips lest she alienate Adburee and lose all hope of his hiring her.

The sardonic smile curled his lips again. ''You win.''

''Win what?'' Lee looked up in genuine surprise.

"You know something about that chain, don't you? Something I don't know. Something I want to know."

"How can I say?" Lee held back her information, enjoying her superior position for the moment. "I have no idea what you know about the chain."

"I know next to nothing about it. I just know that on the current gold market it's worth a mint."

"How can you risk keeping it aboard this boat, Mr. Adburee? It may be worth a mint as bullion, but as an artifact from the seventeenth century, it's priceless."

Again the amber fire lighted his smoky eyes. "I keep it here so I can drop it into the hand of a lady like you who has never before felt the weight of gold from sunken Spanish galleons. I enjoy giving ladies a unique experience." He made no effort to keep the suggestiveness from his tone. "Now I'm asking. Tell me about this necklace."

Lee smiled as she found Adburee's gaze both eager and inquiring. Perhaps he *was* interested in the chain's historic value.... "The chain was never jewelry per se. It was called a money chain. Each link had a certain value. When a Spaniard wanted to make a purchase he unfastened a link to use as payment."

"Then he carried this in his pocket?" Burr hefted the chain again.

"Possibly. Or he might have worn it around his neck. Anything the Spaniards wore as they boarded a galleon was nontaxable."

"So they worried about taxes even in those days."

Burr laid the chain in a heap in the corner of the safe, but Lee reached for it and started to stretch it out to its full length, curling it back on itself three times.

"Can't you imagine that chain in a display case in some grand museum, Mr. Adburee?"

Burr reached for the chain, his fingers accidentally touching Lee's as she still worked at straightening the chain to its full length. For a moment she held her hand still and Burr did the same. In that moment they were like two people transfixed. Then Lee pulled away first, conscious of the tingle that feathered up her arm, raising gooseflesh as it went. Her mouth was so dry she couldn't speak, but Burr answered her question.

"Frankly, no, Miss Cameron. I can't imagine this gold in any museum." With those words he scooped the chain into his hand; but his eyes had a faraway look as once more he let the chain fall into a golden puddle in the corner of the safe. "Tell me about yourself, Miss Cameron. What does a lady scientist do with her off hours? What are your hobbies... your outside interests?"

Lee felt more at ease. Maybe this man was human after all. Sometimes his eyes accidentally revealed a softness she liked, a secretive something she would like to know more about. "I collect shells. I used to keep an aquarium before we sold our house. I like to cook. The usual things."

"Ah, we share an interest. I, too, like to cook. Perhaps you'll allow me to treat you to a gourmet dinner sometime soon."

"Perhaps." Lee looked away, wanting to say the

right things without sounding too forward. She wished Margo was still at her desk, but she had left on an errand some minutes ago and had not returned. Lee stood, hoping to bring their meeting to an end but not quite knowing how to.

"I thank you for your time, Mr. Adburee. I look forward to working with you."

CHAPTER THREE

BURRTON ADBUREE CLOSED THE SAFE and Lee heard a metallic whir as he gave the dial knob a spin. Why was she so conscious of his slim tanned fingers? She looked away. She felt herself dismissed, yet she didn't know quite how to handle the situation. One could not just walk away from a boat miles from the nearest land. She waited for a moment, then Adburee led the way onto the outer deck. Clouds like white cotton puffs wiped the bright blue sky and ribbons of yellow brown turtle grass floated on the satin-smooth surface of the sea. She smelled the yeasty scent of the water mingled with the fragrance of sandalwood that clung to Burrton Adburee. Why was she so acutely aware of him at her side? In a bit of fancy she imagined them alone and adrift on the sea beyond hope of rescue. It was a pleasant fantasy until Burr's voice intruded.

"I assume you would like to return to Key West now." Again his eyes held a hint of mocking laughter. Had he read her mind?

"Yes, if it's convenient," Lee said.

"Of course it's convenient. I presume a spunky one like you isn't afraid to fly in a helicopter. I have an early luncheon appointment in town." He glanced at his watch. "If you're ready we'll board the *Silver Ingot* and fly to Key West right now."

Burrton walked ahead of her up the companionway, ignoring any reaction she might have shown. Egotistical, she thought. Unfeeling. She tried to ignore the svelte way his jeans snugged over his hips and thighs.

On the top deck the *Silver Ingot* perched like a giant insect from outer space. Burrton released lines that held the craft in place; then he opened the door and helped Lee into the passenger seat. This time she was prepared for the touching of their hands, for the pressure of his strong fingers as he steadied her until she had her balance and was seated. But being prepared for his touch did nothing to lessen the pulsing thrill that shot up her arm. She was so engrossed in arranging her face passively so he couldn't detect the effect he had on her that she didn't notice her skirt riding high above her knee until his gaze drew her own to it. Quickly she yanked at the green fabric. Burr grinned at her in a maddening way.

"You really know how to spoil a guy's pleasure, don't you? Why cover such an enchanting sight? But now if you'll excuse me, please?"

Blushing furiously Lee slanted her knees sideways and pressed back against the seat so Burrton could slip in front of her and into the pilot's seat. Even so his slim hips brushed lightly against her breasts and she felt a prickling on her flesh. Once Burr started the engine the roar made conversation all but impossible. But that didn't matter. Lee had nothing to say. The *Silver Ingot* lifted off its launch pad easily and

smoothly, and except for the noise and the floor-
board vibration that made her feet tingle, Lee felt
like an ornament sealed inside a glass globe. She held
herself motionless, afraid that movement might
cause the glass to shatter and drop her into the sea.

They had flown only a few moments when she felt
Burrton's hand on her knee. She looked up sharply
to find him smiling sardonically. As she tried to
thrust his hand away he gripped her hand and held
it.

"Relax, Miss Cameron," he shouted. "I was
merely trying to get your attention. Look down.
You'll want to see that giant ray right below us and to
the right."

Lee pulled her hand from his and forced herself to
look. The sea was clear as Perrier water and the huge
ray looked like a great dark bat undulating gracefully
in the thin waves that washed over a sand bar. Burrton lowered the helicopter for a closer look, but the
ray darted into deeper water and disappeared.

"Too bad," Burr shouted. "I frightened him."

You frighten me, Lee thought, still staring at the
sandy bar and trying to forget the touch of his hand.
For a moment she wondered if they were above sea or
desert. Under the shallow water the sand lay swirled
into dunes. The *Quicksands!* Her father had spoken
of them frequently and now she was seeing them
from a great vantage spot! As she watched, a pepper-
ing of cormorants speckled the buff-colored sand.
She tried to memorize the peaceful scene so she could
remember it in the future when she needed a beautiful memory to sustain her.

Moments later Burrton shouted and pointed. "Key West!"

Lee peered at the hazy horizon and made out a red-and-white tower; then the darker forms of buildings near the harbor took shape. The distance that had taken over an hour to cover in the speedboat was being covered in a matter of minutes in the *Silver Ingot*.

Almost directly below them Lee saw uninhabited keys, mangrove-covered isles surrounded by a tangle of brown roots that thrust from the water like arched ropes. White egrets perched in the mangrove branches, and nearby herons and pelicans searched the shallows for food. So entranced was she with birds and sea that she almost didn't see the blue skiff carrying three passengers as it skimmed over the greenish backwaters. Fishermen, she guessed, yet she saw no tackle, no fiberglass pole, to ease them silently over the shallows.

Burrton saw the skiff at the same moment she did, and his eyes that had seemed so smoky and velvet soft suddenly glittered like wet jet. His upper lip curled in a cruel curve and he plunged the *Silver Ingot* into a swift dive, stopping close to the water, hovering only a few feet above the skiff.

Lee's mouth went dry and her knuckles whitened as she clung to her seat cushion in fear and disbelief. What was this crazy man doing! She couldn't bear to look, yet she couldn't bear not knowing. She peered from the window. The passengers in the skiff were just boys—long-haired, bearded, tanned. And frightened. Two crouched low, the whites of their eyes gleaming as they looked up. The third boy manned the tiller, zigzagging across the water in an attempt to escape the sudden menace from above. But no matter how fast the skiff darted Burrton Adburee stayed right above it, threatening to smash it and its occupants. Now his eyes flashed amber fire and his mouth was a cruel slash across his face. Lee saw that he was as white-knuckled as she.

"Mr. Adburee! You're scaring those boys. Stop it!" Lee screamed the words, seeing Burrton Adburee through the red haze of her anger and feeling nausea born of terror and disbelief flick at the base of her throat. Had he taken leave of his senses?

"I intend to scare them. They need...." Then suddenly Burrton Adburee's whole body relaxed. Color returned to his knuckles and he lifted the helicopter away from the skiff. Lee's nausea slid back into her churning stomach and she tried to relax. Burr's eyes lost their glitter, but his mouth held its cruel tight line as he flew toward the airport, received permission to land, and brought the helicopter down, skimming the ground as gently as a feather on silk. He opened the door and eased past Lee without touching her. Had his other touching been deliberate, she wondered. He jumped lightly onto the concrete, then turned to help her down.

"Thank you, sir." Lee faced the terminal building, hoping Burrton Adburee didn't notice that she was still shaking from fear and anger. "I'll expect to hear from you soon."

"Do let me drive you to your quarters here on the island, Miss Cameron."

"I'm quite capable of taking a taxi," Lee said, wanting to get away from this man as quickly as possible. The airport seemed deserted, but she knew there would be a pay phone and a taxi only a short distance away.

"I have no doubt about your capabilities," Burr said. "But it isn't my style to abandon ladies at the airport and expect them to fend for themselves. Please allow me to drive you to.... Where are you staying?" Burrton fell into step with Lee, casually linking his arm through hers in a way that made her feel as if her flesh were on fire.

Lee felt her need to get away from Burrton Adburee dissipate. "Eaton Street, near Simonton. But you really needn't bother."

"It's no bother, Miss Cameron. And I'd like to dispense with our formality. You may call me Burr if I may call you Lee. And it would be my pleasure to see you to your door."

"It's my policy not to mix business with pleasure," Lee said, avoiding saying his name while trying to prevent his sensuous voice from hypnotizing her.

"That's too bad." Burr gave her a sideways glance that Lee could only interpret as suggestive. "Maybe I can persuade you to change your policy."

Burr led her to a white Mercedes, helped her inside, then drove past the East Martello Gallery and onto the highway, easing through the traffic to Eaton Street. Lee supplied her address and he stopped in front of the Gomez home.

"So you like our Conch homes," Burr said. "My great-great-grandfather built a house in the Bahamas like this one. When the wrecking business moved to Key West he dismantled his house, shipped the parts here, then rebuilt it." Burr looked directly into her eyes. "I would have guessed that the Casa Marina would be more your style—elegant, sophisticated, cosmopolitan."

Lee ignored his gaze that now roved boldly over her body. "I can't imagine why, Mr. Adburee. Marine archaeologists are not noted for their large bank accounts. Do let me hear from you about a position with Dive Boys soon."

Burr slipped from the Mercedes, opened Lee's door for her and escorted her to the porch, again linking his arm with hers. "Never fear, Lee. You'll be hearing from me."

His voice held a promise, but Lee wasn't sure it was the promise of a job. When he pressed her fingers gently in farewell it was all she could do not to respond to his touch. Her heels tapped against the hard pine of the porch; then she heard the Mercedes drive on down the street. Although she was tempted to look back, she forced herself not to. And before she could turn toward the stairway to her room Maria Gomez appeared in the yard, her eyes and lips flashing a smile.

"*Buenas días,* Miss Cameron. You look so warm. Won't you come into my kitchen and let me pour you some limeade?"

Lee smiled, feeling sure Maria had seen her arrival and was eager to pump her about Burrton Adburee. For a moment she hesitated, then she realized that some gentle pumping could work both ways. She would really like to know more about this provocative man she hoped to work for. In return for a job, would he make demands she would be unable to grant?

"Why, thank you, Maria. I'd love a limeade."

Maria invited her into the oregano-scented kitchen, a boxlike room with hard pine walls, floor and ceiling. The avocado-green stove and refrigerator-freezer seemed out of place in this home that had been built in another age and another time.

"Sit down, please." Maria nodded toward a round oak table where a single golden hibiscus blossom lay in a shallow crystal bowl. She brought out green tumblers, clinked ice cubes into them, then poured limeade from a plastic pitcher that she had stored in the refrigerator. "Tell me, did you get your job?"

"I don't know yet, Maria. Mr. Adburee will call me tomorrow. I really would like to work for him."

"As would many girls, miss. Burr Adburee is much sought after by the ladies. I will be the talk of the neighborhood now that his car has been seen here." Maria smiled in an impish way that told Lee she would enjoy every scrap of the talk. "Tell me, what is Burr Adburee really like?"

Lee laughed and looked at Maria with genuine liking as she sipped her tart-sweet drink. "I was going to ask you the same question. All I know about him is what I've read in the society pages." Lee chose her words carefully, wanting to hide her strong reactions to Burr's voice, his suggestive remarks, his touch. "To me he's merely a playboy who has discovered by happenstance a sunken galleon and who plans to enjoy the romance of salvaging its riches.''

"You fault him for that?'' Maria asked.' "A galleon! Old Spain! Gold!''

"I don't fault him for it if he'll go about the excavation in a scientific and scholarly manner.''

When Maria looked puzzled Lee continued. "I'm a marine archaeologist. I don't want to see the wreck site destroyed without scholarly records being made that can be studied by other scientists at a later date.''

"I understand.'' Maria nodded, but Lee doubted if she really understood. "Is he as handsome as his pictures? I only caught a glimpse of him—just enough to recognize him. Is he as gallant as the stories that circulate about him?''

"He's handsome,'' Lee said. "You could see that, surely, even from a glance. And yes, he seems gallant. At least he wouldn't let me take a taxi from the airport.''

"I saw the *Silver Ingot* come in,'' Maria said.

Lee sipped her limeade, unwilling to reveal any more of her personal reactions to Burr Adburee. She was not one to confide to a stranger that a man had just set her heart racing by the mere sound of his voice, the touch of his fingers against hers, the look in his eyes as they roved her body. Nor did she want to admit that he had frightened her by his unprovoked cruelty to innocent boys, nor that she considered him egotistical and arrogant and greedy. She had a hard time reconciling her negative evaluations of Burr Adburee with her growing desire to work for him, with him.

"What do you know of Mr. Adburee, Maria? Is there anything I should know that would help me in working with him?"

"What can I say? I am only a homemaker who runs a rooming house. I know nothing of Key West's society figures. The Adburee family owns a chain of boatyards along the Gulf Coast. That's how they made their money. This treasure operation is just a hobby, I guess. They say old Mr. Adburee runs the business alone now that Burr's caught up in this diving venture. . .and since Zack died."

"Zack? Zack Adburee?"

"Burr's younger brother. He died on St. Patrick's eve. They say his parents haven't been the same since. Nor Burr. They were a very close family. They say Burr still goes into black moods and sudden rages. But that is just hearsay. Gossip. I should not be passing such trivia on to you."

Lee thought of the photographs in Burr's office. Surely they were of Zack Adburee. Now she felt sure she had not imagined that Burr's eyes had misted as he looked at the pictures. He must have been deeply attached to his brother. She thought of her own feelings for Raul and empathized with Burr. "What caused the brother's death?" Lee asked, wanting any information that would illumine Burr's character for her.

Maria shrugged. "Nobody knows. The details were hush-hush." Maria glanced up as heavy footsteps sounded on the porch, then in the hallway. "My Juan is home for lunch, Miss Cameron. Will you join us?"

Lee stood. "Thank you, Maria, but I must get upstairs. I enjoyed the limeade and thanks for inviting me in."

Maria walked with Lee to the outside door. "I hope you get your job, miss. Good luck."

"Thanks, Maria. I have a feeling I'll need it." Lee climbed the stairs wondering why she thought she would need so much luck. Burrton Adburee had been impressed with her credentials, her experience and her knowledge of galleons and Spain. And had he been attracted to her physically? She wished she knew. Burrton Adburee knew his way around women. She would be on guard. She would not be taken in by his smooth lines. She felt almost sure that he would hire her and she felt she would need luck along with great wisdom as she dealt with him. But even as she thought of his brooding moods, his egotistical arrogance, his. . . cruelty she remembered the grief he had shown for his brother. There was a softness under his hard exterior, a tenderness that she liked.

Once in her room, Lee realized that she was quite hungry, so she freshened up, then went out again in search of a restaurant. She strolled along the red-bricked sidewalk of a narrow, palm-shaded street where cactus grew behind a coral-rock fence. About midway down the block she stepped into a hole-in-the-wall sandwich shop called the Pink Turtle where she enjoyed a leisurely lunch. Then returning to her room she disrobed and stretched out on her bed, glad that her quarters caught snatches of trade wind.

But her nap was broken by dreams of Burr Adburee, and around five o'clock she took a cool bath then slipped into a sleeveless blouse and slacks the color of tangerines. Both garments snugged over her curves in a way that told her her weight was just right. She applied her makeup carefully, accenting the gray of her eyes with blue green eye shadow and applying just a hint of blush to her high cheekbones. She fluffed her short honey-blond hair with a blow dryer, casually slanting her fringe of bangs to the right. When she was satisfied with her appearance she walked toward Front Street and Mallory dock. She had read of the crowds that gathered there to watch the sunset and tonight she decided to be a part of the throng.

Everybody on the streets and sidewalks seemed to be heading for Mallory. Some drove cars, parking free a block away in the Pier House lot instead of paying the tab to park directly behind the dock. Others rode bicycles. A group of girls arrived on roller skates, and three long-haired boys balanced on skateboards. Shouts and laughter filled the air as friends greeted friends. Lee inhaled a medley of odors—banana bread from a vendor's cart, the salt air, the sweetish scent of marijuana and wine. A boy with a trombone in one hand and a brown cigarette stub in the other stepped in front of her and she read the logo on his T-shirt: Trombonists Do It in Seven Positions. She blushed, and the boy grinned as he joined other amateur performers who were staking out places on the dock, getting ready to do their thing for whomever they could get to stop and watch.

The dock took on the air of a three-ring circus. A

girl in a flowing red caftan set up a portable harpsichord and began playing folk tunes. A jeans-clad boy with a guitar joined a look-alike pal with an alto recorder and they performed duets, while a third young man, barefooted and wearing an orange kerchief that contrasted with his pajamalike garment fashioned from bleached feed sacks, danced a hornpipe on top of a dock piling not more than a foot in diameter. Lee watched fascinated as the dancer stopped now and then, bowed to the setting sun, and with arms outstretched, recited rhymed poetry in a voice soft as the pink and lavender hues that shaded the gray clouds near the horizon.

Lee didn't see Raul until she eased into a thin ring of spectators around him. She caught her breath sharply. She should have known Raul couldn't resist a street scene such as this one. Surely there must be something she could do to help him mature in his thinking. He caught her gaze and glanced away quickly. Now he was Raul the magician, barefooted but dressed in an Ali Baba suit of green pantaloons, a saffron balloon-sleeved shirt, and a blue headband. He wore a scarlet satin vest with a yellow daisy painted on its back. Raul gave three raps on a tambourine, then stood smiling and waiting for more people to gather.

"Ladies and gentlemen," Raul called. "Come closer. Meet Manfred the Magician. See coins, balls, scarves appear from thin air." As the crowd pressed closer Raul knelt and opened a cardboard suitcase worn out at the corners. He removed a set of steel rings. "Now I'll make a deal with you." From his kneeling position he whispered to the crowd, drawing them even closer. Even Lee stepped closer although she knew what was coming next.

"What's the deal?" a man called from the back row.

"I want you good people to clap and shout and make lots of noise," Raul whispered, smiling his most engaging smile. "When I have a really big crowd, I'll give you a really good show. Is it a deal?"

Lee moved back, not wanting to encourage Raul in his magic act, but the crowd went wild, clapping and shouting and stamping their feet. Raul's trick worked. People from all around flocked toward him, eager to see what he would do next.

"Now see these rings." Brushing his tawny hair from his eyes Raul held his nine steel rings up for inspection, tossing three of them into the crowd. "See the rings? Each one separate from the others? No holes in the rings."

Lee moved even farther back as the members of the crowd nodded. Then Raul collected the rings, manipulated them in his hands for a moment then held them up linked in a chain. The crowd applauded, their enthusiasm now genuine. Lee wished she could turn her back and leave, but Raul's act held even her captive. He wasn't half-bad as an entertainer. Raul continued his act, making coins appear, making scarves disappear, performing card tricks that left the audience smiling in wonder. Then before the crowd left, Raul tossed a hat onto the concrete.

"If you've enjoyed my show, let me know. Sweeten the kitty, okay?"

Lee watched as people stepped forward dropping coins and bills into the hat. She was surprised that Raul had worked up such a professional act. By the time he had packed his rings and scarves into the battered case most of the crowd had dispersed. Lee sat down on a nearby bench that overlooked the harbor, watching as a barefoot young man in tattered cutoffs approached Raul. She tried to hear their conversation, but the sea slapping against the dock, along with the talk and laughter of the crowd, drowned out all but snatches of their words. And even more distracting, she saw Burr Adburee standing on the edge of the crowd as if watching a juggler nearby. But his eyes weren't on the tenpins being tossed into the air. Burr was watching Raul through narrowed lids.

"...food...bail bond...friends...." The words came from the tall boy who limped slightly and whose shaggy hair was salt-crusted and sun-bleached to the color of polished brass.

Not wanting to attract Burr's attention Lee sat very still and continued to watch from the corner of her eye as Raul emptied the bills and coins from his hat and gave them to the brassy-haired boy.

"Thanks, pal...another time...." The boy slapped Raul on the back, then he was gone.

Now Raul approached Lee, glancing over his shoulder as if afraid he might be seen.

"Who was the panhandler you gave your money to?" Lee asked.

"A friend."

"Apparently. What's his name?"

"Spike."

"You don't even know his last name?"

Raul shrugged. "Is a name so important? Is money so important? Spike needs it more than I do. I got my kicks performing for the crowd. They liked me, Lee. They really did. That's what's really important— pleasing people."

Lee felt a combination of irritation and exasperation at Raul's words, at his outlook on life. Deep down, she admired his good-heartedness, but she knew he would never make something of himself if he didn't save some of his money, at least. She glanced around, relieved to see that Burr had left the dock. She didn't want him to see her with Raul any more than Raul wanted Burr to see him with Lee. Being seen with Raul could ruin her image as a professional archaeologist.

"Where are you going now?" Lee asked.

"To find something to eat."

"And where do you plan to . . . look?"

Again Raul shrugged. "Don't worry about it. Someone will give me a handout. I'll find friends."

Lee felt her nails bite into her palms and she struggled to keep her voice low. "Have you no pride? How can you go begging? Why didn't you at least keep enough to buy yourself a meal?"

"Lee, a guy's in the slammer. A cop busted him for no reason at all. That money I collected will spring him. Which is worse, being hungry or being in jail? I can't imagine anything worse than being locked up. The guy would have done the same for me."

Scorn boiled into Lee's tone. "If you've got such good friends, why are you standing there hungry and with no money?"

Raul stared at the sea as if he hadn't heard.

"Come on." Lee sighed in defeat. "I'll buy you dinner. I haven't eaten yet. Can you change from that outfit?"

Raul picked up his case and stepped into a public rest room. When he returned he was wearing shirt and shoes and jeans. "How about hunting for a quarter-pounder with an order of fries?"

"I intend for you to eat a good meal, Raul. And I intend to dine in a restaurant with at least a little atmosphere. Come on. I've seen ads for a place called The Deck. Let's try it."

Raul walked beside Lee through the blue gray twilight that misted Duval Street, past the red brick bank and to The Deck. He pushed open a gate fashioned of silver gray driftwood and they walked single file along a short narrow lane lined with rusty-colored crotons and lush green sea grape until they reached an open-air dining area with round cloth-covered tables set under the dusky sky. The scent of jasmine hung in the air and the clink of ice against crystal gently punctuated the low drone of voices. The hostess eyed Raul's frayed jeans, then seated them near the back of the area at a table in front of a living screen of bamboo. Lee ordered two seafood dinners when the waitress arrived, and Raul didn't argue.

"Tell me about your work day, Raul *Johnson*," Lee said when they were alone.

"You didn't expect me to use my real name, did you? I mean I knew you'd use yours and—"

"It's okay, Raul. I understand."

"Did he hire you?"

Lee felt her throat tighten. Just talking about Burr made her tense. "I'll know tomorrow. No doubt you're hoping he won't."

"Right. That's exactly what I'm hoping. But I saw the way he was eyeing you. And he's so rich he could hire you for an office decoration if he wanted to."

Lee felt herself flushing. "If he's so rich, why doesn't he pay his divers a decent wage? He's parsimonious and arrogant. And he's...mean, Raul. Downright mean." Lee started to tell him about the boys in the skiff, but Raul nudged her, picked up a menu and hid behind it.

Lee glanced up and her mouth suddenly felt cotton dry as she saw the hostess welcome Burr and Margo and seat them at a table near the front of the dining area. A philodendron in a redwood tub partially hid them from view, and Lee eased her chair a bit to one side so her back was almost to them.

"Let's get out of here," Raul whispered. "I can't have them seeing us together."

"You'll really draw attention if you try to leave now," Lee said, wishing she had worn something green that would blend with her surroundings rather than the bright tangerine outfit. "Eat, Raul. Their backs are to us."

The waitress brought their shrimp and snapper and as they ate Lee plied Raul with more questions, wishing she weren't so conscious of Burr's presence. "What are your working hours?"

"Sunrise until sunset if the weather's good. Most nights the divers sleep aboard the *Sea Deuced*. I just had to come ashore today for supplies. I'll return with Harry tomorrow and be out there for ten days. Then we have a few days off."

"Where will you spend them?"

"Burr provides a place and we pay him rent. No big deal."

"He's using you. He pays barely a living wage, then...." Lee heard the shrillness in her voice and she looked down, embarrassed. But the outburst had been too much for Raul. He had almost cleaned his plate and now he finished his baked potato, stuffed two slices of bread into his pocket, and slipped between the bamboo behind them, leaving Lee alone.

Lee's appetite was gone and she felt abandoned and lonely as she lingered over a cup of coffee. How was she going to get out of here without Burr seeing her? She refused to sneak away as Raul had. There was nothing to do but rise and leave. By now many diners crowded the area and she didn't feel quite so conspicuous, yet her heart pounded at the thought of meeting Burr under these circumstances. If only she had an escort. She made plans. She would pass by Burr's table, nod casually and leave The Deck. But before she reached Burr's table he rose, took Margo's hand, and led her onto a miniscule dance floor that Lee hadn't even noticed.

Burr was wearing tailored silk slacks in an off-white shade that highlighted his tanned skin. His black shirt matched his hair and he wore it in an open-throated way that made women look twice and then once more. Margo was wearing a halter-topped dress, bias cut from an apricot-hued fabric that clung to her figure like Saran Wrap.

When Lee passed them they were locked in each other's arms and Margo had her eyes closed, her head nestled against Burr's chest. Lee denied the unwelcome thought that flashed into her mind. Of course she was not envious of Margo King. Just before she turned her head Burr looked straight at her and winked.

CHAPTER FOUR

THE STRAIN OF HER TRIP to the keys, her interview aboard the *Sea Deuced*, and her dinner with Raul left Lee drained, yet as she lay in bed she couldn't get to sleep. Burr Adburee...Burr Adburee...Burr Adburee. His name became a mantra filling her thoughts until at last she dozed off. She came half-awake in the gray of the following dawn as footsteps thudded on the outside stairway and a sharp knock sounded on her door. She wanted to cover her head with her pillow and drift back to sleep, but Maria's voice intruded.

"Miss Cameron! Miss Cameron! You have a telephone call." Maria knocked on the door again. "Miss Cameron, are you awake?"

"Just a minute, please." Lee's voice grated in her ears like a rusty hinge. She forced her eyes open and squinted at her bedside clock. Only five o'clock? She preferred to think that it was five in the afternoon.

"Miss Cameron? Are you awake?"

"Coming, Maria." Lee felt the lick of the cool pine floor against her warm feet as she groped for her slippers. Robe? Where was that robe? She couldn't appear in this citron-colored wisp of a nightgown. She blinked away protecting veils of sleep, shrugged into her robe and hurried to the door. Raul! Something must have happened to Raul. Who else would be calling at this hour? Jail? She remembered the tough-looking character who had approached Raul at the dock. Didn't every suspect get one telephone call? Had they read Raul his rights? Lee raked her fingers through her hair, then flung open the door and faced Maria.

"Who is it, Maria? Who's calling me at this hour?"

"The gentleman didn't give his name, ma'am. He is waiting."

"I'm so sorry you've been awakened on my account."

Lee followed Maria down steps still wet from night mists and the dew on the banister left her hand cold and clammy. Maria's telephone was mounted on the kitchen wall and now the receiver dangled from the cord almost reaching the floor. Lee bent and snatched it.

"Hello...Lee Cameron speaking." She held her breath, dreading to hear Raul's voice, his bad news.

"Good morning, Lee. Burr here. Pack your bags and I'll pick you up in thirty minutes."

Burr! Not Raul! Relief and surprise choked her and she failed to grasp the significance of hearing Burr's voice. "Thirty minutes?" she asked weakly. "Whatever for? I mean—"

"You did say you wanted to go to work for Dive Boys today, didn't you?"

"Of course I said that." Lee groped for words. "But do you realize it's only five o'clock?"

"I realize that. Move along. We'll have plenty of time to settle you in at Marvista and be aboard the *Sea Deuced* by nine o'clock. I'll expect you to be ready in thirty minutes."

What arrogance! Lee groped for polite words to understate her negative feelings. "This is a most unusual arrangement."

"Dive Boys *is* a most unusual enterprise. I'll call for you in half an hour, Lee. Be ready."

It irritated Lee that Burr's voice was as assured as hers was hesitant. She heard the click of his receiver, then the line hummed hollowly. Didn't anyone ever say no to this man? He had allowed her no time to protest, no time to accept. He simply took it for granted that she would obey his order and be ready when he arrived. How dare he snap his fingers and expect her to jump! Yet what else could she do? She wanted the job, didn't she?

"Is bad news?" Maria asked, still hovering like a shadow in the doorway.

"I'm not sure." Lee laughed. "Burrton Adburee just asked me to go to work for Dive Boys, so I guess it's good news in that respect. I have a job."

"A job that begins. . . ." Maria yawned and peered at her watch. "It's—"

"I know. I know. It's five o'clock, and I apologize again for disturbing your sleep. Maria, I'm truly sorry, but—"

"Is all right, Miss Cameron. We go back to bed now."

"You can go back to bed," Lee said. "But I'll be leaving shortly. If you'll allow me to, I'll settle my bill now. And I do thank you for opening your home to me and—''

"You really start to work at this hour?"

For some reason Lee felt a need to defend herself. Or was it Burr she felt needed defending? "A salvage operation doesn't run on an eight-to-five schedule, Maria. The weather, the tides, you know. Burr is picking me up in thirty minutes, so. . . ."

"I see." Maria's eyes had a glazed look, and Lee knew that her landlady didn't "see" any more clearly than she herself did. She hurried back to her room, wrote Maria a check, then dressed more prudently than she had the day before. She slipped into trim-fitting lime-green slacks and a sea-gray top that enhanced her figure and matched her eyes. Gray deck shoes and a shoulder bag completed her outfit. She brushed her hair until it gleamed and added a touch of lip gloss. *Not bad for five in the morning,* she thought, checking her appearance in the mirror. What would Margo be wearing, she wondered. But how silly. What did she care about Margo's wardrobe?

She packed her things, folding garments carefully, wondering just why Burr had ordered her to move from Eaton Street. Did he expect her to take up permanent quarters on the *Sea Deuced*? She wouldn't do it. If her job depended on it? She would do it. Sighing, she wondered how she would be able to maintain her independence from Burr Adburee if she went along with all his ideas so willingly. Yet she wasn't going willingly. She had no choice. Adapt or perish.

Lee carried her bag to the front porch, feeling foolish and vulnerable to be standing in the cool gray morning waiting for Burr Adburee to meet her. And what of her car? Did he expect her to abandon it?

In moments the Mercedes stopped at the curbing, a white cocoon protecting its contents from the mist-filled dawn. Then the cocoon opened and Burr slid from behind the wheel, his long-legged stride relaxed and unhurried as he approached the porch where she waited. He moved with an unstudied slowness born of complete assurance, she thought as she determined to match his calm manner.

"Good morning, Lee." Burr let his gaze travel over her from head to heel as if memorizing the lime color of her slacks, the gray of her sleeveless shirt as well as the pleasing contours beneath the fabric. Then he gave a nod of approval. "I like your outfit. I like your punctuality. I like a lot of things about you, Lee."

Lee felt her heart thudding at Burr's compliments, but she kept a businesslike manner. "And I'd like you to tell me why you're calling for me at this hour. Why have you asked me to give up my room here?" Lee kept her direct gaze on Burr's eyes, but her side vision took note of his casual elegance. Designer jeans...silk shirt that almost matched her own lime-green slacks...matching sweater carried casually over one arm...black deck shoes. Everything Burr wore enhanced his taut figure, his dark good looks; and his craggy features seemed more finely honed in the soft dawn light. She vowed to be immune to his charm.

"We can't very well talk here in this residential

area, Lee. Voices carry. Granted, it is early. Come along with me and I'll find a private spot where I can spell out the details of your employment."

"Shall I follow in my car?" Lee asked.

"Of course not. I want you beside me. I'll send someone for your car later. Come along now." Burr picked up her suitcase as if it weighed nothing, placed it in the back seat of the Mercedes, then opened the front door for her. She slipped into the seat, feeling like a trained porpoise doing its keeper's bidding. Why couldn't she stand up to this man? Driving her own car would have given her a bit more independence.

Burr drove to the other side of the island and parked near an old fort whose brickwork had weathered to the color of ripe plums during the years since the Civil War. Lee edged a bit closer to the car door as she gazed across the shimmering expanse of silver gray water. Early morning had an untouched quality about it that made her feel uneasy. Or was it Burr's nearness that made her uneasy? Sunlight glinted on the waves, each crest like a mirror flashing light back into her eyes. Gulls screamed and dived for their breakfast. Lee inhaled the misty salty air that hung around them like scent from an atomizer.

"What are you thinking?" Burr asked.

"About Spanish gold," Lee lied. She couldn't tell him she was thinking of him and the morning, could she?

"A girl after my own heart. I've been thinking of Spanish gold for some time. There must be an untold fortune lying on the sea bottom just waiting to be discovered."

Now Lee's thoughts really did center on gold. "I wasn't translating long-ago treasure into present-day wealth. I was thinking of what that gold means."

"If not wealth, just what does it mean?"

"Its very presence means that someone lived and loved here before us, that someone will live and love here after us. We like to think we're all-important in the scheme of things, while in reality we're just captives in a fragile bubble of time that all too soon will burst."

"My, my, aren't we philosophical this morning! But aren't captives in time allowed to live and love?" Burr grinned down at her, and while his lips curved in a smile, his eyes held a somber thoughtful quality. Maybe she had been wrong about him. Maybe he wasn't totally a captive of the lure of Spanish gold. She had seen that quick unguarded look once before—yesterday, when he had gazed at the pictures of his brother. Then he spoke again, scattering her thoughts.

"I want to tell you what I expect from you on this job, Lee. For starters I'll expect an eight-hour day, and you'll be paid for an eight-hour day, but you'll be on call twenty-four hours a day."

"On call?" Did this man think he could buy her whole life?

"It's simple enough. I'll need to know where you are at all times if your effort to make the *Santa Isabella* treasure historically valuable is to be successful. I have dive crews working for me during all daylight hours. If some big discovery should be made at dusk or in the early morning hours, then you'd need to know immediately, right?''

"That sounds reasonable. I didn't realize you had crews working so extensively."

"I'll expect you to live either aboard the *Sea Deuced* or at Marvista." Burr's tone was seductively low as he continued. "You've seen the Spartan quality of the quarters aboard the dive boat, so I'm presuming you'll opt for a small suite at Marvista."

"And just where and what is Marvista?" A cold finger of apprehension traced a line up Lee's spine. If this arrogant man thought she was going to move in with him in some—

"Marvista is the Adburee family home."

"I'm not prepared to move in with you, if that's what you're leading up to, Burr. Really now—"

"Really now, I'm giving the orders and you'd better hear me out. I said you could live aboard the dive boat, but I really don't expect that of you. You needn't worry about being compromised. Marvista has many built-in chaperones. My parents live there. My divers live there when they're off duty. Margo lives there."

"How cozy." Lee's voice sounded more sarcastic than she had intended it to. She certainly didn't want to give the impression that she cared where Margo King lived.

"You'll come with me now to see Marvista, Lee. *That*'s an order."

"I much prefer requests to orders, Burr, especially in matters concerning my private life. Of course I'll be glad to take a look at your home, but I can't imagine that I could live there."

"Why not? My other employees live there quite willingly. I pay well. And you'd better face it, it's a take-it-or-leave-it situation. If you want to work for Dive Boys, you'll work on my terms."

Arrogant. . .conceited. . .high-handed. Lee could hardly control her temper. "Your terms are very hard, Mr. Adburee. And I don't think you're being totally honest with me."

"In what way am I being dishonest? And why am I suddenly Mr. Adburee again?"

"You say you pay well, Burr, but you certainly expect your divers to exist on substandard wages." Lee saw a flush spread under the tan of Burr's cheeks.

"I have my reasons, Lee. Any diving enterprise attracts a certain number of drifters, and many drifters are on drugs. I keep the divers' pay low so it won't support a drug habit."

"Isn't that rather making the innocent pay for the misdeeds of the guilty?"

"You've been listening to Raul Johnson, no doubt." Burr's voice grated. "I saw you with him at The Deck last night. You do make friends quickly, Lee."

Lee felt her nails dig into her palms. Was he insinuating she was a common pickup? "My friends are my personal business, I believe."

"Of course. Of course. Your choice of companions just surprised me, I guess. I didn't think you'd go for the barefoot-diver type."

How dare Burr make a stock character of Raul!

Yet Raul did ask to be easily categorized when he dressed as he did. "Raul Johnson seemed nice enough," Lee said weakly.

"We'll see. I never make snap judgments where divers are concerned. But enough talk of Raul Johnson and diving. I presume you are willing to come with me now and let me show you Marvista."

"All right. But will anyone be expecting us at this hour?"

"I hope not. That is the beauty of early morning. One usually has it all to oneself. I will enjoy sharing it with you today, Lee. You impress me as a most enchanting early-morning type."

Lee felt a pulse dance near her temple but she said nothing, and she pretended great interest as she watched a pelican dive for a fish. Burr spouted orders one minute, but the next minute he was trying to mesmerize her with his charm. She was on guard. She guessed he knew little of early mornings. From what she had read about him he was more the late-night type. Of course his late nights might merge into early mornings.

"What are you thinking?"

Lee felt herself blushing. "Why do you keep asking me that?"

"Because I want to know. Most girls chatter. I can tell what they are thinking or not thinking, but you're different. There's a silence about you that intrigues me. I want to know more about you. Where have you lived all your life? What have you done? Who are your friends?"

Burr spoke in a tone that made Lee want to pour

out her life's story to him, but she curbed the desire. Maybe silence could be her secret weapon against him. "I'm sure there's nothing in my past that you would find remotely interesting."

"You might be surprised at what I consider interesting." Burr smiled at her in a way that could melt coral as he started the Mercedes and pulled lazily back onto the highway. There was no traffic and they drove slowly until they came to a palm-lined driveway. Burr waved to a jogger who smiled but didn't break his pounding rhythm.

"Dr. Haynes," Burr said. "He's the only other early riser in the neighborhood. Lives next door."

Lee glanced casually at the jogger, then studied the trees. The palms were like graceful dancers leaning into the wind, their fronds etched against the sky, which was now whitened with a powdered-sugar sifting of clouds. Lee thought the two coral-rock gateposts that marked the entry to the Adburee lane looked as if they once might have guarded Neptune's court—they were so grand. And arched above the gateposts was a green sign with the word Marvista painted in white. Burr turned into the long graveled drive, easing the car under the canopy of palm branches until they reached the single-story green-stucco house.

A wide bricked path led to the square-set double doors where a lush growth of coppery-green crotons guarded the entryway. Lee saw no jasmine, but the sweet scent hung in the air as Burr slipped from behind the steering wheel and strolled around to open her door. *He fits perfectly into all this elegance,* Lee thought. *Can he tell I'm awestruck?*

"Shall we go in?" Burr asked.

"It's still early," Lee said, alighting from the car. "We'll waken everyone."

"Not so." Burr shook his head and took her arm. "Everyone here is a sound sleeper. Maggie and Elmer may be stirring, but nobody else will be up."

"Maggie and Elmer?" Generally Lee didn't like people who called their parents by their given names. It was pretentious.

"Maggie and Elmer are our retainers. Maggie's the best cook in the keys, and Elmer has a green thumb when it comes to tropical plants. They've cared for our family for years."

"How nice for you." Again Lee tried to keep the sarcasm from her voice.

A green chameleon ran the length of the door screen, and Burr gave it time to take cover before he opened the door and let Lee step inside first. He was kinder to animals than to humans, she thought. Then suddenly she shivered. The house was air-conditioned and very cool. At first glance and from the outside Lee had thought the house was built in the shape of one long rectangle, but now she could see that it had been constructed in a U-shape, with the open end facing a junglelike tropical growth, a private beach and the sea.

"How beautiful!" Lee exclaimed.

"I knew you'd like it," Burr said. "You'll find it much more comfortable here than on the dive boat, and Maggie and Elmer have prepared a suite for you. But let me show you around here first."

Lee was still awestruck as Burr showed her the spacious living room with its parquet floor and brightly cushioned rattan furniture. The picture window overlooked the sea as if it were framing a magic, ever changing painting. They strolled through the dining room with its crystal-topped table and ebony chairs and Lee felt as if she had stepped into a picture from *House Beautiful*. Nobody was stirring in the kitchen, and its sea-green fixtures, along with its light paneled walls, gave a feeling of luxury uncommon to most work areas. In the distance Lee could hear a radio playing beguine rhythms.

From a coffee maker Burr splashed coffee into umber-colored mugs and led the way outside to a redwood table shaded by a lime-green umbrella. Lee noted the picture they created, her shirt and Burr's slacks picking up the hue of the umbrella as if an artist had set them against a backdrop of sea and sky, planning to create a scene on canvas.

"We'll wait until after breakfast to tour the guest wing of the house," Burr said.

"We're having breakfast here?" Lee asked.

"Promptly at half-past six. I've ordered Maggie to make it private. We'll eat here beside the sea. The others have breakfast in their rooms."

Lee sipped her coffee, hardly able to believe the loveliness of Marvista. The palms whispered, alive with trade wind. Many smaller trees grew in the rectangular courtyard—pepper trees, limes, bananas. In protected corners cacti grew almost as tall as Lee's head, and everywhere the scent of jasmine hung in the air, wafted by the trade wind. Lee let her gaze rove beyond the growth that surrounded them. Three egrets waded near the shore and overhead a gull made mewing sounds like a hungry kitten. In the shallows a frigate bird perched on a rock with wings outstretched as if trying to sun every dark feather. She heard a coconut plunk onto the soft sand a few feet beyond the protected patio where they sat. She could be happy here forever. Then she checked her thoughts.

How could this arrogant man bring strangers into this lovely home? How could he be so insensitive as to invade his parents' privacy by ensconcing divers and other employees here? Clearly he thought of nothing but his diving operation. He was totally wrapped up in himself and his quest for treasure.

"Tell me what you're thinking," Burr ordered.

"Not that again!" Lee scowled. "You wouldn't like my thoughts, I'm afraid."

"I can guess them. You think I'm a clod for turning Marvista into a high-class rooming house."

Lee felt herself flush as he caught her thoughts so accurately, pinning them down like butterflies in a collector's book. "You're a mind reader?"

"I don't have to be. Your thoughts are written on your face."

"Then, since I'm all so transparent, maybe you'll explain your motives to me. Why? How can you do this? How can you take strangers into your family home like this? Me, Margo, Harry, the other divers?"

Burr's tone was one he might use with a dim-witted child. "Let me explain the arrangement. You saw the living room, dining room, kitchen. Then this wing to our right is my parents' wing. They have their bedroom suites. I have my suite there... now. And there are guest suites. The wing to our left had been sitting there unused since my two sisters married and my brother... since the family left home. To have the rooms occupied by people involved in Dive Boys gives us a tax break, and mother and father say it keeps them young to have young people coming and going. All in all the arrangement works out quite well."

Lee felt mixed emotions. It seemed clear that Burr would do anything for money and she didn't admire that, but she remembered how her mother had enjoyed having her friends and Raul's friends around the house. Rooms that stood idle seemed to die, seemed to drain vitality from the living. It would be a crime to let this lovely place sit lifeless and unused.

"I've never seen such a lovely home as this, Burr."

"I know," Burr said complacently. "That's what everyone says. And those who live here respect the place. Even the divers."

"Raul Johnson says the divers pay for their quarters here. What will my rent be if I decide to stay?"

"The divers pay because I believe that people don't appreciate what they get free. You and Margo and Harry receive living quarters as part of your pay. There will be no added charge. I know you'll agree to live here, Lee." Again Burr's voice became so soft and sensuous that it, along with the early-morning quiet and the ever present mystique of the sea, almost held her spellbound.

"I'd like to see my quarters before I decide," Lee

said, knowing all the while she had already decided, yet hating to grant Burr too easy a victory.

"Here comes Maggie with our breakfast. We'll eat first, then we'll finish our tour." Burr hurried to take the heavy tray Maggie was carrying, scowling at her as he spoke. "How many times do I have to tell you to use the tea cart, Maggie? I won't have you taxing your strength by carrying these heavy trays."

"The cart is in use, Mr. Burr. I appreciate your concern, but I can still manage a tray quite easily, thank you."

Lee looked away to hide a smile. It pleased her to know that Burr could be considerate of others and it amused her to hear Maggie speak up to him, to assert herself in a way that allowed no argument.

Maggie was a tall reed of a woman, middle-aged and with a ready smile, and when Burr introduced her, Lee liked her immediately. Maggie set individual plates before them, each bearing a melon slice garnished with a baby orchid, scrambled eggs and toast.

"How lovely, Maggie!" Lee touched the soft petals of the orchid. "I can see you have an artistic nature. Imaginative."

Maggie blushed in pleasure. "Mr. Burr always demands an orchid with his breakfast. Been that way all his life. An orchid does a lot to perk one up, don't you think?"

"You're quite right." Again Lee felt awed as she imagined a person growing up always knowing orchids for breakfast. Burr Adburee was that sort of person—an orchids-at-breakfast type.

Maggie refilled their coffee cups and left them.

Suddenly Lee felt totally caught up in Marvista. Orchids and melon, sunshine and sea, the romantic quiet and peace. Burr's arrogance and egotism were the only imperfections in the scene.

"I agree," Burr said, his voice almost lost in the sound of waves easing onto sand.

"Agree with what?" Lee frowned at his intrusion into her thoughts.

"I agree with you that this is the most romantic spot in the keys on this day, at this time and with the present company."

Lee's heart pounded. Could he really read her thoughts? "But this is a business day." She tried to cover her vulnerability, knowing instinctively, yet reluctantly, that she could not afford to be open and receptive to this man. He was arrogant and egotistical. But he could be kind and charming, too. Charm. Surely that was his stock-in-trade with the society ladies. His charm was the thing she must guard against. She couldn't risk being hurt again.

"You're right. It is a business day. As soon as we eat I'll show you to your suite, then we'll take the helicopter out to the dive boat."

"You're assuming I'll accept these living arrangements, aren't you?"

"Of course."

"I hate being taken for granted, but at least you're honest."

"I'm always honest. You intrigue me, Lee. I've never known a girl like you before—quiet, self-possessed. You're like a sea sprite on a music box.

Anytime I expect to hear strains of 'Over the Waves.' ''

"Is that why you've hired me?" Lee felt insubstantial, like smoke in the wind, as she considered Burr's compliments, but she kept her voice firm. "I've only come here seeking to advance myself in my profession. That's really not very intriguing."

"I've hired you to help me because you've convinced me that your knowledge will benefit Dive Boys. I must prove that the wreck I've discovered is the *Santa Isabella*."

"Why?" Lee leaned forward, suddenly feeling hopeful. Maybe this man was interested in more than the monetary value of the sunken treasure. Maybe she had reached him with her talk about preserving the underwater heritage. Maybe he did see the artifacts as historical treasures. He must have a reason for wanting to prove the identity of the wreck. "Why, Burr?" Lee repeated her question. "Why is the identity of the wreck so important to you?"

"I should think you could guess," Burr said. "You've convinced me I need you to help me prove the absolute identity of the wreck I'm salvaging. I'm interested in getting the support of any museums or historical organizations that might offer financial aid for the search."

Lee felt as if a cloud had masked the sun although she could see sunshine still glinting on the sea. Crass. Burr Adburee was totally money-oriented. The tragedy of the *Santa Isabella* meant nothing more to him than dollar signs in a bankbook. If it hadn't been for her promise to her mother, if it hadn't been for Raul, she would have left Burr sitting at his marvelous breakfast table staring at his marvelous orchid.

"Is something wrong?" Burr asked. "You're scowling, you know."

At least he can't read all my thoughts, she thought. "I'd like to see my suite, please." Lee pushed her breakfast plate aside, almost spilling her half-filled coffee mug.

"Of course. Time is getting away. Come with me." Burr stood, but before he could help her ease her chair from the table she scraped it back herself and rose. He led her across the courtyard into the wing on their left through a side entry, down a narrow hallway illumined by a skylight, and to a closed door. Burr opened the door and motioned her inside.

"This is it, Lee."

Someone had left the air conditioner on and the suite was frigid. Lee looked around, wishing she could find fault, but there was no fault to be found. Cool fiber matting covered the floors of the sitting room and the bedroom. In both rooms picture windows gave a palm-fringed view of the sea. Bedspread and draperies in a cool cotton floral print blended with the paneled walls. Through another doorway Lee saw a bath with porcelain fixtures the color of sea oats. Velvet-cut bath sheets hung on the towel racks and a matching sand-colored bath mat lay fluffed beside the tub.

"I'll have Elmer bring your bag inside," Burr said, not waiting for her okay.

Lee shivered, looked around for the air-conditioner

control. Seeing it beside the thermostat, she turned it off.

"You're cold." Quickly Burr took the sweater that he had been carrying and slipped it around Lee's shoulders. "Wear this until you warm up." His arm lingered on her shoulder as he eased the sweater in place and Lee felt immediate warmth surging through her. The scent of sandalwood clung to Burr's sweater and she was conscious of it as well as of his hand on her shoulder. His nearness disturbed her and she was just ordering herself to ease away from his touch when he stepped back, excused himself, and strode toward the door.

"I'll have your bag here in a moment. It's time we're getting to the dive boat."

"I haven't said yet that I'll be staying here," Lee reminded him.

"But you will. If you want to work for me you really have no choice but to do as I say." Burr's words were steely hard, yet his voice was as soft as a caress. There was a determination in him that defied Lee's understanding. His eyes held her mesmerized, and the heady sandalwood smell clinging to his sweater distracted her. As he said, she really had no choice.

"Yes, Burr. I'll be staying here."

CHAPTER FIVE

TRUE TO HIS WORD Burr did return quickly, bringing with him three people. Lee guessed their identities before he introduced them. Elmer Buell, Maggie's husband, placed her bag on the bed. For a tall muscular man, he moved with surprising grace, and Lee wondered if he might at one time have been a boxer. Surely his presence at Marvista would discourage the divers from any rowdiness. The other two people were obviously Burr's parents. Lee detected a closeness among the three of them in the way Burr linked his arm through his mother's and in the way he smiled at his father.

"Lee," Burr said. "I'd like you to meet my family. Catherine and Burrton Hastings Adburee. Father prefers to be called Hastings though. I've told them all about your love affair with marine archaeology."

Lee felt her hackles rise as she sensed Burr making fun of her career choice in spite of his need for her professional services. It infuriated her that he was using her to reach his own goals, which were incompatible with hers.

"I'm pleased to meet you, Miss Cameron." Hastings Adburee offered his hand and Lee shook it, conscious of his firm grip. Hastings Adburee was a briefcase-in-one-hand, morning-paper-under-the-arm type. Sixtyish. He looked like an older edition of Burr, and he gave an overall impression of grayness: crisply curling gray hair, gray suit, gray shoes. Yet he countered all the somberness with a white shirt, a red bow tie and anchor-shaped cuff links.

"Father's the skipper at the helm of the Adburee business interests," Burr said. "He's president of Adburee Enterprises."

"I understand you're in the boat business," Lee said, taking note of the pride in Burr's voice as he spoke of his father.

Hastings Adburee smiled and nodded. "That sums it up nicely. We own a string of boatyards along the Gulf Coast as well as one here in Key West. We do repair, hauling, dry-docking."

"It sounds fascinating, Mr. Adburee," Lee said, trying for a note of sincerity. Then she turned to Burr's mother. "You have a magnificent home, Mrs. Adburee. It's most generous of you to open it to Burr's business associates."

"I enjoy having young people around," Catherine Adburee said. "Since Burr feels a need to have his associates close at hand, Hastings and I are pleased to cooperate by opening the unused wing of Marvista."

Catherine Adburee was tall, almost as tall as Burr, and her body seemed to have more planes and angles than curves. Handsome. That was the word that flashed into Lee's mind. And like Burr she showed signs of being at odds with herself. She wore diamond earrings with her denim jumpsuit. A trowel,

clippers and rubber gloves protruded from a cob-
bler's apron tied around her waist. Clearly she
intended to work in her yard, yet she wore party sandals that revealed toenails enameled in crimson. A
working glamour girl? Lee guessed that whatever
Catherine did she did with a flourish.

"We must be going," Burr said after they had
chatted for a few moments. "This may be the day."

"The day?" Lee asked.

"The day we find the hull of the *Santa Isabella*."

"Every day could be Christmas in the treasure-
diving business," Hastings Adburee said with a toler-
ant smile.

"Do take care." Concern and sadness showed in
Catherine's blue eyes. "I couldn't bear another...
accident."

Burr stepped closer to his mother, slipping his arm
around her shoulders in a protective manner. "We'll
take care, mother. Don't worry. And when we find
the big pile I'll deck you out like a *señora* in Spanish
gold."

Lee wondered what accident Mrs. Adburee re-
ferred to and she felt a bit guilty at having judged
Burr so harshly. There was a family warmth here that
touched her. Perhaps there was more to Burr's character than the conceit and arrogance he had shown
her. Burr was an enigma.

Burr gave her no chance to ask questions about his
family, nor did he allow her time to unpack. Taking
her elbow he guided her through the hallway, out the
front entry and to the Mercedes. "Shall I take my
sweater, Lee? Surely you've warmed up by now."

Lee nodded, surprised that she felt reluctant to relinquish the comfort of the soft cotton, the scent of the sandalwood. Before she could shrug the sweater from her shoulders Burr reached to help her with it. His fingers felt warm where they brushed her collarbone, then as he eased the sweater off she felt bare and exposed. His gaze touched her shoulders, her arms until she felt as if she had performed a striptease instead of merely removing a sweater. Quickly she eased into the car.

Burr drove directly to the airport and they boarded the helicopter. Lee suddenly felt tense as she remembered their previous flight, the boys in the skiff. But today there were no boys in skiffs. She was only conscious of a vast expanse of sea and sky and two incompatible people suspended in a man-made miracle somewhere between the two elements. How remote the world seemed. She and Burr might be the only two people alive. What a frightening thought!

Lee welcomed the engine roar that made conversation all but impossible, for surely Burr would have demanded to know what she was thinking. And she wasn't sure what to answer. Any thoughts she was willing to share with him were so muddled she couldn't express them. Then suddenly she felt the helicopter dip. A skiff? Her hands clenched into fists as she peered below at a large yellow workboat. A fishing boat? She glanced questioningly at Burr.

"Galleons Unlimited." Burr shouted to make her hear. "My competitors."

So he really did have competition in his quest for the *Santa Isabella*. Lee saw her knuckles grow white as she waited for Burr to skim threateningly low over the yellow boat as he had over the skiff. A cruel twist curled his lips and his eyes glowed with amber lights, but he lifted the helicopter and in a few moments he set it down on the landing pad atop the *Sea Deuced* as casually as he might set a paperweight on his desk top.

"So you don't harass Galleons Unlimited?" Lee hid her relief. "I was prepared for the worst."

"Why would I threaten them?" Burr shrugged. "They're legitimate businessmen. Competitors. As long as I maintain a physical presence at my wreck site they won't intrude, and they have as much right to explore the rest of the sea as I do."

Lee puzzled over Burr's words, but she didn't ask the question uppermost in her mind. Why had he dived on the boys in the skiff? Burr was a paradox. There were many things about him she didn't understand.

"We're just in time," Burr said. "A dive team is surfacing at the stern right now. We'll get their report, then you can watch the second team go down. I want you to observe, to get the feel of our operation today. Follow me."

Burr led the way down the steep companionway like an admiral, knowing his orders would be obeyed. On the main deck they stood by the stern rail as two divers emerged from the choppy waves and climbed the boarding ladder. In their black wet suits and scuba gear they looked like creatures from another planet. Once aboard they removed flippers, masks, air tanks, and laughing and dripping brine, they joked with each other. Lee gripped the railing to steady herself against the roll of the boat and against her surprise at seeing that Raul was one of the divers.

"Raul," Burr called. "Where did you get that air tank?"

"From the supply room, sir."

"I told you not to dive today until you talked with me."

"But sir, I thought—"

"I don't care what you thought. When I give an order I expect it to be obeyed. I've a notion to fire you on the spot."

"Burr!" Lee spoke up, then lapsed into silence. This was none of her affair. Raul might be better off if he were working elsewhere. But she hated to see him unfairly treated.

"Get below deck," Burr ordered. "Clean the bilge. I'll talk to you later." Burr glared after Raul until he was out of sight, then he introduced Lee to the other diver, Scotty. Didn't divers have last names, Lee wondered. Or did Burr think last names were important only when they had a numeral following them?

"Any luck?" Burr asked Scotty.

He shook his head, sending a spray of seawater flying through the air. Lee stepped back a pace to avoid being splattered.

"Yo!" Scotty walked across the deck and shouted to an unseen companion in the hold and almost immediately an engine was shut off and the only sound remaining was that of waves splashing against the hull.

"How long have you been down?" Burr asked.

"Two hours. Henry showed up to help us, but still no luck."

"Where is he?" Lee peered over the side of the boat expecting to see another diver emerge from the depths. Burr and Scotty guffawed.

"Henry's our pet 'cuda," Burr explained. "He sometimes hangs around to oversee our operation."

"But isn't he dangerous?" Lee asked, knowing any barracuda was a potential danger and sensing that these boys were daredevil types who would deny that truth.

"Sometimes the brain becomes dulled to danger," Burr said mildly. Then turning to Scotty, he continued, "Take a break. Rest up. I'll want you to go down again this afternoon if the weather holds."

"Sure thing," Scotty said.

As Scotty disappeared into the enclosed cabin and headed toward the galley two more divers appeared from the hold. They already were in their diving gear and they plunged into the sea and disappeared before Burr could introduce them. For a few moments Lee watched the surface.

"The sea seems to have swallowed them," she said, thinking more about the barracuda than the sea. "Sometimes the surface is like a rippling curtain hiding the drama on the stage far below."

"Would you like to go down and see the show?" Burr asked.

"Of course." Lee looked him in the eye to reinforce the fact that she wasn't afraid to dive. "Do you have extra gear? I have my own, of course, but it's in my car."

"I have plenty of extra gear. But first I'll show you to your office and let you begin determining how you want to approach the work at hand. We'll dive this afternoon just before we go in for the day." Burr fixed her with his smoky gaze. "It'll give you something to look forward to."

Lee studied Burr's face. Was he trying to frighten her, to build up tension over the dive? Or was he being seductive, planting in her mind the romantic idea of the two of them alone in the mystic sea, yet making her wait for the event as a child might have to wait for a birthday celebration? Did he consider himself a gift from the sea? She wished she knew Burrton Adburee better. Until she did she would be on her guard.

"Why were you so tough on Raul?" Lee asked, hoping to put Burr on the defensive.

"I have my reasons."

"And I'm asking what they are. You didn't even give him a chance to explain his actions."

"I don't want explanations. I want obedience."

"I think you were unfair."

"All right. I'll level with you. I know you're... seeing Raul, but I have reason to believe he's on drugs. Maybe a pusher."

"You're wrong."

"Naturally you'd defend him. But I saw him giving money to some longhair and that usually means just one thing. Drugs. I won't have anyone bringing drugs aboard this boat. I can't actually prove anything against Raul... yet. But I'll fire him if he gives me half a chance. Come along with me now, Lee, and

I'll show you to your office. I ordered Margo to fix it up for you late yesterday."

"That was very thoughtful of you." Lee's heart was with Raul but she followed Burr to a cubicle behind the galley that was hardly big enough to turn around in. True, it contained a desk and chair, a file cabinet and a bookcase, but that was all. There was no carpet to soften the grate of shoes against aluminum, no easy chair to offer a visitor. Clearly Margo had shunted her to the corner farthest from Burr that she could find.

"It will be satisfactory, I'm sure," Burr said as Lee viewed the office in silence.

"Yes, I'm sure it will be quite satisfactory." She repeated his commanding words. "What would you like me to do first?"

Burr hesitated so long before answering that Lee felt herself flushing, but she looked at him with a direct gaze that she hoped conveyed the message that her question concerned business activities only.

"What would you like to do first, Lee?" Burr's voice carried the velvet-and-wine quality she had heard so often before. "You'll have to teach me, to show me what you want done." Burr's eyes roved over her body in a way that made her furious.

"I'd like to get right to work cataloging the artifacts you've found, the ones in your safe. There's a form in common use for that purpose, but it's usually used only when the salvagers know the exact identity of the galleon they're diving for." Lee opened a desk drawer and saw that Margo had fitted it with paper and carbon. "I'll make up dummy forms, number each artifact and record pertinent data about it.''

"That sounds like a good starting place," Burr agreed. "Come, I'll open the safe."

"You'll have to help me by supplying information on where each artifact was found," Lee said. "Will that be a problem?"

"Of course it'll be a problem." Burr scowled. "I can remember the approximate locations where some of the pieces were discovered, but I don't see how I can phrase an exact location that would be meaningful to posterity."

"Good."

"Good?"

"Good in that you now see the need for a way to identify place even though that place is on the sea bottom. I'll need some archaeological equipment to work with."

"I've never known a woman yet who didn't cost me money." Burr winked at her and Lee looked away, recalling his wink the night she left The Deck after Raul deserted her. What sort of a man winked at one woman while he held another woman in his arms? Lee thought she knew the answer.

"Then the equipment will be forthcoming?" Lee asked.

"Within reason," Burr replied. "Come, let's open the safe."

Lee walked the length of the boat with Burr to Margo's office, smiling a bit to herself. Margo was doing her best to keep the "other woman" at bay. Lee tried to think of some way to put Margo at ease, to let her know Burr was safe as far as she was concerned. She would need everyone's cooperation if her work was to be successful and she sensed that Margo could be a formidable enemy or a useful friend. As they entered Margo's domain Lee inhaled the cloying scent of heliotrope perfume even though Margo wasn't present. Did Burr notice it, too, she wondered. Perhaps he liked it. Perhaps he had given it to Margo. Lee forced her mind back to the business at hand. It was none of her concern what gifts Burr Adburee gave to his girl friends.

Burr opened the safe and scooped the artifacts into the "out" basket from Margo's desk. "Here. You can take these back to your office and begin work on them."

"Aren't you going to count the items?"

"I trust you, Lee. Take the loot and get to work on it."

"I prefer not to be responsible for the treasure," Lee retorted. "If you'll please wait, I'll leave an itemized list of the contents of this box here in the safe."

"If you insist." Burr sat down on the edge of Margo's desk, his lean legs thrusting out before him, taut, ready. Lee could feel his sardonic gaze, but she took her time, letting him know she was in charge of her part of this business. When she finished her listing she gave him the sheet of paper.

"Place it in the safe, please. When I return the items, we'll check them off the list."

Lee carried the treasure items to her desk and began working. She lifted the first coin, feeling its heavy coolness against her fingers. Denomination: 4 reales. Date: 1625. Mint: P. Assayer: T. Location: ?

Ruler: Philip IV. When she finished with the first coin she went on to the next one. She worked the morning away almost before she knew it, and she went to Margo's office for advice.

Margo had arrived and she was wearing a chocolate brown sheath that molded her figure and set off her chunky gold jewelry. Lee cleared her throat although she knew Margo was aware of her presence.

"How's it going?" Margo asked without greeting her.

"Fine. But I have a problem." Lee held out the sheets she had been working on for Margo's inspection. "I need a ledger so I can make more permanent recordings."

Margo studied the sheets. "Mint, P? What's that?"

"Potosi. That's the mint maker."

"And the assayer mark?" Margo asked. "You know about that, too?"

"I'll have to check some of them for sure," Lee admitted. "In my car I have books that I'll bring out tomorrow. But the locations will be the big puzzle. There's no way I can accurately fill in those blanks."

"Does it matter?" Margo asked. "We know the general area where they were found. Right here."

"It'll have to do, I suppose," Lee said. "But in the future. . . ." She paused as Burr entered the office.

"What about the future?"

"I'll need equipment for pinpointing exact locations," Lee said.

"You mentioned that before." Burr's tone exuded boredom, and Lee felt her hackles rise.

"I intend to impress you with the fact," she retorted.

"Have you finished with the items in the safe?" he asked, ignoring her sharp reply.

"Not quite," Lee replied. "I want to enter the material on these sheets in a ledger that will be housed in your safe."

"I'll bring you one from town in the morning," Burr said. "It's lunchtime, girls. Shall we go to the galley?"

"I've brought lunch for the two of us, Burr," Margo said. "My special avocado sandwiches."

"But there are three of us today, aren't there?" Burr smiled, yet his voice held an edge.

Lee spoke up quickly, not wanting to cause any friction between them. "I really don't care for lunch. When I eat a big breakfast I often skip a midday meal."

"Not out here you don't," Burr said. "We're going diving today and diving's strenuous work. You'll need a good lunch to keep up your strength."

Lee shrugged as Burr led them, calling over his shoulder, "Come on, girls. I'll toss a salad and we'll share the sandwiches." Margo frowned, pretended to straighten her desk, then when Burr was out of earshot she glared at Lee.

"I'm not sure just what you're up to, Lee. But remember one thing." Margo took a step closer to Lee. "I saw Burr Adburee first."

"I'll remember that, Margo." Lee kept a tight rein on her temper. "And you needn't worry. My only interest in Burrton Adburee concerns the treasure he is disturbing, the underwater heritage he is destroying.''

"You really expect me to believe that?" Margo snorted. "I've seen your type before."

"I doubt that." Lee spat the words, furious that Margo should misjudge her so.

"Ladies, do come along," Burr called, turning to wait for them.

When Lee glanced up, Burr's knowing smile told her that he knew she and Margo had been arguing over him. Her throat felt tight and her hands balled into fists. Burr Adburee might be used to having women argue over him, but she didn't intend to be one of them. And she did intend to make her position clear to both him and Margo.

Working slowly and casually Burr tossed an elegant salad for their lunch, surprising Lee completely. She had expected the galley refrigerator to house little more than wilted lettuce and limp carrots. She should have known such fare was not Burr's style. They dined on a mixture of leeks, romaine and endive with blue-cheese dressing, and the tang of the salad contrasted pleasantly with the blandness of the avocado sandwiches. Burr rose a notch in her estimation when Margo suggested wine and he vetoed the idea.

"Lee and I are diving later, Margo. No wine. You know the rules."

Lee noticed how subtly Burr emphasized the word "later," letting it roll off his tongue like an enticement. He was baiting her with his delaying tactic. Only when she was back in her office cubicle did she realize he was succeeding. She was growing so eager to get on with the dive that the thought of it was distracting her from the work at hand. She didn't hear Burr's approach until he spoke.

"Put this stuff up for now, Lee. It's time to see about your diving gear."

"Fine, Burr. I'll check these artifacts in with Margo." And Lee did just that. She asked Margo to watch while she checked off each item on the list. Then she in turn watched Margo lock the treasure into the safe.

"What will you do tomorrow?" Margo asked. "The divers really haven't found enough stuff to keep you busy."

"She'll work at the bank in town," Burr said, arriving in time to overhear Margo's question. "Lee, we have some silver stored in the basement of the bank. It's all in Styrofoam chests and covered with seawater. It'll be messy to work with, but—"

"I'm used to working with artifacts in seawater, Burr. No problem." Lee felt elated to know she and Margo would be separated for a day at least.

"Shall we get on with our dive now? You can change down in the hold. I've prepared a private cubicle for you."

Lee followed Burr down the companionway into the hold, breathing shallowly to avoid the stale fishy odor in that area. Again they passed the grimy cots where the divers slept; then Burr opened a narrow door in a bulkhead and snapped on a light.

"This is it, Lee. You'll find everything you need here except air tanks and fins. My divers always wear full wet suits at this time of year. The water temperature is over twenty degrees below body temperature today. One chills quickly under such conditions. Come topside when you're dressed. I'll have your air tank ready at the stern."

After Burr left, Lee examined the wet suit he had laid out on the cot that all but filled the tiny cubicle. Then she spied a bright red bikini. New. Tags still on it. When had Burr purchased that? Now she knew that this was no casual dive that was thought of just this morning. Burrton Adburee had planned this session well. But how had he known her size? And why had he chosen red? With her blond hair she usually avoided wearing red, thinking it a bit too flashy. She was glad it wouldn't show under the wet suit.

Lee stripped off her clothes and as she guessed, the bikini was a perfect fit. Burr had an exact eye for the female figure. She felt a pulse pound at the hollow of her throat as she dragged the wet suit on over the bikini and found it fit perfectly, too, molding to her body like black paraffin. The suit seemed hot as a steam oven now, but she knew from experience that it would feel comfortable once they reached a depth in the sea where the sun failed to warm the water.

She inhaled the rubbery scent of the neoprene and heard the swish of the heavy fabric as she climbed the companionway from the hold. Her heart raced as she saw Burr dressed in diving gear and waiting outside the enclosed deck. He wore only the top half of a wet suit and her gaze lingered on his tanned legs, his taut thighs. She joined him, hoping he wouldn't notice how nervous she was, and praying Margo was nowhere in sight.

"Is the suit satisfactory?" Burr asked.

"It's fine."

"And the red suit?"

"It's fine, too."

"I thought it would be." Burr smiled and stared at her as if he could see right through the wet suit to the bikini underneath. "Do you need weights?"

"No. The air tank will be enough."

Burr helped her into the harness and she felt the weight of the scuba tank heavy between her shoulder blades. She rubbed saliva over the edges of the face mask and tested it for fit, then she adjusted the mouthpiece. The routine took her mind off Burr and the scuba gear made her feel protected from his gaze. She looked over the side at the choppy waves where the currents seemed at war with the tide. She wasn't afraid. But why was she feeling so shaky? She hated to admit that Burr had this effect on her.

"Ready?" Burr asked.

Lee nodded.

"I'll go in first. Give me ten seconds, then follow me, okay?"

Again Lee nodded, waiting for Burr to adjust his mask and mouthpiece. Burr plunged over the side. Lee counted to ten, then she plunged in, too. In moments they were swimming side by side, gliding effortlessly like sea creatures through cool water that sparkled with light; and as usual Lee was stunned by the beauty of the underwater scene. The glittering silver of a school of ladyfish flashed to their right and a spotted grouper darted at their left. They swam over a reef that was made up of canyons, narrow slits in rock, dark mysterious caves. Lee saw bright red corals, brown staghorns, purple fanlike plants, and brain coral in all colors of the rainbow. Minnows flashed by like bits of animated sand. She was breathing easily through her mouthpiece, mesmerized by the silent beauty of the scene, when a distant churning started a roiling of the water.

She jumped, startled, but Burr, swimming close at her side, took her hand. For a moment she clutched it in fear and surprise. Then she relaxed. He had planned this, she thought, as she looked back at the boat and up a few feet to where the props of the *Sea Deuced* gently churned the water. He had planned to startle her. Now he placed his arm around her waist like a dancer urging her to their right, pointing in that direction with his free hand. Could she really feel the warmth of his touch through her wet suit? Surely not, yet she felt her blood rushing, her heart pounding. Lee nodded that she understood he wanted her to follow him, but she felt slightly bereft as he removed his arm from around her and glided away. As she watched Burr he seemed to enter a different dimension. His dark hair streamed away from his face and the skin on his slim powerful legs gleamed like dark alabaster. As she followed him she was amazed to find he was leading her into a column of clear water that rushed like a river all the way to the bottom of the sea. And as they were pulled nearer the bottom, the column expanded like a crystal balloon, growing larger and larger until it was the size of a football field. Two football fields.

Burr took Lee's hand again and she made no protest. His touch, along with the underwater scene, sent shivers through her body. They were standing on fine sand about twenty-five feet beneath the surface. No plant life grew here and no rocks poked through the sand. Overhead Lee could see the dark hull of the *Sea Deuced*, the silvery swish of the props slowly turning as they sent water splashing back against the deflector and then down to the bottom. She could imagine the force of the water had the props been going at full speed.

Lee held a lifeline grip on Burr's hand as the sand carpet beneath her feet began to slip away like a half-remembered dream. Now a large crater began to form and rocks and shells showed through the sandy haze. Some of the rocks were football size and Lee guessed them to be ballast stones carried in a galleon's hull from Spain. Just as she felt the force of the water was about to sweep them up and over the back of the crater someone stopped the engine, and the sand that had been hanging and clouding their vision began to settle like a shimmering veil, once again blanketing the rocks and shells in silence and mystery.

So this was how Burr's treasure-hunting device worked. Lee was impressed, so impressed she forgot she was still holding his hand. But when she tried to release it, his grip tightened, holding her captive. She felt her heartbeat throbbing in her fingertips. Surely Burr could feel it, too. As they kicked to the surface Lee felt Burr's thighs brush hers. Deliberately? She couldn't be sure. And she couldn't be sure whether or not she really welcomed the protection of the wet suit. She felt buoyant and vibrantly alive and she wished she were wearing only the red bikini or perhaps nothing at all. She could imagine herself and Burr gliding, gliding on through the crystal green sea until.... Until what? Her imagination ceased to function as Burr released her hand. They had reached the boarding ladder and he swam back, waiting for her to climb up first.

Lee felt reluctant to leave the underwater world. She felt she and Burr had shared a unique experience of such beauty that all her sensibilities had been honed to a new sharpness and she would never be the same again. After she removed her diving gear she kept her head averted from Burr so he couldn't guess her tumultuous feelings.

CHAPTER SIX

LEE'S WONDERFUL FEELING of buoyancy and animation vanished and her body felt leaden when she came aboard the *Sea Deuced* and found Margo waiting with the information that Burr was needed immediately in Key West for an unexpected business meeting. It was hastily decided that Margo should take her steno pad and accompany him. By the time Lee was dressed again Burr and Margo had already left in the helicopter, and Harry was waiting to take her back to Key West in the speedboat. As Lee picked up her shoulder bag and a few notes from her office she saw a group of divers playing poker at a table near the galley. Raul was with them. She looked his way but he avoided her gaze.

The ride back to the Garrison Bight dock where Harry planned to moor the speedboat was long but uneventful, and to Lee's surprise Elmer was waiting there for her in her own car.

"Burr said you'd be needing a ride, ma'am," Elmer said, holding the door for her.

"How kind of you, Elmer. I appreciate your thoughtfulness." And she appreciated Burr's thoughtfulness. Maybe he wasn't as totally self-centered as she had thought. It seemed strange to sit in the front seat and let someone else drive her home in her own car, but Lee sensed that Elmer wasn't the type to be comfortable with a woman at the wheel. Once they reached Marvista and Elmer left the Chevette, Lee drove back to Roosevelt Boulevard, stopped at The Pizza Huddle and ordered a small pizza to go. She was eating it in her room when Margo knocked and entered without invitation.

"Lee, I'm expecting a superimportant phone call this evening." Margo adjusted the spaghetti strap on her short raspberry-colored evening gown. "Would you take the message for me? I'll probably be out when the call comes."

"Of course, Margo." Lee had changed into jeans and she felt frumpy and foolish sitting there munching pizza while Margo, dressed to the nines, stood watching her. "Do you have any message for me to give to your caller?"

Margo cinched in the belt that spanned her tiny waistline and smiled coyly. "Burr and I are dining at Logun's, but I'd really rather not be disturbed there. Just say I was unexpectedly called out."

"Fine." Lee washed the last bite of pizza down with a sip of Coke.

"Put your scraps in the kitchen disposer," Margo said loftily. "Catherine hates roaches."

Lee clenched her teeth to keep from spitting out a tart remark, but she needn't have bothered. Margo was gone. Now that she was alone Lee unpacked quickly, then settled down to peruse some of the research books she'd brought in from the car. Reign. She needed to know dates of the Spanish kings for her record sheets. Surely some of the coins stored in the bank would have dates intact. She searched for a moment then came up with the information she needed. Philip II, 1556 to 1598. Philip III, 1598 to 1621. Philip IV, 1621 to....

Lee paused as she heard voices in the hallway.

"You look lovely tonight, Margo," Burr said. "As always."

"Between the two of us we'll turn every head in Logun's," Margo said. "You're some hunk of man, Burr. Shall we go?"

Lee marveled at the change in Margo's demeanor when she was around Burr. Her stentorian voice softened like chocolate left in the sun, her bossiness dissolved into mellowness. Lee guessed that Margo knew two autocrats could never get along well. And Margo also knew Burr was used to having women defer to his every whim. But what did she care how Margo behaved around Burr? Their private lives were none of her concern.

Margo's superimportant telephone call never came and Lee guessed the discussion of it had just been a ruse, Margo's not-so-subtle way of letting her know she was having dinner with Burr. Lee retired early but didn't drop into a sound sleep until after she heard Margo return at two in the morning. She wished she hadn't looked at the clock. Did Logun's stay open that late?

THE NEXT MORNING it was raining when Burr called for her. She had dressed carefully for her day at the bank. Her sea-green tailored suit managed to make her look businesslike without masking her femininity and she wore high-heeled straw sandals that matched her straw shoulder bag.

Yesterday's speedboat ride had left her wind-burned and now her skin felt as if it had been pulled taut over her high cheekbones. She wore a wide green scarf that pulled her hair back from the sides of her face while it let her bangs spread freely across her forehead. Holding two reference books under her hooded raincoat, she made a dash for the Mercedes. The clouds hung low like pewter-colored smoke and the windshield wipers were hard put to keep the glass clean as the rain slanted in from the sea. Thunder and lightning provided terrifying audiovisual effects, but Lee felt protected by the white plush of the Mercedes's interior...and by Burr. She had been afraid of storms all her life, but how crazy to think now that Burr could protect her from the elements. It was far more likely that the elements would protect her from Burr, by requiring him to devote his entire attention to driving.

"Rain suits you, Lee," Burr said, his gaze frankly admiring her as he turned the Mercedes toward Front Street. "I can never decide what color your eyes are. They change. Blue...gray...greenish. You're like a sea sprite flourishing with the humidity rather than letting it wilt you."

"Thank you, Burr." Silently Lee was grateful to her mother for having taught her how to accept a compliment graciously with poise and without protest, but it surprised her to realize how much Burr's words pleased her. Sea sprite. Raul had used the same word. "Maybe you'll find a guy who goes for the sea-sprite type." But regardless of what Burr said, it was clear that he went for the glamour-girl type. Margo. Yesterday's dive that she had considered so romantic had been no more than a working dive to Burr.

"I'm glad I chose today to work at the bank," Burr said. "There won't be any diving going on at the wreck site unless this weather clears."

"You'll be working at the bank, too?" Lee knew she should have guessed as much. Today Burr had forsaken his macho jeans and deck shoes and dressed in tailored, biscuit-colored slacks, silk shirt and Gucci loafers. The nubbed brown fabric of his shirt set off his tanned skin and he wore the shirt unbuttoned to mid-chest, revealing a gold escudo dangling from a heavy-linked chain around his neck. Had pirates worn gold coins on chains? In spite of his casually elegant clothes Burr still reminded her of a pirate.

"I said do you mind?" Burr asked.

"Mind what?" Lee flushed, realizing that she had been so engrossed in Burr's looks, his nearness, as they sat ensconced against the storm, that she had missed what he had said.

"Do you mind that I'll be working at the bank, too?"

"Of course not." She kept her voice steady but her heart raced at the thought of working with him all day. "I've brought some reference books. You can help me double-check dates and mint marks."

"Oh, I won't be working directly with you. I'll be

meeting with Roscoe Murdock, the president of Key West First National. We have some investment details to work out.''

''I see.'' Lee couldn't decide whether she was glad or disappointed and she was afraid to examine her feelings too closely. Now Margo's warning rang in her memory. ''I saw him first.''

When they reached Front Street Burr parked the Mercedes in the lot across the street from the bank and they waited a moment for the pelting rain to slacken before attempting to make a dash for the old structure.

''This bank has to be one of the most interesting buildings on the island,'' Lee said. ''The columns and arches. The combination of buff and red brick. Is it Spanish in origin?''

''I suppose so,'' Burr said. ''I've never thought much about it. Where a bank is concerned, it's what's inside that counts.''

Lee was saved from making a retort she would regret when Burr opened the door on his side. ''Here's a break in the storm, Lee. Let's go.''

Lee waited until Burr opened her door, then she slid from the car quickly. Burr took her books, linked his arm through hers, and propelled her across the street at a much faster pace than she liked. When they reached the protective overhang of the bank Lee pushed the hood of her coat back and paused a moment to catch her breath. She was steaming hot. Was it the humidity? Or was it Burr's nearness that made her need to cool off?

''Let's go in, Lee. We're a bit late as it is.''

Inside the bank the air was cool and impersonal, as were the tellers and clerks. Lee hated the way the atmosphere of a bank always made her feel like an urchin with dirt on her nose and scabs on her knees. Burr offered to take her coat, but she felt a need to keep it on. It made her feel less vulnerable to whatever was about to come next.

What came next was Roscoe Murdock. Burr performed the introductions and Lee managed a smile, a nod, a handshake. In spite of his tailored business suit, his carefully styled hair and his perfectly manicured nails, Roscoe Murdock was a beefy man who looked as if he would be more at home in a skiff counting lobster traps than in a bank counting dollar bills. Roscoe led them to the basement of the bank, unlocked a door at the far end of a musty corridor, then stood back to let Lee enter the small whitewashed room first.

"Dive Boys has rented this security room," Burr told her. "We haven't much stored in it yet, but there'll be more. And soon, I hope. You'll work here today."

Lee gazed around the room, which seemed more like a prison than a security chamber. It was stark and bare except for a sturdy oak table, four oak chairs and a few Styrofoam picnic coolers sitting in one corner. Lee laid her books on the table, inhaling the dank odor of damp brick and listening to a faraway drip of water against concrete.

"Is this satisfactory, Miss Cameron?" Roscoe Murdock asked.

"Yes. This will be fine." Lee walked to one of the

coolers. "Could you gentlemen lift this to the table for me, please?"

"Of course." Roscoe stepped toward the cooler, but before he reached it Burr strode past him, picked up the cooler and hoisted it onto the table. Lee watched the way his shirt strained over his muscled shoulders, the way the gold escudo and chain swung out and settled back against the mat of dark hair that furred his chest. Burr lifted the lid and a rank odor rose from the cooler.

Lee glanced at the contents that half filled the chest and gasped. "I didn't realize you had found so many coins, Burr."

"We try to keep the exact tally of what we've brought up a secret," Burr said. "But of course there'll be many more coins than this before we're through."

"Bank security rules require that you be locked in this room while you're working here, Miss Cameron," Roscoe Murdock said. "The rule is for your own safety as well as for the security of the treasure. You understand?"

"Of course." Lee nodded, hiding her reluctance to be locked in. What if there was a fire? "I'll have a key in here with me as I work, will I not?" she asked.

"Of course," Roscoe replied. "And Burr will have a second key. You are free to come and go as is necessary as long as you check in with our security guard at the head of the stairs." Roscoe gave Lee a heavy black key. "If everything is satisfactory, I'll leave you to get to work now. Burr, we'll meet in the room right down the hall. Very private down here."

Lee slipped the key into the pocket of her suit, removed a magnifying glass from her coat pocket, and prepared to begin studying the coins. Burr left for a few moments, then returned with a roll of paper towels.

"Looks as if you'll need these, Lee. This is going to be a messy job."

"I'll manage, thank you." Secretly Burr's thoughtfulness pleased her. He did think of others now and then.

"Keep the table well padded with this paper," he ordered. "I don't want anything to mar those coins."

Scratch my last two thoughts, Lee told herself. Why did she keep trying to assign attributes to Burr that clearly were not there?

At last Burr left her and she settled down to work, dipping into the brine in the cooler and removing pieces of eight that had known sun and moon of another age. The treasure stank. Black goop rubbed off onto her fingers. Yet the coins were like a silver stream flowing her to another place and time. Ancient Spain. What widows had wept over the tragic fate of the *Santa Isabella*? What children had wailed for their lost parents? What men and women had moaned in their sleep for lovers who would never lie in ecstasy beside them again?

Lee wiped the black residue from the coins as best she could. She was not a professional coin cleaner. Burr would have to hire an expert for that job. She had heard there was a reverse electrolysis process that was quite effective. For today she would merely sort the pieces of eight into groups of twenty-five each, record dates, reign and mint marks if she could, then bag the coins in mesh with plastic tags before replacing them in the brine.

Potosi? Was that mint mark a P or an S? Lee was squinting at the coin when the lights flickered, brightened momentarily, then went out. For an instant she sat quietly in the total darkness trying to quell the panic she felt rising inside her. Her throat ached. Her palms were slippery with sweat. The rank odor of the coins made her stomach churn. The air conditioner had expired with the lights and now the room began to close in on her, to suffocate her. She squelched a scream as she dug into her pocket for the key.

"Don't scream. Don't panic." She heard her own voice talking. There. She felt her fingers close over the cold metal of the key. She knocked over her chair as with arms outstretched she groped her way to the door and felt for the keyhole. Metal scraped metal as she thrust the key this way and that against the lock plate in search of the keyhole. Now she clenched her teeth against her rising panic. Lightning. Surely lightning had struck the bank. What if the building were on fire! Did she hear a siren?

"Help!" Lee shouted, giving clear voice to her panic. "Help! Someone help me!" She pounded the door with her fist and as she did so she heard her key drop, clanking against the concrete floor. Stopping, she groped for it. Where was it? Gone. Her fingers found a wide crack in the concrete. She gasped. She had lost the key. Panic was like an ever tightening vise gripping her and she pounded on the door again.

"Help! Help!" She felt tears streaming down her cheeks. Then suddenly a key scraped in the lock from the other side. The door opened and Burr called to her.

"Lee? Lee?" And she was in his arms, pressing her cheek high against his shoulder, her breasts against his chest. Her hips and thighs molded against his as she inhaled the sandalwood scent of him.

"Lee, what is it?" Burr asked, still holding her tight. "The lights have gone out, but...."

"Trapped," Lee muttered. "Dropped the key. Fire. Trapped." She couldn't control her shaking.

"Everything's all right," Burr said. "There's no fire. The door's open. We'll find the key when the lights come on."

As the calmness in Burr's tone reached her, Lee got a grip on herself. Embarrassment flooded through her. She tried to ease away from him, but he dropped his hands to her hips, molding her to him even more tightly. Moments ago she had clung to him as a refuge in a time of supposed danger, but now their nearness was something quite different and her shaking had changed to an expectant trembling, a vibrancy like that of the wings of a hummingbird searching out sweet nectar.

She felt his ragged breath hot upon the hair beneath her scarf as he continued to pinion her against his body. Then his hands slowly began to burn a deeper meaning into her as they moved over the hollows and rises of her body with a fundamental understanding. Slowly. Slowly. There was no rush to him and his slowness made her ache as she longed for his touch and hated herself for her weakness.

She could not say that his lips found hers because hers had been just as seeking as his when they met. At the same time his lips defined their priorities the slow exploring movements of his hands carried the promise of pleasures yet to come. Lee felt a deep wanton longing within and there was nothing of the neophyte in the way she responded to him. Somewhere from the crevices of her mind a monitor warned her to withdraw, but her reflexes ignored the warning. She was powerless to defend herself against his exquisite torture as his hands again ranged downward, cupping her hips with maddening deliberation at the same time his tongue slowly traced liquid fire on her lips. The soaring vibrancy continued for a few moments even after the lights flashed back on again, and Lee pulled away from Burr with great reluctance.

Neither of them spoke for a moment, their breath coming in ragged snatches, and it was the grating of Roscoe Murdock's step in the hallway that plummeted them both back to the saner realms of reality.

"Sorry, Burr," Roscoe said. "And Miss Cameron. Hope the power failure didn't inconvenience you too much. Everything's fine now. No damage done. Air conditioner's back on. All signals are go. Is everything okay down here? I thought I heard some shouting a few minutes ago when I was called upstairs to the phone."

"Everything's fine, Roscoe," Burr said with a

calmness Lee could not have matched herself. "Lee just dropped her key and couldn't find it in the dark. But see, there it is." Burr stooped to retrieve the key from a shallow crack in the concrete.

"Glad there's no problem." Roscoe beamed at them. "Shall we continue our business, Burr?"

"Of course." Burr started to leave, then turned to Lee. "I'll call for you at lunchtime, Lee. Wait."

Lee nodded mutely, but once the door was closed and locked again she sat staring into space. What a fool she had made of herself. What must Burr be thinking of her! And how could she possibly face him at the lunch table?

Lee's hand shook as she held the magnifying glass over the next piece of eight she fished from the briny cooler. 1631. Whose reign? Her mind was a muddle of Philips and at last she gave up really studying the coins. She merely counted them into groups, then made a shopping list of things she would need to complete the day's work.

When Burr called for her at lunchtime she was outwardly calm, but inside she was still quivering. Did he feel the same? There was no way to tell. Outside the storm was over and the sun was turning the island into a steamy kitchen. Burr drove her to a secluded restaurant on White Street, but he made no mention of her panic or of their prolonged kiss. They washed red snapper and French fries down with light beer and almost no conversation, and when they finished eating Burr asked her to dance. In a far corner of the restaurant there was a handkerchief-size dance floor where a jukebox was playing ballads.

"I never dance on my lunch hour," Lee said, grasping at any wild excuse that would keep her from Burr's arms.

"I think you're afraid."

She met his direct gaze and hoped her eyes didn't reveal her fear. "What would I be afraid of?"

"Me."

"You flatter yourself."

"Then maybe you're afraid of you, of your own reactions. I had no idea a sea sprite could generate such heat waves."

Lee looked away. "I apologize, Burr. I pushed the panic button over that storm. I assure you it won't happen again."

"Did I say anything to indicate I didn't want it to happen again? I've never minded having a lovely lady pursue me."

"Pursue you! I certainly wasn't pursuing you."

"Oh? I had hoped you were. I thoroughly enjoyed that kiss, Lee, and I'd like to think you enjoyed it, too."

"I can hardly deny it." Lee laughed in spite of herself, remembering.

"Good. I like an honest woman." Burr winked at her. "You just happened to get panicky in the dark. Just *happened* to drop your key in that terribly deep crack."

"You're being unfair to tease me, Burr. I really did panic for a few minutes."

"I suppose you would have clung to King Kong if he had produced the key to that room."

"I'm glad it was you with the key, Burr. But I

apologized for my behavior and the apology stands."

"All right. I'll accept it. . .for now. Tell me, how did the work on the coins go?"

"Very well. I'll need some supplies. Some mesh bags. Some plastic tags. But Burr, nothing more should be brought up from the wreck site without pinpointing its location before removal."

"And how do you intend to do that?"

Lee relaxed a little, glad that the talk had turned to business. "I'll need a steel grid. And if you can afford it, I'd like a plane table and an underwater camera. I used such equipment at school, but they didn't belong to me."

"What you need you shall have," Burr said. "Where will you order such equipment?"

"It's available in Miami, but. . . ."

"But what?"

"Ordering takes a long time. Maybe I could drive to Miami, pick up what I need and drive back. I could do it in a single day if I call the order in ahead. And I really do need to do some research in the library, too. Many of those coins stump me."

"It won't be necessary for you to drive to Miami, Lee. I'm flying there tomorrow on business. You can come along, do your research, buy your equipment and return with me."

Lee hesitated. She hadn't counted on spending a day with Burr in Miami. "I don't know, Burr. Perhaps I should drive."

"I'll make that decision, Lee. You'll fly with me and we'll be leaving at eight o'clock sharp."

"All right." Lee took a gulp of water to cool her

temper, to help her remember that a good employee obeyed her boss. "I'll be ready."

"Pack an overnight case," Burr said. "My business in the city will take two days. We'll be staying over."

CHAPTER SEVEN

LEE FINISHED her afternoon's work in the bank's security room, dreading to have to face Burr again for the ride back to Marvista. The memory of their kiss haunted her, tantalized her, and the thought of taking an overnight trip to Miami with Burr unnerved her completely. How could she have behaved so poorly that morning! In Burr's eyes her actions probably placed her in the same category as all the other women who pined for him. Pined for him? That seemed an old-fashioned term. Lusted for him might be more accurate.

"We'll be staying over." The echo of Burr's words clogged her mind. Had his tone been suggestive? In his arrogance and conceit was he taking for granted that she was programmed for instant sex? If that was in his thinking she supposed it was her own fault. She had flung herself into his arms, hadn't she? And her body had responded to his kiss in a way she had been unable to control. But on the other hand he had certainly taken advantage of her panic. But what was past was past. She would see that such a scene was never repeated.

When Lee emerged from the bank's basement she found to her relief that Burr had left sometime earlier and that her own car was waiting for her in the parking lot. Magic? She guessed the name of the magic was Elmer and she silently thanked him. She stopped at a steak house for an early dinner, then she drove on to Marvista. After making a reservation at a Miami hotel near the library she changed into blue shorts and halter then pulled her scarf off, brushing her hair until it shimmered in a golden halo around her head. She read for a while before she stepped outside into the U-shaped courtyard. In the distance where uninhabited keys mounded from the sea, flocks of white egrets descended on the mangroves like salt spilled from a shaker. Lee walked some distance toward the golden-sand beach where tangles of greenish brown turtle grass marked the high-tide line before she heard the metallic sound of clippers and saw Burr's mother pruning a small tree.

"Good evening," Lee called, strolling toward the lush greenery that almost hid the older woman. "You're keeping busy, I see."

Catherine smiled and slipped her pruning clippers into her pocket. "Yes. I like to prune the lime trees myself to be sure it's done correctly. Hastings and I enjoy the fruit so much."

Lee started to step back to view the tree more carefully, but Catherine touched her elbow and restrained her with a glance. "Excuse me, but I don't want you to fall."

Lee looked back and saw she was near the edge of a yawning hole. "A well?" she asked. "A well right here in the middle of the courtyard?"

"A cistern of long ago," Catherine corrected.

"There are several of them around here. In the old days when the island was very small, before building contractors began marl-filling to create more land, several homes occupied this lot where Marvista stands today. And each house had its cistern."

"The steep pitch of the old Conch house roof was put there for a practical purpose, right?"

"Right. Before World War II the cisterns were the only sources of fresh water. But they're obsolete now, and my next project is going to be to turn them into reflecting pools that will enhance the grounds."

"With some low plantings, some lily pads, the overall effect should be very pleasing," Lee said.

"Much better than capping them and trying to hide them."

Lee visited with Catherine for a few moments longer and when she returned to her suite she was surprised to find Margo at her inner hallway door. Clearly Margo was not going out that night. Her hair was in rollers and she was wearing a faded terry-cloth robe and scuffs.

"How did your day go?" Margo came in and sank down uninvited on a rattan chair near the small desk in Lee's sitting room.

"I found the silver artifacts most interesting," Lee answered, guardedly. Instinctively she knew Margo had come to pump her, to learn whatever she could about Burr's activities.

"I understand you're going to Miami tomorrow." Margo's green cat eyes gazed at her through narrowed lids.

That is getting right to the point, Lee thought. So

she had seen Burr and he had told her. But that was only natural, wasn't it? Margo was his secretary, his business manager, his.... "Yes. I need some special underwater equipment and I need to work at the library. I wanted to drive up, but—"

"Burr told me you'd be flying to Miami with him." Margo's tone told Lee that Margo wanted her to know the flight was common knowledge and nothing at all special. Lee was willing to go along with that. More than willing. But Margo's eyes belied her tone of voice, their green glitter speaking louder than any words.

"Perhaps you'll accompany us, Margo. Burr said he was going on business."

"He's going to raise money," Margo said.

"Oh?" Lee looked at her as she sat down in a chair across the room. "I supposed Burr's operating expenses came from the family boatyard business or perhaps from the sale of some of the artifacts."

Margo snorted. "Hastings isn't about to let any of his money go into Burr's salvage business. Salvage is expensive work." Margo spoke in a patronizing manner. "Dive Boys suffers from periodic money shortages and when that happens something has to be done. Sometimes Burr can get bank loans if he's found enough treasure to put up as collateral."

"Then Burr's going to Miami to try for another bank loan?" Lee asked, wondering which pieces of treasure he was willing to part with. What had he parted with in the past?

"No bank loan this time. He's going up to talk to some potential investors and he usually comes home with a pocket full of checks and a head full of promises."

"People are *that* eager to risk their money on such a precarious venture?" Lee wanted to believe Margo and she had no reason to disbelieve her. Burr Adburee would rise a notch or two in her mind if she was sure he wasn't a leech sucking money to support his fun-and-games search for the *Santa Isabella* from his father's business.

Margo lighted a cigarette and puffed smoke toward the ceiling for a moment, then she continued. "Burr works on the theory that most people lead very dull lives and that no matter what they're doing they'd much rather be out searching the sea for treasures from sunken Spanish galleons. So he offers them a way to enjoy his quest vicariously. He sells shares of stock in Dive Boys. You should see him in action."

Lee looked away, thinking that she had already seen Burr in more action than she had been able to handle. "No doubt he is very persuasive."

Again Margo looked at her sharply through narrowed lids. "Why do you say that?"

Lee groped for a quick answer at the same time she forced glibness into her voice. "Because anyone who raises large sums of money has to be as persuasive as the Pied Piper himself. I've worked for some university projects and I know raising a sufficient amount of money was always a problem."

Margo relaxed and stubbed out her cigarette. "I write letters for Burr, setting up appointments with moneyed people in Miami and other big cities. Then

Burr calls on them personally. That's what he'll be doing tomorrow. He'll carry with him some of the gold pieces you saw in the safe.''

"But isn't that risky?'' Lee asked. "Those artifacts are priceless. Even their bullion value would be staggering. I can't believe he carries them with him.''

"Well, he does. And loose. In his pocket. He carries them the way you'd carry a comb or lipstick. When he goes into a potential investor's office he nonchalantly reaches into his pocket, pulls out a few escudos and that chain and drops them on the man's desk. Burr's shrewd. If he can manage it he sometimes lets one of the coins roll onto the floor so the businessman will have to reach to pick it up. Once that man feels the weight of the gold and sees its gleam, he's usually hooked.''

"That sounds incredible.''

"But it's true. I can understand it. A lot of investors do not want to put all their money in tax-free bonds and blue-chip stocks. So they might invest in Dive Boys. They find that reading about Burr's activities—which are then their business, too—is a lot more interesting than reading the Dow-Jones averages.''

"How much do they usually invest?''

"See?'' Margo laughed. "Even you are more than halfway hooked, aren't you?''

"My interest in the treasure isn't monetary,'' Lee said. "I was just curious as to how much money these investors come up with.''

"It depends. An unlimited share in the venture might sell for ten thousand dollars. A limited share might sell for much less.''

"I don't understand those terms," Lee confessed.

"A limited share would be defined by certain dates. The investor would be buying a share in any treasure found between the specified dates. If nothing was found during that time, he would be out of luck. That's why limited shares cost less."

"But an unlimited share would allow the investor to claim a part of whatever treasure is found no matter when it's found, right?"

"Right." Margo laughed. "Care to buy a few shares? You might be able to save Burr the flight to Miami."

"Afraid not," Lee said, refusing to let Margo goad her in any way. "Investing in a treasure operation is quite out of my reach. I'm just a poor working girl."

"Me, too." Margo lighted another cigarette. "But some girls have more to work with than others."

"Did you know Burr's brother?" Lee asked, changing the subject completely.

"Zack? Yes. I knew him. . . well. Why do you ask?"

"I'm curious. Are those his pictures in Burr's office?"

"Yes." Margo looked at her fingernails and although Lee sensed her reluctance to discuss Zack Adburee, she asked another question.

"How did he die, Margo? Was it an accident?"

Just then the telephone rang and Margo reached for it, seeming to welcome the interruption in their conversation. Lee bristled at first, then she relaxed. All the phones in this wing of the house were on the same line. The call might be for Margo. If so, Lee hoped Margo would take it in her own suite. She had no desire to listen in on a private conversation between Margo and Burr.

"It's for you." Margo thrust the receiver toward Lee. "A man." She rolled her eyes. "Voice like satin. I could go for that."

Lee took the receiver, wondering who could be calling her, wishing Margo would take the interruption as her cue to leave. But Margo didn't budge.

"Hello?" Lee turned her back to Margo and pretended to look out the window. Raul's voice flowed across the line. Satin. A good description.

"I need some money, Lee. Can you help me out?"

"Tell me about it." Lee tried to choose words that would reveal nothing of importance to Margo, but she was immediately on guard. Raul had to learn to be responsible. He couldn't expect money to appear at the sound of a dial tone.

"Are you alone?"

"No, I'm not."

"Who's there?"

"I really can't say at this time."

"Burr?"

"Of course not. Why do you think...." Lee caught herself before she blurted Burr's name.

"Margo?"

"Yes."

"Get rid of her."

"I can see no easy way of doing that."

"Then come meet me where we can talk privately."

"All right."

"The Deck?"

"No way." Lee refused to accept a meeting place where Burr might appear.

"Mallory dock?"

"All right. Can you be more specific?"

"It's not all that big, Lee. Just show up. I'll find you."

"All right."

"In fifteen minutes."

"Fine."

Lee hung up the phone and faced Margo. She said nothing, hoping Margo would take the hint and leave. Margo stayed.

"I don't suppose you'll reveal who Satin Voice really is?" Margo asked.

"That's right, Margo. I won't. After all, one's private life is. . . one's private life. A girl's entitled."

"I don't mean to pry." At last Margo stood. "I'm really glad you've found a boyfriend so. . .quickly, Lee. Sometimes a new girl in a new town is rather at loose ends. Sometimes she goes for the first male who presents himself."

"You mean Burr, of course." Lee made no effort to keep the irritation from her voice. "You needn't worry about my being interested in him, Margo. I got your earlier message loud and clear. As far as I'm concerned Burr is all yours."

"That's easy to say. But Burr's very much a man, and when you're thrown with such a person day after day—well, things can happen."

Lee flushed, remembering the kiss that morning.

"But *things* aren't going to happen. At least not between Burr and me." It surprised Lee that a girl with Margo's looks and brains would feel so insecure in her ability to hold her man, yet she guessed that Margo was being guided by past experience. Margo knew Burr Adburee much better than she did. Margo had probably watched a whole string of women fall for the Adburee charm.

"Margo, you never did answer my question about Zack. How did he die? Catherine hinted at an accident."

Margo hesitated. She shrugged. Then hostility blazed from her eyes. "If you're so interested, why don't you ask Burr?"

"I just may do that," Lee replied, knowing she wouldn't.

Margo relaxed a bit and forced a smile. "Good night, Lee. If there's anything I can help you with in Miami tomorrow, let me know. Phone calls to the right people? Reservations?"

"Thanks, Margo. I'll manage." *She wants to go along,* Lee thought. Lee guessed Margo also wanted to know where she would be staying, where Burr would be staying. And as a matter of fact, so did Lee. She had made her own reservation; but wasn't it strange that Burr's business manager and secretary hadn't made his reservation for him?

Lee waited a few moments after Margo returned to her suite before she slipped through her outside door into the courtyard; then she walked around Marvista's guest wing and on to her Chevette. She drove to Mallory, parked in the lot behind the dock and scanned the area for Raul. Why wasn't he watching for her? They could talk right here in the car. Was he in trouble, she wondered. Or was he already realizing that his diving pay would barely meet his needs?

Lee waited for a few moments and when Raul didn't arrive she left the Chevette and went to the dock. It was almost deserted. A long-haired boy playing a melancholic tune on a recorder sat with his feet dangling over the edge of the dock. At the far end of the concrete an olive-skinned man and woman were tossing a circular net into the water, hauling in shiners and transferring them to a tin bait bucket. Maybe Raul had been delayed. Lee sat down on a concrete bench to wait. Behind her she heard a whir of tires and the honk of horns from Front Street; ahead she heard waves splashing against the gray dock pilings. Now and then tarpons jumped, their huge gleaming bodies silvered by the glow of the dock lights. How mysterious the gleaming black sea looked at night. Mysterious and changing and mesmerizing and endless as time itself. Then before she knew it Raul was beside her.

"Thought you'd never get here," he said.

"And I thought you weren't around," Lee replied. "I really don't enjoy sitting here alone at night, Raul."

"Let's go sit in your car. It'll be more private there."

Lee rose and they walked back toward the Chevette. When they came to the steps leading down into the darkened parking lot Raul took Lee's hand, offering support; and just at that moment a car entered the lot, catching them in the glare of its head-lights. Lee glanced up quickly just before the car turned. The white Mercedes.

"Burr!" Lee exclaimed involuntarily. "What's he doing here? Raul, did you call him?"

"Calm down, sis. Why would I call Burr? And, anyway, it isn't Burr. Take a better look."

Lee had looked away and lowered her head, hoping that maybe Burr wouldn't recognize her, but at Raul's words she turned and stared. The car had swung around the second tier of parking places and was now heading away from the lot, but she knew who the driver was. The platinum blonde with her hair in rollers had to be Margo. Of all the nerve! Lee leaned up and gave Raul a kiss just for Margo's benefit.

"What's the deal?" Raul asked. "You don't want her to think you're my sister, do you? She must have followed you here, but why, Lee?"

"Curiosity, I suppose. Your voice over the phone intrigued her. She wanted to know who my boyfriend was, and since I wouldn't tell I guess she decided to find out for herself. Margo is a woman of determina-tion and action."

"She must have a nose ring in Burr to be able to jump into his car any old time she pleases. Someday I'm going to drive a Mercedes like that, Lee. Real class. That's what that is. Real class."

"On three bucks an hour you're planning to drive a Mercedes? Be realistic, Raul. It just isn't possible."

"Anything is possible for those who believe," Raul teased.

"For those who believe what?" Now they had

reached the car and Raul opened the door for her, slipped in beside her.

"For those who believe their dreams will come true," Raul said. "I hope you're not going to fall for Burr, Lee. I saw the way you looked at him yesterday."

"This is why you called me here?"

"No, but I was wondering if you were trying to get me in trouble with him. He rode me unmercifully yesterday."

"That's your own fault. He's got a thing against drugs and he thinks you may be into them. He'll fire you if you give him the least reason to."

"That's not fair!"

"But that's how it is. You could quit. Go back to school."

"No way."

"Why did you ask me to come here, Raul? You said you needed money. Why?"

"It's not for me, Lee. I wouldn't ask you to help support me, knowing how you feel about that and all. I'm asking for a friend."

"What friend?" Lee kept her voice stern, knowing that Raul had a way of wheedling whatever he wanted from her.

"Spike."

"Spike who? Does he have a real name?"

"Are names that important? Spike's a human being who's in trouble and who needs help. He's got no friends down this way except me."

"And when did you and Spike get to be such buddies?"

"We're friends, Lee. That's all that matters. I need a hundred bucks."

"I thought Spike was the one in need."

"He is. It's for his bail bond."

"No way, Raul. I'm not providing bail bonds for your live-in-the-street friends. How did he land in jail? Drugs?"

"The cops said he was a vagrant just because he was dozing on the beach by West Martello. He had sixty bucks when they picked him up. They took it. He'll never see it again. And now he's in the slammer. Just a hundred, Lee. I'll pay you back. A hundred dollars will buy this guy's freedom. Be a sport."

"No, Raul. Spike sounds like bad news to me." Lee thought Raul would argue some more, but instead she felt anger coming off him like a mist. He flung the car door open and leaped out as if he couldn't get away from her quickly enough. Then he banged the door shut so hard it made the whole car shake. He was halfway to the gate of the parking lot before Lee recovered from her surprise and started the motor.

She paid her parking fee then drove toward Marvista, her thoughts churning. She couldn't help feeling sorry for the boy in jail. Maybe the police had treated him unfairly. And again, maybe they had not. That wasn't for her to judge. She felt she had done the right thing in refusing to lend Raul the money. A person wasn't apt to learn effective lessons in self-reliance if big sis came through with money at every request.

At first Lee resented Margo's intrusion at the

dock, then she smiled to herself. Perhaps it was just as well that Margo thought Raul was her boyfriend. Maybe it would relieve Margo's fear that Burr might stray from her side. Lee realized that Burr appreciated Margo's business acumen and also her more obvious attractions. Lee needed Margo's friendship. Margo could be a strong ally in time of need. But what sort of need was she anticipating? She wasn't sure. She drove on home with a feeling of unrest as she thought about Raul and Margo and about Burr and their trip to Miami the next day.

CHAPTER EIGHT

BURR WAS WEARING a well-cut brown business suit, a white silk shirt and a saffron-colored tie as they took off for Miami the next morning in the twin-engine Cessna. Lee had dressed carefully, trying for a look that was businesslike yet comfortably casual. She had used only a little blue green eye shadow to enhance her eyes and she had brushed her hair until it lay smooth and flat against her head. She thought her sea-green tailored skirt and white short-sleeved blouse gave her a dignified look; a tan braided belt that matched her shoulder purse and her sandals completed her outfit.

Burr had ordered Raul to drive them to the airport, and all during the ride he had goaded Raul and emphasized the fact that Lee would be staying overnight. Lee had barely been able to control her anger. And she had felt at ease with her appearance in her suite, but now that they were in the plane and under way, Burr's sidelong scrutiny unnerved her.

"You should always wear that sea-green color, Lee. It does wonderful things for your eyes."

"I'll remember that in the future," Lee said lightly, thinking it was hard to bring off subtle voice inflections when she had to make herself heard above the roar of the plane.

"I've made reservations for us at the Moonraker Hotel on Miami Beach," Burr said.

"I've already made reservations to stay in Miami," Lee shouted. "The Seashore Hotel."

"I'll cancel for you."

"But I'd rather stay at the Seashore," Lee shouted. "It's easy walking distance from the library."

"I can drive you wherever you need to go." Burr spoke in an it's-all-settled tone that infuriated her.

"I suppose it's useless to argue with you."

"Right." Burr winked at her. "But I admire your spunk. We'll have separate rooms," Burr added, his eyes twinkling. "I knew you'd be concerned about that."

"I wasn't worried at all. I took separate rooms for granted." She flushed under Burr's amused gaze, knowing he must be remembering her wanting kiss, the way she had flung herself at him less than twenty-four hours ago. She peered out the window to avoid having to meet his gaze. The sky was a bright clear blue with no clouds in sight. Below them the overseas highway was a slim thread stitching the islands to each other and to the sea. Sometimes the waves reflected such a glare from the sun that they reminded Lee of a distant expanse of crumpled aluminum foil throwing back the light. Then moments later the water would look a dull bottle green, and sailboats bobbing on the surface would seem almost within touching distance. Lee felt a sense of remoteness that made her uneasy. Yet there was something very romantic and exciting about flying, about being alone high in the sky with Burr. And sharing the experience of flight tended to draw her to him in a way that frightened her. For a moment she wondered if he felt the same sensation, then she guessed that he didn't. The exhilaration of flight would only serve to enhance Burr's feeling of his dominion over ordinary creatures such as she.

They circled Miami airport for almost fifteen minutes before being granted permission to land. Burr touched the Cessna down gently. When he leaned in front of Lee to open the door and slip from the plane she was aware of his shoulder brushing against her breasts and she guessed the touch had not been accidental. Did he think she would be flattered that he wanted to touch her? How boorish he could be! Now there was nothing to do but allow him to help her from her seat and to the ground. The distance was too great for her to manage without assistance.

"I've reserved a rental car," Burr said as they crossed the breeze-swept airstrip and headed for the terminal building. "I'll drive you directly to the library...unless you want to stop by the hotel and...freshen up."

"The library will be fine, Burr. I have everything I need here in my attaché case."

Burr gave her a sidelong glance. "You have everything you need without the attaché case, Lee. If I haven't told you, you're beautiful. Make a record of it, okay?"

"How very flattering. Perhaps you should have Margo make a memo of it, so you won't forget. Do remember this is a business trip, Burr."

"I'm sure you won't let me forget."

They entered the air-conditioned comfort of the terminal where crowds gathered around the gift shops and the departure gates. Voices babbled in Spanish, English, French. A cat yowled from its carrying case. Uniformed stewardesses hurried toward the next concourse, pulling their overnight cases behind them on tiny two-wheeled carts.

Burr headed directly for the Hertz desk, produced his ID and credit card, and waited until he was summoned to accept his car.

Lee admired the expert way he handled the car in the heavy traffic. But in spite of the traffic, the heat and the humidity, she loved the sprawling city. Sometimes she thought it seemed like a maze of gray concrete, then she would look up at green palms set against the cloudless sky and somehow the gray concrete would become a part of the beauty.

After only a few minutes Burr pulled up in front of the library. "I'll meet you here at five."

"You'll be wasting your time. I'll only need to spend the morning here. This afternoon I'll track down equipment."

"Bill it to me, of course."

"That's what I intended to do."

"How will you get about the city?"

"There are buses. And cabs. I much prefer to be on my own. I know the city; I lived here for years."

"I'll see you at the hotel shortly after five."

"I didn't know I was required to keep curfew." Lee tried for a teasing tone. "But if you want me to punch a time clock...."

Burr scowled. "You seem to forget that I give the

orders around here, Lee. The Moonraker. Don't forget the name of the hotel. I'll see that your room key is at the desk. But I want you there shortly after five. You may know the city upside down and backward, but I'm responsible for you while we're on this trip and I intend to know that you've reached the hotel safely."

"All right, Burr. I didn't intend to be obstinate." For a moment Lee really appreciated Burr's concern for her safety in spite of his overbearing manner. "I'll be at the hotel shortly after five."

Lee watched after the car until it disappeared in the maze of traffic; then she felt irritated at herself for watching. Did Burr really worry about her safety, or was he merely concerned about the safety of his archaeologist who could perhaps help him to fame and fortune by finding a means of identifying his treasure galleon? She guessed that the second reason was probably the right one.

It was an old-fashioned library where hushed silence was the order of the day and where the smell of freshly bound books permeated all other odors. Lee went to the card catalog, then took an elevator to the floor where stacks housed books on ancient Spain.

For two hours she read, Xeroxed off needed data, took notes. Philip IV. She wondered what it must have been like to be king of Spain at age sixteen. Some historical texts she had read had called him dim-witted. Surely by today's standards he would have been called an exceptional child, or a child with a learning disability. Had Philip minded that he couldn't even sign his own name, that his guardians had had a stamp in his name made for official use?

Lee forced her attention back to the *Santa Isabella*. She searched in many volumes without finding any pertinent information about the galleon Burr thought he had found, or was about to find. A few pieces of eight and gold artifacts certainly didn't constitute proof. He needed to find the hull and the primary cultural deposit. What if Galleons Unlimited found it first? It would mean the end of her job, the end of her chance to help preserve the underwater environment. Burr had no other galleon to seek.

Traveling by bus Lee visited camera shops and archaeological supply houses, trying to be conservative in what she ordered, yet wanting instruments and equipment that would take her where she needed to go in her work. It was just before five o'clock when she took a cab to the hotel.

The Moonraker was the tallest high rise in the bay area. More gray concrete. Even the doorman wore gray. But the hotel had lots of windows to give it a sleek appearance. It was the sort of hotel she would have expected Burr to choose. She checked in at the registration desk and picked up her key. A sudden unnerving thought struck her. What if Burr had lied about the separate rooms? She was glad she had arrived early. She could check out her quarters and if they were unsatisfactory she could make other arrangements without his interfering.

She took an elevator to the fourteenth floor, the top floor, then followed the bellhop to room 1414. The boy unlocked the door and waited for his tip.

Lee half expected to find Burr inside waiting for her, but the room was unoccupied. It was plush, as she should have known it would be. That was Burr's style. He turned plush into an art form.

She felt her heels sink into the thick sea-green carpeting as she walked to the bed covered with a quilted spread of the same color. Sea-green. "You should always wear that sea-green color, Lee." The memory of Burr's words drifted back to her. Had he requested a room done in this special shade? The color was everywhere—in the draperies that hung at the sliding doors that opened onto a balcony overlooking the sea, in the bath fixtures and in the bath sheets. It was too much, too overpowering. Lee tested the door on the opposite side of the bath, expecting to find it locked, but to her surprise and irritation it opened into an adjoining room. Burr's room. She recognized his bag on the luggage rack, the hint of the scent of sandalwood. Quickly she closed the door and locked it. No. That would never do. She couldn't lock him from the bathroom. He would only come to her room seeking entry. She left the door to his room unlocked and locked the bathroom door to her room instead.

Glancing at the dressing alcove off her bedroom she stopped, startled. Someone had unpacked her bag. Her clothes were neatly hanging from hangers on the clothing rod. Who had done this? Burr? How dare he go through her things! Quickly Lee jerked open a drawer. Yes. There were her underthings all neatly arranged. Bra over panties...slip over hose. How dare he! Well, she would surprise him. If he thought she was going to wait here ready to fall into his arms he was sorely mistaken. Quickly she changed into her bikini and cover-up and went down to the pool. She was surprised that the water didn't sizzle when she dived in—she was so hot with anger.

"Beautiful, Lee," Burr called when she surfaced. Then he glanced at his watch. "You're early. I'm flattered."

What was he doing here? For a moment Lee stared at Burr's tanned leanness, wondering if she had brought out the latent exhibitionist in him. His citron-colored swimsuit was of the latest brief style, clearly designed to flaunt his body. She vowed not to be impressed.

How had he known she would come to the pool? Lee glared at Burr through mists of anger as she pulled herself dripping up the pool ladder and walked to the deck chair where he was sitting. She knew her eyes were blazing as she stood before him, arms akimbo, and she didn't care.

"How dare you, Burr!"

"How dare I what?"

"You know good and well what. How dare you open my suitcase and go through my things!"

"You're lovely when you're angry, Lee."

"Don't try that threadbare line on me. And I'll thank you never, but never, to touch my luggage again."

"I'm the one who gives orders, remember? And I'll touch what I please." Now Burr's eyes roved over her scantily clad body in a way that revealed his total enjoyment, and people at the poolside were beginning to stare. She was creating a scene. *She* was creating a scene? This whole thing was none of her doing. She had merely come to the pool to swim, to cool her anger. She strode to a chaise lounge and snatched her cover-up from where she had dropped it before entering the pool. Quickly she shrugged into it, then returned to Burr's chair and faced him.

"Sit down, Lee, and that's another order. Do make yourself comfortable. You've spoiled the view for everyone with that nasty jacket affair, but I'll let you join me anyway."

"Who gave you permission to rifle through my luggage?" Lee held her voice to a mere whisper although her inclination was still to shout.

"I didn't know I needed permission, Lee. You didn't lock the bags, you know. There was no keep-out order posted. But that's neither here nor there. I was really checking to see if you'd brought the proper clothing with you. If you hadn't brought a dinner dress I would have gone out and purchased one for you."

"And why, might I ask?" Lee dreaded what she knew was coming next.

"Because I'd like to take you out to dinner. I'm glad you've brought along something appropriate. I'll be proud to be your escort."

"I'd really prefer to stay in tonight, Burr. I've put in a fair day's work today. My evening is my own."

"Under ordinary circumstances it would be your own, but these are not ordinary circumstances. In fact when we're together the circumstances get less and less ordinary. Please have dinner with me?"

Lee smiled and relented with less reluctance than she cared to admit. "All right, Burr. You win. We'll have dinner together."

"Now you're being sensible. Can you be ready about two hours from now?"

What choice did she have? She could imagine him bringing the dinner to her—right to her room if she said no. That would be even worse than going out. He had said it would be a business dinner. She had to eat somewhere, didn't she? She might as well enjoy some companionship. She could see to it that the conversation never veered from business.

"All right, Burr. I'll be ready around seven."

"I'm pleased, Lee. Really pleased."

Lee nodded, then turned and left the pool area. Back in her room she prepared to take a bath, a leisurely bath, and she carefully locked the door leading to Burr's room.

She poured bath bubbles into the tub, turned the tap, then submerged herself in warm water, relaxing with eyes closed against the smoothness of the tub. It was almost an hour before she heard Burr enter his room and rap on the bathroom door.

"You in there, Lee?"

"Yes."

"Are you about through?"

"I'm bathing."

"Too bad there isn't a keyhole."

She'd been in the tub long enough. She began to let the water down the drain. She couldn't relax now, knowing Burr was on the other side of the door waiting, imagining her every move. She stepped out of the tub and wrapped herself in the bath sheet. She could almost feel Burr's gaze on the other side of the door and she pulled the sheet more tightly around her body, patting it to her curves in an effort to dry herself quickly. Making sure the door to her room was open, she unlocked the door to Burr's room, darted to her own quarters, then locked the door to ensure her privacy. She leaned on the door waiting, listening. It was a full five minutes before she heard Burr enter the bath. She felt chagrined. Had she really expected him to pounce on her the minute he heard the key turn in the lock?

Lee dressed quickly but carefully in the brandy-colored sarong-type gown she had brought along, feeling the soft jersey fabric flow against her skin as it fell from the elastic top to just below her knees. She cinched the waist in with a narrow pearl-studded belt, then put on high-heeled sandals. The humidity of the bath had given her fine hair body and she fluffed it up, brushing it forward over her ears so that wisps of it just touched her cheekbones and drew attention to her gray blue eyes. She snapped on pearl earrings. When Burr knocked on her door she was ready to go.

"To say you look lovely is an understatement," Burr said.

"Thank you, Burr. Where are we going to dine?" She kept her voice crisp, trying to set a businesslike pace for the evening. But she couldn't help noticing the way Burr's silky shirt clung to his broad shoulders, the way his slacks fitted over his slim hips and flat stomach.

"I've made reservations at the Blue Dolphin, and

if you don't mind we'll walk. It's just half a block down the beach and there's seating under the stars.''

"Fine." She showed no reaction when he took her arm, although she could feel her breath catch in her throat as if she had been running. Seating under the stars—and he said this was to be a business dinner!

The hostess at the Blue Dolphin led them to a candlelit table for two overlooking the sea and Burr ordered a bottle of champagne.

"Your day was that successful?" Lee asked. "I mean Margo told me you were coming here to raise money."

"Of course my day was successful. And I hope my evening will be equally so."

Lee looked into the distance where sandpipers poked along the shore investigating seaweed and stones and shells. The pristine triangular canvas of a sailboat was silhouetted against the dusky sky, and the cry of a gull sounded muted and lonely. The breeze carried a yeasty scent from the water, and Lee welcomed the coolness against her face, her bare shoulders. Burr couldn't have selected a more romantic spot. Presently the waiter brought their champagne, poured it into hollow stemmed glasses, then nested the bottle in the bucket of ice.

"Here's to the *Santa Isabella*!" Burr lifted his glass and touched it against Lee's.

Lee sipped her champagne, feeling its bubbly coolness against her nose, and the tang of the sweet liquid against her warm tongue. She rarely drank and the pleasant effect of the champagne made her wonder why. They both had second glasses before the waiter returned with the seafood dinners that Burr had ordered when he made their reservation. Lee thought she had never tasted such excellent shrimps and scallops. And the hot rolls were the kind that made her want to ask for the recipe. Without seeking her opinion Burr ordered baked Alaska for their dessert, and when they had finished that he ordered an after-dinner liqueur for them to sip over their business discussion. Lee was frankly surprised that there really was to be a business discussion.

"I need your help in arranging an exhibit of the artifacts," Burr said. "Granted, it will have to be a small exhibit, but hopefully we'll have more things to add to it before the date arrives. Such an exhibit can serve as a trial run for a larger exhibit here in Miami after we find the big heap."

"Would it be safe to exhibit such treasure? Think of the security precautions that would be required."

"I've talked with Roscoe Murdock about that. He says he can arrange all the security I'll need. We might hold the exhibit at his bank. It would attract customers for him and investors for Dive Boys."

"And what help do you want from me?" Lee asked.

"I would want every item we displayed to be tagged and identified. Perhaps you could write up a brief description of each item, telling about its use in old Spain—you know, the sort of thing you told me that first day when Harry brought you to the boat for your interview. Would that be possible?"

"I'm sure it would be possible, and I think it's a great idea. This is the sort of thing I had in mind when I spoke of sharing the heritage with the people. Such an exhibit should draw a big crowd. Reporters would flock in to write about it for newspapers and magazines, I should think.'' Lee gazed out over the water. It was dark now, but starshine washed the sea with silver and an orange crescent of the moon was beginning to peek above the horizon. She wondered if she and Burr would always be working at cross-purposes. To him an exhibit would mean a fund-raising endeavor; to her it would mean the sharing of a heritage. Yet if they were both satisfied with the end result, that was all that mattered, wasn't it?

"You'll not slow my divers down with your grid and camera, will you, Lee?''

"I'll try not to, but look at it this way. The grid and camera will help give authenticity to your arti-facts. Your exhibit will attract scholars as well as the curious. Why, you might even get the National Geo-graphic Society or the Smithsonian Institution inter-ested in your search.''

They talked for an hour or so, making tentative plans for an exhibit, and when Burr suggested they leave Lee was reluctant to go. It had been a pleasant evening, an exciting evening, yet it had been a busi-ness evening, too. Perhaps one could mix business and pleasure. She took a last sip of her liqueur, then they strolled back to the hotel.

She had not intended to invite Burr into her room, and she didn't, but somehow, as she was opening the door, he slipped in before she could prevent it. He followed her to the balcony high above the surround-ing buildings and overlooking the bay just a block away. Below the traffic sounds were distant and muted. Above moonglow streamed through a thin cloud cover and starshine stippled the sky. A pervading scent of the sea hung in the heady humid air, mingling with the ever present scent of sandalwood that clung to Burr. He looked down at her knowingly.

"What are you thinking?"

"Personal thoughts."

"You had planned all along on going out to dinner with me, hadn't you, Lee?" His silky voice matched the soft evening and all hint of business was gone from his tone as well as from his words.

"Why do you say that?" Lee looked up at him through a haze of drowsiness induced by wine and food.

Burr let his eyes glide over her body, lingering first where the gently gathered bodice of her gown clung to her full breasts. Then his gaze dropped to her waist and lower, to the flare of her hips where the bias cut of her skirt snugged her body. His smoky eyes gazed directly into hers as he answered.

"No woman packs a dress like this one you're wearing unless she plans to dine with a man."

Lee looked away and tried to hide her nervousness with flippancy. "I used to be a girl scout, Burr. Their motto has always stuck with me—be prepared."

Burr chuckled and tilted her chin with his forefinger, forcing her to look directly at him. Even in the moonlight Lee could see the amber fire flicker in his eyes as he reached toward her. Somewhere inside her warning bells rang, but they were far too distant to galvanize her into action. She didn't back away, nor did she make access any easier for him. He took her hands and placed them on his waist.

She felt her heart flutter then pound as his hands released hers. His thumbs discovered her navel through the filmy fabric of her dress and pressed gently into it as his strong fingers circled her waistline, almost meeting at her spine. For a moment the fingers held her taut, then they relaxed and roved in soft circles on her back, gently stroking. In a moment his hands slowly slid up her sides until they reached the top of her gown.

Now each of his forefingers traced a fiery line on her skin, using the top of her gown as a guideline. Why was she letting him do this to her? She tried to coax a protest through her drowsiness and failed. She stood as if hypnotized with her hands on his waist, while his fingers continued their exploratory course.

He moved with a deliberate and maddening slowness, gently inserting his forefingers beneath the fabric of her bodice and easing it to her waistline. He seemed unsurprised that she wore no undergarment, and now she was sorry she hadn't; not that she desired the protection of a bra or a chemise, but rather because she would have enjoyed letting him remove it as much as he would have enjoyed doing so.

"You're beautiful, Lee...beautiful." He gazed at her for several moments as if transfixed, then she felt the cupping upward thrust of his palms moving in a slow circular motion as his fingers splayed gently up and over her breasts. Goose bumps rose on the inside of her arms, her thighs.

She could have pushed him from her, his touch was that light, or she could have backed away from his nearness. But she did neither. Deep within her a new desire brimmed like a fountain of molten gold, drowning all thought of protest and holding her in a position of quietude as she waited for what his commanding hands would do to her next.

"I like a woman who can show great restraint," Burr murmured huskily. "It makes the eventual capitulation all the more enjoyable."

"You've had wide experience, no doubt?" The raggedness in her voice threatened to betray the pent-up emotions her body still hid from him.

"You would hardly enjoy the blundering of a novice now, would you? And you are enjoying me, aren't you?" His seductive voice matched the slow, probing motion of his hands still cupping her breasts. She wanted to fling herself into his arms, yet her enjoyment of the exquisite pain of not doing so overcame her desire.

"You didn't answer me, Lee. You are enjoying me, aren't you?"

"Yes. Oh, yes!" Her voice was almost a sob, her desire for him was so great, her shame of her own weakness so supreme.

"Tell me what you want me to do, Lee."

Her loins tingled but still she didn't move. Through her drowsy haze she realized he was deliberately tantalizing her. "Tell me what you want me to do." He was purposely using his irresistible masculine appeal to bring her to him in a rush of passion that would seem of her own doing rather than a result of his force. Somewhere in the recesses of her mind she heard a voice wondering how many other women had succumbed to his sensuous voice, his eyes, the slow motion of his hands.

"I like your style, Lee. You keep a man guessing. One day you fling yourself into his arms, the next day...this. You know how to enjoy a man."

"And you seem to know how to enjoy a woman," Lee countered.

"The secret is in enjoying one thing at a time, making the very most of a pleasurable experience." Now his voice had grown as ragged as hers. "How long are you going to stand there quietly driving me wild?"

Silently she tried to answer the question. She was still her own woman. Or was she? She could still back off. But could she really? No, she couldn't. She was mute with desire.

Now he bent toward her, touching his warm lips to the throbbing pulse in her throat. Although his hands and fingers remained on her breasts in a state of quiet born of total self-assurance, she felt his thumbs apply a subtle pressure against her flesh, keeping time with her heartbeat. She could stand no more. She didn't want to give in to her desire, but she was helplessly caught in his power. Dizzy with wanting she reached toward him, bringing her arms up under his in a careful way that wouldn't distract him from the wonderful things he was doing to her.

Her fingers shook as she fumbled with the top button of his shirt; then he lifted his head.

"Easy, darling. No hurry. Let's enjoy each other slowly and deliberately, and intentionally...until we can't. . . ." His words trailed off raggedly as his lips found her forehead, her eyelids. She unbuttoned his shirt to the waist, then let her hands slide upward over his chest, feeling the crisp hair catch in her fingers then spring free.

"Lee. . .Lee. . . ." His mouth found hers and now his hands released her breasts and his arms went around her waist and shoulders, crushing her to him. At first he kissed her tenderly, then his tongue parted her lips and she felt a surge of desire rush through her like a hot flame invading her body.

Then there was a shrill ring from the telephone. Burr's arms jerked in a startled reflex, but he didn't take his mouth from hers until the third ring. As he left her Lee felt the evening air cool her in all the places Burr had warmed with his hands, his body. And with the coolness reason returned. Quickly Lee eased her dress up to cover her nakedness and went inside.

Burr had rushed to his room to answer the phone. Lee could tell by the conversation that the call was from Margo. And it went on and on. Something about Raul. She listened for a moment through the open door between their suites.

"You're calling me at this hour to tell me Raul wants to borrow money? What's he want it for?"

Silence.

"Of course I won't lend it to him. Let him learn to live on his salary. Let him learn thrifty habits."

Quietly Lee closed the door to her room and locked it. The champagne and liqueur had been a mistake—a mistake she would not want repeated.

She hardly remembered slipping from her clothes, and when Burr knocked on her door she didn't answer. Let him think she was asleep. She owed Margo a debt of gratitude. What might have happened had that telephone not rung! She was too tired to sort out the wild disorder of her thoughts now, yet she lay awake for a long time before she dozed and dreamed of Burr bending to kiss her. She wakened before the kiss took place. And each time she fell back to sleep the dream was repeated. Burr's first kiss had been the result of her fright, his second the result of her imbibing too much wine. At dawn she was still wondering how Burrton Adburee kissed a woman under ordinary circumstances. But then perhaps there were no ordinary circumstances when Burr kissed a woman....

CHAPTER NINE

A RAP ON HER DOOR awakened Lee the next morning. She sat up sleepily, peered at her travel clock and gasped. Ten o'clock. She had overslept. "Who's there?" she called.

"Burr. Who were you expecting?"

How could she face him after last night? How could she have been so weak when she had wanted to be so strong! "You'll have to wait a minute." She hurriedly dressed, determined that Burr wouldn't see her in anything but businesslike clothes. When at last she opened the door to the bath she was surprised to find him smiling, surprised and sincerely pleased to see the equipment she had ordered stacked in neat piles in his room.

"You picked up my things! Thank you so much, Burr."

"Is that all you have to say?" Burr grinned at her sardonically.

"What were you expecting me to say?" she asked, knowing intuitively she shouldn't have.

"That you love me. That you can't live without me. That we belong together forever and ever."

"Why would I say things like that?" Lee glanced away, unable to meet his gaze.

"I hoped you'd say them because they're true."

"But they're not true." She knew she was lying. She was falling in love with him. Against her will her emotions were betraying her, but Burr must never guess that.

"Look at me, Lee." He waited until she reluctantly met his gaze. "No girl leads a man on as you did, kisses as you did, unless she's in love. How can you deny it?"

Lee pulled indignation over herself like a quilt. "I did *not* lead you on. The whole scene was your doing. You gave me too much champagne and too much liqueur. Then you...took advantage of me. I really think it was rotten of you."

"You didn't think so last night. You said you were enjoying me, remember?" Burr's voice was like a caress. Her every inclination was to go to him, to kiss his sensuous mouth, to seek out the knowing touch of his hands. Then she remembered Margo's phone call, how Burr had talked on and on, forgetting her completely. It was Margo he loved. Or maybe he just passed out his favors like candy to whatever girl was handiest. She refused to be taken in. She remembered all too well how deeply Ben had hurt her. She wasn't ready to wear her heart on her sleeve again no matter how she felt.

"I want to forget about last night, Burr. I want you to forget it...pretend it didn't happen."

Burr tensed. The soft smile left his lips and a thin white line appeared around his mouth. She had seen that look before, seen it the day he dive-bombed the boys in the skiff. For a moment she was afraid he might strike her and she backed away. If only she had backed away last night! She breathed easier when he turned, then called over his shoulder, "Get packed and let's go. Be at the front desk in ten minutes."

They flew in an electric silence all the way to Key West, transferred from the Cessna to the helicopter, and traveled in a more highly charged silence on to the *Sea Deuced*. Margo and the divers were waiting on the main deck to greet them, to find out what luck Burr had had in his fund-raising trip.

"We made some finds yesterday, Burr," one diver called out. "Ballast stones. Are we still in business?"

"We're still in business." Burr pulled several checks from his pocket, fanning them out for inspection.

Lee hadn't seen the checks before and she was as interested as the rest of the group, until she noticed Margo and Raul. Margo was gazing up into Raul's eyes as if she adored him and Raul was gazing down at her in the same manner. Lee could sense sparks passing between them. What was going on here? Casually Lee approached Margo.

"We purchased the underwater camera and the grid," she said. "Now I'll really be able to go to work."

"How nice," Margo said coolly. Then she batted her eyes and looked up at Raul through her heavy fringe of lashes. "Raul has promised to bring me up a special piece of treasure today. He believes in hunches; don't you, Raul?" Margo batted her eyes at Raul again, but she gave him no chance to respond to her question. "He has a hunch that this is going to be his lucky day."

"I hope he's right." Suddenly Lee felt as if everyone were against her. Burr was angry over last night, Margo was steaming because Lee had gone to Miami with Burr, and Raul was livid because she had refused to lend him money. But she could stand all their anger. What really bothered her was Margo's flirting with Raul. Clearly Margo was trying to even a score. Lee could almost hear Margo's thoughts. "You flirt with my man in Miami and I'll flirt with your man while you're gone." This was insanity. Margo was using Raul but there was nothing she could do about it. Then Lee shuddered as she saw Burr watching the sparks fly between Margo and Raul. Burr could do something about it, and he did.

"Raul, step over here, please." The white line was clearly visible around Burr's mouth again and now Lee was frightened for Raul.

"I have a chore for you in the hold." Burr's voice was icy. "You'll do no more diving until that chore is completed to my satisfaction."

"Yes, sir." Raul waited silently with a bewildered expression, and Lee saw the telltale slump of his shoulders. All the divers knew Burr used certain hated chores as punishment, and Raul had a fair idea of what was coming next. But it was obvious he didn't know why. Lee bit her lip. Didn't Raul realize he couldn't openly flirt with Margo without arousing Burr's wrath? For a ladies' man Raul was sometimes very unwary.

"I want you to transfer the fuel in the starboard

tank to the port tank. We're getting a slight list to the starboard and a shift of weight in the hull should remedy it."

"Yes, sir."

Lee could detect no list and she was surprised that Raul hadn't protested.

"Well, what are you waiting for?" Burr demanded. "You have your orders. Carry them out."

Raul cleared his throat and took one step closer to Burr. A twist of fear tightened Lee's stomach. Was there going to be a fight? The rest of the crowd evidently didn't think so. They began to disperse, and for the first time Lee noticed the new man aboard. She recognized him. Spike. He had approached Raul after his magic act that first night at Mallory dock. Now a second twist of fear brought an ache to her stomach and she stood nearby frankly listening as Raul spoke.

"Burr, before I go to the hold I want you to meet Spike. He's a friend of mine and a diver. He'd like to work for Dive Boys so I invited him out to meet you. I think we need him."

Burr scrutinized Spike for several moments before he spoke. "You're a certified diver?"

"Sure, man." Spike took a limping step forward, reached into the hip pocket of his tattered cutoffs and produced a dog-eared paper, which he handed to Burr. "I'm certified."

"Good." Burr nodded. "I've got a rule around here. No certification, no air."

"I'm certified, man. I'm certified."

"Had any experience in salvage work?" Burr asked.

"Put in a month with Galleons Unlimited."

Lee saw a faraway look in Spike's eyes, as if he was remembering some exotic experience with Burr's competitor.

"How soon can you go to work?"

"Right now, man. Right now."

"I'll give you a trial, Spike. You're on." They shook hands. *Is it this simple,* Lee thought. No references required. No credentials presented. If you were certified, you rated air and a trial period of diving. She could hardly believe the way Burr operated his business.

Burr gave Spike the ground rules for working for Dive Boys, and Lee thought Spike might have second thoughts, but apparently he did not. When Burr dismissed him he headed for the hold to check out a wet suit and an air tank. Lee stood glaring at Burr, yet not realizing she was glaring until he spoke.

"You disapprove of my hiring Spike?"

"What right do I have to approve or disapprove? You're the boss."

"I'm glad you realize that."

"Why did you hire him, Burr? He looks like bad news to me."

"Sometimes bad news can be turned into good news. I'm not above pumping him for information concerning Galleons Unlimited and what they've brought up so far. And I'm not above using him to trap Raul. Spike could be very useful to me."

"Trap Raul!" Lee let the words out before she thought.

"You've really got a thing for that kid, haven't you?"

Lee refrained from answering. What did she care what Burr thought?

"I told you once I'd fire Raul if I could, if I had legitimate cause. Spike just may provide me with legitimate cause."

"In what way? I think you're being very unfair."

Burr lowered his voice. "I think the two of them are into drugs. I told you my sentiments about drugs and this boat. If I give those two enough rope I think they'll hang themselves. I want them both off this boat but I don't want to get the reputation of being a hard man to work for. Nobody will bad-mouth a captain for firing a drug pusher."

Lee felt hot anger surge through her. How could she have let this man touch her! How could she stand to go on working for him! "I can't bear a person who lies to himself."

"It takes one to spot one, I always say." Burr grinned at her. "You lie to yourself, too."

Lee forced herself to ignore that remark. "Your real reason for wanting to fire Raul is because you think Margo's looking his way. It wouldn't do for a lowly diver to walk off with the boss's girl, would it? With Raul off the boat you'd have a clear field where Margo is concerned, right?"

Again the white line appeared around Burr's mouth and his smoky eyes smoldered. "Prepare to dive, Lee. I want to see some action with that underwater camera and the grid." Burr checked his watch and seemed to relax a bit. "Can you be ready to go over the side in five minutes? I'd like to help you set up the grid.''

"Yes, sir." Lee left Burr with so many conflicting emotions churning inside her that her head was threatening to ache. She hated Burr's suspicious attitude toward Raul and Spike. She hated Margo's flirting with Raul to make her jealous, but she softened a bit as she thought of Burr's offer to help her set up the grid. Sometimes he could be thoughtful. She welcomed the chance to really get to work underwater and was glad Burr was going to be with her. She couldn't forget the aftermath of their Miami dinner date. She tried to tell herself she wasn't in love with him, yet she was eager for him to share the underwater scene with her, eager to see if the divers had tagged yesterday's finds properly, eager to see just what the finds were. Maybe there was something more than the ballast stones.

Lee hurried to her cubicle in the hold, slipped on the red bikini, then dragged on the top half of her wet suit.

"About ready, Lee?" Burr called down to her.

She left the bottom half of the wet suit on the cot and hurried up the companionway. When she stepped back onto the main deck Burr was waiting at the stern to help her with the air tank. Even through the wet suit his touch, as he adjusted the tank, sent shivers coursing along her arms and legs.

Lee carried the camera strapped around her neck while Burr carried the grid as they plunged into the sea. After the initial shock of the entry Lee welcomed the satiny feel of the water against her face, her

hands, her legs; welcomed its pressure against the wet
suit as it molded to her body. How graceful Burr
looked gliding through the greenish brine, the plum-
dark waters. How privileged they were to view this
esoteric underwater realm. Today the *Sea Deuced*
was anchored farther from the reef. New territory
was being searched. They swam over the coral ledge,
and this morning the colors were different than they
had been that first late afternoon she had seen them.
The cave mouths had a purplish cast and the valleys.
were a deep inviting blue. Sunlight slanting through
the water showed the staghorns, the sea fans, the
brain coral in paint-box tones like splotches on an
artist's smock.

They swam over the holes dug by the water forced
down by the deflectors. Craters. Here the sea bottom
looked like a blowup of the moon's surface. Craters...and more craters. Lee's heart pounded when
she saw five tripletails dart in front of her. One left a
string of bubbles in the crystal water that reminded
her of the bubbles in last night's champagne. She
tried to put that thought from her mind.

Snag drifters! Fish that had a habit of hanging
around wrecks! These were young fish, dull black,
mottled with yellow spots. She wished she could tell
Burr. Maybe these fish could lead them to the hull of
the *Isabella*. Fat chance! The fish flashed out of sight
before she could get Burr's attention.

They swam on across the coral ledge and Lee saw
the dark cannon shape for the first time. Her initial
reaction was disappointment. At first glance the cannon looked like a length of sewer pipe. Parts of it

were encrusted with coral and shellfish and others
with a smooth dull-black coating. She approached it
and touched it, and suddenly she felt that she was being transported back through the centuries. What
Spanish hands had polished this cannon? What galleon captain had aimed it at the enemy? And who
had been the enemy? The Dutch?

Lee coaxed her thoughts back from old Spain. This
cannon would be a major landmark in her work.
They would have to submerge other buoys to serve as
markers and points of reference. Burr would have to
fly over the site to get gyrocompass bearings of the
main grid lines. From now on each crater dug by the
Sea Deuced's deflectors would be numbered, reference buoys submerged, grid patterns established. But
for today this cannon would be enough of a marker.
Her heart raced as she saw three small buoys attached
to tagged objects.

She knew these were yesterday's finds, which had
been left where they had been found as Burr had
ordered. Burr was hovering over them, and as she
joined him a surge of current tossed their bodies
together. For a moment Lee was completely thrown
off-balance both mentally and physically. The pressure of Burr's thighs and hips against hers made her
head reel.

She swam away from him for a moment until she
felt in control of herself again, then she returned to
examine the tagged objects. Ballast stones, that was
all. She saw Burr shrug and knew he was disappointed. But he had no real reason to be. Every galleon
carried ballast and there was always a chance that a

trail of these football-size rocks might lead to the galleon's hull. They must be photographed in place.

She helped Burr with the grid, positioning it so her photographs would include a bit of the cannon. Burr had ordered this dive far too hastily. They needed the plane table to set up elevations and projections, but that could come later. For now the grid and the cannon would have to suffice. As Burr held the steel mesh in place, Lee swam above it and snapped several shots of the tagged objects. It was a start. She vowed to do far more careful work in the future. She would impress upon Burr the need for accuracy.

After they surfaced Burr sent divers down to bring up the ballast stones, but there was little rejoicing. Ballast stones had been found before and nothing had come of them. They ate lunch, and Lee was working in her office when high excitement broke loose.

"Treasure!" The hoarse shout came from the stern deck.

"Gold!"

Feet pounded against the aluminum deck, approaching the stern from all directions. Lee dropped the reference book she had been reading and joined Margo, Burr and the divers near the deflector. Apparently Raul had served out his disciplinary stint for he was the diver thrusting a golden pitcher above the surface while Burr reached for it.

"What is it?" Margo asked, dropping to her knees to examine the dripping pitcher, unmindful that seawater was soaking her Gloria Vanderbilt skirt.

Burr relinquished his hold on the object and helped

Raul and Spike from the water and onto the deck, slapping them on the back, shaking their hands.

"Where did you find it? Was there anything else nearby? Did you look carefully?" Burr spouted questions faster than the boys could answer.

Now Margo was holding the pitcher above her head. She had kicked off her spike-heeled sandals and was jumping up and down like a crazy lady. "Gold! Gold! Gold! It must be worth a mint, Burr."

Lee saw tears in Burr's eyes, which he made no attempt to brush away, and Spike and Raul were just wandering around the deck with dazed expressions on their faces.

"This is it, man," Spike said. "This is it. This is it! Would you believe! This is it!"

Burr slapped Spike on the back again, but Spike's dazed expression remained. The sun glinted on the gold, and the pitcher looked as if it might have been removed from Tiffany's display case only moments before. Through her rising anger Lee reflected on the qualities of gold. Did it carry a curse as some people believed? Men and women had killed for it since the dawn of time. How many slaves had given their lives for the sake of some master's gold? Lesser metals were destroyed by the sea. Even silver became blackened and encrusted. But the brine of centuries had no derogatory effect on gold. It survived unchanged. It reigned supreme, more stable than man himself. Then Lee shook her head, as if shaking scales from her eyes.

"All right!" She was surprised at the wrath and volume of her voice. A hush fell over the wild celebration, and everyone looked at her expectantly.

"What is the meaning of this?" She faced Burr,

her fury growing. "You promised me a disciplined operation, yet the first item of real significance that is found is brought up with no regard for your order, my request, that every artifact be photographed in place before it is disturbed."

Mouths dropped open and everyone stared at her as if she had taken leave of her senses.

"Raul was excited, Lee," Margo said, finding her voice. "Surely you can understand that. Gold! He found more gold today than has been found on this search to date. It was his first find. You expect him to swim up and leave it down there?"

"That is exactly what I expect," Lee replied. "Pinpointing the location of each find is my first priority. Celebration comes second."

"Well, it's too late now." Margo's voice carried a triumphant ring. "The pitcher's aboard and I for one intend to continue the celebration."

"The pitcher must be returned to the spot where it was found," Lee insisted. "After I photograph it you can do your celebrating."

"Lee's right," Burr said at last, surprising Lee. "The pitcher will be returned to the spot where it was discovered. Since Raul found it and brought it up contrary to my orders, he will be the one to tag and return it. Then his services will no longer be required aboard the *Sea Deuced*."

"You mean he's...fired?" Margo took a step toward Raul as if to protect him from Burr's wrath.

"I think I made myself perfectly clear," Burr said. "A diver who disobeys my orders is no longer needed. Raul will leave immediately."

"If Raul goes, I go," Spike said, scowling and stepping forward.

"I'll accept your resignation," Burr replied evenly.

Lee was nonplussed. Again she felt trapped. If she was going to be able to live with herself she had to be true to her profession, yet she had never intended to cause Raul to be fired. It infuriated her to realize she had been the one to provide Burr with the excuse he had been waiting for. How ironic! Raul had falsely accused her of working against her best interests, and now he would be convinced that he had been right, convinced she was betraying him. There was only one thing for her to do. She faced Burr boldly.

"Raul is a good diver, Burr. He just made a mistake. If he goes, I will tender my resignation as your archaeologist immediately." Lee tried not to hold her breath, tried to breathe evenly as she realized what she had done. If he let her go she would have failed Raul and herself and future generations who might have benefited from her work on the galleon *Santa Isabella*.

She waited for Burr's reaction.

CHAPTER TEN

BURR GLARED for several moments, then he pulled himself to his full height. "I spoke hastily, Raul, Spike. Return the pitcher to the bottom for photographing and we'll carry on as usual."

"Yes, sir," Raul said.

"Sure thing, man." Spike grinned, grabbed the pitcher, and limped after Raul as he adjusted his diving gear and plunged into the sea.

Lee felt sudden tears spring to her eyes. She knew they were not just tears of relief because she had saved Raul's job, but also an expression of joy because she had also kept her own job. She was surprised that Burr had let her get away with her maneuver, yet his reaction told her things about him that she liked. Surely he felt something for her. He would never have backed down on his order unless he realized that he definitely didn't want to lose her. She was still silently congratulating herself on her small victory when Burr approached her, his face stern and unsmiling, his eyes hooded and inscrutable.

"I hope you're satisfied, Lee. I don't know what you see in Raul, but I do know what I see in you."

Lee waited for Burr's voice to grow soft and sensuous as it had last night, this morning, but it didn't.

As he continued to speak his tone grew even more crisp and businesslike, if that was possible.

"I need your scholarly approach to this salvage operation, Lee. I know you're right about the importance of the exhibit we planned—are planning. Without your help I know there'll be no chance of attracting the interests and financing of any national organizations such as the National Geographic Society or the Smithsonian. But if Raul makes one more mistake, he's going to be off my payroll and even you can't save him."

Lee felt as if her heart were on a teeter-totter. Up one minute and down the next. And now it was down. Rock bottom. She should have known Burr's only interest in her concerned what she could do to give scholarly credibility to Dive Boys and the quest for the *Santa Isabella*. She was nothing more to him than a valued assistant. Their relationship was strictly employer-employee.

They dressed for diving again and went down to photograph the gold pitcher, but after they completed the work and surfaced there was no more celebrating. The firing and rehiring had cast a pall over everyone. The curse of gold? Some people believed that gold was cursed, that bad luck would follow any find of the precious metal. But that was crazy. Lee was above such superstitious belief.

"Will you take the pitcher to town?" Lee asked. "Some reporter from the *Citizen* would welcome the opportunity to photograph it, to splash a human-interest article with inch-high headlines right on the front page. This artifact is priceless, Burr."

"There'll be no photograph, no article," Burr said with finality. "The pitcher will go straight into the safe here with the chain and the other stuff. I don't need any self-serving publicity that might give useful information to Galleons Unlimited. Let them guess what we're bringing up until I'm ready for them to be privy to the information."

Lee rode back to Key West that night with Harry in the speedboat, watching as Margo climbed into the helicopter with Burr. She tried to tell herself she didn't care. She cared, but surely Burr couldn't guess that. Once she was at Marvista she snacked on some instant soup and crackers and went straight to bed, exhausted by the activities of the past two days and chagrined at her increasing involvement with Burr.

THE NEXT MORNING on the boat was uneventful. Dive teams went down for their hourly stints and surfaced with nothing to report. In the afternoon Burr weighed anchor and moved the *Sea Deuced* to a new location, but one still close to the cannon. Raul and Spike plunged in for a routine dive while Scotty and Mac, two of the other divers, dived in with spear guns, intent on bringing up snapper or grouper for their shipboard supper.

"Get ready to dive, Lee," Burr said at last, stepping into her office. "I want to go down to look over this new area."

"I have to work on the records, Burr. I'll dive later if the boys find something of interest."

Burr glared. "I'm still captain of this ship. I want you to prepare to dive. Now."

Lee glared back at him. "All right. If you insist."
What else could she say to such an order?

"Don't bother with a wet suit this time," Burr
added. "We'll just take a quick look and come right
back up."

"Fine." Lee hurried to the hold and slipped on the
red bikini, more conscious now of the expanse of
skin it revealed. Burr was waiting in the same citron-
colored suit he had worn in Miami. She looked away,
hating to be reminded of that night. The air tank felt
cold against her bare back, and Burr offered her only
a minimum of aid. She helped him on with his tank,
being careful not to let her hands touch him any more
than was absolutely necessary to get the tank properly positioned.

They plunged in. The underwater site looked very
similar to the others she had seen. Sand... a crater
that the deflectors were busily blasting, exposing the
bedrock... fish. Today there was an abundance of
fish swimming like silver slivers through the water.
Yellow perch. Soapfish emitting bubbles through
their gills. Lee saw a dark shadow hovering above her
and thought it was one of the other divers until she
looked up and saw a huge sea bass hanging almost
motionless in an undulating swell. Where was Scotty
and his spear gun? The bass would provide fish for
the table for a week.

She and Burr glided through the satiny water side
by side like actors in an underwater documentary.
She watched the way the current smoothed Burr's
hair back from his face, the way the sea snugged his
muscled shoulders and thighs like a fluid cocoon. She

sensed him watching her in the same way she was watching him.

Although Lee tried to keep out of touching distance, Burr stayed close enough to her to reach her hand anytime he saw something he wanted to point out to her. The tides and currents did battle in this spot, frequently sweeping her against Burr's taut body. Every time they touched she felt a thrill feather through her. She could sense Burr smiling behind his face mask as she struggled to widen the distance between them and he struggled to narrow it.

Once a trailing tendril of seaweed caught against her shoulder, wrapping one end around her neck, looping around her arm, and brushing against her thigh. Lee jumped, always alert for eels or some other undesirable sea creature. Now she wished she had worn a wet suit. She brushed frantically at the clinging weed, eager to rid herself of its slimy touch, but it clung stubbornly. Seeing her predicament Burr swam closer, found the end of the weed near her left breast and began pulling the entangling greenery away. His touch was like liquid fire against her skin as he followed the trail of the weed over her breast, around her neck and along her upper arm, down to her thigh. A chill rippled gooseflesh to the undersides of her arms as his deft fingers finished their job. Then he ran the flat of his hand over her arm and thigh to remove the small leaves and debris that still clung to her skin. At last she found the will to swim away from his touch, but she jerked in fright as she bumped into something solid right behind her. One of the first sea-safety rules she had learned was always to search about for danger, but today she had been so distracted by Burr's nearness that she had ignored the rule. Now she looked around.

Raul! It was Raul, and he was pulling at her arm and motioning to Burr to follow him. Had there been an accident? Lee peered in the direction Raul pointed. It was like peering at 7-Up through the green bottle. At first she saw nothing unusual; then as they approached the crater that the water from the deflectors had been digging, she saw what Raul had wanted them to see. Spike was not present and she guessed he had surfaced to order the deflectors turned off.

Overhead the *Sea Deuced*'s props were still, and in the crater Lee could make out a huge form that could only be an anchor. Burr swam away without her. Everyone was converging on the anchor and more men were free-diving to the scene, alerted to the find by Spike, Lee guessed. Even Margo appeared, her white bikini matching her platinum hair, which flowed out behind her, giving her the look of a voluptuous mermaid.

How frustrating to be unable to talk through the mask and the mouthpiece! Burr was gesticulating to the divers, but most of them were just hanging above the sea bottom like suspended flotsam, staring at the huge anchor. Under ordinary circumstances Lee would have shot to the surface to grab her camera and photograph the find before anyone had a chance to touch it, but there was no hurry this time. This artifact was so huge and heavy it would take a winch to move it. There would be plenty of time for photographs later.

In spite of the craters that the deflectors had dug, part of the anchor shank was still buried in sand. How much could be buried, Lee wondered. Surely sixteen feet of it still showed. The gigantic flukes were at least eight feet wide, and Raul, with air tank on his back, was able to swim through the anchor ring with inches to spare.

Lee swam closer, running her fingers over the dark metal. Iron. In some places it was encrusted and in others it was smooth. In still other places sand and sea had pitted it badly. Lee searched the anchor, not knowing quite what she was searching for. Did she expect to see the words *Santa Isabella* engraved on the shank? But maybe there was a serial number. The cannon had a number, but what did that prove? They had no manifest to compare a number to.

When the initial shock of the wonderful new find wore off Lee swam up, boarded the *Sea Deuced*, then returned to the anchor site with her camera. When Burr saw her he nodded his approval and pointed out various angles from where he wished the anchor photographed. Lee was not surprised that he could give orders with his hands.

As if I don't know which angles are best, Lee thought to herself. *He's the only man I know who can give orders even when he's unable to talk!*

When Lee felt something brush against her arm she thought it was Burr trying to get her attention, but a scream froze in her throat when she looked down and saw a five-foot-long barracuda eyeing her. Had the monster been attracted by some flashing metal on the camera? Should she stay in position? Or should she try to swim away? She didn't have to make that decision. Burr swam to her, easing his body between her and the fish, easing her away from danger. His arm circled her waist, his hip and thigh pressing against hers as he guided her to safety. But what if the barracuda followed? Burr was risking his life to save her. In spite of her fear she enjoyed the sensuous feel of his smooth skin against hers as they glided through the water and took refuge behind the anchor.

The 'cuda didn't follow them, but Lee couldn't relax. She knew the fish could dart through the sea with the speed of a bullet anytime it wanted to. Her heart pounded and her ears rang. But now Raul had grabbed Scotty's spear gun and was stalking the creature, moving in for the kill.

Lee turned her head, brushing it against Burr's chest, and as if sensing her fear and revulsion, he pulled her to him again, protecting her with the circle of his arm. She basked in his nearness. She didn't see the spear shoot through the water, but the next time she looked, the 'cuda was impaled on the spear tip, and it was thrashing and churning the water. Blood spewed, spreading a rusty tinge through the greenish brine. Raul fought the fish, sometimes letting it drag him along behind it, sometimes pulling it in line and trying to force it to the surface. Lee feared for his safety, yet there was nothing she could do to help.

Nobody was prepared for the swirling rush of water that announced the presence of the hammerhead. In the next instant half of the barracuda disappeared and the spear fell from the other half, cut from the line by the shark's teeth. The shark swam only a short distance away, turned with a lash of its great tail and hung in the water like a dark cigar-shaped bomb as it shook its head; then it devoured the 'cuda. Margo and some of the divers swam quickly to the surface, but Lee and Raul and Burr remained in place behind the anchor as if frozen in time. Raul moved to Lee's side and as he did so Burr grabbed the spear gun.

The shark made a second run, snatching at what remained of the dead 'cuda and then turning on the divers. How big was it? Lee guessed it was ten feet as she stared at the grayish body, the pale underbelly, the evil-looking crossbar on the head with eyes on the extreme ends. As the shark made a wide circle around them Burr motioned to Raul to take Lee and surface, but before they could leave, the shark turned and zeroed in for an attack. Burr hit it a glancing blow with the disabled spear gun and kicked at its head. Lee felt its dorsal fin scrape her thigh like a comb with knife-sharp teeth. They were going to die. The anchor didn't offer enough protection. The shark was going to get them all. She saw it turn for another attack. Again Burr motioned for her and Raul to surface. Lee glanced around. There were only three of them left at the scene. She clung to an anchor fluke as the hammerhead made a much smaller circle this time, its powerful tail churning the sea around them. But as it faced them once more Burr held the spear gun like a club and advanced to meet it. Lee could not have moved had Raul not broken her grip on the anchor and pulled her along behind him. Then suddenly their upward motion brought her to her senses and she kicked strongly toward the boarding ladder, climbed it and turned to give Raul a hand. They were safe!

"Burr!" Lee shouted as soon as someone had helped her out of her mask and air tank. "Someone help Burr. He's still down there."

"Spike's gone down with another gun," Margo yelled.

Lee grabbed her breath to scream something else, then everything wavered and went black. The next thing she knew someone was stroking her head and speaking into her ear.

"Lee! Lee! Say something!"

Lee opened her eyes and stared up at Raul for a moment before she remembered what had happened—the horror of the barracuda and the marauding shark. "Where's Burr?" she asked. Yet she was afraid of the answer.

"He's okay. Spike scared the shark off. Burr and Spike are both aboard. Everybody's aboard. Everyone's safe."

Lee felt a warm flood of relief course through her body as she let herself go limp in Raul's arms. She felt as if she might never have the strength to stand again. She felt herself trembling as Raul set her on her feet, and as she continued to cling to him he supported her with the circle of his arm.

"It's all right, Lee. It's all right. Snap out of it, will you?"

"Raul, Burr saved our lives. If it hadn't been for him...."

"He did what anyone would have done, Lee. We were all in a very bad spot."

"And he saved us. How can you minimize the importance of that?"

"I'm not minimizing. I'm just stating facts. But you can express your gratitude personally in your own inimitable way. Here comes Burr right now."

Lee turned, still unable to move from the protective ring of Raul's strong arm. "Burr! Thank heaven you're safe! How can I ever thank you for what you did! We all could have been killed!"

Burr eyed her coldly, his gaze taking in Raul's arm around her. "You seem to have little trouble finding a protector. Perhaps you'd like to have us take numbers and wait our turn."

"I felt faint a moment ago," Lee said, self-consciously trying to ease away from Raul's nearness.

"How convenient for you." Burr's eyes glittered as they left her and focused on Raul. "Johnson, get below. Clean the bilges until you're assigned another position."

"Yes, sir." Raul turned and left them, and once he was gone Lee leaned against the bulkhead. How unfair! She wanted to scream the words, yet how could she scream at the man who had just saved her life! Her mind felt fogged. Surely Burr must care for her. He had risked his life to save her. And why would he send Raul to the bilges if he wasn't jealous of Raul's attention to her?

"How can I say thank you for saving my life, Burr?"

"I can think of lots of ways, Lee, but I'm sure none of them would appeal to you." Burr turned and

walked away, leaving her leaning against the bulkhead, leaving her feeling quite guilty. How wanton
she must seem to him, seeking refuge in Raul's arms;
yet she could do nothing to straighten out that mis-
understanding without revealing her true relationship
to Raul.

The finding of the anchor seemed almost anticli-
mactic after the death-threatening shark attack. Burr
was ready to call it a day and nobody argued with
him. The speedboat ride back to Key West seemed
endless.

Lee was exhausted, yet once in bed that night she
couldn't sleep. She rose and sat up reading for a
while. When she could no longer keep her mind on
the printed page, she slipped into the courtyard and
sat in the deep shadow of an almond tree. She was
still sitting there when she heard footsteps approaching. She started to leave, but it was too late. She
didn't want to be seen in her filmy nightgown. She
settled back into her chair to wait out the intrusion.
Margo. She recognized Margo's throaty voice, her
distinctive laugh.

"It was a wonderful evening. Simply wonderful.
You're a darling, and you were so brave this afternoon."

Lee heard the murmur of Burr's voice, but she
couldn't make out his words.

"And that anchor!" Margo exclaimed. "It's the
most glorious find of all—for Dive Boys, that is.
You're the most glorious find I've discovered lately."

Lee was sitting where she couldn't see Margo and

Burr, but she saw their shadows cast on the stucco wall of Marvista as Burr took Margo into his arms and their bodies merged. She could hardly bear to watch those shadowy figures, yet she couldn't force herself to look away. She bit the inside of her cheek, unmindful of the pain. Only a short time ago she had been the one crushed in that embrace. She had been the one feeling those burning kisses...enjoying them? She couldn't deny that.

"I want you, darling," Margo murmured. "What on earth are we waiting for?"

Lee heard Margo's door open and the shadows disappeared from the wall. For a few moments a light shone from behind the louvered shutters at Margo's window, then all was dark. Lee slipped into her own room and went to bed, glad that the walls in this wing were thick and soundproof. The very thought of Margo and Burr in the next room making love was almost more than she could bear, and the sound of it would have been intolerable.

What a fool she was to think that Burr cared for her. He had saved her life, true. But Raul had stated the truth of that matter. "He did what anyone would have done, Lee." Raul was right. Burr had done what anyone in the same position would have done. She was not minimizing his act of bravery, but she was facing the truth. Burr loved Margo.

CHAPTER ELEVEN

THE NEXT MORNING as they rode to the wreck site in the speedboat Margo instigated a conversation with Lee. Lee had determined not to let on that she had seen Margo and Burr the night before, or that she thought they had spent the night together. Their ride would have been a silent one had it been up to her to speak first.

"I owe you an apology, Lee," Margo said.

"Why?" Lee asked, trying to sound totally disinterested in Margo and any apologies she might make. Yet she was curious. Margo wasn't the apologetic type.

"How serious are you about Raul, Lee?"

"What makes you think I'm serious about him at all?"

"Seeing you together. Hearing him call you on the phone. I hope it isn't too serious."

Lee remained silent, but she was feeling edgy. What was Margo leading up to?

"Well, whether or not you're serious about Raul I want you to know I'm seeing him, Lee. That's what I'll apologize for—if my seeing him matters to you. Fair is fair. Last night we were out together and— well, you know how it is sometimes. I'm sorry if I've invaded your territory. But it sort of evens a score at that. A night in Key West for a night in Miami.''

Lee felt and heard a roaring in her ears. Raul! So it was Raul Margo had been with last night, not Burr. For a moment elation buoyed her up, then a turgid sickness spread through her. She tried not to imagine her brother in Margo's bed.

''Aren't you going to say anything?'' Margo demanded.

''What do you expect me to say?''

''Hands off. That's what I told you.''

''And would you obey a hands-off order?'' Lee asked.

''Maybe. Maybe not. I'm not really mad about Raul, you see. I just think Burr needs a little comeuppance. He's too used to female attention. He hasn't taken me out for several nights. It never hurts any man to know he has a little competition. So if you don't really mind, I'll use Raul for that good purpose for a while; then you can have him back all safe and sound and unharmed.''

For a minute Lee was too angry to speak. Anything she might say would jeopardize her own position as well as Raul's. How dare this slinky blonde use Raul for her own devices! Raul had been around plenty, Lee knew that. But no man was made of steel. Raul could be hurt. Deeply hurt. Margo was taking unfair advantage of him. Lee tried to keep her voice calm as she spoke, presenting the only point of view she could think of that wouldn't reveal her true intent.

''It really wouldn't be fair of you to get Raul fired,

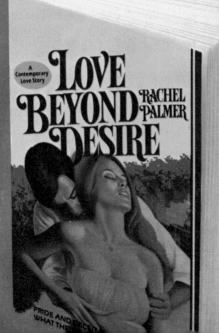

Yours FREE, with a home subscription to SUPERROMANCES™

Now you never have to miss reading the newest **SUPERROMANCES**... because they'll be delivered right to your door.

Start with your free *Love beyond Desire*. You'll be enthralled by this powerful love story...from the moment Robin meets the dark, handsome Carlos and finds herself involved in the jealousies, bitterness and secret passions of the Lopez family. Where her own forbidden love threatens to shatter her life.

Your free *Love beyond Desire* is only the beginning. A subscription to **SUPERROMANCE** lets you look forward to a long love affair. Month after month, you'll receive three love stories of heroic dimension. Novels that will involve you in spellbinding intrigue, forbidden love and fiery passions.

You'll begin this series of sensuous, exciting contemporary novels...written by some of the top romance novelists of the day...with three every month.

And this big value...each novel, almost 400 pages of compelling reading...is yours for only $2.50 a book. Hours of entertainment every month for so little. Far less than a first-run movie or pay-TV. Newly published novels, with beautifully illustrated covers, filled with page after page of delicious escape into a world of romantic love...delivered right to your home.

Begin a long love affair with SUPERROMANCE.
Accept *Love beyond Desire,* free. Mail the postage-paid card below, today.

SUPERROMANCE
1440 South Priest Drive, Tempe, AZ 85281.

Mail this card today.

FREE! Mail to: SUPERROMANCE
1440, South Priest Drive, Tempe, Arizona 85281

YES, please send me FREE and without any obligation, my **SUPERROMANCE** novel, *Love beyond Desire.* If you do not hear from me after I have examined my FREE book, please send me the 3 new **SUPERROMANCE** books every month as soon as they come off the press. I understand that I will be billed only $2.50 per book (total $7.50). There are no shipping and handling or any other hidden charges. There is no minimum number of books that I have to purchase. In fact, I may cancel this arrangement at any time. *Love beyond Desire* is mine to keep as a FREE gift, even if I do not buy any additional books.

CI013

| Name | (Please Print) | |

| Address | | Apt. No. |

City

| State | | Zip |

Signature   (If under 18, parent or guardian must sign.)

This offer is limited to one order per household and not valid to present subscribers. Prices subject to change without notice, offer expires June 30, 1982.

SUPERROMANCE

A compelling love story of mystery and intrigue... conflicts and jealousies... and a forbidden love that threatens to shatter the lives of all involved with the aristocratic Lopez family.

Mail this card today for your FREE book.

Margo. That's about what will happen. You know Burr's out for Raul. You goad him too hard and Raul will be the one to suffer."

"Oh, I won't let that happen," Margo said. "I come on tough around the office, but I can sweet-talk Burr into almost anything. If he threatens to fire Raul, I'll accuse him of being afraid of competition. He'd lose face if he fired him then." Margo chuckled as if enjoying herself greatly. Lee said no more and they finished their trip in silence.

FOR THE NEXT TWO DAYS Lee kept to her desk away from Burr's sight, diving only when it was necessary to photograph artifacts. Nothing much of interest was found—some pottery shards, an encrusted spoon, more ballast. But that wasn't surprising when one knew that each galleon had carried two hundred tons of stones to counterweight its high superstructure. If only those ballast stones would lead them to the hull. . . .

It was on Friday night that Burr knocked on her door at Marvista. "Be ready in twenty minutes. We're going out to dinner."

"No way," Lee said.

"A business dinner."

"Still no way. I remember our last *business* dinner." She had expected Burr to argue, to insist, and when he didn't she was disappointed. He just walked away, leaving her door open, but before she could collect her wits and move to close it he returned, with Margo following close behind.

"You needn't dress," Burr said. "We'll eat right

here. But don't think you're calling the shots. We're eating here because I decided Marvista will offer more privacy than a restaurant. Maggie will bring us dinner in the courtyard." Burr led the way through the outer door, motioning Lee and Margo to follow. At Lee's questioning look Margo shrugged, letting Lee know that Burr's impromptu plans were as much of a surprise to her as they were to Lee.

It was almost dusk and the sea breeze was pleasantly cool, bringing with it the salty scent of the water, the sad haunting cry of gulls. The setting sun put on a spectacular show, blazing sky and sea with a red glow that held for several minutes before gradually fading and disappearing into mistlike grayness. It reminded Lee of her relationship with Burr, the red blaze of their passion that night in Miami along with its fading and disappearance and the grayness that had filled her ever since. But why was she being so melodramatic? She was the one who had put an end to their relationship, insisting that everything between them be strictly business.

"What is it, Burr?" Margo asked after they were seated at the round umbrella table. "I'm expecting a caller a little later. I hope this will be a brief meeting."

"You'll be free a little later," Burr replied curtly. "But now I want you both to consider this." With an angry flourish Burr slapped the evening paper onto the table. "Look at this." He jabbed at the headlines with his forefinger. Lee read silently. Then she repeated the words aloud.

"Galleons Unlimited Find Santa Isabella Manifest." Lee met Burr's gaze. "Burr!"

"Where did they find it?" Margo demanded. "Their search area is miles from ours."

"The manifest would have been found in some archive," Lee said in a more patronizing tone than she had intended or that was polite. "In Seville, probably. A manifest is a *document*, Margo, not a piece of treasure."

"Oh." Margo continued to read the article and Lee read along with her.

"They've found a complete list of what the *Santa Isabella* carried on that last voyage," Lee said. "Just imagine! More than nine hundred pages in that manifest. It must have taken months to translate it."

Burr jabbed at the paper again. "The galleon carried hundreds of silver ingots and each is described minutely by weight and serial number."

"And it carried pieces of eight and gold pieces." Margo looked up and scowled. "But what does all this matter to Dive Boys, Burr? It's all just a paper listing. Galleons Unlimited still hasn't found any real treasure."

Burr looked at Margo as if she were simpleminded. "Now that they have the manifest they can match any treasure they might find that has a serial number with the serial number in this manifest and prove without a doubt that they have discovered the first *authentic* treasure from the *Santa Isabella*. If that happens, Dive Boys will be out of business. I'd feel like a pirate if I continued to search for the hull of a galleon claimed by another salvage company."

"No sensible investor would buy any more stock from you, either," Lee said.

"Of course I don't intend to let Galleons Unlimited beat me to the first authentic treasure," Burr said.

"They haven't found anything," Margo said hopefully.

"Not yet," Burr admitted. "But they might. We have a cannon with a number on it. And there may be a number somewhere on that anchor."

"Numbers won't help us unless we have a copy of the manifest," Lee said. "Would they share the information?"

"Don't be crazy!" Burr slapped the table with the palm of his hand, making Lee jump.

"Maybe you could buy the information," Margo suggested. "Everyone has his price."

"They'll guard that manifest information with their lives," Burr said. "I've known for a long time that we were in a race with Galleons Unlimited, but now time is running out on us."

They sat in silence as Maggie served conch chowder and a tossed salad. Then Margo spoke again.

"Can you read ancient Spanish, Lee? You're a scholar. Was that part of your training?"

Lee hesitated, wishing Burr didn't already know the answer. "I've had some experience with it, but not a whole lot."

"Then there's just one thing to do," Margo said glibly. "Burr, you've got to send Lee to Seville. If someone from Galleons Unlimited found that manifest, then Lee can find it, too. Archive is just a fancy term for library, isn't it? Let Lee go over and look in their library and find what we need. That way we've still a chance to claim the first authentic treasure."

"Finding the manifest wouldn't be that easy, Margo," Lee said. "Professor Hoskin told me a little about the archive. It contains millions upon millions of handwritten documents and it's managed by a very small staff. There are no librarians to hunt up what you want. There are no card catalogs offering easy access to the location of the bundles."

"Bundles?" Burr asked.

"Bundles," Lee repeated. "Professor Hoskin says the documents from old Spain are tied in bundles, and the bundles are stacked floor to ceiling in the rooms and the corridors of this huge building that used to be the center of Spain's commerce."

"And people have to go poking through all the bundles?" Burr asked.

"Nobody, but nobody is allowed to poke," Lee assured him. "If a scholar can figure out what bundle he needs to see, a porter will bring it to him and he can sit at a table in the scholar's room and go through the hundreds of pages." Lee stopped speaking abruptly, remembering Burr's words about professionals always trying to play up the importance and difficulty of the work they did. She hadn't meant to go on and on. She just didn't want to be sent to Seville on some whim of Margo's.

"I think Lee should go and have a fling at the archive, Burr," Margo said. "What can it hurt? She just might turn up something valuable among all those musty bundles of documents. Obviously someone from Galleons Unlimited was able to do so."

"They may have hired a Spanish researcher to do the work for them," Lee said, grasping at straws. "You might consider doing that, Burr."

"I don't think so," Burr said. "There would be too much danger of a mix-up in translation. I wouldn't feel secure working with a Spanish translator."

"I would write letters for you," Lee said. "My modern Spanish is fine."

"I said no." Burr scowled and thumped the table again.

They ate in silence. Lee tried to enjoy the hot spiciness of Maggie's chowder, but her throat felt tight. There was nothing Margo would like better than to get rid of her for a few weeks or forever, and there was nothing Burr would like better than to have a copy of the *Santa Isabella* manifest to keep Galleons Unlimited from being one up on him. And she was the logical one to try to get a copy of that manifest. Mentally she began forming and phrasing her refusal, yet when Burr's order came she was unprepared to oppose him.

"You'll leave for Seville just as soon as you can get a passport, Lee. All your expenses will be paid, of course. And you'll stay as long as is necessary for you to find the manifest and have it microfilmed."

"As easy as that, is it?" Lee's voice dripped sarcasm. "I'll simply fly over to a foreign land, take up residence who knows where, and bury myself in halls of gloom where I'll spend the summer trying to translate worm-eaten documents."

"On the contrary," Burr said. "Just get the manifest on microfilm. You can bring it back here for translation. The Monroe County Library has microfilm equipment you can use."

"I took this job to help protect the underwater environment here, not to do research in the Seville archive. I won't go."

"Then you're through as my archaeologist," Burr said.

"And who will give credibility to your continuing search for the *Isabella*?" Lee felt sure Burr would give in. He had given in once before when she threatened to quit, hadn't he?

"Any credibility you could lend to my search would be totally outweighed by just one authentic find by Galleons Unlimited. Just one find of a numbered object that matches up with the listing in the *Santa Isabella* manifest and Dive Boys is out of business." Burr rose and began pacing around the table, his chowder untouched and cooling in its bowl.

"You will go, Lee."

"I won't."

"Then I'll fire you and hire someone who will go."

"Where will you find that someone? Scholars who can read ancient Spanish aren't lolling on every street corner."

"I'll give you just twenty-four hours to change your mind, Lee. No, I'll give you even less time than that. When you board the *Sea Deuced* tomorrow morning I want your decision. In fact, if it's still negative, just send the message out to me with Harry. Don't even bother to report for work."

Lee stood up. She glared at Margo, who had started all this go-to-Seville business; then she stamped back to her suite. She was aware that Margo and Burr left together a short time later, but she hardly cared. Burr loved Margo and there was nothing she could do about it. For all his macho arrogance Burr listened to Margo when she wanted him to listen.

Lee sat in her room for a while trying to think of what she should do. When no solutions were forthcoming she walked down to the beach, still struggling with the problem. If she abandoned her job with Burr she would have to leave Raul permanently and find other work. What other work? What else could she do but go back to Professor Hoskin in Miami? Or maybe she could go to work for Galleons Unlimited. She wondered if they had an archaeologist working for them. But no. She couldn't do that. That would be too much like betraying Burr.

Maybe she *should* go to Seville. It would mean leaving Raul, but only temporarily. She would be back sooner or later. And the archive experience would advance her in her career. It would be an excellent credit in her portfolio when she had to go jobhunting again. Surely that's what she must do. But why was it so loathsome to her? Seville. Spain. The change could be exciting. Was it Raul she hated to leave or Burr?

Lee stumbled over the form on the beach before she realized she was not alone. For an instant fear held her in its vise, then she regained control of her actions and turned to flee. She hadn't even taken one step before a strong hand reached out and clamped her ankle in a steellike grip. Panic and fear weakened her until she heard Burr chuckle. Then anger exploded within her like a burning fire as his hand crept from her ankle to her calf, then her knee.

"Have you nothing to do except frighten ladies on the beach?" Lee demanded. "I thought you were a drunk or a...drifter." She struggled, but she was unable to free her knee from his grip.

"Come off it, Lee. This is private property. You know the drifters keep to the public beaches. Have you nothing to do except walk the beach where you *know* you'll tantalize me?" Burr rose just long enough to grab Lee's hand and pull her roughly onto the soft sand beside him.

Lee gasped from the sudden jolt and from the anger and indignation that filled her. "I had no idea you were out here. I heard you leave with Margo. I came here to be alone...to think."

"If you heard Margo and me leave, surely you must have heard us return. We made no pretense at keeping silent."

"I didn't hear you," Lee insisted. How dare he insinuate she had planned this encounter?

"You knew Margo had other plans for this evening. She told us so."

"I forgot." Her words sounded weak even to her own ears, but why did she have to explain?

"It doesn't really matter, does it?" Burr asked. "You're here. I'm here. Relax and enjoy the night."

"I was just going inside. I have already enjoyed the night." Again he had made her look like a man-chaser.

"Have you reached any conclusions or decisions?"

Lee hesitated. Why should she tell Burr now of her decision? Let him fret about it until morning. He was the one who gave her the ultimatum, the deadline for decision. Let him wait it out. "I've reached no conclusions yet, Burr. But I'm still thinking about what you said." She braced her hand against the sand, preparing to rise.

"Maybe I can help you think." Burr slipped his arm around her waist, unbalancing her as he pulled her to him.

Lee pushed herself away, trying to avoid his touch. "Please don't, Burr. You only confuse my thoughts."

"That's because you love me."

"I don't love you."

"Then I'll phrase it more bluntly. You *desire* me."

"You needn't be vulgar." Again Lee tried to pull away but her strength was no match for his. He pulled her to him again then pushed her back onto the sand, applying more pressure to her shoulder each time she tried to rise until she stopped struggling and lay quietly at his side. Her anger was a loud ringing in her ears, a white heat behind her eyes.

"There's nothing vulgar about desire, Lee." Burr's voice grew lazily sensuous. "Not to my way of thinking. With some people desire comes before love and with some love comes before desire. Who can say which is right? And who wants to worry about such details on a night like this? Look at that moon, Lee. It's a lovers' moon. It's a shame to let it go to waste."

Lee looked at the moon because it was hard to look anywhere else while being forced to lie so vulnerably close to him. Ragged clouds scudded in front of the moon, casting a moving shadow on her face; then they rippled on, leaving nothing but milky, silvery brightness to heighten the gentle sound of waves lapping on the shore. Lee closed her eyes, gathering the will to make a strong thrust for freedom. When she opened her eyes again Burr was leaning over her. Now he wasn't touching her at all but his closeness made her tremble. She could feel the warmth of his breath on her ear, in her hair. She could hear his soft intake of air and smell the sandalwood scent of his skin.

"Why don't you leave, Lee?" His voice taunted her. "I'm doing nothing to hold you here now."

"I'm going." She whispered the words, yet she could find no strength to move.

"Go then."

She lay motionless, angry that she could find no will to rise.

"You can't leave, can you?" Burr's voice grew soft and vibrant. "You want me as much as I want you, don't you?"

"I can leave. And I'm going to leave." With great effort Lee rose onto one elbow and thrust herself to a sitting position before Burr forced her roughly back onto the sand. She felt an invading grittiness in her hair as his mouth found hers, its force pushing her head more deeply into the soft sand. This time his kiss was surprisingly tender and sweet. But its very gentleness bespoke a strong demand, and the demand increased in intensity until it conquered her.

She let her lips part because his will negated hers. At first she vowed to make no response to his advances. She would lie there in the sand like a discarded rag doll. If he used her, he would do it knowing there was no invitation on her part. If she enjoyed his using her, she would never let him know. But as his marauding tongue probed more deeply she felt an awakening she couldn't deny. Every pore of her body seemed to open to his magic, and as she felt a throbbing glow, she came vibrantly alive in spite of herself.

Her arms went around his neck, pulling him closer; then she let her hands slide down his sides, along his thighs. As his kiss became even more insistent she felt ashamed of her own weakness. Why was she allowing his invasion? Why was she encouraging it? Their tongues investigated this new realm cautiously at first, like explorers intent on conquering and claiming new territory; then they probed with greater and greater confidence and a consuming urgency.

"No, Burr, no," Lee groaned when he released her mouth.

"You want me, Lee. Don't deny it. Why deny it? Tell me what you want me to do. I want to hear you say it." His lips found her eyelids. "I can take you to places you've never been before." His lips found her throat as his fingers unbuttoned her blouse, insinuating themselves around her breasts, stroking, moving slowly.

She felt a hot thrilling need as she let Burr push her blouse aside, working slowly and deliberately as was his style. She hated him for what he was doing to her, yet at the same time she loved what he was doing. And again she despised her own weakness. He was acting with the consent of her body if not the consent of her mind.

"Undress me, Lee. Start with my shirt."

"No."

"You think it's okay to enjoy my undressing you, yet you refuse to return the favor? Is that fair? I need you, Lee. Don't make me beg."

Of course it wasn't fair. Nothing was fair. It wasn't fair for him to hold her under his macho spell like this, to force her yielding body to do things her mind found unpardonable. She began undressing him, starting with his shirt, working as slowly as he had worked. She felt a new tension building within her, a tension that demanded release.

"Saving the best for last, are you?" Burr chuckled, pulling her to him once more. The crisp growth of hair on his chest prickled against her breasts as he kissed her. The soft cotton of his walking shorts did little to conceal the power of his body. His fingers stroked her, lingering in ways they should not have lingered, ways that made her every nerve rise to new heights of expectancy.

With one last shred of will she pushed him away, only to have his tongue sear a circle around her nipple, branding her with his passion. Her body had long ceased to resist and now she tried to wreak the same devastation on his body as he was wreaking on hers. They were both so caught up in their hot yearning that as the wave crashed down on them, it caught them totally unawares. It wasn't a large wave, but it was cold. The tide. They had forgotten about the tide. Lee screamed, and her scream, along with the water, brought them both to their senses, sent them scampering for higher ground.

In the next moment Lee heard feet running toward

the beach and she hastily pulled her blouse together and buttoned it.

"Is someone down here?" Margo called out. "Who's there?"

Burr groaned. "You hide, Lee. I'll face her. Here, slip into the shadow of this sea grape and I'll turn her off your trail."

"Lee, is that you?" Margo called before Lee could hide. "Don't you know it's dangerous to go swimming at night? And alone? Nobody in his right mind goes swimming...." Margo paused as she drew closer and saw Lee was fully clothed and soaking wet.

Lee held her breath, hoping that Burr was out of sight. She knew then that a person could blush over her entire body. Her skin felt as if a heat lamp were turned on it.

"Lee!" Margo gasped. "You weren't trying to commit.... I mean you aren't really desperate about not wanting to go to Seville, are you?" Margo grabbed Lee's arm and kept babbling as she urged her toward the house. "I mean, if you feel this strongly about Seville, I'll ask Burr not to send you. I never dreamed you'd try this. This is the exact spot where Zack...."

Lee's embarrassment died and curiosity consumed her. She lowered her voice and walked more quickly so Burr couldn't hear her question. "Margo! Did Zack Adburee commit suicide?"

Margo hesitated. "No. No, of course not. His death was an accident."

Lee sensed that Margo was lying. She had hesitated

too long before replying. Burr's brother had taken his own life. Lee could only wonder why.

"Were you trying to scare me?" Margo asked. "Or maybe you were trying to scare Burr out of... trying to make him think...."

"I was just out for a walk, Margo. I happened to get caught by the tide. There's absolutely nothing to be so excited about."

"Then why did you scream?"

"A wave just caught me by surprise. That's all. I've thought over the Seville business carefully and fully and I intend to give Burr an affirmative answer first thing in the morning. Experience in the Seville archive will be a grand boost to my career."

"Well, get back to your suite, now," Margo ordered. "A person never knows who may be walking the beach, even a private beach, and you've no business swimming alone or being in the surf even accidentally."

Lee walked faster, hating the feel of her skirt and blouse as they dragged and stuck against her wet skin. But what she had said to Margo was true. Nothing had changed. She was going to Seville. She would forget all about Burr Adburee in the cool recesses of the Archive of the Indies.

CHAPTER TWELVE

LEE SPENT A SLEEPLESS NIGHT, knowing that some wild wanton part of her was in love with Burr and that a saner part of her couldn't bear his arrogance, his egotism, his cruel hostility. What was the real Burr like? She had seen him struggle to hide his grief for his brother that first day in his office. She had seen him show tenderness toward his mother. And he had shown great courage in protecting her during the shark attack. Burr was an enigma. She remembered his kisses. He could be gentle in a way that made her melt. But even if the whole of her loved Burr, she could never let him know. She would never allow herself to be one of the many women who carried a torch for him. She would never let herself be vulnerable to the heartache she had known all too well in the past. Burr loved Margo. Let Margo deal with him.

Burr was in his shipboard office when she entered the next morning. For a moment the pictures of Zack that dominated the room exerted a powerful force that held her silent. He looked so young. So alive. Why would he have snuffed out his life in the sea?

"Well?" Burr let the word hang between them like a caress and Lee was suddenly conscious of her appearance. She had worn blue because she knew it gave her eyes an innocent, guileless look. And she had sleeked her hair back in a way that drew attention to her face, to the hollows beneath her cheekbones.

"Cat got your tongue?" Burr teased.

Lee forced herself to lock the memories of the previous night in the deep recesses of her heart as she spoke of current matters. The past was gone forever. All that mattered was today and the future.

"Since I left no message with Harry, since I'm here, you surely have guessed that I'm ready to go to Seville."

"Just like that?" Burr eyed her coldly. "You're ready to go to Seville?"

She tried to make her voice flat as a slap. "That's what you wanted, wasn't it?"

"Past tense. Yes, that's what I wanted. But I think the circumstances have changed, haven't they? Did last night mean nothing to you?"

Lee had to fight to control her voice, her words. She mustn't let him know how close she had come to letting him take her last night. "I'm ready to go to Seville. If you can use your influence to speed up getting a passport I'd appreciate it."

"I'll make a bargain with you. Tell me you'll let me love you and we'll forget all about Seville. You wanted me last night, Lee. We wanted each other."

His voice had gone soft as moonlight, but she found the will to hold firm. "Why should I lie to you?"

"To deny me would be lying."

"I'm surprised you're willing to bargain." Anger made her voice shrill, but it didn't tremble. "I'm surprised you don't just order me to say whatever you want to hear. That's more your style."

He leaned back in his chair studying her. "I think you wish I would give that order. You do, don't you?"

"Why do you say that?" Lee held her hands stiffly at her sides so Burr couldn't see their shaking. Did he think his line was foolproof? She wondered how many women had been fooled by it, or how many had used it as an excuse to give in to their desire for wanton pleasure.

"If I ordered you to say the words, then you'd be relieved of the responsibility of making the decision, wouldn't you? You're copping out." His face darkened and his voice grew dangerously quiet. "But you needn't worry that I'll order you to say you love me. Even I know one can't order love. It's no good unless it's freely given. I'll fly you back to town and you can make preparations to leave for Seville."

Lee felt strangely let down. Was Burr right? Had she wanted him to order her to love him? Well, she wasn't going to. Burr's demands were one-sided and unfair. Never had he said he loved her. She would do quite well with an ocean between them. That wanton part of her wanted to give in to him so badly, but she knew that only separation from him could save her from herself.

IN THE NEXT FEW DAYS Burr managed to speed up the procurement of her passport, and on the day of her departure, he drove her to the airport although she would much have preferred driving her own car. She dreaded their farewell. How should she handle it? A verbal until-we-meet-again? A handshake? What if he kissed her? Surely he would never let her go without a farewell kiss. She steeled herself to be strong, not to let her lips respond to his.

"You will keep in touch by letter at least once every week?" Burr asked with a touch of genuine concern in his voice that surprised Lee. He was actually learning not to order her around. But she suddenly realized with a sinking of her heart that his interest no doubt stemmed from the business purpose of her trip.

"Of course."

"You will call the minute you turn up anything really important."

"Just what do you consider really important?"

"The *Santa Isabella* manifest, of course. The complete listing. You have the cannon number?"

"I have it." The ride ahead seemed a million miles long. How could she bear to leave him? Suddenly everything around her seemed intensified, as if an unseen hand had twisted a knob that brought the world into sharper focus. Had the sky ever been so blue? And the clouds! Some were like white puddles, like cream that had refused to whip, while others were as stiffly precise as mounds of meringue. And the sun shimmering behind the clouds backlighted Burr's profile until she knew his craggy features were etched in her memory. How could she bear to leave? Why didn't she throw herself into his arms and stay there? That's what she really wanted to do, wasn't it?

Then they were at the airport and the flight was leaving on schedule. Burr checked her luggage through, then sat with her in the crowded waiting room near the departure gate. When her flight was called they stood. Lee inhaled deeply to get control of her emotions. In a few moments she would be far from the temptation of his voice, his hands, his lips. . . .

"Goodbye, Burr. I'll keep in touch."

"I'll expect to hear from you." Burr smoothed silky seductiveness into his voice and leaned a little toward her. Instinctively she took a step back, and as she did so, Burr ran his tongue over his lips and smiled at her sardonically, letting her know he knew she expected a kiss. She felt her face flame, then she hurried across the concrete to the plane, climbed the boarding steps, and settled herself by a window facing away from the terminal. The stewardess did the seat-belt check; and when all the passengers had been trussed like turkeys awaiting the oven the plane took off.

Had she really expected Burr to kiss her? He cared nothing for her. He wouldn't be letting her go to Seville if he cared for her.

They touched down in Miami where she changed planes, then she dozed most of the way to Spain. Blessed oblivion. She wakened when the plane touched down on the tarmac and sleepily she joined the general scramble for carry-on cases, papers, books. After she deplaned and settled into the taxi for the ride to the pension Burr had selected, she knew immediately she was in another country. The heavy pungent odor of orange blossoms hung in the warm evening air, and Spanish flowed from the radio. As they drove along the banks and quays of the Guadalquiver River, she tried to identify the Seville landmarks she had read about in a tourists' guide. The Giralda Tower? The Alcazar? The Tower of Gold? She tried to put all thought of Marvista and Burr Adburee from her mind, but she was unsuccessful. Burr's image was still on the back of her mind.

Presently the taxi screeched to a stop, and after paying the driver, she stood and studied the pension where she would live. Moorish archways... creamy stucco walls... three stories. Pots of geraniums, miniature palms and marigolds hung from iron-railed balconies exuding a sharp fragrance. A hoarse cry drew her eye to a partridge in a wooden cage that was hanging from a balcony high above the street. Lee walked up three marble steps and entered the recessed doorway to the pension. Should she have knocked? Cautiously she peered into a deserted parlor on her left where massive carved furniture was arranged in a formal touch-me-not manner.

"Señorita Cameron?" The voice flowed from another direction and Lee looked to her right, then crossed the polished marble floor between her and a carved oak desk.

"Yes, I'm Lee Cameron," Lee said. "And you must be Señora Pedraza. Mr. Adburee has made arrangements for me to live here, has he not?"

"Sí, sí, Señorita Cameron. Welcome. You are expected and your rooms are ready. Come with me."

Señora Pedraza was a short woman who hid her obesity behind the folds of a brown caftan. Middle-aged, Lee guessed, yet the hair sweeping back from each side of her face was as dark as a raven's wing and it accentuated her pale olive complexion. Her eyes fascinated Lee. The huge black pupils almost concealed the pale brown iris. Owl eyes.

"Gracias, señora," Lee replied. Then as she followed the Spanish woman toward a stairway she glanced outside at the iron-fenced garden with its fretwork gates where orange and palm trees bordered beds of roses and azaleas. Charming. No doubt she would have plenty of time to investigate it later at her leisure.

"You are here to stay for a while?" Señora Pedraza asked, as if she weren't quite aware of the arrangements Burr had made.

"Perhaps," Lee said. "It depends on my work."

"Your work?"

Lee sensed she was being pumped for information. Señora Pedraza made little effort to hide her curiosity about the American lady whose bills were being paid by Dive Boys, Inc. "I'll be doing research in the archive."

"Oh! You are a scholar working on an advanced degree?"

"No," Lee said. "Or perhaps. I could apply my research to an advanced degree one day if I chose to do so."

"What is your subject?" Señora Pedraza was panting by the time they reached the second floor, although Lee was carrying both her heavy suitcases and the *señora* was carrying only a light attaché case.

"My subject is old Spain," Lee replied blandly as if the archive might house other information.

"I see." Now Señora Pedraza unlocked the arched oak door to a small suite of rooms. Burr had chosen well. Her heels sank into thick sea-green carpet. White wicker furniture cushioned in sea green gave a cool light touch that she welcomed. Sea green. Had Burr ordered it especially for her? Didn't Spanish taste run more to ornate carved furniture like that in the downstairs parlor? She couldn't help wondering if Burr was trying to remind her of that other room in Miami.

Sitting room...boudoir...kitchenette...bath. And a balcony. Burr had said it was more elaborate than most pensions and that the kitchenette was the room that made it special. She stepped to the arched doors filigreed with wrought iron and opened them. The balcony overlooked a rose garden with a small fountain where a young girl was feeding goldfish. Even in the twilight Lee could see the flashing bodies in the water. But it was the girl who attracted her interest. There was a sadness, a loneliness, about her.

"You find the suite suitable?" Señora Pedraza asked smugly.

"Quite," Lee replied. "It has an old-world charm I thought existed only in books."

"I have rules here, *señorita*." Señora Pedraza cleared her throat. "Where there are both men and women in residence we must have rules. And we must practice economy—the inflation, you know."

"Of course." Suddenly Lee felt like a schoolgirl being reprimanded for breaking curfew.

"You will have no gentlemen callers after seven in the evening. Lights must be turned off when not in use. The mattress on the bed will be turned side for side and end for end each week. Personal phone calls will be made at the pay phone in the lobby."

"I understand, *señora*. Thank you for showing me in. My rent has been paid in advance, I believe?"

"Quite so. Quite so." Señora Pedraza stood there for a moment eyeing Lee's bags as if they might contain contraband, then realizing there were no more details to discuss she reluctantly took her leave.

Once the door closed behind the *señora*, Lee stretched out for a moment on the satin-quilted bed. This lovely room might inspire her to be very slow in finding the necessary information in the archive. But of course she had to get back to Raul. To Burr? He kept intruding into her thoughts. She relaxed for a few minutes, then she sat up and began unpacking. Perhaps a new life was unfolding before her.

After hanging her clothes in the wardrobe Lee freshened up, changed into a skirt and sleeveless top that matched her hair and strolled downstairs and outside to look at the tiny formal garden. She paused, touching the wrought-iron gate still warm from the afternoon sun. Then, stepping through the gateway, she wandered for a few moments among the fragrant-smelling roses before she sat down on a stone bench beside the tiny fountain and pool. How restful. She sat for a long time just watching the fish playing among the lily pads and listening to the gentle splash of water. Now and then she thought she heard the faraway clap of hands—or was it the snap of castanets? She wished Burr were here to share the moment with her.

"I saw you arrive, miss. Perhaps I can help you with directions?"

Lee jumped, startled and irritated by the sound of the bass voice at her elbow when she had heard nobody approach. Clearly she was in no need of directions. But when she turned to gaze up at the owner of the voice, she smiled in spite of herself. Suddenly it was good to see another American.

"I'm Julio Hunter," the man said. "And you're Lee Cameron."

"And how did you learn that?" *Be on guard,* she warned herself, erasing her smile.

"Señora Pedraza sees all, hears all, tells all."

Now Lee frankly studied her unexpected companion. She liked his friendly smile. It went well with his copper-colored hair, his rangy, loosely jointed build, his denim suit that was as American as apple pie. Thirtyish, she guessed. But what did that matter? She wasn't going to allow herself to form any instant friendships in Spain. She rose.

"It's nice to have met you, Mr. Hunter. Now if you'll please excuse me. . . ."

"Call me Julio, okay? I live on the third floor. Have you had dinner?"

What nerve! Did she really look like a cheap pickup? Lee stepped around him, retreated through the iron gateway and hurried back to her suite, angry that Julio Hunter had interrupted her enjoyment of the garden. The airline had fed her well. Eating could wait until tomorrow.

As moonglow flooded through her balcony doorway she took a leisurely bath, thinking of how strange it was to be in a land that many centuries past had known Arab caliphs and harem girls and also Roman legions. She retired, falling asleep to the scent of orange blossoms, roses and the even more powerful fragrance of night-blooming jasmine. She wondered if Burr knew how lovely Seville was in the springtime.

The next morning Lee awakened to the lively chatter of wren song and knew immediately she had overslept. But it really didn't matter. Professor Hoskin had told her the archive didn't open until nine o'clock. She dressed in a cinnamon brown skirt and rust-colored shirt, a won't-show-the-dirt outfit, because Professor Hoskin had told her the archive materials were sometimes musty. Señora Pedraza was watching from the entryway desk as Lee left the pension; she had a feeling that the *señora* would always be watching. Were there such things as watch owls? Señora Pedraza reminded her of an owl, with her pale face, her penetrating eyes, her flowing caftan. She would have to tell Burr about the *señora* in her first letter. But no. She had decided that letters to Burr would only pertain to business. She would not be his pen pal.

She found the small café right where Professor Hoskin said it would be, ordered juice, toast and coffee, then as soon as she had eaten she strolled to the archive. One really couldn't miss it. It loomed right across the street from the cathedral and its Gothic arches and massive stone walls gave it the appearance of a castle.

The archive was set well back from the street, and Lee thought that the formal garden in front of it, with its palms and orange trees, looked much like the smaller garden at her pension. The fragrance was the same: orange blossoms. Heady. Pervasive. Stone pathways crisscrossed the garden and in its center was a marble fountain where stone lions rested their paws on a stone globe of the world. Did the lions represent the long-ago power of old Spain? Lee scowled as she realized it was a fountain Burr would admire since he admired both power and treasure.

Lee strolled on past the garden and a massive bronze cannon, then climbed the pink marble staircase. For a moment she studied the display of a treasure chest that had been salvaged from some ancient galleon. Four feet long, two feet wide and as many feet deep, it had a lock so massive Professor Hoskin had told her it required the strength of a horse to turn the key. Then she walked through the archive entryway where great iron doors had been flung wide to admit the day's scholars. The cool interior air seemed to surround her like an aura and she inhaled its dank musty smell. The smell of the Old World?

"My credentials," she said, presenting papers from the university for the inspection of the attendant at an official-looking desk.

The lady studied the papers for a moment then smiled. "*Sí*. You are welcome."

"Will you please direct me to the index shelf?" Lee asked.

"This way, *señorita*." The attendant spoke in broken English, leading her toward a massive shelf where about thirty giant-size volumes and many smaller ones sat stiffly upright like sentries. Lee felt dwarfed by the very size of the building, the size of the index volumes. And after the attendant left her she felt very much abandoned and alone. Why had Burr done this to her? How could she ever cope?

She forced herself to open the first of the index volumes. Handwritten. Her heart dropped to her left toe. What had she expected, an IBM printout? She began turning pages, having no idea exactly what she was looking for. She knew the name of the ship. She knew the date it had sunk. She decided to look for material pertaining to those two facts.

"Perhaps I can help you with something?"

The familiar voice. Lee turned and gazed up at Julio Hunter, and his infectious smile was like a magnet coaxing a smile from her own lips. Today he wore loafers with the same denim suit he had worn the evening before. Lee noticed the way the dim light in the archive glinted on his coppery hair, giving it the look of newly minted pennies. But it was his eyes that held her. They were friendly gray eyes, kind eyes that looked right into her soul and saw only the good things about her. Surely that was true or why would he be smiling so sincerely? She thought of

Burr's smoldering eyes and felt a prickle along her nape. Why couldn't she rid herself of Burr? Why did thoughts of him cling to her like filings to a magnet?

"Really, I'll help if I can," Julio said. "This place confuses even the skilled scholar, but I've never before seen a skilled scholar with honey-colored hair and—"

"I can manage," Lee said. "But thank you."

"I'm sorry," Julio said. "I didn't intend to be fresh. But if you do find you need help, let me know. I'll be working in the scholar's room." He started to walk away and suddenly Lee hated to see him go.

"Mr. Hunter, er, maybe I could use a little help at that."

Julio turned immediately. "What's your subject?"

"The *Santa Isabella*. A galleon that sank in 1639."

"Sounds fascinating. But you won't find anything about it in that volume." Julio studied the books a few moments, then pulled out another selection. "Here. Try this one. It's an index relating to the House of Trade. If you don't find something there, call me. The scholar's room, you know."

"Thank you, Mr. Hunter."

"Julio, okay?"

"Thanks, Julio. I really appreciate your help."

It took Lee several minutes before her eyes adjusted to the look of the script in the index. The words were all run together. There was no punctuation. The lines looked like a child's drawing of the sea itself, an endless scribbling sketch of waves. *I'll never be able to do it,* Lee thought. *I'm not going to be able to read any of this.* She hated Burr for putting her in a situation where she was destined to fail.

Then her eye caught some familiar terms. Armada Papers 1630-1640. She copied out a request slip for the documents; then, while the blue-smocked porter went to find the bundle, she parted the red velvet draperies that gave admission to the next room.

The scholar's room reminded her of the peep boxes she used to make as a child when she created precise scenes in a long narrow shoe container. She felt as if she were standing at the opening of a giant-size shoe box. Then she stepped inside the room and chose a chair at a heavy oak table near one of the great arched windows because the only other lighting in the room came from dim fixtures set high in the vaulted ceiling.

The marble floors and stone walls kept the room cool. At least she would be comfortable as she worked. She saw Julio sitting at a table near another window, but she didn't look his way. Instead she pretended to be very interested in the picture of Columbus that gazed down at her, at the brass studs that rimmed the leather seats and backrests of her chair. Presently the porter returned with a heavy bundle, thumped it on her table and departed.

Other blue-smocked porters stalked about the room shushing for silence although silence seemed to drip from the very ceiling beams. The room was already so quiet it seemed like a place where time had stopped. Lee untied the pink ribbon that bound her bundle of documents, flipped it open and began poring over the pages. How many there were! One thousand? Five thousand? It was hard to guess. Where should she start? If she took time even to glance at each paper in this bundle she would grow old in the Archive of the Indies.

She studied the documents until her eyes watered and when Julio paused at her table and asked her to take a break with him, she went willingly. Julio stopped on the pink marble steps and they sat down.

"How's it going?" he asked.

"Terrible. There's absolutely no order to the documents. Not alphabetical. Not according to date. And the ink has faded and—"

"It was made from oak galls. It's a wonder it's held up at all."

"And there are bug holes in the pages and—"

"Are you on a limited time schedule?"

Lee laughed and shook her head. "I can stay forever. And I may have to."

"Listen, I'll give you one clue that may help. Don't try to read each page. Just scan it. Scan it for two things. *Isabella* and 1639. If you spot either of those items you can stop and read more."

"That makes sense," Lee admitted. Then she grew embarrassed because she had expressed no interest in Julio or his mission at the archive. "What is your research subject?"

"I'm a meteorologist," Julio said. "I'd like to get a Ph.D. and I'm working on my dissertation. The subject matter is rather complicated, but it concerns storms and hurricane patterns that affected early commerce between Spain and the New World.''

''Sounds fascinating.''

''Not as fascinating as lunch sounds. How about having lunch with me, Lee? The archive closes for a couple of hours. We could have lunch at the café down the street, or we could buy some bread and cheese and picnic by the river.''

''You're overwhelming me with choices.'' Lee laughed. ''I really should go back to my suite and rest my eyes. They'll never be the same again.''

''You rest mine,'' Julio said, letting his gaze rove over her body, yet grinning in a way that kept her from taking offense. ''Surely you're not going to deny a poor tired scholar the chance to refresh his vision, are you?''

''That would really be quite inconsiderate of me, wouldn't it?'' Lee replied, matching his teasing voice with her own.

''You're absolutely right. Come on. Let's go back, return our bundles to the porters and escape that tomb for a while.''

''Will they check the bundles out to us again later this afternoon?''

''Sure. No problem. You wait here and I'll take care of it for both of us.'' Julio left, and in a few moments he returned and they crossed the Avenida Queipo de Llamo and found seats in the café. Lee felt at home in the casual setting of pine tables, straight chairs and red-checked linens. And the smell of olive oil and fresh bread made her mouth water.

Julio ordered coffee for them from a slim heavily made-up woman who waited on them, then he turned his attention back to Lee. "Tell me about yourself. Where are you from? What are you doing here? Who are you working for?"

"Nobody has asked as many questions of me since I met Señora Pedraza."

"That's a low blow. I assure you my intentions are quite different from the *señora*'s." He gave her a mock-evil leer.

"I won't even ask what your intentions are in that case." Lee sipped her coffee. How much easier Julio was to talk to than Burr. She frowned. Why couldn't she forget Burr and just enjoy herself?

"Come on, tell me a bit about yourself, Lee."

"Well, for starters I'm living in Key West and sort of looking after my younger brother, Raul, and working for—" she started to say Burr Adburee but caught herself "—for Dive Boys, Inc., a treasure salvaging company that's searching for the lost treasure that was supposedly aboard the *Santa Isabella*."

"Are they having any luck?"

"Some. They've brought up a few artifacts, but the hull of the galleon is still missing, and another company is also searching for it. The first ones to prove that they've actually found the *Isabella* will claim the whole of the treasure—if they can locate it."

"Sounds like an exciting race," Julio said. "Exactly what are you hunting for? The place where the ship went down?"

"No. Dive Boys thinks it's discovered that—approximately, of course. I'm searching for the complete manifest, the document that gives a listing of what the galleon carried along with serial numbers for all the items. We have a cannon with a number, but we have nothing to match that number to."

"Lots of luck."

"Your turn. Where are you from? What are you doing here?"

"I'm from Miami. We have a lot in common, Lee. Both of us are from Florida. Both of us are looking after a younger sibling. Since our parents died last year in a car crash I'm in charge of Claudia. She's fifteen going on thirty in some ways. Quite a girl. I like the continent, Lee. I could make my home here. Don't you think I'm the romantic villain-in-Spain type?" He didn't wait for an answer as he chatted on, "Seville is the most relaxed city I know of—a city for strollers. I could go for the easy life here."

"I like what I've seen of the city, which admittedly isn't much, but I could never consider leaving America and living in a foreign land on a permanent basis."

"Let me show you more of the country, and maybe you'll change your mind."

When the waitress approached again to take their order Lee ordered *paella*, taking a chance that it would be good. Julio ordered *gazpacho* and when their orders arrived he laughed at Lee's look of surprise.

"What were you expecting?"

"I thought I was ordering rice with fish. Guess my Spanish is rustier than I thought. But I love rice, and the ham and tomato and peas look delicious."

After they finished eating they drank more coffee and talked some more. Lee hadn't realized just how long they had been talking until she looked outside and saw that the sun was casting long fingers of shadow on the street.

"Julio! We've talked away the whole afternoon."

"Ah. I've held you mesmerized. You find me enchanting."

"But I can't do things like this! I'm being paid to work and I—"

"And who knows or cares? Relax. Live a little. The archive will be there tomorrow and tomorrow and tomorrow. Have dinner with me."

"We just had lunch."

"But in a few hours it will be dinnertime. We'll buy the ingredients and make a meal in my kitchenette."

"What about Señora Pedraza? Surely my presence in your suite would be against her rules."

"The rules are different for men. Anyway, Claudia serves as a buffer—a chaperone, so to speak. Say you'll dine with me and the three of us will thwart the watch owl."

"Watch owl!"

Julio looked at Lee and grinned. "I'm sorry. I didn't mean to be that rude."

Lee broke out laughing. "Rude! I can't believe it. That's exactly what she reminds me of. A watch owl. You must be a mind reader!"

"Come on. That settles it. We'll have dinner together, then I'll read your mind."

Lee allowed Julio to sweep her into his plans without further protest. How different he was from Burr. Just as handsome in his own way, yet casual and easygoing. No arrogance. No obey-the-master theatrics. No cruel hostility. Again Lee frowned, wishing Burr would stop intruding into her thoughts. She found Julio quite a welcome change.

CHAPTER THIRTEEN

ONCE IT HAD BEEN DECIDED that they would have dinner together they left the café where Lee guessed the owner surely must have thought they intended to take up permanent residence. He had not even bothered them during the siesta hour. Perhaps Julio had tipped him, but if that was so, Lee had not been aware of it.

"We must go shopping," Julio said. "In Seville that takes a bit of time, but there's no great hurry here. It's my kind of city."

"Where's the grocery store?" Lee asked. "And what will we make for dinner?"

Julio smiled down at her. "Don't expect a supermarket, Lee. But come along and I'll show you where the Seville *señoras* shop."

Lee. She liked the lilt he gave to her name. Although Burr had made a point of dispensing with calling her "Miss Cameron," he had seldom said her name in other than a businesslike tone. But once he had called her darling. Lee grimaced. Why was she constantly letting Burr intrude into this soft Spanish afternoon? Why was she feeling this need to compare Burr to Julio? There was no comparison. None.

For a few moments they walked down a residential

street where windows were screened with ornate iron grills and brightly painted shutters. A poodle barked from one window and a throaty voice shushed it in Spanish. Courtyards revealed flashing glimpses of petunias and morning glories, of white and purple clematis clinging to sturdy trellises. Everywhere pale green foliage cascaded on stucco walls. Geraniums grew in pots at every doorway, their pink and scarlet blossoms like jewels awaiting discovery. Lee thought the scene was like a page from an old-world fairy tale. Even the people she passed on the street had a special charm and smiling grace that she had seen nowhere else. Springtime in Seville! The whole city looked like a cathedral decked out for a wedding.

"And always the scent of orange blossoms," Lee said. "I'll never forget Seville."

"You sound as if you're leaving instead of just arriving," Julio said. "Perish the thought. I have only found you, Lee. We have only discovered each other."

"Oh, I'll be around awhile, that's for sure," Lee said, thinking of the archive with all its bundles, its blue-smocked porters shushing. "But the scent of orange blossoms will always remind me of this place."

"The oranges you'll see in the market stalls aren't from these trees that grow along the streets," Julio said. "These trees produce only bitter fruit. It's a paradox."

"Perhaps it's a foreshadowing, a warning that love is not always followed by happiness."

"A very solemn thought for such a pleasant day."

Julio linked his arm through hers and guided her into a passage so convoluted and much too narrow to permit the use of vehicles. The lane was enclosed by a high wall on each side, and their heels clicked on mosaic tile that appeared to be freshly scrubbed. Ahead of them a woman in a green cotton shift carried a bucket of water from some nearby tap, and a dark-eyed boy watched them as he petted a calico cat. Here and there Lee saw little squares with rose gardens surrounded by gaily tiled seats.

"May we sit down and just look?" Lee asked, pausing at one of the squares.

"Not if you want dinner before midnight," Julio replied.

"You said there was no hurry."

"There is none, but let's do our rose-garden sitting another time. Look up ahead. There's the market."

Lee gazed at the large white building with its red tile roof; when they entered she was all but overwhelmed with sights and sounds and smells. At a cheese stall the proprietress, a tiny *señora* with eyes that gleamed like dark agate, ruled over aromatic arrays of soft creamy cheeses and smoke-cured horns. Lee's mouth watered, and as they stood in line the sound effects were like a musical. Feminine voices lilted, masculine voices droned and the staccato clink of pesetas set the rhythm.

They stopped at a stall for wild asparagus and at another for salted almonds. When Julio had made his necessary purchases at the market they stopped at a *carnicería* for some cubed meat and at the *panadería* for a special type of hard rolls. At each shop they had to wait in line to make their purchases. Lee understood at last why there was no time for sitting in rose gardens.

"Spanish housewives must spend half their lives shopping for their meals," Lee said when at last they were on their way back to the pension.

"But I don't think they mind," Julio said. "Shopping's a morning chore and many times one that is performed every day. It gives the ladies time to chat with friends, to catch up on the local gossip. And sometimes the ladies don't do their own shopping at all. They send their servants, who have all the fun of the marketplace."

As they left the winding lane and stepped back onto a wider street Lee sighed. "One almost gets claustrophobic in there."

"You probably wouldn't like it at all during the heat of summer," Julio said. "A canvas awning is stretched overhead by day to foil the sun's rays, and of course it foils the breeze, too. The canvas isn't removed until night. Then it is furled so strollers may stop and visit or sit in the soft night gazing at the stars."

"You make it sound quite romantic."

"Seville is quite a romantic place. I look forward to showing it to you, Lee."

"I feel as if I've been here a month already."

"My company hangs that heavily?"

"You know that's not what I mean. It's just that everything's so new I feel bombarded with a myriad of impressions, sights, sounds, smells—more than my mind can absorb. I can't wait to go sight-seeing."

Now they were passing the cathedral across the street from the archive. "Look." Lee nodded. "A cathedral second only to St. Peter's in grandeur, or so I've heard, and I haven't seen inside it yet. They say Columbus is buried there."

"There is time, Lee. There'll be time to see everything. The cathedral, the Giralda Tower. It's part of the cathedral and it overlooks the old Moorish Court of the Oranges that dates back from the twelfth century."

"May one climb up into the tower?" Lee asked. "I'd like to do that."

"I'll take you to the top to see the bells and the magnificent view of the city. We'll have a great time exploring Seville, Lee. You'll forget that you came here to work."

"No. I mustn't forget that. My work is very important to me."

"Who is your boss? You never mentioned who runs Dive Boys."

"His name is Burrton Adburee." Lee didn't elaborate, didn't want to get involved in a conversation about Burr.

"Of Adburee Boatyards?"

"Yes. The son."

"You must feel quite an allegiance to your boss to travel all this distance and spend your summer in the musty scholar's room."

Lee started to explain that her allegiance was to marine archaeology, to a dream her father had, to a goal she intended to work toward, but she couldn't find the right words. And maybe she couldn't find the words because deep in her heart she knew those words would form a lie. Julio had hit on the truth. She felt a strong allegiance to her boss. Allegiance? I pledge allegiance.... That was a dry brittle term for what she really felt, if she would admit the truth.

When they reached the pension Señora Pedraza nodded to them as they crossed the entryway and headed upstairs together. They nodded back, and Lee could feel the woman's calculating gaze on them. She was like an owl watching a rabbit's nest. Julio had a suite on the third floor, and his sister called out to him the minute she heard the door open.

"Julio! *Where* have you been? You promised to take me to Triana tonight!" Her indignant words stopped abruptly when she saw Lee. "Oh, I'm sorry. I didn't know you were bringing a guest."

This was the girl who had been feeding the goldfish yesterday. Lee thought she would have recognized Claudia as Julio's sister had they met as strangers on the street. She had the same coppery hair, the same gray eyes, the same friendly smile. And Lee understood what Julio had meant when he said she was fifteen going on thirty. Claudia was as tall as Lee was and she held her well-rounded figure in its bias-cut shift with a natural dignity, yet in a way that told the observer she was quite aware of her striking appearance. She was more woman than child and she gave the impression of eagerness like that of a filly racing the wind.

Lee smiled at Claudia. "I hope I'm not interrupting your plans for the evening." She knew from the first quick look of disappointment that had flashed across Claudia's face and had been replaced slowly by a weak smile that she was indeed interrupting plans.

"There were no definite plans," Julio said firmly. "Just sort of a discussion about visiting the old city, the gypsy sector across the river. Claudia, I want you to meet Lee Cameron from Florida. It's a small world, isn't it?"

For a moment Lee thought Claudia might burst into tears, but she managed another smile.

"I'm glad to know you, Lee." Then Claudia brightened. "Maybe you'd like to go to Triana with us."

"Not tonight, Claudia," Julio said. "Another time, perhaps. I've promised Lee a true Spanish dinner tonight. Think we can manage that?" He walked on through the sitting room to a tiny kitchenette.

"Let me see what you've brought." Claudia began to poke into the packages Julio set down on the table, and Lee remained in the sitting room studying the suite that was almost like her own. The same type balcony overlooked the garden. The room had similar wicker furniture, but the cushions were the color of apricots. The only difference in their accommodations seemed to be that here two bedrooms, instead of one, opened off the sitting room.

Lee walked out to the balcony to give Julio and Claudia some moments of privacy. She was surprised that she could see the river undulating like a great umber serpent in the distance. And on the street leading to it she saw couples riding in open horse-drawn carriages. She felt the evening breeze like cool gauze against her face as she listened to the flow of Spanish coming from two gentlemen strolling on a pathway below. Then suddenly the soft strains of music drifted from the sitting room. Spanish guitar. Castanets. She turned to go inside, but Julio joined her on the balcony, carrying two fragile-stemmed wine goblets.

"Spain isn't Spain without the background music. And Spain isn't Spain without *manzanilla*." He gave Lee one of the goblets and pulled two wicker chairs near the iron balcony railing. He returned to the kitchenette for a dish of salted almonds, then he sat down beside her.

"Julio, I feel terrible about Claudia. I've ruined her evening."

"But you've made mine." He sipped his *manzanilla*. "And don't worry about Claudia. Childish disappointments and childish elation fill her life constantly. She's like scales never in balance, always way up or way down. I've already made it up to her for the trip to Triana."

"How?" Lee sipped the white sherry and found the taste pungent yet pleasant. "How does one make it up to one's sister for skipping out on the gypsy city?"

"Oh, I have a way with the ladies. Claudia's birthday is coming up in a few weeks. Her sixteenth. It seems to be very special to her—her step into womanhood or something. Anyway, I promised her not only a trip to Triana, but a dinner there at the Venta de Antequera."

"A very posh spot, no doubt."

"Supersophisticated. Claudia fancies herself a

woman of the world, and now she can dream for weeks of leaving a string of swains pining with broken hearts throughout the pavilions of the Venta de Antequera.''

"Clearly, you don't understand how rough it is to be fifteen going on thirty,'' Lee said with a laugh. Yet her heart went out to Claudia. She could remember her own sixteenth birthday. Even then she had been in love with Ben. How she had tried to impress him with her worldliness. She had felt older then than she felt now.

They sipped their *manzanilla* until the glasses were empty, but when Julio offered seconds, Lee declined. "Perhaps I could help Claudia with the dinner.'' She glanced at her watch. It was already past nine o'clock. "It's not fair to leave Claudia to cope with the meal alone. I thought *we* were going to make our meal.''

"Are you hungry?''

"I won't lie to you. I'm starved. I knew the Spanish dinner hour was late, but *this* late?''

"Ten o'clock is the usual time, but I'll see if I can get Claudia to speed it up a bit.''

When Julio rose to leave the balcony Lee followed him to the kitchenette where Claudia was busy with pans and dishes.

"Can I help?'' Lee asked.

"You could set the table,'' Claudia answered matter-of-factly. "The dishes are in the cupboard to your left.''

"It's impolite to make a guest work,'' Julio protested.

"She volunteered," his sister pointed out.

"That I did," Lee insisted, feeling guilty because Claudia not only had missed an outing but also had drawn kitchen detail. "You go put some more records on the player, Julio. Claudia and I will attend to the meal."

But Claudia had the meal well under control, and after Lee finished setting the table, there was little else to do. "Aren't you in school, Claudia? I mean, how do you spend your days over here?"

"I finished spring term by correspondence, and Julio has hired a tutor for me. I spend two hours of the morning studying and working with him on my Spanish." Claudia grinned. "But sometimes he'll only give me one hour."

"Why is that?"

"He's one of those men who will only work long enough to support himself for the day. When he's earned that amount, he quits work and joins his cronies for a game of dominoes."

"Perhaps his key to happiness lies in relaxation."

"I'm not complaining," Claudia said. "In the afternoon I'm on my own. I go sight-seeing. I read a lot and I take pictures. Photography is my hobby. Someday I'm going to be a professional photographer for a big magazine."

"Here?"

"No, at home. Florida. Julio can use his inheritance to stay here forever if he wants to, but just as soon as I'm old enough I'm going home."

So Julio was living and studying on an inheritance, Lee thought. But what business was that of hers? She admired Claudia's ambition to be a photographer, but that was a long way into the future. Right now she admired the delicious-looking meal Claudia had prepared, and Lee praised her lavishly. "This is some kind of lobster, right?"

"Langostas," Julio replied before Claudia could answer. "Señora Pedraza showed Claudia how to serve them cold with mayonnaise."

"And she showed me where to buy this special thick brown honey," Claudia said. "I love it on hard rolls. And I eat it for breakfast while Julio dips bread in warm olive oil. He's gone native."

Julio held Lee's chair as they sat down at the small table in the kitchenette. Lee ate slowly, enjoying the lobster, the buttered asparagus, the hard rolls. Julio kept up a flow of chatter, but Lee couldn't help feeling sorry for Claudia. How lonely she must be here separated from all her high-school friends, away from the kind of schooling she was accustomed to. How much time did she have to while away with Señora Pedraza each day?

After they finished eating, Lee helped Claudia wash and dry the dishes, then Claudia excused herself and went to her room. "It was a lovely evening, Julio," Lee said as she prepared to leave. "A lovely day, really. Even the archive was rather exciting."

"The day doesn't have to end yet, Lee. The night is young."

"It's almost eleven."

"And does your chariot turn into a pumpkin at the witching hour? Come on. Sit down a while. You can sleep in the morning. The archive won't open until nine. I've been thinking about your work here, about Adburee's work in the keys, and I have a suggestion to make."

Lee let Julio lead her back out to the balcony, where they sat under the stars while the heady scent of the orange blossoms engulfed them. No breeze stirred and the palm fronds on the nearby trees were still as paper patterns a child might have cut out and pasted in a book. Julio offered Lee another glass of *manzanilla*, but she declined, remembering the effect of the champagne she had consumed that night in Miami with Burr. She tried to forget that night. Now that it was totally dark it seemed as if she and Julio were suspended in space, floating in a bubble of moonglow and starshine. Lee closed her eyes, letting the sensuous Latin rhythms flowing from Julio's records mesmerize her. She pulled herself from her reverie reluctantly when Julio spoke again.

"Here's my suggestion, Lee. I told you I'm a meteorologist. With a little extra effort I could look up an account of the exact storm that sank the *Santa Isabella* back in the 1600s."

"That would be interesting, I suppose," Lee said. "But how would it help Dive Boys?"

"Once I find the details of the storm, the direction of the wind currents, the wind velocity, the tides, I might be able to project the course of that storm. The winds and the seas behaved very much the same centuries ago as they do today. Knowing the storm's course might enable me to indicate the location of the ship's hull, or at least it might indicate the scatter pattern of the wreckage."

Lee leaned forward, peering at Julio intently. "Is that really possible?"

"I think it is. I'll certainly try if it would give you Brownie points with your boss and if it would give me Brownie points with you."

Lee leaned back again. "I can't let you do it, Julio. You're working on projects of your own. From the little I accomplished this morning I can see how much time it would take you to find that kind of information in the archive. I can't let you spend that kind of time for Dive Boys."

"I wouldn't be doing it for Dive Boys, Lee." Julio impaled her with his direct gaze. "I'll be honest with you. I would be doing it for me. I would be doing it because I want you to like me."

"I guess that's about as honest as you can get." Lee smiled, a bit confused by Julio's straightforward approach. She didn't want to be indebted to him. She hardly knew him, and although he was as friendly as a puppy she felt wary. "If you really want to take the time to do this, then you must let me arrange it with Mr. Adburee. I'll explain the situation to him and he'll pay you for your work."

Mr. Adburee. How strange it seemed to say the name as if it meant absolutely nothing to her. Mr. Adburee. Someone she had known in the distant past.

"I don't want any pay from your Mr. Adburee," Julio said. "You'll hurt my feelings if you turn my offer down or if you try to make a business deal of it."

"I'm sorry, Julio, but I can't let you do this unless

Mr. Adburee orders it done. I mean I've only known you for—"

"Forever. Isn't that how it seems? I feel as if I've known you all my life. And I thought you surely must feel that way, too."

Lee was surprised that he had pinpointed her feelings so accurately, yet she was unwilling to get involved on the terms he was offering. She was silent for so long that he spoke again.

"Do you type, Lee?"

"Why, yes. Why?"

"Perhaps you'd accept my offer if I'd let you do some typing for me. I'm a two-finger typist myself and typing up my notes for that dissertation is almost more than I can face. Maybe we could work out an exchange of work."

"Perhaps so, Julio. I'll think about it." Now Lee stood again. "Really, I must be going."

She had no more than spoken when a knock sounded on the sitting-room door. Lee followed Julio from the balcony as he hurried to answer it. When he opened the door they saw Señora Pedraza standing in the hallway. A dim overhead light gleamed on her hair, making it shine like black olives, but shadows fell on her face and Lee couldn't see the expression in her eyes.

"What is it, *señora*?" Julio asked.

Señora Pedraza stepped inside and sniffed. "Gas. I think I smell the dangerous odor of escaping gas. Do you notice it?"

Lee and Julio both sniffed and suddenly Lee had to fight her mirth. How could anyone smell anything except the orange blossoms? It was obvious Señora Pedraza had come to the door only to check on their activities.

"I smell nothing unusual, *señora*," Julio said, his expression serious. "I think you are overly concerned."

"I'm just leaving," Lee said as if to reassure the *señora* she didn't intend to besmirch her establishment by indulging in any hanky-panky with Julio.

Adroitly Julio stepped forward in a way that blocked Lee's exit, yet hastened the exit of Señora Pedraza. He literally shooed her back into the hallway and closed the door firmly behind her. They waited until they heard her steps on the stairs before they convulsed with laughter. Then suddenly she was in Julio's arms.

His lips found hers in a light kiss and she relaxed, letting his arms encircle her neck in an easy way. She waited for her heart to pound, for her mouth to go dry, but her body made no special response to Julio's. She felt only a pleasantness at being near a friendly congenial person who seemed to demand nothing of her. How unlike Burr he was!

"Thank you for a lovely evening," Lee said, easing from Julio's light embrace. "It has been a lovely day. I don't know when I've enjoyed myself as much."

"Don't make it sound so final," Julio said. "We've only begun to know each other." He drew her close and kissed her lightly again, and when he withdrew Lee leaned her head against his chest for a moment. A strong chest, a protective chest. She felt

as if she could stay in the easy circle of his unde-
manding embrace forever. But she knew she must
not.

"I must go now, Julio."

"I'll walk downstairs with you."

"You needn't."

"Don't argue. I can't abide a woman who
argues." He took her hand and they walked to her
room. Lee fitted her key into the lock and let herself
inside.

"Good night, Julio."

"Not good-night," Julio said. "Until tomorrow."

Lee waited until she heard him go back upstairs,
then she prepared for bed. What an unusual day. She
felt exhausted and at the same time exhilarated. She
prepared for bed then slipped between the sheets, and
as she lay there in the darkness she tried not to compare Julio's kisses with Burr's. There was really no
comparison. Good. It was comforting to know she
could kiss Julio without losing her head, that she
could enjoy his tenderness without suffering from the
devastating, exploding passion she had known with
Burr. Julio had a calming effect on her. He offered a
platonic sweetness she liked and she looked forward
to seeing him again as she might look forward to seeing Raul or some other good friend.

CHAPTER FOURTEEN

SPRING RACED INTO SUMMER as Lee continued her plodding research in the archive. Each Monday she sent a progress report to Burr, but although she felt sure he received them, he made no response. Julio did the projection of the ancient hurricane that had swamped the *Santa Isabella* and she forwarded that to Burr. Sometimes, as she typed Julio's notes at night or before she went to the archive in the morning, it seemed that she was spending much more time on his work than he had spent on hers, but she never voiced the opinion aloud. The typing for Julio was a welcome change from poring over the worm-eaten documents in the scholar's room.

One day, when she was about to write Burr telling him that she had failed, that she was giving up the search for the manifest, the words *Santa Isabella* appeared four times on one document. Her heart pounded as she went back to the top of the page and began translating as carefully as she could. After many readings she went to Julio for help.

"I've found something, Julio. Will you come take a look? I can't make it all out, but I think it may be the manifest."

A blue-smocked porter held his forefinger to his

lips, motioning for silence, as Julio scraped his chair back from his table and followed Lee.

"It is a cargo listing of sorts," Julio said after studying the document for several minutes. "It's sort of a summary. Not at all complete." He pointed to the all but illegible scribbling. "You see here it says five hundred ingots were to be loaded aboard the galleon from the mines at Potosi, but it gives no numbers for them."

Lee sighed and her shoulders slumped. "That won't help us too much, but I'll have the information microfilmed and forward it to Mr. Adburee. At least he'll know I'm doing something over here. Thanks so much, Julio. You've really saved me a lot of time."

"I'd do anything for you, Lee. You know that." Julio spoke in the half serious, half teasing manner that Lee always tried to take lightly. She had been careful not to lead him on or to give him the impression they were anything but good friends. Yet sometimes she wondered about their low-key relationship. Julio made no demands on her, yet now and then he hinted at marriage. While she let the hints pass without comment she began to wonder about them. Was he serious? Her feelings toward him were tepid compared to her feelings toward Burr, yet maybe a marriage in which feelings didn't run quite so high might be a happier union than one in which one's senses were constantly under bombardment.

Lee ordered the document she had found microfilmed as she continued her search, but that one page was her gem for the day. She found nothing else of interest. She and Julio walked home in the cool twilight and when they entered the pension Señora Pedraza motioned to them.

"A letter for the *señorita*." She held up a thin white envelope and Lee hurried to take it. Burr? Had Burr written to her at last? Maybe he was tired of spending his money and getting no results, no information. Maybe he was ordering her back home. Did she want to go? Was she ready to leave Julio? But the letter wasn't from Burr. Margo's name appeared in the upper left-hand corner, and Lee immediately felt wary. Why would Margo be writing her except at Burr's request?

"Hearing from a friend?" Julio asked.

"From Dive Boys' business manager." Lee ripped the envelope and removed the message. She read it through once and shook her head.

"Not bad news, I hope," Julio said.

Señora Pedraza's dark eyes never left Lee's face, and Lee turned and headed for the rose garden. "Let's rest a moment, shall we?"

Julio followed her into the garden away from the *señora*'s prying eyes and they sat on the stone bench by the fountain where they had first met.

"Listen to this." Lee unfolded the letter once more and read aloud:

Dear Lee,
We are very disappointed that you are finding so little useful information at the archive. The word is out around here that Galleons Unlimited has brought up a silver ingot. They're claiming it's from the *Isabella*, of course. They've leaked

the information that there's a serial number on the bar, but the big question is—does that number match a number on the *Isabella* manifest?

Of course they claim it does, but Burr is insisting that their claim be verified by an authority, probably by someone from the university. Maybe even your Professor Hoskin.

The whole thing has caused a bit of a flap, but there's still hope for Dive Boys. Do speed up your search for the manifest, Lee. I feel sure that cannon number was recorded somewhere.

Cordially,
Margo

"Oh, Julio! What am I going to do? If Galleons Unlimited lays official claim to the *Santa Isabella* I'll truly have failed. I'll be without a job and...."

Julio dropped his arm around her shoulder and hugged her. "Now just calm down and think about this rationally. You've done your best for your boss. Surely he knows archive research isn't an exercise in speed-reading."

"He knows. But Julio, nobody really *understands* until he's looked at some of those documents. Ugh!"

"Is this Margo your friend?"

Lee hesitated, searching for the truth. Was there such a thing as a friendly enemy? "Margo's just a business associate."

"Is her job at stake, too?"

"I suppose so. If Galleons Unlimited has really found authentic artifacts from the *Isabella*, then Mr. Adburee says he will withdraw from the search."

"Then it would be to Margo's advantage to hurry you up if she could, wouldn't it?"

"I suppose so."

"Mr. Adburee hasn't corresponded with you personally?"

"No."

"Then I'd just consider this a prod from a gal who's trying to protect her own interests."

"I think you're right, Julio. When I look at it from that angle your theory makes sense. Tomorrow I'll get back to the archive and—"

"What you need is a break," Julio said. "You're numb from too much work. Tomorrow I'll take you sight-seeing." He continued to make plans over Lee's protests, and when they went inside again it was agreed that the next day they would sleep late, meet after siesta and see some of the sights of Seville.

After Julio left her at her suite Lee shredded Margo's letter, made herself a light supper, then took a long leisurely bath. She slept well and in the late morning after she got up she listed some places from a tourist guidebook that she wanted to see. When Julio called for her he had rented a horse-drawn carriage and they began their afternoon with a relaxing ride along the river where a cooling breeze wafted the pungent smell of the water toward them. Cafés and flowering trees overlooked the quays, but Julio drove across the Bridge of San Telmo, pointing out to her the Tower of Gold that guarded the east bank of the river. The sun gleamed against the majestic tower.

"Moorish officials once stretched a chain across

the river at this point," Julio said. "They levied duties on passing boats."

"I'd like to see the cathedral," Lee said after Julio had stopped for orange juice at one of the cafés.

"We can go back there anytime," Julio said.

"But we never seem to take the time to do it. In the mornings we're always in too much of a rush to get into the archive, then at night, we're too tired for such sight-seeing."

But Julio didn't turn the horses toward the cathedral. Instead he showed her the tobacco factory, reminiscent of the famous opera *Carmen*, then they proceeded to the shop where supposedly the Barber of Seville once wielded his scissors. After that, they wandered by the haunts of Don Quixote.

"I'd really like to climb the Giralda Tower, Julio," Lee said at last.

"I hate steps," Julio said.

"The lower part of the tower has a ramp. I read that in my guidebook."

But they didn't climb the Giralda Tower. Instead Julio took her to the Museo de Bellas Artes, which was housed in an old convent where vines the color of old jade clung to the walls.

"The collection has been given a complete rejuvenation," Julio assured her. "The present director of the museum has rehung all the paintings. You'll see the best paintings by Murillo in Spain."

Lee followed Julio through the age-old cloister. It reminded her a lot of the archive, with its stone floors, its thick walls, its coolness. It even had the same musty smell, yet Lee knew the humidity must be carefully controlled to protect and preserve the works of art.

Later, when they were tired of sight-seeing they had dinner on Julio's moonlit balcony, and when he returned her to her own door at midnight she was exhausted. And she still hadn't seen the cathedral. She had enjoyed the break in her routine, yet she was eager to get back to work.

THE NEXT DAY Lee felt refreshed and ready to tackle old Spain again. She pushed the velvet draperies aside and entered the scholar's room with renewed enthusiasm. It was midafternoon when she found it. She translated the first page, then retranslated it just to be sure she had made no mistake.

"The registry! I've found it!" She stood and called the news to Julio, forgetting the archive rule of silence. Three porters rushed toward her and for a moment she feared she would be evicted, but Julio calmed the porters and they returned to their stations.

"Where is it? Let me see." Julio studied the page Lee pointed to, then he smiled and nodded. "You're right. This is it. This whole bundle."

Lee stared at him for a moment. "The whole bundle?" Then she remembered the Key West news article about Galleons Unlimited finding nine hundred pages in the manifest.

"Those galleons carried a large cargo," Julio said. "And if what you tell me is correct, they kept track of everything, down to the last tin of biscuits in the galley."

For a moment Lee felt as if a tug-of-war was raging inside her. She was elated because she had found the manifest, dejected because of its size. She studied the pages again. Some of the writing looked like Arabic script, some seemed Gothic in style, and much of it was in a flowing, cursive slant that was almost impossible to read. It didn't take her long to realize one important fact.

"Julio! Just look at this. Even the numbers are written out in script. There are no numerals! I have the cannon number, but I . . . I thought it'd be an easy matter to match the cannon number with a number in the manifest. But *this*!"

"Don't panic." Julio grinned down at her. "The thing to do is to order this whole manifest microfilmed. Then at your leisure you can translate it."

"My leisure during the next decade." Lee sighed, unable to face the thought of such a task.

"You can hire translators," Julio pointed out. "If your Mr. Adburee is in such a snit for the material, he'll be willing to put out some money for translators, won't he?"

"I'll have to write to him and ask. No, wait. I'm supposed to call him if I've found anything really big." Lee felt herself shaking at the thought of talking directly to Burr again. It was well into summer and she hadn't even received a card from him.

Julio glanced at his watch. "It's almost closing time now. Why not order the microfilming and let the call go until tomorrow? Tonight I want to take you out on the town. We'll celebrate. Okay?"

Julio's enthusiasm was contagious. All during the

past weeks she had known him he had been ready to celebrate anything, from the sighting of a robin to the advent of a cool day. Sometimes she had felt that her own diligence at the archive was the only thing that had kept Julio at work on his dissertation. But finding the manifest was really cause for celebration and she agreed. She felt light as a balloon ready to waft into the clouds.

"Where shall we go?"

"I know a flamenco place near the river," Julio said. "We'll dine. We'll watch the performance. We'll. . .celebrate!"

"I'm ready for it." Lee made the arrangements for the microfilming and they left the archive. Back in her suite she dressed carefully for her evening with Julio, thinking for a moment that it was a shame he would have two big celebrations in a row. Tomorrow was Claudia's birthday and she had been talking of nothing but the Venta de Antequera for weeks. But Julio was up to two celebrations, and Lee knew he would look forward to both of them.

What did one wear to view flamenco dancing? Lee studied her wardrobe. The sea-green gown with the empire waistline? No. The very color of it reminded her of Burr. The scarlet sheath? No. Julio had mentioned once that he really didn't care for fire-engine colors on his women. His women. If there were others Lee hadn't noticed them. He had seemed quite content with her company during the whole time she had been here. At last she chose a deceptive-looking wraparound dress. At first glance it looked very demure and simple, but when she put it on, the silky

fabric clung to her curves and the clear lemon color
did pleasant things for her hair and tanned skin. The
V-neckline of the dress attracted the eye, again pointing up her well-proportioned figure. She wore pearl
earrings, a lovely bracelet that had belonged to her
mother, and a necklace that hung in an oval pattern
that drew attention to the perfect oval of her face.
Then she brought out a thin evening purse that hung
from a gold shoulder chain and sandals with spiky
heels so high they would surely raise her almost to
Julio's chin at the same time as they complimented
her legs.

She finished dressing early and used the extra time
to gift wrap the book on photography she had
ordered from New York for Claudia's birthday.
When Julio knocked she paused just long enough to
touch plumeria scent on her earlobes, on the warm
bend of her elbows.

"You look luscious," Julio said, brushing a kiss
onto her cheek.

"And you look very handsome yourself." Lee
smiled her approval of his outfit. He had a knack for
choosing nutmeg-colored shirts that were perfect
foils for his hair and eyes, tailored slacks that called
attention to his flat stomach and lean strong legs.
And tonight he wore a lime scent that she hadn't
noticed before. It suited him. Clean and fresh and en-
ticing.

They took a taxi to the Venda del Oro, and the
place captivated Lee immediately. They walked down
rough stone stairs to a cellar-type room with iron-
studded doors, and the odd but pleasant fragrances

of jasmine and olive oil greeted them. A waiter in tight black trousers and a balloon-sleeved white shirt led them to an oak-topped table mounted on an old olive barrel. In one dimly lighted corner a guitarist played softly, as if more for his own entertainment than for the entertainment of the diners. Muted voices murmured. Candlelight glowed from hurricane globes on each table. Old Spain, Lee thought. Moorish. Charming.

The waiter brought *manzanilla* with the menus then departed as silently as he had arrived.

"What would you like for dinner, Lee?" Julio asked. "I understand the prawns here are delicious."

"That sounds like an excellent choice," Lee agreed. "And I'd like mine with lemon wedges rather than hot sauce."

Julio gave their order to the waiter then studied their setting. "I love beamed ceilings. When I have a home of my own it'll have nothing but beamed ceilings. They lend an informality, a special warmth to a room, don't you agree?"

"I agree."

"We agree on many things, Lee. Have you noticed that?" Julio looked deep into her eyes. "I think we're really quite compatible."

Lee managed to avert her gaze, to change the subject. "Do you think those are authentic Roman pillars by the hearth?"

"They may be," Julio agreed. "I like the way they're topped by those country-style capitals. They seem just right for this rustic room."

The *manzanilla*, the prawns, the cellarlike atmosphere put Lee in just the right mood for the flamenco dancers when they appeared later in the evening on a slightly raised platform in the center of the room. A hush fell over the crowd as the guitarist began to strum an introduction. The tones that had seemed staccato and brittle moments before now grew profound.

"Look," Lee whispered. "There are five of them." Then she hushed. Julio could see as well as she could. The three men, guitarist, singer and dancer, wore tight dark trousers above their high-heeled boots, white frilly shirts and red cummerbunds. The two girls with scarlet roses in their ebony hair wore sleeveless white bodices with low-cut necklines above bias-cut black skirts that hugged the hips then flared at mid-calf. Their high-heeled shoes and castanets tapped out intricate rhythms as the guitarist played and the singer sang a melody Julio told her was called *Petenera*.

The performers chanted, performed whirling arabesques, clapped their hands and snapped castanets. As Lee watched enchanted, she felt transported back to Moorish days. Surely that distinctive wail that expressed such stark grief was an echo of the muezzin's cry. And surely the darkling passion of ancient gypsies was expressed here, too. She tried to remember what she had read about Flemish courtiers of Charles V bursting on the drab Spanish scene. Was it 1520? She wished her memory of history and dates was better. But why try to identify the origins of such a dance? It was to enjoy here and now.

When the dancers finished their performance there

was a moment of silence; then the crowd burst into wild applause and stamping.

"*Olé!*"

"*Bravo!*"

"*Bravissimo!*"

The last cry came from Julio, who had risen and was clapping and shouting. But the performers returned only long enough to take bows, then they disappeared again.

"It was wonderful, Julio! I'll never forget this night."

"Is that a promise?"

"A solemn promise."

A few moments later they joined the crowd that was leaving the café, and Julio managed to get them a taxi back to their pension. "Let's go to my suite, Lee. I've discovered a new wine I'd like you to try, okay?"

"Okay, but just for a few minutes. And just a sip. I'm still so high from that marvelous flamenco that I don't want to spoil my reaction with wine."

Julio took her arm and they climbed to the third floor, but when they arrived they heard rock music blaring from the record player.

"Oh, no!" Julio slapped his forehead. "I forgot. Claudia is having a friend overnight."

"Let's go down to my suite," Lee said. "You left a bottle of *manzanilla* there, I think. Will you settle for that?"

"Most gladly. Thought you'd never ask."

In Lee's suite Julio sat down at the kitchenette table while Lee poured the sherry, then they carried their drinks to the balcony and sipped them in the moonlight.

"It was a wonderful celebration, Julio. But it may be the beginning of the end. Now that I've found the manifest Mr. Adburee may want me to come home." Lee couldn't decide if she was glad or sorry.

"Don't even think about Florida, Lee. Why, you can delay for months in translating all those pages."

"There is a hurry, remember?"

"I wanted to forget. I'll hate to see you leave, Lee."

"I've enjoyed Seville. I've enjoyed it more than I ever thought I would. You've been such fun, Julio. It's been a memorable time."

"Have you ever thought of staying here, of making this your home? I'd like that, you know."

"No. Home is Florida. I must go back when my work here is finished." That was the truth. Whether she wanted to go or stay, she had to leave. Florida was home.

"Let's not spoil a perfect evening talking about unpleasant things," Julio said, taking another sip of wine. "Lee, there's a concert I'd like to take you to tomorrow night. Manuel Rodriquez will be singing at a small music house down by the river. He's fantastic. Does arias from the Italian operas—the ones with Spanish settings."

"But, Julio! Tomorrow is the night you're taking Claudia to dinner—her birthday dinner. You haven't forgotten, have you?"

"No, I haven't forgotten. But Rodriquez will only be in Seville the one night. I don't want to miss him and I don't want you to miss him. We'll take Claudia with us, okay? We can bring her home early, then...."

"Not okay." Lee began to feel a rising irritation. Couldn't Julio understand how important a sixteenth birthday was to a girl! "Tomorrow is Claudia's entry into womanhood. I've helped her pick a new dress. You'll love it, Julio. It's sophisticated, yet—"

"I don't want to hear about Claudia's dress. I want to hear that you'll go to the concert with me." Julio gulped the rest of his wine. "I won't take no for an answer."

"But I'm afraid you'll have to. Tomorrow night you're taking Claudia to dinner at the restaurant of her choice."

For a moment Julio stared at her. It was the first time she had really thwarted him or argued with him over anything important. Usually he was so easygoing that no argument had ever been necessary. But tonight he seemed different. There was a determined glint in his eye and a firm set to his mouth. He stood, set his wineglass down with deliberation, then he walked to her and swooped her from her chair.

"Julio! Put me down." His breath reeked of wine and she remembered that he had sipped *manzanilla* all through dinner, all during the flamenco performance.

"I will put you down when and where I want to put you down." Julio carried her to the sitting room and eased her onto the sofa, sitting down beside her. When she tried to sit up he pushed her back against a pillow.

"Don't fight me, Lee. I've waited far too long for this moment. A man can exist on soft words and moonlight kisses just so long, then.... I've really been very patient, I think."

Lee pushed against his chest with both hands, but he merely clasped both her wrists in one strong hand, held her hands above her head and smiled down at her.

"I think that perhaps women really like to be over-powered, don't they? Tell me, is that true?"

"Of course it isn't true, Julio." Suddenly Lee didn't know whether to be angry or afraid. This was a side of Julio she hadn't seen before, a side she never dreamed existed. She struggled harder against his re-straining grasp. "Let me up, Julio. Right now. Let me up."

When Julio's lips found hers she relaxed a bit. There was no violence here. It was just the same ten-der Julio she had known all summer. He'd had too much wine, that was for sure, but she could handle him.

She returned his bland kiss willingly but without passion, thinking he would be satisfied and release her hands. But the kiss seemed to excite him and he found her lips again. Lee turned her head aside.

"You've kept me at arm's length all summer, Lee. Don't you know I want to marry you? I'll build us a villa in the country and we'll make Spain our home."

Suddenly Lee's reaction was pure anger. With a quick jerk she managed to free her hands and in the next instant she leaped from the sofa. With great ef-fort she managed to control her voice.

"Julio, will you please leave at once?" *I'll count to ten,* she thought, *then if he doesn't go, I will.*

But something in her tone reached him and for a moment he just sat there looking up at her as if through a haze. He stood.

"I'm sorry, Lee." He faced her, but he made no effort to touch her again. "I'm really sorry this happened. I love you, Lee. I want you. But I also respect you and...."

"It's all right, Julio. I understand...I think. Just leave me alone now, please." Lee smoothed her dress, her hair, thinking that she and Julio must have a long talk the next day when they were both more calm. She walked purposefully toward the sitting-room doorway, but before she could open the door someone knocked.

"Señora Pedraza," Lee said, exasperation and anger filling her again. How could a day that had started out so nicely end so badly? She flung open the door ready to do verbal battle with her landlady, then she stopped and stood staring.

"Burr!"

CHAPTER FIFTEEN

FOR A MOMENT the three of them stood staring at one another, then Lee spoke again, her voice shrill with anger at Burr's ill-timed intrusion. "What are you doing here at this hour of the night?"

"I might ask you the same thing," Burr replied, glaring at Julio.

"She lives here," Julio retorted. "Why wouldn't she be here?"

"And who are you?" Burr demanded.

"Burr, this is Julio Hunter." Lee forced her voice into a false calm. "He's responsible for much of my success here at the archive. When you find out. . . ."

"*Por Dios! Por Dios!*" Señora Pedraza came puffing up the stairs, her brown caftan flapping in the breeze her motion created. "What is this you are holding in my corridors? A festival perhaps? A *feria*? Silence! I beg of you. Silence."

"I'm sorry, Señora Pedraza," Lee replied, realizing only then that they had been creating a disturbance. "We'll be more quiet." Then she turned to Burr. "Come inside, Burr." Lee stepped back so Burr could enter, then she added, "Julio was just leaving, weren't you, Julio?"

"I should hope so," Señora Pedraza said, interjecting herself into the conversation once more.

"I'm not leaving until we have one thing straight, Lee." Julio glared at Burr as if they were sworn enemies of long standing. "Either you attend the concert with me tomorrow night or...you'll see no more of me."

"I am ready to see no more of you right now," Señora Pedraza advanced toward Julio, stamped her foot, and stood before him with arms akimbo. "Off with you."

While Señora Pedraza shooed Julio up the stairs to his own quarters Lee seized the opportunity to close the door and lean back against it while she tried to collect her thoughts.

"That was quite a scene," Burr said. "Who is that man?"

"I just told you. He's a scholar...."

"A gentleman and a scholar, I presume." Burr's gaze roved over her body until Lee found her hands easing self-consciously to the tie on her dress. Was it in order? Were there telltale signs of her struggle with Julio? But what did she care what Burr thought? And why, oh why, did she have such a crazy desire to fling herself into his arms?

"I think I deserve an explanation," Lee said at last. "What are you doing barging in here at this time of the night?"

"This time of the morning, you mean, don't you?" Deliberately Burr checked his watch. "Three in the morning to be exact. Perhaps you'd like to tell me just what your research scholar was researching at this hour."

Lee straightened to her full height, relinquishing the support of the door. "My private life is none of your concern, Burr. What are you doing here? You'll send Señora Pedraza into fits when she stops concentrating on Julio and realizes you're still present.''

"I'm here to congratulate you on finding the manifest.''

It took a moment for the words to sink into Lee's mind, then she stared at Burr unbelievingly. "How did you know? How could you possibly know? I was going to call you in the morning. I only found it a short time before the archive closed for the day.''

"Money talks, Lee. Oh, I'll have to admit that part of my learning about the manifest was coincidence. Shall we sit down while I tell you about it or do you prefer to hold the door up again while I remain standing?''

Lee started toward the couch, but Burr shook his head. "I prefer the balcony. I've had a long day and I'd like to relax in the cool morning air. Come.'' He grabbed her wrist, tugging her after him as if she were a balking child. "Be wary. Be on guard.'' Lee summoned all her prickly thoughts about Burr, weaving them into imaginary barbed wire around her heart. They sat down in the moonlight and she tried to ignore the way the soft glow silvered Burr's rugged features, giving a sensuous fullness to his lips that she could almost feel. The shadow of his brows fell across his eyes in a way that kept her from seeing into them, kept her from reading their expression. It was just as well. She knew all too well how those eyes could make her melt.

"When Galleons Unlimited began to get serious about matching their ingot number with a corresponding number on the manifest I decided I'd better get over here and see how you were progressing with your research in the archive. I arrived this evening just before the scholar's room closed and I asked for you.''

''I wasn't there,'' Lee said inanely. Was he going to ask her to account for her whereabouts?

''I know you weren't there, Lee.'' He paused and when he saw she wasn't going to let the awkward silence goad her into speech, he continued. ''I flashed my identification at the officials and since you had billed the microfilming of the manifest to Dive Boys, Inc., they let me call the shots from there on. I ordered extra help with the microfilming, and I stayed to see that they began the work immediately and that they remained on the job. It will take a lot of time to get the job done because the manifest pages are so old and fragile.''

''When will you have it?''

''They are to have it done as quickly as possible. They'll mail it to me in Key West.''

''Oh, Burr! I'm so glad you've instigated some action. For weeks everything has progressed so slowly.''

''That's the understatement of the year, Lee.'' For a moment Burr's voice softened. ''I owe you a lot for being sharp enough to find that manifest.''

Lee. He had called her Lee. ''You owe a lot to Julio, too, Burr. I didn't realize how little I actually knew about reading ancient Spanish until I faced the documents in those worm-eaten bundles. Julio compiled a vocabulary list of ancient terms for me. He compiled a list of abbreviations that were unfamiliar to me, and—"

"I've heard quite enough about Julio. He may present me a bill for his services if he desires to do so."

"I seriously doubt he'll do that. Moneygrubbing isn't uppermost in his mind."

"You should know about that." Burr gave her the sardonic smile she remembered so well.

"Well, now that you have the manifest, do you think it will enable you to claim the remains of the *Santa Isabella* before Galleons Unlimited moves in?"

"It takes me several steps closer to that goal. But I need your help once more."

"In what way?" *Be wary.* Again Lee heard a warning voice.

"I need you to pave the way for me with Professor Hoskin. I want you to call him and ask him if he'll verify the cannon number when we find it in the manifest."

"You're totally confident of finding it, aren't you?"

"One must think positively. Professor Hoskin will no doubt want to come to Key West to inspect the cannon first, then to study the microfilm."

"Well, surely you can just order him to do those things. Money talks, you know." Lee was intentionally sarcastic, yet she knew Burr's money probably would talk. It usually did.

"As long as you're working for me, you'll take my orders. Professor Hoskin wouldn't work for Galleons Unlimited. Doesn't want to be a part of their destroying the underwater environment. But I think he'll work for Dive Boys for the simple reason that you're working for us, too. But time is at a premium. You'll call him first thing in the morning.''

"All right." Of course she would call Professor Hoskin. Of course she would do anything Burr wanted done. As always, their motivations were completely different, yet the goals they aimed for were the same. They both wanted verification that the treasure Burr had found was from the *Santa Isabella*. For several minutes they sat in silence, Lee wishing he would leave at the same time as part of her wanted him never to leave.

"What will happen to the treasure, Burr? You know how I feel about it. I feel that it belongs to the people."

Burr sighed. "But some of it *has* to be sold to support the project. Some of it *must* go to the investors. If they care to sell it or donate it to museums, fine. That would please me very much. But it must be their choice."

"What if they prefer to sell some of the gold as bullion? It would be melted down and its value as an artifact would be lost forever."

"That's a risk I have to take. But surely you can understand that a galleon's treasure must be located and raised by private enterprise. Can't you just hear the taxpayers screaming if any tax money was spent on a pie-in-the-sky treasure-hunting operation?"

Lee had to smile at the thought. "I suppose you're right at that." For the first time she was beginning to see the treasure from Burr's point of view.

"The treasure means more to me than you think, Lee."

Lee wanted to pursue that line of thought, but Burr changed the subject.

"May I have a drink, Lee?"

"Of course. I'm sorry I didn't offer you one sooner; I was distracted."

"I'm aware."

At least he had asked for the drink. He hadn't ordered it, Lee thought as she splashed *manzanilla* into a goblet and returned to the balcony. Again they sat in silence as he sipped his drink, and she tried to sort through her spinning thoughts. Julio had asked her to marry him, hadn't he? Or was it the *manzanilla* in him that had spoken? Did she love him? If she loved him, why hadn't she answered him in the affirmative? She enjoyed Julio's company. She liked Claudia. Both of them were easy to be around. Yet when Julio had proposed she had jumped up and run. Why? Was it the idea of living in Spain, of being separated from America and from Raul? Or was it the idea of being separated from Burr? How she wished she had never seen Burr again! Maybe if she had been able to mail the microfilm back to him, if she had been able to avoid a confrontation, a meeting.... And now that she understood why part of the treasure had to be sold she found herself empathizing with him. But she mustn't let him know. Never.

"What are you thinking?" Burr asked.

Lee felt her jaw muscles tighten as the question transported her back to another night, another balcony, when Burr had asked the same words. But this time she answered him.

"I'm thinking about home. About Key West and Dive Boys."

"About Raul?"

"Yes. About Raul."

"And Margo?"

"Why do you mention Margo?"

"Because when you think of Raul you might as well think of Margo. They've become quite a two-some while you've been away."

"Oh, Burr! How can you be so foolish as to think Margo would be interested in Raul! She's just trying to make you jealous. She's using Raul in her scheme and she makes me furious."

"Her relationship with Raul may have started out that way, but it's changed. And Margo's changed, too. There's a new softness about her. It's as if she's discovered that love is more important than money. She's in love with Raul, Lee. If you're expecting Raul to be waiting for you with open arms, you're in for a disappointment."

"I can see it breaks your heart to give me the news," Lee said.

"It doesn't hurt me much one way or the other. I didn't think you'd be bent out of shape over it. You aren't one to sit around lonely and lonesome."

Lee began to seethe inside, unable to say more without revealing her true relationship to Raul. They were still sitting in stony silence when another knock sounded on the door.

"Another caller?" Burr raised an eyebrow. "My,

but you do keep a busy schedule." He glanced at his watch. "Four in the morning."

Lee hurried to the door knowing almost instinctively that this time it really would be Señora Pedraza. She willed herself to be polite as she faced her landlady.

"Señorita Cameron, you know it is against the rules of this pension for you to entertain a gentleman caller in your quarters at this hour."

"I'm sorry to have broken your rules, *señora*. But Mr. Adburee is a very special person, you see—"

"I see quite well, *señorita*." Señora Pedraza's nostrils flared and her eyes grew wide. "I have had enough. Too much. I must ask you to vacate."

"Vacate?"

"You know," Burr said, coming up from behind her. "Get out."

"He is correct," Señora Pedraza said. "Get out is what you must do. You I have been lenient with. You take advantage of me many time. Now you must go."

Lee could feel Burr's ill-concealed mirth and she turned to face him. "How dare you laugh when I'm being evicted and for no real reason!"

"For consorting with male guests," Señora Pedraza said, spelling out the offense in no uncertain terms. "It is a very real reason. You will be out before the siesta hour tomorrow."

"You can just bet I will," Lee said, her anger flaring. "I won't stay a moment longer than it takes me to pack my things. You're unfair and you have an evil mind and—"

"You have until tomorrow afternoon," Señora Pedraza repeated, "but that one must go right now." She glared at Burr.

"It so happens that I don't take orders," Burr said. "I give them. And I'm not finished talking with Miss Cameron just yet."

"I will call the *policía*," Señora Pedraza threatened. "You are breaking my rules. They are clearly down in writing on a board near the entry desk."

"You needn't call the police," Burr said. "I'm leaving. I'll finish talking to Miss Cameron in the garden. That is not forbidden, is it? Are there written rules posted about the garden?"

Señora Pedraza shook her head. "No. The garden is not forbidden. You may talk there if you must."

Burr grabbed Lee's wrist, pulling her after him, and she followed without protest. She had faced all the arguments, all the encounters she could handle for one day. And now she was disgraced, evicted from her quarters due to unseemly conduct. She had never been so mortified. She felt Señora Pedraza's disapproving gaze like a hot brand on her back as she and Burr retreated down the stairs.

When they reached the garden Burr led her to a private corner where the scent of roses permeated the Andalusian night like a heady wine, and they sat on a stone bench beneath a palm tree. At the whimsy of the breeze moonglow filtered through the palm fronds now lighting them, now shading them, and Burr eased his arm around Lee, drawing her close. For a moment the moon silhouetted him, washing away his hard arrogance with a pale light, and in that instant she could imagine him as a romantic Moorish lover escaping from centuries past to revisit a fondly remembered place. But when Burr's touch grew more insistent, the Moorish vision vanished. She tried to shrug away before he felt her heart begin to race.

"Burr, I've had quite enough for one day."

Burr drew her even closer. "If you've been passing out your favors in the way the *señora* indicates you have, I certainly intend to get my share."

"She's a busybody. A nosey-poke."

Suddenly Burr laughed outright. "Nosey-poke. I haven't heard that expression since I was a kid."

"I'm glad you find me amusing. I'd hate to think I was boring you."

"You've never bored me, Lee. Infuriated me. Maddened me. Aroused me. But you've never bored me." Now Burr encircled her with his arms and his mouth found hers, tenderly at first, then hungrily. He cupped her head in his hands as if that's all there was of her, and his tongue and lips showed her his intent in a way that burned into her heart. She went limp with longing.

"This is a public place," Lee gasped when his lips released hers and she could speak again.

"But it's a very private public place at four in the morning. I love you, Lee." Now he pulled her to him again and began commanding her body in the slow sweet way she remembered so well. He had said "I love you." She wanted to believe him, yet she knew the words were just a line he used to get what he wanted. Once more that golden fountain within her brimmed and her mind protested silently and fruitlessly while her body protested not at all. Surely he could tell she was his.

"You wear provocative clothing intentionally, don't you, Lee?" His voice grew husky and he tilted her chin with his forefinger in that way of his that forced her to look him in the eye. "Bodices suspended with no more than an elastic. Dresses that give way with the loosing of a sash."

She met his gaze, but there was no need to reply. She felt the bow at her waist untie like a shoestring, felt the silky fabric fall back at the brush of his fingers. Then his hands defined a tantalizing slow motion, cupping her breasts gently while his lips found her mouth and reinforced the message of his hands.

"You are very slow with the shirt buttons this morning, darling."

At his invitation Lee reached for his shirt, pulling the buttons from their holes as she might pull roses from a bush. When they were all undone she spread the shirt fabric wide, baring his skin to the moonlight and the breeze. She skimmed her fingers over his virile chest, up and up until her hands throbbed with her pulse beat. With the balls of her fingers she rotated a teasing circle on his chest that inflamed him. She could feel his male strength as he pushed against her.

"I love you, Lee," he whispered in her ear. Then he blew his warm breath into that ear until she closed her eyes and buried her face in his neck, unable to stand the delight any longer. Yet he continued his slow enticement, running the sharp tip of his tongue over her earlobe while all the time his hands suggested a preview of delights yet to come. Surely his hands were meant for this. If she shrugged one shoulder then the other her dress would fall away completely. She shrugged. And the dress dropped to the ground with no more sound than a leaf dropping from one of the orange trees. Her half-slip and panties dropped like two more leaves, then Burr's flesh felt warm against hers as his fingers traced the curve of her back, her hips, then rose to find the tender soft places of her underarms.

She melted, and he swooped her into his arms as if she weighed nothing. He carried her to a more secluded corner of the garden. The grass felt cool and lush under her hips, her back, and his body felt warm and hard and powerful and she wanted him more than she had ever wanted anything in all her life.

"Tell me what you want me to do," Burr said. "I need you. I love needing you."

A shudder wracked her body as his words hit a raw nerve. And that nerve gave her the strength to protest. She would be a fool to believe he was sincere. Again he was deliberately tantalizing her, trying to make her the instigator of what was to come next. She could still hide the extent of her desire. His words, so reminiscent of that night in Miami, the night on the Marvista beach, gave her the strength she needed to push away from him. This was neither the time nor the place to give in to her weakness. There was no telephone to intrude. There was no tide to surprise them. She had only herself to save her from herself.

"What's the matter, darling?" Burr asked. "A moment ago I thought you were ready for me, but now...."

Lee sat up, still pushing him away. "My body is ready for you, but my mind is not."

"Tell me what you want me to do, Lee. Tell me."

"Leave me alone, Burr. I can't give myself to you unless I truly love you in all ways—mind and body. It wouldn't be fair to either of us."

Lee could feel Burr's fury as she left him, picked up her dress, and slipped it on.

CHAPTER SIXTEEN

As Burr watched in astonishment Lee picked up her underthings, folded them into a small soft bundle, then started to leave the garden. Before she reached the gateway Burr was at her side. He grabbed her arm, spinning her around until she faced him. His eyes were like steaming tar and his gritty voice forced his words through clenched teeth.

"You're going to walk off as easy as that? You think you're going to walk away from me?"

"That's exactly what I'm going to do, Burr. That's what I should have done much sooner."

"I have a low gag threshold when it comes to women who tease."

She jerked her arm away from his grip, knowing there would be bruises on her skin the next day. "I've never been a tease."

"Then what are you?" He grabbed her arm again, increasing his pressure.

In love with you, her mind shouted. But she made no reply. "Let me go. Let me go right this minute."

Burr flung her arm aside as if the very touch of her was repugnant to him. "I'll let you go. You can depend on that. But hear this. We are leaving for Key West on the next afternoon flight."

"You may be leaving for Key West. I'm not. I have more work to finish up here."

"I don't know what work you're referring to," Burr said, "but you'll receive no more money from Dive Boys for research. That's behind you. If you value your job in Key West you'll be at the airport ready to board the afternoon flight. That should give you time to pack your things and to attend to any... business that may be at loose ends."

"And if I don't board that flight?"

"Then you're through working for Dive Boys. You have a choice."

"You're absolutely masterly at delivering ultimatums, aren't you?" Lee stamped her foot, thinking that she had never been so angry in all her life. How dare this man barge in on her in the middle of the night, use the rest of her night, then tell her to be ready to travel with him in less than.... She gazed through palm fronds at the eastern sky where the sun was already turning the horizon to a shade of pale bisque. "You expect me to be ready to leave Seville in less than ten hours?"

"Of course." Burr cocked his head to one side. "Seems to me I've given you a lot more time than the *señora* gave you. And I don't believe I caught Julio Hunter's deadline. You seem to be gathering ultimatums like sticky tape collecting flies. Perhaps you have a talent for it. Are you going to be on the plane?"

"What do you think?"

Burr looked at her for a moment. His eyes still smoldered, but his smile was supercilious. "I'm sure you'll be there." And with those parting words he turned and walked into the pale newness of the dawn.

Lee felt like spluttering. She felt like hitting. She felt like doing anything except walking through the entry of Señora Pedraza's pension carrying her undergarments in her hand. Slipping back into the garden, she stepped into the deep privacy of a box hedge and slipped on her underthings. Then she left the garden again, this time hurrying through the entry of the pension, up the stairs and to her suite. She heard Señora Pedraza's labored breathing as she followed her, but she didn't look around. How dare the woman wait for her, spy on her!

"Out!" the señora cried. "You will be out of my sight before noon."

Lee ignored the señora, entered her suite quickly and closed the door. Then she flung herself onto the bed and squinted her eyes shut to keep angry tears from flowing out of control. She had received too many ultimatums. Señora Pedraza's she couldn't ignore. She must pack and prepare to leave the pension by the appointed time. But Julio's ultimatum? Burr's? What to do?

Julio wanted her to stay. Burr wanted her to leave. Julio was offering her marriage. Burr was offering her only arrogance and hostility. The choice seemed easy enough when stated on those terms. Choose joy. Choose love. Choose Julio.

Yet why was she being forced to make choices? Who gave either man the right to demand decisions of her? Perhaps her own actions had made her vulnerable to them both. Choose love. It seemed like an easy choice until she thought about it more carefully. Did Julio really love her? Or did he merely love Spain and think she would make a nice ornament for his villa as he drifted through life. For the first time she admitted to herself that basically Julio was totally self-centered. The thought shocked her when she brought it right up front and examined it. But it was true. Everything Julio did he did for Julio. True, he had helped her greatly with the archive work, but he had done that because he wanted her companionship. Always his desires came first. They had seen the sights Julio wanted to see. They had dined where Julio wanted to dine. He even put himself before Claudia, knowing how disappointed she would be if he failed her on her birthday. Yet she knew Julio would manage to get his way, using some smooth maneuver in a way that would hurt Claudia least. Julio wanted people to like him, and people did, including Lee. Julio seldom made waves or rocked the boat. Life with him would be smooth and pleasant.

And what of Burr? She had known before she came here that he had a powerful macho magnetism that made her lose control of herself, that made her self-destruct right before his eyes. And although he had said "I love you," the words had been uttered so glibly. He had used them in the age-old way as bait in a trap. And he had never even hinted at marriage. Marriage would tie him down too much.

Lee sighed and rolled on her stomach, burying her head under the pillow to shut out the sunlight that was starting to filter into her room. Darkness. She needed darkness like a blotter to blot out all feeling.

She rose and closed the doors to her balcony and the shutters at every window. She had to get some sleep even if just an hour or two. As the room was once more shrouded in near darkness, she stretched out on the bed again, and when she awakened later she sat up with a start and glanced at her watch. Nine in the morning. She could have slept round the clock. Her eyes ached and she felt numb, but she rose and flung open the windows and doors, letting the daylight in.

Although her body felt draggy, even the few hours sleep seemed to have rested her mind. At least she knew what she was going to do next. She picked up the telephone and called Claudia. What if Julio answered? But he didn't. Claudia's voice flowed over the wire.

"It's Lee, Claudia. Are you busy?"

"My tutor is here."

"I'm sorry. I'll only take a minute. Could you meet me at the airport for lunch?"

"Sure. I suppose so, but why?"

"Because I'm leaving Seville on the afternoon flight and I'd like to see you before I go."

"Why don't you just stop by our suite before you go?" Claudia asked.

"Personal reasons, Claudia. Please meet me."

"Does Julio know you're leaving?"

Lee hesitated and the line hummed vacantly. She decided to ignore the question. "I want to take you out to lunch for your birthday, Claudia, and lunching at the airport is the only way I can work it in. I'd take you out in the cab I hire, but I have several errands to attend to. Meet me there and I'll take care of your cab fare, okay?''

"Sure, Lee. I've never lunched at the airport. What time?''

"One o'clock? Okay?''

"Okay. See you then.''

Lee felt weak when she replaced the receiver, yet she thought she had handled the call well. Surely Julio had gone to the archive, but he would report home during siesta. Claudia would tell him Lee was leaving on the afternoon flight. If he really cared for her, really wanted to marry her, he would try to stop her, wouldn't he? Somehow she knew deep in her heart that he wouldn't. And what would she do if he did?

She was surprised at how little time it took her to pack her things. She hadn't accumulated too many extras because she hadn't taken time out from her research work to go shopping. Had she known she would be leaving so soon she might have picked up some souvenirs, something special for Raul, something for herself. But too late to think of that now. She dressed in a tea-colored travel suit, brushed her golden hair until it gleamed, then carefully applied some makeup to cover up the dark hollows under her eyes. A touch of blusher on her cheeks helped her appearance, but nothing could totally hide her exhaustion. She brewed herself a cup of tea once she was packed. Promptly at noon Señora Pedraza knocked.

"You are ready to go?'' Señora Pedraza's owl eyes darted around the room as if checking to see if everything was in order.

"I'm ready." Lee nodded toward her bags. "I've called a taxi."

"Fine. It is with regret that I have asked you to leave."

"And it is with regret that I'm leaving." Lee picked up her bags and headed downstairs. What else was there to say? "If you're ever in Key West, look me up. I'm in the book." But she wasn't in the book and she never wanted to see the *señora* again.

"Where to, *señorita*?" the taxi driver asked, stepping inside for her bags.

"The airport, please."

She was barely settled inside the car before the driver took off with a start that pinned her to the seat's back for a moment. When she was able, she leaned forward. "There's no rush, *señor*. I have plenty of time."

"Gracias, señorita." He smiled at her in the rearview mirror, but he didn't slow down. She clung to the seat cushion to keep from being flung into the door as they rounded corners, and she breathed a sigh of relief when they reached the airport. Inside the terminal some people rushed here and there. Others dozed behind newspapers, starting to attention now and then to glance at their watches, then dozing off again.

Lee went to the ticket desk to try to check her bags through, but when the official asked for her ticket or her reservation she remembered belatedly that she had none. "Do you have reservations for two in Burrton Adburee's name?" she asked.

The official checked his reservation list then shook

his head. "Burrton Adburee has no reservation, *señorita*."

"Thank you." Lee checked her bags in a locker. Had Burr been negligent in calling for reservations? It wasn't like him, but it made her wonder. She felt guilty now for not sharing the taxi with Claudia, yet how could she have done so? Señora Pedraza had literally kicked her out of the pension and she had preferred not to explain that to Claudia. And she needed Claudia to be home when Julio arrived. How else would Julio know where she was?

Lee found her way to the coffee shop, and the Spanish flowing all around her made her feel so foreign and isolated. She had always thought of Spanish as a smooth, fluid language, but today the talk around her seemed shrill and staccato and disturbing. She was drinking her third cup of coffee when Claudia arrived. Lee saw her before Claudia did and for some reason Lee felt that gave her an advantage. She half rose from her seat, motioned, then settled back, smiling as the girl threaded her way between the tables, joined her, and was seated.

"Your birthday gift, Claudia." Lee filled the awkward silence between them following their greetings by producing the flat pink package with a flourish that demanded both attention and action.

"Oh, how nice of you! Lunch and a gift, too!" Claudia bent over the package, trying to untie the ribbon without destroying it. And all the while she worked Lee watched the coffee-shop entryway, thinking that perhaps Julio had come with her and had been delayed in paying his driver. But Julio made no appearance and Lee felt something inside her shrivel up and die.

"A photography book!" Claudia exclaimed, opening the cover quickly. "And in English! Lee, you're an absolute doll! It's exactly what I wanted."

"I'm glad you're pleased."

"Are you *señoritas* ready to order?" The waitress approached and held pad and pen at the ready.

"May we see a menu, please?" Lee asked.

"Of course." She left, then returned with a menu.

"What would you like, Claudia?" Lee asked. "Live it up."

"I'll have a chef's salad and French fries," Claudia said.

"And I'll have the same," Lee said.

"I keep hoping the French fries will be like the ones back home," Claudia said, "but they never are. I wish I were going home with you."

"Claudia! Enjoy your time here. It'll end all soon enough and someday you'll look back on these months as one of the most memorable parts of your life."

"You've gotta be kidding." Claudia sighed. "Did you know that Julio's not taking me to dinner tonight?"

Lee tried to pretend surprise. The cad. "When did you talk to him last? Maybe. . . ." Lee hoped Claudia wouldn't think it a strange question.

"I talked to him just before I left home. I told him I was meeting you here, and he gave me the bad news about our dinner. It seems that some singer is performing in concert tonight, and of course that's more important than my birthday.''

So she had told him. She had told him and he didn't care. She blinked back sudden tears. ''I'm sure he'll make it up to you, Claudia. You'll have that much more fun looking forward to your big dinner.''

They ate lunch, with Lee trying to make bright conversation. Sometimes she thought she had succeeded and other times she knew she was failing. After lingering over dessert for as long as they could without making Lee miss her flight, she walked with Claudia to the terminal entry, hailed a taxi and put her in it, paying the driver and adding a generous tip.

''Happy birthday, Claudia. Perhaps we'll meet again one day.''

''I'm sure of it, Lee. Have a good flight.''

Then she was gone. And Julio had not appeared. Lee stuffed her pride in the deep recesses of her mind, took her luggage from the locker and walked slowly to the departure gate. Why did she feel... jilted? For that was how she felt. Julio had said he loved her, said he wanted to marry her, yet when it came time to back the words with action, he had been missing. Would she have remained in Seville had he asked her to? She wasn't sure.

When she reached the velvet-roped area for ticketed passengers only, Burr was there. He was wearing a white sport coat and slacks and a black shirt that called attention to his dark features. His eyes seemed more hooded than usual, but other than that he showed no signs of a sleepless night. They didn't speak, but he took her bags and checked them through. He had known she would appear. He had been that sure of himself and of her. She guessed his reservation had been under the Dive Boys' name.

"Nonsmoking," he said to the ticket clerk. "That's what you like isn't it, Lee?"

She felt like a puppet and Burr was the puppeteer. She could feel his maddening, sardonic grin, feel the derision in his eyes. "I bow to your choice, Burr." Lee looked away. She would ignore him. She was too exhausted for the anger the situation really demanded. When the official called their flight, she preceded Burr to the plane, found the correct seat and slipped into it. Takeoffs always scared her and she stayed alert until they were airborne and she saw the clouds pressed against the window like gray velvet. Then she relaxed. Her lack of sleep began to catch up with her and she adjusted her seat into reclining position, asked the stewardess for a pillow and blanket, and settled down to sleep.

She awakened once with her head on Burr's shoulder, her hand in his hand, but she didn't care. She was so tired that nothing mattered to her. Nothing at all. She welcomed the oblivion of sleep.

CHAPTER SEVENTEEN

BURR'S CAR WAS AT THE AIRPORT when they reached Key West and he drove Lee to Marvista. How good it was to be home. She had dozed and wakened throughout the flight, but there had been long delays in New York and Miami. Her eyes felt like gravel pits and her body begged for sleep while her mind begged for solitude. A beggar. She felt like a beggar in more ways than one. Why had she placed herself in a beggar's position, begging for a job, begging for a place to live, begging for Burr's... love? That's about what her life amounted to. She wondered if everyone was a slave to dreams and promises.

Burr drove slowly through the sunlit day and all the things she had taken for granted before she had gone to Seville now stood out like sculptures in bas relief; and it was as if she were seeing the island for the first time. The glorious backdrop of sea glinted in the sunlight constantly changing colors in a range from deep blue to a blinding lime green. Gulls faced the sun with their tails to the wind. Had they always done that? She wished she could face the sun forever, ignoring the winds that carried problems that she would rather forget.

"It's good to be home," Burr said, suddenly breaking the silence between them.

"I was thinking the same thing," Lee said. How often they seemed to think the same thing. But she said no more, preferring to listen to the wash of the turquoise-colored waves against the white sand, the laughter of children playing along the beach, even the roar of the yellow truck as it scooped seaweed from the shoreline, cleaning the beach. Burr stopped at an intersection to let the Conch Train pass. There were few tourists here in the heat of the summer, but a dozen hardy souls sat in the yellow cars with their orange seats and awnings. The slow-moving tourist train reminded Lee of a giant caterpillar as it inched along, with its driver droning facts about the island into a hand-held microphone.

At Marvista Burr carried her bags to her suite, setting them inside the door quickly then retreating to the hallway as if he feared Señora Pedraza might somehow have transported herself to the keys and might be waiting for him with a reprimand.

"Take the day off, Lee. Rest up. Report for work tomorrow morning as usual."

"Thank you. I will." How could she do anything else? She was practically walking in her sleep. She would have been absolutely no good at the wreck site. Once Burr was gone she bathed, went to bed, and slept almost around the clock.

THE NEXT MORNING she celebrated her return by relaying the news of her finding the manifest to Professor Hoskin and asking his help in translating it.

He was eager to help and to be included in the excitement, and when Lee finished talking she felt she had two things to celebrate—the finding of the manifest and the procuring of professional help. She indulged herself with coffee and key-lime pie at the Pie Palace before reporting to the dock for her ride to the *Sea Deuced*. She was hardly situated in her office again before Burr joined her, looking her over in a way that made her conscious of her appearance. She was glad she had worn the blue slacks and shirt that brought a bright color to her eyes.

"Good morning, Lee. I want you to see some of the work I did in your absence. The divers have done a good job of following your orders to tag the artifacts in place before disturbing them, and I took care of photographing the finds."

"I appreciate that, Burr. May I see the photos?"

Butt slapped a Manila folder onto her desk, flipped it open and stood waiting for her reaction. "A lot of it isn't very exciting. At least not to me anyway. Pottery shards. Ballast stones. Always ballast stones. I'm more interested in gold and silver."

"The ballast stones could be significant." Lee began poring over the pictures and growing more excited by the minute. "Burr, look! These are cannonballs. Iron. And these! These are marble cannonballs."

"How can you be so sure?"

"I've seen similar artifacts before. Professor Hoskin has a display case with artifacts from other galleons."

"Look at this, Lee." Burr jabbed his forefinger at the next photo.

"A musket!"

"A harquebus," Burr said. "I've been reading about them. A musket invented by a guy named Harquebus. He had to convince the old-timer kings that a musket could be more effective as a weapon than a knight on a charger."

Lee looked up at Burr with new respect. "I do believe the lore of the *Santa Isabella* is getting to you. Three months ago you would have cared nothing about an encrusted musket."

"Let's hope it's the lore of the *Santa Isabella*," Burr said with a sigh. "I paid the head of the archive to be speedy with that microfilming. Lee, I want you to call Professor Hoskin today. Be persuasive."

"I've already done that, Burr." Lee felt a bit superior at having acted ahead of Burr's order, at least ahead of his order now that they were back home. "He's eager to help us."

"Congratulations, Lee. I'll see that you get a bonus."

"What's the latest word from Galleons Unlimited?" How easy it was to talk to Burr when the subject was treasure.

"The silver ingot was authentic—ancient Spanish loot from the New World."

"Have you seen it?"

"I don't associate with those guys. But there was a picture of the ingot in the *Citizen*. The number on it matched a number on the manifest—so they say—but when they weighed it, the weight didn't match the weight specified in the manifest. So they still lack proof that they've found the *Isabella*."

"That's a relief," Lee said.

"It buys us a little more time," Burr said. "That's all. Look at that next picture. Now you're getting to the good stuff. This is the kind of thing that will draw people in for our display. The plans are still go for that exhibit, Lee. Roscoe Murdock and I are in the process of finalizing the details."

Lee hardly heard Burr's words, so engrossed was she in the next few photos. "Another gold chain! And another!" She turned to the next picture. "And a ring! Gold with a coral set, it looks like. A lady's ring, I'd guess. But the next one." She turned to the next photo. "Surely this heavy ring belonged to a man. There must have been wealthy passengers aboard the *Isabella*, Burr. Where are these new pieces? In Key West?"

"No, they're in our safe right here."

"I want to see them."

Burr smiled down at her. "I thought you might. Come on. We'll go take a look."

Lee followed Burr into Margo's office, where Margo was seated at her desk, wearing a fire-engine red jumpsuit and matching combs in her platinum hair. Lee nodded to her in greeting and received a nod in return. What had she expected, a fanfare? She would have to speak to Margo about Raul. She only hoped Margo would be reasonable. Surely she could see she wasn't being fair to Raul by using him so. Then a little finger of worry nudged her mind. Margo hadn't jumped up when Burr entered her office, hadn't sidled to him in that possessive way of hers. Something seemed to have cooled between them. But Burr had opened the safe and was demanding her attention. There was no time to think about personal matters now.

"Here, Lee. Feast your eyes."

For a moment the flash of the gold held Lee speechless. Each chain had been dropped in a heap and she stretched them to full length. "Burr! This one must be six feet long. The owner must have had a stiff neck from carrying such weight."

"I thought the chains were carried in the pocket," Burr said.

Lee held the chain up. "That would make quite a bulge in a pocket. It was probably worn necklace fashion." Lee laid the chain down and picked up the smaller of the two rings, slipping it on her finger and holding her hand out to admire it. Then she slipped it off quickly, trying not to think too carefully about another lady in another age who might have admired the same ring on her own finger.

Now Margo had joined them at the safe and she slipped the larger of the rings on her thumb. "Wish I had known the fellow who owned this one," she said. "I'm sure he would have been my type of guy."

"Quite possibly, Margo," Burr said, chuckling.

Margo laid the ring back in the safe and Lee saw a puzzled expression on her face. "What is it, Margo? What's the matter?"

"I thought we had three gold chains," she said. "Where's the other one?"

Burr and Lee exchanged worried glances; then one

at a time Burr lifted all the artifacts from the safe, examined them and checked the interior of the safe.

"It's gone!" The words came out a hoarse whisper. "It's gone.... But it can't be gone. Nobody has access to this safe but you and I, Margo."

"Well, I didn't steal it!" Margo grew indignant. "If that's what you were thinking you can...."

"Easy, Margo," Burr said. "Nobody's accusing you of stealing the chain. But it's gone. The two of us are the only ones who knew the safe combination."

"Lee might have known it," Margo said.

"Of course not," Lee said, bristling. "I had no way of knowing the combination. And this is the first time I've been near the safe since I returned from Seville." She scowled, irritated that Margo could make her so defensive.

"That first day you came out here Burr opened the safe in your presence. It wouldn't take a genius to figure out the combination. Anyone could do it just by carefully watching Burr's fingers on the dial knob."

"But I didn't watch."

"All right," Burr said. "That's enough of that kind of talk."

"Are you going to notify the police?" Margo asked.

"Let's just think this through for a few minutes," Burr said. "Who else has had access to this safe?"

"Nobody." Margo began tapping her toe. "It's time to radio the police. And Burr, I think you should know that Spike's missing. He hasn't reported aboard for three days."

"Are you insinuating. . . ?"

Margo shrugged. "A gold chain disappears. A diver disappears. I'm just putting two and two together."

Lee wished Margo would hush. Spike was Raul's friend and she didn't want to see Raul linked with the theft in any way.

"But Spike had no access to this safe," Burr said.

"Don't be too sure of that," Margo said. "There was such excitement aboard when those new chains were brought up and when those rings were found that the safe might have been opened and left unguarded for a few minutes. Or even for more than a few minutes. I certainly can't remember and I doubt that you can, either."

Lee gathered the things Burr had removed from the safe and replaced them. "I don't understand it. The chain's gone. That's obvious. But who would be dumb enough to think he could sell an artifact like that without attracting all sorts of attention? I mean you just don't go up to someone and say, 'do you want to buy a solid gold chain? I just happen to have one here for sale.' "

"Call Raul in here," Burr ordered, looking at Margo.

"You can't blame Raul for the theft," Lee said, feeling lightning flashes of anger almost before Burr finished speaking.

"Get Raul in here," Burr ordered.

Margo left and in moments returned with Raul, who had on the top half of a wet suit and appeared to be ready to dive. "What is it, Burr?" Raul looked at

Burr in such a questioning way that Lee knew Margo had revealed nothing about the theft. She held her breath waiting to see what Burr would say, ready to come to Raul's defense if he needed her.

"Where's your friend, Spike?" Burr asked. "Margo tells me he hasn't reported for work for the past few days."

"He's gone home," Raul said. "He asked me to tell you when you got back."

"And why didn't you? Why didn't you tell Margo?"

"I didn't tell you because I didn't know you were back yet. And I didn't tell Margo, because she knew he was gone and I didn't think his reason would matter to her."

"Why did he leave?" Burr spat the words.

"His mother died."

"I don't believe you. Guys like Spike don't even have mothers."

"All I know is what he told me. He said his mother died and I believed him. What's the big deal anyway? Lots of divers come and go. I've never seen you get uptight about it before."

"That's all, Raul," Burr said. "Go on down and see what you can find for us today."

Raul left, scowling, and Lee breathed again. "You're going to radio the police?"

"No. Not yet. That would instigate unfavorable publicity. Our investors don't need to be hearing that sort of news. This loss is to be kept a secret between the three of us, you understand?"

Margo and Lee nodded, but Lee wasn't sure she

understood the full ramifications of the loss. Spike's leaving coinciding with the discovery of the theft seemed suspicious to her, yet Burr wasn't making plans to find him and bring him back.

"Everyone will stay aboard ship tonight?" Margo asked. "There'll be a search?"

"No." Burr shook his head. "I don't want anyone to get suspicious. We'll come and go as usual, and in the meantime I'll do my own personal investigation aboard ship."

"You think someone's dumb enough to steal the chain and hide it right aboard the *Sea Deuced*?" Margo asked.

"That might arouse a lot less suspicion than for someone to take it and split. And don't worry. I'll put a tail on Spike. Not police. A private investigator."

The rest of the morning passed in a haze of confused thoughts for Lee. The loss of the gold chain was devastating enough, but Burr's plan to investigate without the aid of the police frightened her. Spike was gone. She knew Burr had never been able to catch Spike or Raul in any drug involvement or they both would have been fired long ago. But Burr still suspected both of them of dealing in drugs. Burr would blame this theft on Raul if it was at all possible for him to do so. Surely he now hated Raul more than ever for his involvement with Margo.

Could she persuade Raul to give up this job? No. She had tried before and failed. Why did she think she might succeed now? Anyway, Raul's quitting at a time like this wouldn't be practical. Anyone who left the *Santa Isabella* operation at this time would be highly suspect. But she had to talk with Raul, to warn him. Warn him of what? Surely he knew Burr was out for his hide. Surely he knew that only Burr's pride, his great ego, had kept him from firing him long ago. To fire Raul with no good reason would be to admit he had made a mistake in hiring him in the first place. It would also be an admission that he resented Raul's involvement with Margo and it would make him look like a hard-to-please boss.

Finally Lee managed to talk with Raul briefly after he came up from his dive and he promised to meet her that night at a little café on Stock Island.

Lee was surprised when Burr ordered her and Margo to ride back to town that night with Harry, saying that he would be staying aboard the *Sea Deuced* with the divers. Margo looked haggard from worry over the chain, Lee thought. Or perhaps Margo was just exhausted. Burr had kept her at her desk all day, issuing orders as only he knew how.

"He's going to search the boat," Lee said on the way back to town.

"Hush." Margo scowled and nodded to Harry.

They rode in silence back to the dock, back to Marvista. Then Margo grew talkative. "He couldn't search the whole boat single-handed. There are too many nooks and crannies."

"Maybe he's just going to keep an eye on the divers, to watch for suspicious actions."

Margo would have talked longer, but Lee pleaded tiredness; and when Margo suggested they have dinner together, Lee refused. She didn't want to be involved with Margo and have to explain leaving to meet Raul. She wasn't going to risk having Margo follow her this time. Although it was past her appointed time for the Stock Island meeting, Lee waited until she heard Margo leave before she slipped away. She thought she might pass Raul hitchhiking along the way, but he was already seated in a back booth at the Blue Marlin when she arrived. Lee hardly noticed the interior of the place except to note that the decor was a total cliché. Fishing nets on the walls with a few conch shells wired to them for effect. Porthole-type windows. Menus shaped like brassbound sea chests. The smell of stale grease permeated the air, and the clatter of crockery in the kitchen almost drowned out the music blaring from the jukebox.

"You're late," Raul said.

"Couldn't be helped. I didn't want Margo following me."

"How was Seville?"

"I enjoyed it, Raul. And working in the archive was an educational experience. But I didn't come here to talk about Seville. There's a gold chain missing from Burr's safe. It's supposed to be hush-hush information known only to Margo, Burr and myself, so don't let on that I've told you. But do you know anything about it?"

"Nothing like getting right to the point." Raul scowled at her. "And no. I don't know anything about it. But I think Spike left on legit business—his mother, you know. I think he'll be back in a few days. He wouldn't have lied to me. Had no reason to."

"Unless the reason was a gold chain and he didn't want a two-way split."

"It's possible, I suppose. But not probable."

"How's the work going?" Lee asked, glad to change the subject. "Do you like treasure-diving as well as you thought you would?"

"I suppose you want me to say I'm fed up with the hard work, the low wages."

"Well, are you?" Lee waited hopefully for his answer.

"No way. If anything, I feel more deeply involved than before. It started when I found the gold pitcher. And then, I found that ring. The small one. I'd been down almost two hours and I was about ready to go up. The deflectors were digging sand like crazy, then I saw this flash of gold. I swam above it, hovering over it until I was sure it was something gold and not just my imagination playing tricks. Then I swam away from it, but I watched it every second. When the force of the current carried me back over it, I snatched it up and let the rush of water pitch me out of the back side of the crater. When Burr turned off the deflectors I replaced the ring for the photographing. Lee, would you think I was crazy if I told you that finding that ring changed my life?"

Lee thought of the ring, thought of the way it looked, the way it had felt on her finger. She thought of the strong feeling for the past it had evoked in her. "No, I wouldn't think you were crazy. Not at all, Raul. There's a profundity about the sea and its secrets that leaves me in awe. I can understand how finding a priceless treasure from the past could change your thinking. And once a person's thinking changes, his whole life changes."

Raul pulled a small thin book from his shirt pocket and placed it on the table before Lee just as the waitress came to take their orders. Lee didn't look at the book until after they had made their selections from the menu and the waitress had left them. Then she picked up the book.

"A savings passbook, Raul? You've opened a savings account?"

Raul grinned at her. "Right at good old Key West First National. I don't have much socked away yet, but I add to the account every payday. I'm saving for my own scuba gear and a course in deepwater diving."

Lee looked at Raul with admiration. "I'm proud of you, Raul. You're making a start in the right direction."

"I'm through drifting, Lee. I'd like to start my own salvage operation or maybe work as Burr's partner. Salvage diving can mean a lot more than just fun and games."

"Your own business!" Lee could hardly believe the change in Raul's thinking. "I'll help you all I can, of course."

They talked of many things as they ate conch chowder and salads, then over dessert Lee approached the subject of Margo.

"Are you dating Margo, Raul?"

"You're not going to pry into my love life, are you, sis?"

"I suppose not." Lee laughed. "I guess there's

not much a girl can do about her brother's love life, is there? I just don't want you to be hurt. Sometimes Margo...uses people to her own advantage and—"

"Stow it, Lee. Stow it. Let's get out of here."

Lee was sorry she had mentioned Margo. Now Raul stood up, picked up the check, pulled out his billfold. Lee reached for the check. "I'll make this my treat," she said. "It was my idea."

"No way," Raul replied. "This is payday. I'm loaded."

Lee grabbed the bill. "Then unload into your savings account. I invited. I'll pay."

Lee paid the tab, but as they headed for the Chevette in the parking lot two long-haired boys approached them. Lee felt her hackles rise and she was immediately on guard as she got into her car and started it.

"Raul, man." One boy slapped Raul on the back. "Long time no see. Can you let me have a fiver? You see, I've got this chick—"

"Sorry, Lew. No way." Raul opened the car door.

"Pay you back double on Friday, friend."

"Sorry." Raul shook his head and eased into the car. "Let's go, Lee. Okay?"

Lee drove from the parking lot, hardly able to believe the change in Raul. It would take some getting used to. At Raul's request she let him out a few blocks from Marvista so they wouldn't be seen arriving together.

Once back in her suite Lee busied herself with more unpacking, with hand laundry, with a general resettling in. She had brought written reports of the divers' finds home to study and she marveled at what a good job they had done of recording their finds. It would smooth the job of filling out the official forms. She didn't realize she had stayed up so late until she heard voices coming from the hallway. Margo. She listened. Raul. Feeling only a bit guilty at eavesdropping, she walked closer to her door. She had expected to hear Margo flirting with Raul, but their conversation surprised her.

"You're crazy to think of taking a deepwater diving course, Raul," Margo said. "You're already a deepwater diver."

"I'll learn to be a better deepwater diver," Raul said.

"That makes no sense." Margo's voice took on authority. "If you want to start your own salvage business, that's great. But you need business experience, not more diving experience."

"But—"

"I know diving is a glamorous occupation, Raul, but lately I've begun to realize that lots of things are more important than glamour."

"Name one."

"Love. I love you, Raul. I want the best for you."

"I love you, too, Margo. *You're* what's best for me."

"If you love me, prove it. Get yourself out to Community College and enroll in some down-to-earth business courses. And I don't think much of the idea of your trying to buy into a partnership with Burr. You haven't got that kind of money. And besides, the two of you simply don't get along.''

"I like Burr. He's an okay guy.''

"But he doesn't return your sentiments. He's on your tail all the time. I don't think you'll ever convince him you're not a pusher or a dealer of some sort.''

"What's his big thing about drugs?'' Raul asked. "I don't get it. I've never shown up stoned.''

"But Spike did.''

"What's that got to do with me?''

"Guilt by association, I guess. Face it, Raul. Burr's been highly suspicious of your activities ever since he saw you giving money to Spike. He told me about it. To Burr that just meant one thing—drugs. Burr doesn't like you. He puts up with you because you're a good diver and a hard worker, and that combination is hard to come by in this business. If you're smart you'll get yourself enrolled in a business course and begin to lay groundwork for the future.''

"I'll think about it. Aren't you going to invite me in?''

"Not tonight, Raul. See you tomorrow, okay?''

There was a long silence, then Lee heard Margo's door open and close. She slipped into bed and turned out her light, still thinking about the conversation she had just overheard. It wasn't quite the lovers' sweet talk she had expected. Margo sounded sincere. In a way she wanted to thank Margo for talking sense into Raul, yet in another way she resented her bossing him so. What was Margo building anyway? Lee couldn't help thinking Margo was still trying to rouse Burr's interest, yet she had seemed genuinely engrossed in Raul's plans. Lee yawned. She was still suffering from jet lag. She turned over and fell asleep, wondering about the theft of the chain and about Burr. Would she always fall asleep with Burr uppermost in her thoughts?

CHAPTER EIGHTEEN

THE NEXT MORNING aboard the *Sea Deuced* Lee was in her office making entries in the ledger on the artifacts that had been raised in her absence. She had worn a honey-colored jumpsuit that matched her hair and she had used light blue eye shadow to bring out the blue of her eyes. But she had soon forgotten clothes and makeup as she concentrated on ancient Spanish tax stamps, mint marks, dates. She glanced up when Burr entered, but she was unprepared for his black expression. The shadows beneath his eyes were like soot smudges and she guessed he had been up all night. The thin white line showed around his mouth and she wondered what she had done to call up his anger.

"Report to my office immediately," Burr ordered. Without giving her time to reply, he turned and strode across the deck to the business office where Margo was working on the ledgers. In a few moments Lee saw a look of shock cross Margo's face as she followed Burr. They reached his office at about the same time and Lee waited in the electrifying silence for Burr to speak.

Burr said nothing and waited as all the divers filed into the office with them. At first Lee had been fascinated with the pictures of Zack Adburee, pictures that seemed to follow her with their gaze no matter where she stood or sat. How could Burr stand the overpowering and constant reminder of his brother? She wondered exactly what his memories of Zack were. Did he think of the good times they had shared? The bad times?

Margo eased into Lee, pushing her a bit to one side as another diver entered the small office. Lee inhaled deeply. With so many people crowded into such close quarters the room was becoming stuffy and hot. Burr said nothing until Raul arrived, then he cleared his throat. The sound was like a great scraping rumble, the silence in the room was so complete. Then Burr reached under his desk, pulled out a battered cardboard suitcase and laid it on his desk.

Lee gasped. Raul's magic kit. The suitcase he used for his magic act. She glanced at Raul from the corner of her eye without turning her head. A muscle tightened at the corner of Raul's mouth and tendons stood out in his neck, yet only shock showed in his eyes.

"I owe all of you dive boys except one a sincere apology," Burr said. "For the past twenty-four hours or so you all have been suspect in my mind." Burr paused dramatically for a moment, then he continued. "Yesterday we discovered one of the gold chains missing from the safe."

Now a murmur of voices rose as the divers muttered to one another, but Burr spoke above the muttering. "Every one of you was suspect until I found the chain."

"Where, Burr? Where did you find it?" Lee spoke out, asking the question all their minds were screaming, dreading the answer.

"I found it hidden in this suitcase of magic supplies." Moving with maddening slowness Burr snapped open the suitcase clasps, raised the lid, and stood aside. Lee tiptoed and peered into the case. She could see nothing of special interest—scarves, silver rings, skull cap. Then Burr reached for Raul's velvet vest, lifted it up for their inspection, then pulled the chain from a large secret pocket hidden in the lining of the vest.

At first the divers froze, then there was a shrugging of shoulders, much whispering and a shuffling of feet. Lee wanted to scream fraud as a nausea made her stomach growl. She swallowed and tried to calm herself.

"Raul, perhaps you'd like to explain the presence of this chain in your case."

Raul looked grim faced and his tan took on a greenish tinge. "I can't explain it, sir. I have no idea how it got there."

The thought flashed through Lee's mind that Burr himself might have planted the chain in Raul's case to provide the excuse he needed for getting rid of him. But no. In spite of Burr's capability for cruelty she couldn't quite believe he would do that. Yet she couldn't quite believe he would *not* do that either. She wanted to rush to Raul, to defend him, yet she knew she dare not approach him and she dared not speak out until she had considered her words carefully.

"If you can't explain the presence of the chain in your suitcase, who do you think can explain it?" Burr demanded.

"I don't know." Raul's voice shook. "Someone's trying to frame me."

"That's an old line," Burr retorted. "I'm not buying it."

"Do you think I'd go to the risk of stealing the chain, then leave it where you could find it? I'm not that stupid."

"This evidence proves otherwise." Burr pounded his fist on his desk. "You're through, Raul. I don't ever want to see you again. Get. . .out!"

"Burr!" Margo cried out in protest. "You're not being fair. Maybe someone did try to frame Raul. All you have here is circumstantial evidence. You have no firm proof that Raul stole the chain."

"I have all the proof I need," Burr said. "I have my reasons for not making a police case of this theft. And since it's a private matter between myself and the thief, I'll handle it in the manner most expedient to Dive Boys. Get your things together, Johnson. I'll fly you back to Key West. Then I never want to see you again. The rest of you are dismissed. I called you here to witness this because I wanted to squelch any rumors about the theft before they got started. It will be to your advantage and to the advantage of Dive Boys if this information goes no farther. Now get back to work. On the double! We've lost enough time as it is."

"You're making a mistake, Burr," Lee said when the other divers were gone. "You're playing God.

You're ruining a man's reputation on circumstantial evidence.''

"What does that matter to you?" Burr demanded. "Surely the woman scorned isn't going to plead for her former lover, is she? Margo's interest in Raul I can understand, but *yours*?" Burr shook his head.

Once more Lee thought of resigning in righteous indignation, but they had played that scene before. And now due to her own actions she had much less leverage. Since Professor Hoskin had agreed to help with the translating of the *Santa Isabella* manifest, he might well become so fascinated with the other archaeological work that he would take over her position if she resigned. Or if he wouldn't take over, he might at least supply names of other students who might be interested in the work.

Burr thrust the gold chain at Margo. "Lock it up, Margo. Then be sure the monthly financial report is ready for my inspection. I'll expect it on my desk in exactly forty minutes.''

Lee felt sick, actually nauseated, as she returned to her desk. How could this be happening? Just when Raul had seemed to be discovering himself as a person, just as he seemed to have found a goal in life he had been shot down before he had a fair chance to work toward that goal. She couldn't believe he was guilty.

Raul had few possessions other than those in the magic case. Lee turned her back when he and Burr climbed the companionway to the helicopter pad. She tried to ignore the sound of the engine and she refused to watch the takeoff as she usually did. Finally she put all pride in her pocket and went to Margo's office.

"Can you think of anything we can do?" Lee asked. "To help Raul, I mean?" She was surprised at how pale and drawn Margo looked. Mascara had run onto her left cheek. Clearly she had been crying.

"You know Burr," Margo replied shortly. "There's no countering his orders." Margo went on with her work on the ledger, dismissing Lee with her actions more thoroughly than she could have dismissed her with words.

Lee returned to her office, but she couldn't concentrate on itemizing the artifacts. She could only sit there staring at the blank forms. When she heard the helicopter return she knew it would be exactly forty minutes later than when it had left. Burr's punctuality didn't surprise her. The thing that surprised her was the woman who accompanied him as he came down the companionway. The impression of a long-stemmed rose flashed through Lee's mind. The woman was tall and willowy. Maybe early thirties. And her figure did justice to the bottle-green jersey shift that obviously had been chosen because it did such wonderful things for her auburn hair and hazel eyes. Lee pressed her lips together in a thin hard line, hating the way one woman could size up another so accurately, yet knowing the redhead would be doing the same thing to her the moment they met.

But they didn't meet. Burr ensconced himself in his private office with the woman for over two hours, then they left in the helicopter. Lee was so frustrated she felt like sobbing, sobbing for Raul, sobbing because Burr had required so little time to find a new girl friend to take Margo's place. But why did that surprise her so? She had known all along that Burr was a playboy. Why didn't she resign and leave this job? Raul was gone now. She no longer needed to stay here to keep her promise to their mother. Yet she couldn't leave. To leave now would be to abandon the beginnings of her own career. She had no other job to go to.

Somehow the rest of the day passed and Lee went to a movie that night to try to distract herself from all the problems that pressed in on her. She didn't even know where Raul was. His things were gone from the divers' quarters at Marvista. At least he had money. He wouldn't be forced to sleep on the beach. Yet if he reverted to his old ways, the beach would be the first place he would hit. Should she go looking for him? She decided against it. There were too many beaches. Raul would have contacted friends by now. She shuddered.

The next morning on their ride to the *Sea Deuced* Margo looked as if she had spent a sleepless night.

"Have you seen Raul?" Lee asked.

"No."

"Do you have any idea where he is?"

"No."

Lee gave up further attempts at conversation. Surely Raul would contact her when he was ready. He knew she was for him all the way. Once aboard the *Sea Deuced* Lee was surprised that work progressed much as usual. What had she expected? Had she thought the world would stop spinning if Raul left? Burr called a midafternoon meeting to outline search plans for the following day.

"I have now had time to formulate ideas that should speed up our search for the *Isabella*," Burr said. "Some time ago Julio Hunter—a scholar Lee met in Seville—sent me information on the hurricane that sank the *Isabella*. I wanted to search our present location thoroughly before moving on, but tomorrow we will move and use Hunter's projection of the storm to select our new location."

"Where are we moving to?" one of the divers called out.

"To another deep-water area near here. From now on we'll execute a more logical method of search. We'll lower some concrete blocks that Harry brought out this morning and that you boys will have painted white before tomorrow. These will be our markers. Lee, can you use such markers to plot out large squares of the ocean bottom?"

"Of course. The white blocks will show well in photos. A photographer can hover over the site with a plumb line attached to the camera so he can stay a fixed distance above the area. Another man can swim below the photographer moving a calibrated surveyor's rod into each picture to indicate scale. This would have to be done for each marked area."

"Good," Burr said. "We'll start this work tomorrow. We'll number each square. Then we'll anchor the *Sea Deuced* over the area, working one square at a time with the deflectors until every inch of the area has been searched."

"It sounds like a good plan to me," Lee said. "Thorough."

"We have Julio Hunter to thank for helping us with the storm information," Burr said.

Lee looked away, surprised at how few times she had thought of Julio since her return to Key West. Had he thought of her? And what of Claudia? Perhaps she could invite Claudia to come for a visit sometime. It would be a nice gesture. She knew how homesick Claudia was. Lee was still thinking about Julio and Claudia when she heard Margo say her name.

"I want you in on the meeting, too, Lee," Margo said.

"What meeting?" Lee asked.

"I just told Burr I want to talk to you both in my office. Please."

There was a pleading note in Margo's voice that alerted Lee to trouble of some sort. Her curiosity rose like a kite in the wind. Margo wasn't the kind to plead. "Of course, Margo."

As Lee sat down in front of Margo's desk, her curiosity mingled with old memories and she felt like a school child being called in for a reprimand until she saw a tear trickling down Margo's cheek. This was completely out of character for Margo. Lee looked away in embarrassment.

"What is it, Margo?" Burr asked. "If there's a problem maybe we can help."

"I stole the chain." Margo blurted the words and they hung in the air like four live grenades with the pins pulled.

"*You* stole the chain?" Burr asked the question then he laughed. "Come off it, Margo. There's no point in your trying to protect Raul. Noble of you, but useless."

Margo shook her head sadly, and Lee realized she was telling the truth. Her anger flared, but she squelched it, knowing she must hear Margo out. "I stole the chain," Margo repeated.

"But why?" Burr asked, now giving Margo his complete and serious attention. "And if you did steal it, why did you hide it in Raul's things?"

Margo's voice broke, but she continued her confession. "I was out of my mind, I guess. All this treasure coming up. It didn't seem as if one chain more or less would make much difference to you, Burr. And it would make a lot of difference to me. Are you going to radio the police?"

"I didn't tell the authorities when I thought Raul had stolen the chain. Why should I call them in now? Investor confidence is all-important to me. But you keep talking. I want to know why."

"That should be clear enough," Margo said. "I'm in love with Raul."

"So you try to frame him by hiding a stolen chain in his suitcase!" Lee spat the words. "Some sort of love that is!"

"Hear me out." Margo took a deep breath. "I took the chain from the safe and hid it in Raul's things. Then I paid Spike to leave the operation and never return. I told him I was in love with Raul, that I thought he, Spike, was a bad influence on Raul and wanted him out of our lives."

"And Spike believed you?" Lee asked.

Burr nodded and scowled at Lee. "Of course he would have believed her if she paid him enough. Money talks."

"It took a chunk of cash," Margo said, "but I thought it was worth it at the time. I thought all evidence would point at Spike, but I thought he would be gone. I thought he wouldn't be found and made to suffer. I didn't want to hurt Spike."

"But you forgot about Burr's obsession to be rid of Raul, didn't you?" Lee snorted, wondering at Margo's capacity for deception.

"I hid the chain in Raul's things thinking he would find it later. He doesn't use that magic case much and I thought that by the time he discovered the chain the theft would have been forgotten and there he would be with all that gold."

"And your object in life is to make Raul rich?" Burr asked, sarcastically.

"I wanted him to have enough money to marry me." Margo glared at Burr. "Being rich isn't really all that important to me anymore, not since Raul and I...." She let the sentence dangle, then continued. "I knew Raul would never be able to afford marriage on the pay you put out, but he does love me. I know that. And now he's saving what little he can for... for other things. I guess I rationalized that Raul had really earned that chain by risking his life every day diving. Those boys do risk their lives, you know. And for a pittance!"

Lee stood up. "Your story's crazy, Margo. But I believe you. Nobody could make up such fiction. But do you realize Raul is out there somewhere angry at the world? Frustrated! Why, heaven only knows what he might do. We've got to find him."

"And just how do you propose to do that?" Burr

asked. "He could be anywhere." Burr's fury showed in his grating voice, the terrible white line around his mouth, his glaring eyes. "He's no good. A pusher."

Lee glared back at Burr. "You don't really believe that, Burr. You have no evidence to prove that Raul has had anything to do with drugs. You're just jealous because Margo preferred Raul to you." For a moment Lee thought Burr was going to strike her. His hands balled into fists and he took a step toward her. Then he got control of himself.

"You're wrong, Lee. Dead wrong. I don't know why you're so defensive about another woman's man, but you take me to Raul and I'll apologize."

"It's all my fault," Margo said. "I'm the one who should apologize...if it isn't too late. But how are we going to find him?"

"I have an idea," Lee said. "I don't know why I didn't think of it sooner. All Raul had besides his belief in himself as a diver was his belief in himself as a magician." She glanced at her watch. "He may be at Mallory tonight putting on his magic act."

"It's a starting place," Burr said. "That's where I saw him his first night in Key West. Let's go. We'll fly in the heli. Move it."

The flight to Key West was a blur for Lee. Burr managed the craft stiff-jawed and silent. Margo cried the whole distance. They arrived too early. Raul might spot them and run if they went to the dock before the sunset crowd gathered. They waited in the courtyard at Marvista until they knew the performers would be gathering at Mallory before they headed in that direction. Would Raul be there? The question raced in Lee's mind. He had to be there.

Burr eased the Mercedes into a spot in the far corner of the Mallory parking area and they walked quickly to the dock. The artsy types were out in full force. A juggler tossed semiripe avocados, three girls dressed in ponchos and jeans played tunes on recorders, the thin piercing tones wailing into the soft evening. One of the girls had a baby strapped into a carrier on her back and the infant smiled and gurgled at a Great Dane that stood at attention beside the trio. A barefoot poet was dancing on the dock piling reciting to the sun between dances with his hands folded in an attitude of prayer.

"Looks like we've got a high freak count tonight," Margo muttered.

Then Lee saw Raul. The crowd around him was so dense that she could only catch a glimpse of his crazy cap, the quick flash of the silver rings he used in his act. She nudged Margo and Burr.

"There he is!"

"Better let him finish his act before we close in," Burr said. "If he sees me he might run. No use causing a street brawl in all this crowd."

So they waited and waited. Lee's head began to ache from the tension. Then when Raul threw out the hat for the coin collection, the crowd began to disperse. Lee approached Raul first before either Margo or Burr could protest, thinking he would be more likely to listen to her than to either of them.

"Margo and Burr are here, Raul. They want to talk to you, to apologize."

Raul glared at her for a moment, then he looked

around at the crowd as if doubting her words. But Margo and Burr pushed forward. Lee linked her arm through Raul's to try to prevent him from running, but he made no attempt to run. If Burr and Margo thought her actions strange, let them. She owed them no explanations.

"If this is some sort of a trap..." Raul said. "If you're going to call the cops after all, go ahead. I can face that. There's no way I'll spend the rest of my life running."

"Sit down, Raul," Margo said. "I have something to tell you. Something terrible. Something important." Lee led them to the raised safety ledge at the edge of the dock where she and Raul sat while Burr and Margo remained standing.

Margo repeated her confession to Raul, begging him to forgive her. Raul just nodded, staring at her as if he didn't quite understand or couldn't quite believe. When he spoke Lee felt as if she were eavesdropping on a private conversation.

"I didn't know you loved me that much, Margo," Raul said. "You're no thief. You love me enough to *steal* to get to be my wife?"

Margo nodded. "I love you much more than that, Raul. I did a crazy thing. Money's important, but not as important as love. It's taken me a long time to learn that."

Lee was struck by the sincerity in Margo's voice and the glow shining from her eyes. She was no longer the cold glamour girl that Lee had first met. Lee still could not believe that Margo and Raul, her brother, had fallen in love. It was definitely an attraction of opposites, but maybe they would be good for each other.

Raul took Margo's hand, pulling her down beside himself, but before they could speak again, Burr intruded. He stooped so he and Raul were on an eye level, then he extended his hand, and when he spoke, sincerity in his tone replaced the usual arrogance.

"I'm sorry for my part in all this, Raul. I was wrong."

Raul accepted Burr's hand, shaking it, his expression solemn. "I'm sure an apology doesn't come easy for you, Burr. But I accept it and I respect you for offering it."

"You'll come back to the diving boat?" Burr asked. "Your job's still open if you want it. I'd like to have you back."

"Are you firing Margo?" Raul impaled Burr with his gaze.

"No." Burr didn't elaborate, but neither did he look at Margo.

"Then I'll be back. Tomorrow."

"I'm pleased." Burr shook Raul's hand again, and Lee got the impression that maybe Burr meant his words. But then why shouldn't he mean them? What did he care for the relationship between Margo and Raul now? He had his new redhead, didn't he? She would restore his pride and salve his wounded ego. Lee tried not to hate her.

CHAPTER NINETEEN

LEE PICKED UP fried chicken and a carton of cole slaw from a fast-food establishment and ate in her room that evening. The air conditioner had gone on the blink and it was hot, but she needed to be alone to think. So much had happened since she had returned from Seville that her mind seemed to be constantly in a whirl. Margo's startling confession along with the rest of the day's happenings convinced her that Margo was truly in love with Raul. But would Raul marry her? Some sister-in-law! Despite all the antagonism between herself and Margo, Lee couldn't bring herself to think of Margo as a thief although there was no escaping the fact. She could only try to rationalize by saying that what Margo had done she had done out of love for Raul. People stole for far worse reasons than that. She would try not to be judgmental.

She thought of Julio and wondered if he was at the archive. Had he taken Claudia out for her birthday dinner? She could only look back on her hours spent with Julio with fondness. It had been pleasant going out with him, knowing he wouldn't arouse her as Burr had, wouldn't cause her to do things that would make her feel ashamed afterward. Julio was the kind of man a girl could build a pleasant life around. But she had turned that chance down. She had nobody to blame but herself.

The next morning the speedboat arrived at the *Sea Deuced* before the helicopter, but the crew waited to weigh anchor and move to their new location until Burr was there to oversee the operation. After they had sped to their new anchorage Lee sighed. She realized she had been spending lots of time and thought on clothes and makeup lately and she knew it was for Burr's benefit. Yet he didn't seem to notice. She had new sea-green shorts and shirt and she had applied eye shadow in a way that made her eyes look even larger than usual. She had highlighted her cheekbones and dabbed some rouge on her cheeks in an attempt at glamour, but Burr had made no comment.

"This new anchorage doesn't look much different from the old spot, Burr. There's a lot of sameness about the sea."

"A mysterious sameness that I like," Burr said.

Lee wondered if he meant that. She had guessed that the sea had taken Zack's life. No, that was wrong. Zack had taken his own life. The sea was just the tool he had chosen to use.

Burr passed out paintbrushes, and after Harry helped the divers hoist the concrete blocks from the speedboat to the *Sea Deuced*, everyone helped paint. As they worked Burr talked to Lee.

"The first half of the microfilm arrived from the archive yesterday. It was at the house when I got home last night, and I sent it to Professor Hoskin by special messenger."

"The first half? What happened to the second half?"

"I asked the archive officials to mail the manifest to me in two parts in order to speed up our work on it. I don't envy Professor Hoskin the job of reading through all that gibberish."

"It's the hardest kind of work, Burr. Not physical work, of course. It's the mental strain that tells on a person. But I'm sure Professor Hoskin will work much faster than I could. He should have a report to you soon."

They covered the blocks with quick-drying paint and by the time the divers who had gone down to inspect the new location returned with their report, Burr was ready to toss the blocks over the side, dive after them and start measuring out the squares that would mark the bounds of their treasure search for the next several weeks.

Lee and Burr plunged into the sea together and Lee found that although the water looked the same on the surface, the undersea life was a bit different. She started at Burr's touch on her arm, then she looked where he was pointing, trying to hide from her reaction to his touch. Would it always be this way? Would he always have the power to send chills racing through her body by merely touching her arm? She swam to one side of him, well out of his reach.

A flying fish. That's what he had been pointing out to her. She looked in awe at the small fish's great fanned fins, diaphanous as grasshopper's wings. Even as she watched, the creature took off in a sudden burst of speed, sculled rapidly with its tail, then taxied along, splashing the surface. When the fish disappeared she knew it was gliding through the air, then moments later it plopped back into the sea again. Magic. She had never seen such a performance from below the surface before. But she wasn't here to view the scenery. She swam farther down toward the bottom where the white blocks lay scattered on the sand like nougat bars spilled from a sack. Here and there spiny lobsters skittered through the sparse meadow of sea grass that grew in the sand.

Burr had brought her plane table, a measuring tape, and they went to work, using the farthest block as their first marker. Now Burr stayed close to her, watching her work, his body brushing against hers as the current and tides clashed about them. He had brought along a special book with waterproof pages on which he wrote down measurements, elevations, checking with her for accuracy after each entry. They stayed down until they were almost out of air, and when they surfaced the sea bottom looked as if it had been marked off for a great game of checkers or maybe ticktacktoe.

She found Burr a pleasant diving companion. Maybe it was because he couldn't shout orders. Or maybe it was because he found so many excuses to touch her hand, her arm, gentle touches that she pretended to ignore but that in reality she liked to store in her mind and remember.

When they were aboard and dressed again Burr stopped at Lee's office. "Did you see the baby moonfish as we came up, Lee?"

"Yes. Weren't they gorgeous? It seems impossible

that a silvery creature hardly as big as a half-dollar can support such long threadlike rays several times its own length. Someday I'd like to study a specimen in a saltwater aquarium."

"You find sea creatures as fascinating as I do, don't you?"

"That's a hard question to answer, Burr. But, yes, I find them fascinating." It pleased her that Burr was interested in something besides treasure. Yet, what difference could his interests make to her?

"You'll be working overtime tonight, Lee. We need to have a meeting."

As usual Burr's commanding tone made her bristle. "I prefer that we keep our meetings scheduled during the business day," she said.

"That's impossible this time. But no dinner. No champagne." He smiled at her knowingly. "Just business. I'll pick you up around eight o'clock, so be ready."

"Yes, sir." Lee felt her heart pounding as Burr left her office. She knew she hadn't fooled him with her protest at an evening meeting just as he hadn't fooled her about his motive for choosing such a time to meet. Surely he had designed their meeting more for pleasure than for business. And why had she let him get by with it? Because she wanted to be with him, that's why. At least she could admit the truth in her own mind, even if she could never admit it to him. But tonight she would be on guard. She would remember the redhead and Burr's roving eye. She would enjoy herself and enjoy Burr's company, but she would keep her emotions under control. She had managed to do that in Seville, hadn't she? Burr had been furious when she had withdrawn before he was ready for her to go, yet he had come back to her now, knowing how she felt about love. . . .

That night she enjoyed a sit-down meal at a sidewalk café where she could listen to the ocean, see the gulls etching circles against the sky, see the setting sun turn the whole bay to crimson. After she finished eating she drove leisurely to Marvista and prepared for her date with Burr. Her business meeting. The air conditioner was still off so she relaxed in a cool bubble bath, then instead of patting herself dry with the bath sheet, she stood in front of the louvered window and let the soft breeze dry her body.

For a moment she hesitated in deciding what to wear, then she pulled out the lemon-colored wraparound she had worn that last night in Seville. She grinned at her reflection in the mirror. Burr had liked the dress. With Margo out of the picture maybe she could win him in the way she wanted to win him. Maybe the next time he said "I love you" he would mean it. But that was crazy. There was the new redhead on the scene now, and who could guess how many other girls were in the wings waiting to go on-stage the minute Burr spotlighted them! Nevertheless, she highlighted her eyes with green shadow, then made her lips look their fullest with coral-colored lip gloss.

When Burr knocked on her door she was ready. But she wasn't ready for the look on his face when he saw her. His eyes smoldered and his nostrils flared.

"That dress won't do, Lee. Go change."

"Why should I do that?" She felt ready to match him glare for glare. "The dress pleases me and I'm the one wearing it."

"I said go change."

Lee stood her ground. "You have no right to—"

"Are you going to change quickly or do you want me to help you?"

"I suppose you've had lots of experience."

"It doesn't take much experience to deal with a dress like that." Burr reached and jerked on the bow string at her waist. "Who'll it be? You or me?"

Furious, Lee retreated into her room, flung the wraparound on her bed and began looking through her closet for something else. Then suddenly she saw the humor of the situation. Burr was afraid of the wraparound. He didn't want a repeat of that scene in the Seville rose garden. Well, she would give him what he wanted. Quickly she pulled out a long-sleeved dress. Nubby cotton. A shirtwaist that buttoned to her chin. When she appeared again for his inspection she had expected him to scowl. But he neither scowled nor smiled.

"That's more like it, Lee. Come along now."

Lee followed him through the hallway to the front entry, then one glance at the Mercedes left her all but speechless. Raul and Margo were in the back seat and the redhead was on the passenger side of the front seat.

Burr opened a rear door for Lee, and she slid onto the seat beside Raul. Why hadn't Burr told her there would be others at this meeting? Yet she couldn't blame Burr. She's the one who had jumped to the conclusion that it was a business meeting for two. She felt mortified. What if he had let her appear in the partyish wraparound?

"Lee, I'd like you to meet Whitney Deleveau. Whitney, Lee Cameron."

Lee leaned forward to nod and murmur a polite greeting as Whitney turned in her seat to smile. "I've never known a marine archaeologist before," Whitney said in a whispery voice that gave the impression she classed marine archaeologists right along with five-legged horses and calves with two heads. Lee could think of no response. She could only stare at Whitney in her green softly-tailored suit. Was green her trademark? Lee decided she hated green.

"We're meeting Roscoe Murdock at the bank," Burr said. "He's ready to help us finalize our plans for the treasure exhibit."

Lee wondered why Raul was present at such an official-sounding meeting. And Whitney Deleveau? But she didn't ask questions. She was too furious with Burr for not telling her there would be others present this evening, that the meeting would be held at the bank.

When they reached Key West First National Roscoe escorted them to the basement and to the Dive Boys' security room. "Thought we'd meet right here where we can see the treasure if we need to," he said.

Tonight Roscoe wore dark slacks and a red sport shirt that called attention to his florid complexion, his beefiness. Even out of banker's gray he retained a solid "money" look about him. Maybe it was his carefully manicured nails or his Gucci belt. Lee couldn't be sure.

"Are you sure the bank can handle such an exhibit as this one promises to be?" Lee asked as soon as they were all seated around a large table.

"That's all been decided while you were in Seville," Burr said. "All we have to decide now is the best way to show off the treasure. That's why Miss Deleveau is with us. She's a professional artist and I thought her background would prove helpful to us in arranging the artifacts in an eye-pleasing way."

An artist! Lee fumed. Why would Burr bring an artist in when an archaeologist was the only professional he needed? Clearly, Miss Deleveau was a lady of many talents. Lee watched the way she looked up at Burr through her lashes, the way she sat with her profile toward him. She'd be on him like paint if the rest of us weren't present, Lee thought.

"I've asked Raul to be at the exhibit to speak for the divers," Burr explained. "Raul has had enough performing experience to assure me he'll be able to speak about the various pieces of treasure in a special way that will appeal to the crowd we expect to pass through the bank."

Lee knew Burr was appeasing Raul, trying to make up for his earlier error. Surely Raul was enjoying his elevated status. "Then the exhibit will be held inside the bank?" Lee asked.

Roscoe nodded and handed a scaled drawing toward her. "Here's how Whitney sees the exhibit. The setting will be upstairs in the main foyer. Regular banking activities can proceed as usual in one section. There'll be armed guards at each door as there normally are. And the police have promised extra protection outside the bank. I feel assured that everything will be quite safe.''

Lee studied the scale drawing. According to the plan there would be several glass-topped display cases for the coins, another for the chains, and a third for the rings and other small artifacts. A tank holding brine would be used to display the muskets, thus reducing the risk of their disintegration.

''I wish we could bring up that iron cannon,'' Raul said. ''That would make an impressive exhibit.''

''I'm not ready to bring it up yet,'' Burr said. ''But we can display some pictures of it. You can get pictures of it, can't you, Lee? We'll want pictures that show its size and some close-ups of the markings on it.''

''Of course I can arrange that. And we can have the photos enlarged, framed, if you like.''

The meeting lasted until almost ten o'clock; then Burr thanked Roscoe, ushered everyone back to his car, and drove from the parking lot. He stopped at Marvista first and let Raul, Margo and Lee out, then he snapped on the radio tuning in some calypso music before he eased from the drive with Whitney Deleveau at his side.

Lee went straight to her suite, undressed and slipped into a jersey beach cover-up. Then she applied cream to her face and rinsed out a few underthings. She could hear Margo and Raul talking in the courtyard and guessed they must be sitting at the umbrella table. When she finished her chores she sat down and tried to read, but the heat and the thought of Burr and Whitney together kept her from concentrating. At last she tossed the book aside. The voices outside had ceased. She glanced at her clock. Eleven. Time for bed if she intended to be fresh in the morning. She started to slip into her nightgown, then changed her mind.

"I'll take just a short walk around the courtyard," she said to herself. "Just long enough to get some fresh air, long enough to cool off and make myself good and sleepy." As she walked she tried to put Burr and Whitney from her mind. If only she hadn't made such a fool of herself tonight by appearing in that wraparound. Surely Burr was laughing at her. He might even be telling Whitney Deleveu about his crazy archaeologist who had thought she was going out on a date tonight.

Lee strolled past the umbrella table and started down to the beach. Then she remembered another night of strolling on the beach and decided to be cautious and stay close to the house. The scent of jasmine reached her and she wanted to pick a sprig of it to take to her room. But where was it? Following her nose into some deep shrubbery overrun with crotons, she felt like Moses in the bulrushes. Then suddenly she felt tiny feet scamper across her instep and ankle. She squelched a desire to scream, realizing it was only a harmless chameleon, but the creature had startled her. She swayed for a moment and clutched at the croton, trying to keep her balance. Then she stepped back a pace into...nothingness. Screaming, she felt herself falling, falling, and then blackness enveloped her.

When she came to she smelled sandalwood. Burr? She wanted to open her eyes, but her eyelids seemed to be weighted down. She couldn't lift them.

"Lee? Lee, darling...." Burr's voice crooned her name as if from a great distance and she felt cool fingers on her forehead. Where was she? Sitting down somewhere. No, lying down.

"Can you move your fingers, Lee?"

She did and felt a blur of pain engulf her entire body. Burr kissed her hand and the pain subsided.

"Can you move your toes?"

Lee concentrated through the pain, trying to focus her mind on Burr's strange words, and moved her toes.

"Thank God!"

Where was she? She felt cool grass beneath her and although she didn't have the strength to open her eyes she could sense moonlight on her eyelids. Outside. She was somewhere outside and Burr was with her, asking her to do crazy things. Move fingers. Move toes. The thud of feet sounded nearby, and in a moment she recognized Margo's voice.

"Burr, what's happened?" Margo paused then gasped.

"She fell into one of mother's would-be reflecting pools," Burr said. "I lifted her out, but...."

"Let's get her to her room, her bed," Margo said.

"No. It's not safe to move her again. She may have internal injuries. Her neck and back are okay, I think, but there could be other broken bones."

"She's bleeding. Stay with her, Burr. I'll get some antiseptic, some cotton balls."

Lee heard the thudding of feet again, then she felt Burr's lips on her eyelids, her forehead. She felt his warm breath in her hair. "Lee? Lee? Can you hear me?"

She said yes in her mind, but she couldn't say it aloud.

"Here's the antiseptic, Burr," Margo called, her voice ragged from the exertion of running. "Shall I help you?"

"Get a doctor, Margo. Go. Hurry."

"Doctors don't make house calls. We'll have to take her to the hospital emergency room."

"Go next door. Get Dr. Haynes. He'll come if you tell him I've sent for him and there's an emergency."

Again Lee heard Margo's departing footsteps then she smelled the medicinal scent of antiseptic and felt the cool touch of the saturated cotton against her forehead.

"This won't hurt, Lee. Just have to get you cleaned up a bit. Antiseptic."

She felt him swab her face, her neck. Then he eased her left arm away from her body and ran his fingers gently along her inner arm from shoulder to elbow. She felt herself come alive under his touch. Surely he could feel the heat that suddenly began pulsing through her body. Now he was lifting her right arm, running his fingers gently and slowly over the tender skin with a touch as light as a breeze. When she winced he retraced the path of his touch, applying antiseptic.

As he loosened the belt at her waistline Lee felt the jersey wrap slip from her body as water might flow over flesh.

"Your poor beautiful robe," Burr soothed. "Your poor beautiful body."

Now he skimmed the saturated cotton over the top of her breasts. In her mind she arched her body to meet his. His touch, the cool antiseptic evaporating on her skin in the night air, both acted as aphrodisiacs blotting out pain. The fountain of molten gold brimmed inside her again, burning, shimmering.

Her stomach, her thighs, her calves. He touched her everywhere with the cool cotton and she wanted him never to stop. She begged him never to stop. She pleaded. But although the words sang through her mind she couldn't force them past her lips. Badly as she wanted to she couldn't make herself heard.

"I love you, Lee. Can you hear me? I love you. Tell me what you want me to do. Can you hear me?"

She could faintly hear him as if from somewhere far away. She was floating, in a hazy unreal place. Was her mind playing tricks on her, only hearing what she longed to hear? She could think of many things she wanted him to do for her and an equal number that she wanted to do for him, but the words were locked inside her. She wanted to speak, but she couldn't.

He kissed her again and she thought surely her body would dissolve. Where was she? What dimension of existence had she entered that allowed her to feel with such heightened awareness yet prohibited her from speaking? If only she were fully conscious!

His fingers were like satin against her skin as he eased her robe back into place, tied the sash at her waist. He was through. And she wanted him to do it all again. But he didn't, and now that his touching had stopped she realized that she hurt. Her head throbbed. Scrapes and abrasions burned like fire, and a black cloud was settling over her eyes. She tried to brush it away, but it was too heavy. She let it take her.

CHAPTER TWENTY

WHEN LEE OPENED HER EYES she was in her bed and Margo was sitting in the chair beside her reading *Vogue*. For a moment Lee closed her eyes and just lay there trying to remember what had happened. Burr was hovering in the cloudy depths of her thoughts. Why? Why was her head aching like this? Why was Margo here? She opened her eyes again and spoke.

"Margo?"

Margo laid her magazine aside and leaned forward. "Lee! Are you feeling better?"

"I feel terrible." Lee put her hand to her head and touched an egg-sized lump. "What happened to me? What time is it?"

"I guess you were out walking last night. Burr said you fell into one of the old cisterns. He heard your scream, found you, then fished you out. Dr. Haynes came and gave you a going-over, a checkup. No broken bones. No internal injuries. Just cuts and bruises and abrasions. You'll be stiff and sore, but you'll live."

Lee tried to sit up, but when the room began to whirl she relaxed back against her pillow.

"I'll get you some tea and toast, Lee. Maggie left

things in the kitchen and said to help myself to whatever you wanted when you came around.''

"Thank you, Margo. Some tea. With sugar. Maybe I can drink that.''

Margo left, and as Lee closed her eyes again memories of the previous night began to agitate her mind like flying fish sculling in the depths, breaking the surface for a moment, then disappearing again. Burr had rescued her. Burr had.... She felt herself blushing as memory returned and she recalled all the things Burr had done to her. And then she felt even more heat as she recalled all the things she had wished him to do. Or perhaps she had imagined the whole thing. She wished she could be sure. When Margo returned with the tea Lee tried to make discreet inquiries.

"Was Burr angry?" Lee asked. "I mean, I must have caused him a lot of trouble and bother.''

"Oh, I don't think you put him to too much bother. You know Burr. I was the one he ordered to get the doctor. I was the one who ran all the errands. Dr. Haynes was out for an evening jog and I had to hunt him down on the beach. It took a while.''

Lee concentrated on her tea. So she had been alone with Burr, alone with him for some time, if she could believe Margo's story. "Thank you for all you did, Margo. I'm sorry to have caused so much trouble, but I'm beginning to feel better already.''

"Burr left orders that you're not to report for work today no matter how well you say you feel.''

"And you? Did he give you the day off too?''

"I'm supposed to report to the bank as soon as you feel you don't need me any longer. We're going to begin setting up the exhibit. Guess we'll only get the cases ready today. Whitney is going to help with the placing of them.''

"I'm going to feel fine after this tea, Margo. You go ahead to the bank. I know there'll be a lot of work to be done. I'll get down there this afternoon if I get to feeling better."

Margo looked at her and shook her head. "It *is* afternoon, Lee. Late afternoon. Dr. Haynes gave you a sedative. Said you needed to rest. But if you're feeling okay now, I'll run on down to the bank. Can you stand?"

Lee set the teacup aside and swung her legs over the edge of the bed. Suddenly she realized she was in her nightgown. Who had dressed her?

"I did," Margo said, as if sensing her unasked question. "I got you into your gown and I threw your robe into the trash. It was ruined beyond help."

"You're sure?"

"Positive. You'd probably go into shock if you even saw it, it was so bloody."

Margo left when she felt sure Lee could get up and around on her own, and once Lee was on her feet she felt better and stronger. Margo hadn't been gone over two hours when Burr knocked on her door bringing a supper tray.

"You gave us a real scare, Lee. How are you feeling?"

"Much better," Lee replied, surprised at the calm in her voice despite the inner confusion that his sudden presence had aroused. "I'm sorry I was such a bother. I understand you fished me from a cistern."

"Yes. You had quite a fall. Do you remember anything about it? How did it happen?"

"I was going to pick some jasmine. I remember the chameleon running over my ankle. That's when I lost my balance, but after that...." She let her voice trail away, unable to tell Burr what she remembered or what she thought she remembered. Maybe it was just wishful thinking that made her remember that he had said "I love you" even when he thought she couldn't hear the words. Was Burr the sort who would lie to himself? She would like to think that in his own private thoughts he was honest with himself. And if he had said "I love you".... No. It was merely wishful thinking on her part. Maybe the blow to her head had triggered the erotic thoughts that she had translated into reality.

"I thought you might remember more than that." Burr gazed deep into her eyes.

"Was there more to remember?" She gazed back at him, her eyes equally direct.

"Sometimes the mind blots out the unpleasant," Burr said. "I'm glad you didn't see yourself, your robe."

"Margo said she threw the robe into the trash. I guess that's the proper place for it."

Burr sat with her while she ate her supper, then he took the tray and left. "He only did what anyone would have done." Raul's words the day of the terrifying encounter with the shark flashed through her mind. Did those words hold true for this experience, too? Had Burr done only what anyone would have done, or had he done all the very exceptional things she remembered him doing?

The following day Lee still was feeling stiff and sore, but her headache was gone and she was eager to get back to work. Raul and the other divers were at the *Sea Deuced*, but Burr and Margo were working at the bank when Lee joined them. The display cases were in place. The brine tank had been filled. Margo had cut out paper replicas of the treasure and placed them in the display cases so they could visualize how they would look as they arranged and rearranged them.

"I wish we could place the real items out right now," Lee said. "That's the only way we'll really be sure how the display will look."

"Security won't allow that," Burr replied. "This afternoon after the bank closes Roscoe will let us start arranging the displays."

Lee looked in each case, planning brief speeches about the history of the artifacts. She felt it was going to be a good exhibit. With herself to present artifact history and with Raul on scene to give accounts of the actual discovery, of how the treasure was brought up, they should hold their audience spellbound.

THE NEXT DAY Lee felt stronger as the day wore on. It was midafternoon when Raul appeared at the bank, wild-eyed and excited. Burr drew him into a private room before he allowed him to say a word, and Lee and Margo followed close behind.

"We need you and Lee at the dive boat," Raul blurted when the door closed and they were assured privacy. "The second dive team found a necklace and some sort of a gold pitcher without a handle."

"They didn't bring them up?" Lee asked.

"No. Relax. They tagged them, left them in place, turned off the deflectors. But they're important finds. I think they're artifacts you'll want in this exhibit."

"Then let's go out," Lee said. "I'll photograph them in place then we'll bring them in for cleaning and...."

"You aren't going to do any diving today," Burr said. "You're still weak from your accident. It would be foolish. I won't allow it."

"You'll be making a mistake if you don't include these finds in the exhibit," Raul insisted. "Come on, Lee. Don't you feel up to just a short dive?"

"No, she doesn't, and that's final." Burr glared at Raul.

Lee wanted to argue, yet she knew Burr was right. She had no business diving today no matter how short a time she would be down. It pleased her to know Burr was concerned with her well being. "Burr, I won't dive, but there's no reason you can't. Someone did my work all the time I was in Seville and I'm sure you supervised it. Why don't you get out there and have divers hold the grid in place while you take the photos? Then you can bring the stuff up."

"You wouldn't mind?" Burr asked.

"Of course I wouldn't mind. I'll just die at not being able to go down myself, but I won't keep you from going down. We need everything we can get for this exhibit. The more impressive the artifacts, the more investors you'll attract. Jump in the heli. Go on out and dive."

"I can't jump in the heli because it's being over-hauled. We'll have to take the speedboat."

"We?" Lee asked.

"Sure. You're coming along. Even if you can't dive I want you there to help analyze the finds we bring up."

"What about me?" Margo asked. "I'd like to go, too."

"No." Burr shook his head. "You and Raul stay here and keep working. Raul, you might go to the security room in the basement and see if you can clean any more crust off the muskets. Margo, you sort out the coins in order, so all we have to do is carry them upstairs and lay them in place. Is Harry around, Raul?"

"He's at the site. I came in alone. The speedboat's at the dock."

Once Burr had given the orders for the afternoon he and Lee left the bank. He made one stop on the way to the dock, picking up two box lunches and a cooler of ice.

"What's that for?" Lee asked. "There'll be food aboard the boat."

Burr grinned at her. "I want to have instant energy on hand in case you grow faint."

Burr took the helm, piloting them out to the *Sea Deuced*, and the air blowing from the Gulf Stream seemed to revive Lee. She felt stronger when they reached the diving boat than she had felt cooped up in the bank. The climb from the speedboat up the boarding ladder to the deck of the big boat taxed her strength, but she made it. She poured herself a cup of coffee in the galley as she waited for Burr to get into his diving gear and check the underwater camera. She finished the coffee in one last gulp when she saw him standing on the stern deck ready to plunge overboard.

One diver went into the water with him as Lee and the rest of the diving crew watched; then the sea looked as it had before, vast and undisturbed. Lee checked at what seemed like two-hour intervals, each time noting with surprise that only five minutes had passed. What could be taking so long? Sharks? Barracuda? The waiting divers murmured among themselves and Lee tried to relax, but she had to pace the deck and draw on deep reserves of willpower to keep from dragging on her own diving gear and going down in spite of Burr's orders and her own better judgment. Than at last Burr's head broke surface and he raised something in his left hand.

"What's he got?" a diver at her side asked. "Can you make out what it is, Lee?"

"Not from here, I can't. But I see a glint of gold." Her voice caught in her throat and her tongue felt like a blotter. Then the diver with Burr surfaced empty-handed. Lee felt some of her eagerness vanish. Raul had said there were two important finds. Maybe he had been mistaken. Burr swam to the side of the boat, then as a swell raised him high, he stretched his arm up and set a golden chalice on the stern deck. For a moment everyone just stared at it, then a diver lunged for it, held it overhead and started doing a war dance, jumping and yelling as if he had gone berserk.

"Gold! Gold! This is it! Gold! Well, all right!"

"Get Burr aboard," Lee shouted to another diver, and he rushed to lean over the stern and help heave Burr from the sea. Moments later he reached for the other diver and helped him aboard, too.

A golden chalice! Lee could hardly believe their luck. It was one of the best artifacts yet. Priceless. She could only wonder why it had been aboard the galleon. Perhaps some priest had carried it among his religious items. She helped Burr from his tank and mask and he was the only one aboard who wasn't literally shouting and jumping for joy. Lee had noticed in the past that the person who made a find was usually thrown into a state of semishock by the impact of the discovery. Burr was no exception. He wandered aimlessly around the deck, staring into the distance.

When some of the excitement died down, the second diver, who Lee thought had come up empty-handed, stepped forward. He had removed his tank and mask, but he still wore the top of the wet suit and his gloves.

"Okay, guys, look at this." He stood grinning but motionless until the other divers formed a semicircle around him, then he eased back the gauntlet of his diving glove and spilled a chain onto his other hand. Silence. Awed silence.

"What is it?" someone asked. "It's not a money chain like the others."

Lee stepped forward and picked the chain up, suspending it from her forefinger. A rosary! She felt tears well in her eyes as she examined the exquisite piece. Gold beads alternated with coral beads, all threaded onto a fine gold chain, and a slender golden cross dangled from the center, linked to the chain with a golden hook.

"A rosary." Lee whispered the words. "The most magnificent rosary I've ever seen." She offered the rosary to Burr for his inspection, and he studied it in speechless wonder.

"If only we knew these things came from the *Isabella*," he said at last.

"If only we could make that firm announcement at the exhibit," Lee said. "If only. If only. I don't suppose you've heard from Professor Hoskin."

"No. Not yet. We don't even have the second half of the microfilm yet. But let's be thankful for what we have. These two new pieces will have everyone in the keys talking about Dive Boys."

After the excitement died down Burr turned to Harry. "You'll stay aboard out here tonight, Harry. I'm leaving you in charge of the dive crew for the next couple of days. If anything big comes up, radio me at my office."

"Yes, sir."

"Lee, go to my office and get the canvas bag on my desk. We'll put this new loot in it for safekeeping."

Lee hurried to Burr's office while he finished giving orders to the dive crew. She found the bag on the desk, but something in the office seemed amiss. Lee paused, wondering. Then it struck her. The pictures of Zack were gone. All but one. A single framed portrait of his brother sat on Burr's desk....

"Lee! What's keeping you?" Burr called.

"Nothing at all." Lee turned and hurried from the office, wishing she dared ask about the pictures.

Harry helped Lee into the speedboat, then Burr started the engine and pointed the bow toward Key West. They had rushed out to the *Sea Deuced* at breakneck speed, but now Burr set a leisurely pace, as if all the excitement had exhausted him.

"This is my favorite time of day." Burr spoke at last as they glided over the water. "It's a relaxing time. The day's work has ended and it's too soon to begin thinking of the next day's work. Peace and plenty."

"I like early twilight, too," Lee said. "The sea is never lovelier than when the sun is sprinkling it with crimson hues. When I was a kid and our minister talked about the Red Sea, I always thought he meant Miami bay at sunset. That was the only Red Sea I could relate to."

Burr chuckled and smiled at her. "How are you feeling?"

"Fine. How could I feel any other way with the finds we've made today?"

"Are you hungry?"

"A little. Shall I open the lunches?"

"Not here."

"Why not here?"

"Because I'm a foodaholic. It's not safe for me to eat and drive." Burr revved the motor and they sliced across the waves toward an island in the distance, then when they reached it he circled it slowly.

"We're in luck," Burr said. "There's a sand beach

right here on the leeward side. We'll have a picnic lunch and a swim, which is a much less strenuous activity for you than diving. Or perhaps a swim and a picnic lunch would be a better order of activity."

"You forget I haven't a suit," Lee said. "But I'll settle for the picnic."

"I won't." Burr eased the boat into the shallows, then vaulted overboard, grabbed a bow line and pulled the craft up onto the sand.

"I'm not going skinny-dipping with you, Burr. You can forget that."

"Oh, I wouldn't expect you to do that." Leaning toward her, he took her hand to steady her as he helped her from the boat. As she walked higher onto the sand he opened a storage compartment that doubled as a boat seat and pulled out the red bikini.

"Burr! You planned this all along. You...."

"Are you angry?" Burr impaled her with his direct gaze. "Because if you don't want to swim with me, we'll head right back for Key West."

Lee felt herself flushing. How like him to put the decision on her. If Burr wasn't issuing orders he was demanding decisions. "I guess there's no harm in a swim before our picnic. But where will I change?"

Burr gave her the sardonic smile she knew so well. "I'll hide my eyes, Lee. I wouldn't want to embarrass you."

"You've no call to be so sarcastic."

"And you've no call to be so prudish. You know quite well I've seen it all before. Shall I elaborate? Miami...Seville...."

Suddenly Lee laughed because it was so much

easier to laugh than to pretend an indignation that she really didn't feel. She could have added Marvista to his listing, but she didn't. "All right, Burr. Touché! But I'm not going to hide myself in those mosquito-infested mangroves. Do turn your head so I won't feel quite so wanton."

"I like women who are a little bit wicked, a little bit wanton. Spare me from a prudish female." Burr grinned at her, but he turned his head while she undressed and slipped on the bikini. But all the time she was working with elastic, ties and buttons he was humming "The Stripper." Then when she was ready he began undressing, unbuttoning one shirt button at a time and revealing his hairy chest in a seductive, teasing way.

"See, I don't mind if you watch." He unbuckled his belt and let it drop to the sand, undid the button at the waist of his slacks.

"Burr!" Lee turned her head as she heard the whisk of his zipper, then when he spun her around to face him she saw he already had on his trimmed-down suit. It snugged to his body in a way that played up his sensuous leanness of thigh and hip and accentuated the broadness of his shoulders. Lee looked away, embarrassed to realize how frankly she had been staring.

"Don't be coy, Lee. I like a woman who likes my body." Burr grinned and took her hand and they waded slowly into the water. Lee felt the water coming up higher and higher, on her knees and thighs. Then, to cool off the sudden rush of heat that had coursed through her at Burr's touch and very nearness, she ducked under the surface, holding her breath as long as she could before she came up gasping for air.

She turned to float on her back, staring at the changing cloud formations. A wave slapped her in the face and she lifted her chin high, felt her breasts thrust through the surface. Then Burr's arms slid under the small of her back as he buoyed her on the waves. She thought he would kiss her, but he didn't. How often she had expected kisses from him that weren't forthcoming!

Instead of kissing her he turned on his side, pulled her to him until their bodies nestled like two spoons in a drawer, then he swam with a slow strong side-stroke. She relaxed against him as they glided through the water. She could feel his body hard against hers at the same time as she felt the sea slipping between them with a silvery sensuousness that was exquisitely intrusive. She could have gone on that way forever, nestled against him, protected by his great strength.

Then Burr turned on his back, pulling her on top of him, and she grabbed a deep breath as they sank beneath the waves and he kissed her into self-willed surrender. After his lips reluctantly released hers and they surfaced, he carried her from the water and onto the sand. For a few moments they just lay there resting lightly in each other's arms; then Burr pulled her closer to him, his hands defining the contours of her body until all she could think of was her very fundamental need. When his mouth found hers she offered no resistance at all, and just when she thought they might drown in the depth of the kiss Burr gently withdrew, a deep, low groan escaping from his lips.

"I love you, Lee," he murmured huskily, yet there was almost a wary note in his voice.

I love you. The words surged in her head and in her heart like the sea itself, invading the core of her being. Did he mean the words? Or did he merely think that she wanted to hear them before giving herself totally to him? Why should she punish herself by doubting? He had said the same words when he thought she couldn't hear him. Accept. Accept, she told herself. She desperately wanted to believe him. Afterward she never knew if she really did or not, but an echo of his words was suddenly torn from her.

"And I love you, Burr," she said quickly, the words of her heart sounding strange when spoken aloud for the first time. "I told you once before, but you couldn't hear me."

"When was that?" Burr asked in that same strange tone. He propped himself on his elbows and looked down at her. "You have never said those words to me before. I would have remembered."

"Oh, yes. I've said them before," she insisted, gaining confidence. "At Marvista. Under the moon. You undressed me and did wonderful things to me while you told me you loved me. And that's when I told you I loved you—in my mind. I was only half-conscious. I couldn't make my mind and my voice work together."

"You devil," Burr bit out fiercely as he abruptly sat up. "You knew everything that was going on that night, yet you played 'possum. You lay there like a rag doll letting me think. . . ."

"I was speaking to you with my mind, my body. I knew what was going on, but no matter how hard I tried I couldn't talk or move." Lee sat up now, leaning toward him in her earnestness, but a sick feeling was starting to wash through her.

"I don't believe you."

Lee inhaled deeply, feeling the nebulous love that was present between them only moments ago slipping away completely. What could she do to catch it, to save it from destruction? "What do you mean, you don't believe me? I can repeat to you your every motion. They're etched permanently in my brain as well as in my heart. And I loved every one of them. You kissed my eyes, my throat, my breasts. You called me darling. You undressed me...."

"You weren't very well dressed as I recall."

The flatness in Burr's voice frightened her and she tried again to evoke the warmth that had filled his tone earlier. "You untied that sash and let my robe skim from me, then you touched me, deliberately and slowly. You know how you touched me. Surely you can't have forgotten when I remember it so clearly."

"I was cleaning you up."

"And telling me you loved me all the time you were doing it."

"And you took advantage of me, played on my sympathy, pretended to be unconscious, when all the time...."

Suddenly Lee felt an anger surging through her with an intensity that all but overwhelmed her. "What do you want from me, Burr? What do you expect from me? I've told you that I love you, and surely you've known that for some time. I don't understand you. I thought you'd be pleased when I trusted you and trusted myself enough to say 'I love you.' "

"You thought I'd be pleased with a woman who plays tricks, a fickle woman who says I love you when she doesn't know her own mind!" His eyes narrowed.

Her longing for Burr and her anger merged into a deep, prickling sadness that was like a cactus thrusting roots to a great depth to find sustaining moisture. "How can you say that I don't know my own mind?"

"It's easy. Want to hear me say it again?" Burr's eyes were smoldering.

Lee rested her head on her knees, crushed by Burr's words. "No, I don't want to hear you say it again."

"I should guess you wouldn't. But how do you expect me to think you anything but fickle when I keep finding you with other men? First Raul. Then Julio Hunter. And who knows how many others!"

"But Raul's. . . ." Lee stopped midsentence.

"Raul's Margo's man now. Is that what you were going to say? That may be true, but it doesn't heal past wounds, does it?"

"I should have known you weren't to be trusted." Lee stood, glaring. "It must give you great macho satisfaction to have heard me say 'I love you'. You've trumped up this bit of anger to save yourself from getting seriously involved with me, haven't you? As they say, a good offense is a strong defense. Now you can go back to your redheaded Whitney, knowing that...knowing that...." Lee didn't even know how to finish her angry sentence.

"Why, Lee, I do believe you're jealous. Now you understand how it feels to think another person is where you'd like to be." Burr approached her so slowly she didn't even guess his intentions. She thought he was going to bypass her and get back into the speedboat, but when he came even with her, he turned, took her into his arms and brought his lips down on hers with such force she might have cried out had she not been so engrossed in pushing him from her. Then he released her as suddenly as he had taken her and she was pushing at air. There had been no love in his kiss, she realized, suddenly filled with remorse and humiliation at having been coerced into uttering her own senseless love for him.

She climbed back into the boat without his help and sat as far away from the wheel seat as she could. She eyed the picnic cooler with distaste, knowing she would never again feel like eating. Burr started the engine and she watched the angry froth spew out behind them as they cut through the sea toward Key West in a stony quiet the whole way.

CHAPTER TWENTY-ONE

LEE SAW RAUL pacing along the dock when they were still some distance from shore, and she used his presence as an excuse to break her angry silence. Furious as she was at Burr she hated the charged atmosphere between them; and she knew something would have to give if they ever were to manage to survive the next day's exhibit.

"Something must be wrong," Lee said. "Why do you suppose Raul's waiting for us?"

"He's carrying a newspaper." Burr scowled as he eased the speedboat into its mooring spot and waited for Lee to get out.

"Wait'll you see this!" Raul thumped the paper with his forefinger. "A bunch of lies...I hope."

"How about a hand up?" Lee asked, wanting Raul to help her so she could avoid Burr's touch.

Raul reached down for her hand and Lee grasped his, hoisting herself onto the dock. Burr handed up the cooler and Raul almost dropped it, its weight surprising him so.

"Hey! Didn't you even take time to eat? Or wasn't the food good or something?"

"Help yourself to it if you're hungry," Burr said.

"Lee seems to have lost her appetite. What's in the paper, Raul?"

Remembering the paper, Raul held it toward them. "Galleons Unlimited. They claim to have found a silver ingot that matches the weight of the ingots listed on the *Isabella*'s manifest."

Burr grabbed the paper and scanned the article. "Don't see anything about the serial numbers matching, though. Do you?"

"No," Raul said, "but it's just a matter of time. If those guys come up with an authentic find from the *Isabella*, our whole exhibit will have been for nothing."

"Of course it won't, Raul," Lee said. "People will still be interested in ancient Spanish artifacts no matter which salvage company they make rich."

"But they'll ruin the exhibit for Burr's practical purposes," Raul insisted. "Nobody's going to invest money with Dive Boys if Galleons Unlimited has absolute proof that they've found the *Isabella*."

"They're bluffing," Burr said. "This is pure bluff. It's the only thing they can do to confound our exhibit. They evidently haven't brought up enough artifacts to stage an exhibit of their own, so the next best thing they can do is to try to put down our exhibit."

Lee was so engrossed in reading the article, trying to hold the paper steady in the onshore breeze that Raul had to nudge her to get her to listen to him.

"I almost forgot to tell you, sis. There's some guy at Marvista who says he has to see you."

"*Sis?*" Burr's word sizzled between them. "*Sis?*"

Raul looked so crestfallen at his slip of the tongue

Lee felt sorry for him at the same time as she felt relieved. Here was one sham that could be discarded forever. "Raul's my brother, Burr. It's a long story and—"

"And I have plenty of time to listen," Burr said. "Start talking, Lee. Start at the beginning."

"Hiding our relationship was my idea, Burr," Raul spoke up. "Before mom died Lee promised her she'd sort of, well you know, sort of look after me. It was a crazy promise. I'm a grown man and I don't need to be looked after, but Lee was determined to keep that promise."

Lee leaned against a dock piling for much needed support and let Raul finish the tale. Of course he offered an apology, but Burr ended the conversation by giving them both an enigmatic look and no comment at all.

"All this won't make any difference in my job status, will it, Burr?" Raul asked. "I mean, I dive just as well as Raul Cameron as I do as Raul Johnson."

"That seems reasonable." Burr's voice held an even pitch, but there was no friendliness in his eyes and he didn't smile. What was he thinking? Lee held her breath waiting for an explosion that didn't come.

"I'll drive Lee out to Marvista to see this guy who's waiting for her," Raul said. "That way you can get on back to the bank. Margo and Whitney have already started bringing the loot up from the security room, and Mr. Murdock has his armed guards primed and ready."

"I'm in no hurry to get to the bank, Raul." Burr

handed Raul a small canvas bag containing the gold chalice and the rosary. "I'll take Lee to Marvista. And I'm putting you in charge of these new artifacts. You arrange for their display in a way that pleases you and if Margo or Whitney give you any flak tell them they'll have to answer to me."

"Yes, sir!"

Raul was so pleased with his new authority over the artifacts that Lee thought he might leap in the air and click his heels. Burr knew how to reward people.

"I can take a cab to Marvista," Lee said. "My caller is probably just a lawyer wanting to settle something about mom's estate."

"Or he could be someone else you've dragged on the scene to try to arouse my jealousy." Burr grinned at her knowingly. "You surely don't expect me to believe you weren't using Raul for that purpose."

"How dare you—"

"Spare me your wrath, Lee. Please spare me that."

"It was never my idea to pose as Raul's sister. Raul started that without consulting me."

"Methinks you protest too much. Let's think about your caller, Lee." Burr suddenly grew businesslike. "He could be a representative from Professor Hoskin at the university. We'll go together to see who he is. If that cannon number matches.... Lee, what a great thing that would be! The timing couldn't be better." Burr seemed to have forgotten his earlier anger in the face of learning of a report from Miami, and Lee hoped he wouldn't be disappointed.

When they reached Marvista there was a rental car parked in the driveway and nobody was in sight until Maggie appeared in the doorway.

"A gentleman's here to see you, Lee. I told him you were very busy, but he insisted on waiting. He's nursing a limeade in the courtyard."

Maggie held the screen open, and Lee stepped inside the house with Burr right on her heels. Would a business associate have waited here rather than at the bank? They crossed the foyer and the hallway, then stepped through the French doors into the courtyard. The man in the denim suit turned at the sound of their steps against the flagstones, but even before he turned Lee recognized his rangy build, his coppery hair.

"Julio!" Her knees threatened to bend like carrot curls. What was Julio doing here?

"Hello, Lee." Julio stood and devoured her with his eyes as if Burr weren't even present. He took both her hands in his, and at first Lee thought he was going to pull her to him and kiss her, but he didn't. He kept an arm's distance between them and just gazed at her as if he thought he might never get a chance to look at her again. As he lifted her hand and gently kissed her fingers Burr cleared his throat. The sound galvanized Lee into action.

"Julio! How good to see you again. You remember Burr Adburee?" Lee held her breath, uncertain for a moment whether or not Burr would be civil to Julio. Julio offered his hand and Burr shook it. The calm before the storm, she wondered. Then she sighed. Why did she think Burr would be upset if

Julio called on her? His recent anger over trivial and trumped-up matters proved to her he cared nothing for her. Perhaps to Burr the only upsetting thing about Julio's sudden appearance would be over his delay in getting back to Whitney at the bank.

"Good to see you again, Burr." Julio turned and picked up a package from the umbrella table. "The archivist in Seville was getting ready to mail this microfilm to you, but since I was coming here anyway I told her I'd drop it off personally."

"I appreciate it, Hunter." Burr accepted the package. "Appreciate it very much."

"Since I was coming anyway...." The words roared in Lee's ears. Julio hadn't come just to bring the microfilm. Perhaps Claudia.... "How is Claudia?" Lee asked. "Where is she? Has she gone on an errand?"

"Claudia's in Seville," Julio replied coolly. Then he turned to Burr. "If you'll excuse Lee and me, we have some things to discuss."

Lee thought Burr was going to refuse or to ask them to hold their discussion elsewhere, but he nodded. "Of course. I'll be getting on back to the bank. I'll expect you there within the hour, Lee. We need your help."

"Of course." Lee said nothing more, but merely stood looking at the exit until Burr turned and left them alone. Then she sat down across the table from Julio.

"What brings you to Florida, Julio?"

"You."

When Lee said nothing, he continued. "I'm in love

with you, Lee. I'm sorry I lost my cool that last night in Seville. And I've regretted ever since that I didn't go to the airport that afternoon and forbid you to leave Spain, forbid you to leave me. But spouting orders has never been my style.''

"I rather expected you to have come to see me off at least. I'm sure that my telling Claudia of my departure time made it rather obvious to you.'' Lee felt her heart pounding. The moon was rising now and its glow highlighted Julio's coppery hair and his fine features as it might have highlighted a finely carved cameo. *Moonlight becomes you,* she thought. Was that a song title she remembered from somewhere?

"I've come to ask you to go back to Seville with me.''

"For what purpose?''

"As my wife, of course. I love you, Lee. Surely you've known that all along. It was love at first sight.''

I'm getting a second chance, she thought. *Few people are so lucky. Yet I'm not ready to accept that chance.* "Florida is my home, Julio. America. I belong in America, not in Spain. I thought I had made that clear to you.'' What if he offered to remain here? What then?

Julio rose and walked around the table to her. Cupping her chin in both his hands he leaned down and kissed her slowly, lingeringly. The position of her chair kept her from backing away from his kiss, and although his hands coaxed at her chin, she felt no desire to lessen the distance between them. She felt no throbbing at her temples, her throat. She felt nothing.

"You see how it could be between us, don't you?" Julio looked earnestly into her eyes for a moment, then he sat back down across from her. Lee searched for words to express her thoughts without hurting him, but no words came.

"We'll build that little villa in the Spanish country-side, Lee. Near Seville. I'll find work in my field. I wouldn't take you away from Andalusia, rest assured of that."

It was as if he hadn't heard what she had said about leaving America. Suddenly Julio's character and personality came into sharp focus for her. He was kind. He was sweet. Some woman would find him lovable as long as she wanted the same things he wanted. For Julio would give the woman of his choice whatever it was *he* wanted. And he would think he had acted from love because he very much wanted to be loved.

Perhaps that was the trouble with the whole world, Lee thought. Everyone wanted to be loved rather than to love. And some people wanted it more than others. But she respected Julio for one thing—he wanted only her to love him, and he would get over that once he found it was impossible. But Burr! Burr wanted to be loved by her and by Margo and by Whitney and by heaven knows how many others.

"It can't be, Julio," Lee said gently. "You'll always be my friend. You'll always be one of my favorite people. But it wouldn't be fair to either of us for me to marry you because I don't feel a passionate desire to be your wife."

In the distance the sea lapped the shore for some time before Julio spoke. "No, I guess you really don't, do you?" Julio leaned back and his jaw went slack. His expression told Lee that the reality of her words had come to him as a complete shock. "If you had a passionate desire to become my wife, continents and oceans would make no difference at all to you. You would be eager to go where I asked you to go."

"Perhaps. Perhaps."

Julio stood, with the moonlight glowing on him like silver fire, and left without kissing her farewell. And she watched him go with regret yet with a sense of rightness. But his words still echoed in her mind. "If you had a passionate desire to become my wife, continents and oceans would make no difference to you." Was that a true criterion for love? She wondered if Burr had asked her to marry him and live in Seville what her answer would have been. She suspected that she would have started packing immediately. And that's what she did as soon as she entered her suite. And she was still packing when Margo rapped on her door about midnight.

"We expected you at the bank, Lee."

"I'm sorry. I couldn't make it."

"You're packing?"

"Yes."

"You're not going to let Burr down on the eve of this big exhibit, are you?"

"Of course not, Margo. I'll see my part of the exhibit through before I leave."

"Raul told me that you're his sister, Lee. That

changes a lot of things between us. You're not really a bad kid, you know. Now if you'd just shape up and...."

Suddenly Margo's bossiness got to Lee. "Out, Margo. Out. We'll talk in the morning. Right now I've got to get some rest."

Lee lay in bed staring at the ceiling long after Margo left, thinking how wrong she was for Raul. Margo would henpeck a man in no time at all. Raul deserved better than that. Then she thought about Julio. She knew she had done the right thing in turning Julio away, but in doing so had she sentenced herself to a lifetime of carrying a torch for Burr? She hated to give up her job, but there was nothing for her to do but leave Key West. She couldn't bear to work for Burr, feeling about him the way she did and knowing that he didn't return her love, knowing she was merely one of many. Some women might be able to marry a man knowing he was a potential philanderer, but Lee was not one of that group. If she ever married it would be for keeps and she would expect the same fidelity from the man she married. She buried her head under her pillow and fell asleep itemizing the things about Burr that she absolutely couldn't stand.

Arrogant... conceited... cruel. A womanizer....

CHAPTER TWENTY-TWO

WHEN LEE REACHED THE BANK the next morning she had to steel herself to perform her duties at the exhibit. She had shampooed her hair and blow-dried it into a shimmering cap before dressing carefully in a pale blue sheath. And she had applied enough make-up to hide the dark circles under her eyes. At least she hoped they were hidden.

See Ancient Spanish Treasure. Lee studied the sign posted at the corner of the bank. The words were splashed in gold against a sea-green background. Whitney's work, she guessed, since Whitney was the artist. Lee had arrived long before the exhibit was scheduled to open, but a crowd was already milling around the bank door and there were enough uniformed security men in the area to give the place the look of a military camp.

"Good morning, Lee." Burr spoke to her distantly but politely as she entered the exhibit foyer.

"Good morning." Lee looked away from Burr immediately. Time enough later to give him her resignation. She would see the exhibit through to its conclusion, then she would confront Burr with her decision. She pulled her notes from her shoulder bag and reviewed them briefly. She had her short speeches well in mind and she was thankful for them. They would require her to concentrate on something other than the message she must deliver to Burr at the end of the day.

At nine o'clock Roscoe Murdock bulled his way through the crowd outside, opened the doors and asked people to form a single file as they entered the bank. Lee had expected noise and confusion; but instead there was an awed silence as people studied the pieces of eight, the gold chains, the muskets. Then the questions started and Lee fixed a smile on her face as she tried to answer them.

"Yes, the ancient Spaniards did try to salvage treasure from the galleons at the time of their sinking. They kept provisioned salvage vessels in Havana that could reach a wreck site in the keys in nine days. They enslaved pearl divers who could dive to depths of a hundred and fifty feet. . . .

"Yes, the Spaniards knew the reefs were dangerous, but they used the keys as their navigational guideposts. They feared the unknown dangers of the open sea more than they feared the known dangers of the reefs. . . .

"Yes, sir. The round mark on the gold bar is the tax stamp. It showed that the king had received his fifth. Gold without stamps was considered contraband."

And so it went for the whole morning. Lee's throat felt like sandpaper from so much talking and she welcomed Raul's invitation to lunch.

"Where shall we go?" he asked.

"To the other end of the island," Lee said. "Somewhere where it's quiet."

Raul took her to a Greek café that specialized in shrimp, and once they had given the waitress their order, Raul pulled a small box from his pocket, snapped it open, and showed it to Lee. "It's for Margo," he said briefly.

"An engagement ring! Raul! Are you sure?"

"Of course I'm sure, Lee. I've been sure for a long time. We're going to be married in just a few months. Her family's high society, and her mom wants to plan a big affair. Margo hasn't seen the ring yet. I'm giving it to her tonight."

Lee squelched her fears, her true feelings. "I'm glad you're so happy, Raul. I wish you all the best. Margo is a...a beautiful girl." Lee could hardly finish her lunch because Raul's announcement had upset her so. Surely Burr would fire Raul on the spot when he saw Margo actually wearing Raul's ring. It was one thing to know Margo and Raul were dating, but it was quite another thing to know they were actually engaged.

"The exhibit's going well, I think," Raul said.

"Yes, people seem really excited about it." Lee had thought she would tell Raul she was leaving Key West before she told Burr, but now hardly seemed the time. He was so buoyed up over his news about his engagement that she didn't have the heart to say anything that would cast a pall.

They drove back to the bank and Lee knew the moment they entered the building that something had happened. A robbery? Her lunch rose and clumped in her throat.

"I wonder what's up," Raul said.

"Maybe someone tried to steal something. The crowd's going wild."

"Yeah, but the cops aren't. If there had been a theft the cops wouldn't just be standing there. They'd be trying to bust someone."

Lee relaxed a bit as she knew Raul's words made sense. When at last they were able to shove their way through the crowd and get back to their stations at the exhibit, Lee saw that Burr had dragged a small oak table to the center of the foyer and that he was getting ready to step up on it. The security guards were trying to hold the crowd behind the single-file ropes that formed the spectator aisles as they surged forward trying to see and hear Burr. Burr held his hands up for silence.

"I have an important announcement to make."

It was several moments before the crowd quieted down enough for Burr to be heard. Then he cleared his throat and smiled triumphantly as he began to speak.

"I have good news," Burr said. "Exciting news. Dive Boys, Inc. now has scholarly proof that the treasure you'll see here came from the ancient Spanish galleon, the *Santa Isabella*." Burr jabbed his forefinger at a telegram in his hand, then he waved the message above his head as if everyone could see the words. Even before he had finished giving the details of the authentication, Whitney Deleveau appeared with a new sign to place in front of the bank. This sign read: See Authentic *Santa Isabella* Treasure. She was a quick worker in more ways than one, Lee thought. Then she was ashamed of having such negative feelings when the very thing she had been working for, had been hoping for, had materialized. Dive Boys had discovered treasure from the *Santa Isabella*. They had proof!

Raul rushed to Lee and swept her off her feet, kissed her and set her back on her feet again, then pushed across the foyer to Margo and repeated his actions. When Burr stopped speaking the security guards went into action diplomatically quieting the crowd until people were entering the doorway and passing before the exhibits in an orderly fashion. Burr made his way to Lee.

"I have you to thank for this message from Professor Hoskin, Lee." Burr tapped the telegram with his forefinger again, then folded it and slipped it into his shirt pocket. "But not here. Not now. I want to see you when the exhibit closes."

Another order. Lee nodded without speaking. She had planned to seek Burr out after the exhibit closed, but not for the reason he had mentioned. All afternoon her mind churned with so many thoughts she could hardly organize her words and answer the questions people were asking her.

"Yes. Sometimes the galleons did carry indigo dye. It was an excellent place for secreting contraband because it was messy stuff and none of the Spanish officials liked to search it thoroughly.

"Most of the pieces of eight came from the Potosi mines, sir.

"Yes, we've had some close encounters with sharks, ma'am." Lee shuddered as she remembered.

Somehow the day ended. Every few minutes Burr

stood on the oak table and repeated his announcement about the authenticity of the treasure. It was almost as if he couldn't believe the words unless he kept hearing them spoken aloud. When at last the crowd had left and the exhibit had ended, they carried the artifacts back to the security room, checked them in carefully, then left the bank. Success. The exhibit couldn't have been more successful.

Raul and Margo strolled away arm in arm. For a while Lee thought Whitney Deleveau had disappeared, then she saw Roscoe Murdock helping her into his car.

"Lee!" Burr called out then caught up with her. "Lee, how can I ever thank you? If it hadn't been for your research, your connection with Professor Hoskin. . . . Come on!" He took her arm. "We're going to celebrate."

Lee could hardly believe the change that had come over Burr. He seemed to have forgotten his anger, their past differences, as he smiled at her. But she couldn't let him take her out anywhere. She stopped right in the middle of the sidewalk and said the words she had been planning since the night before.

"I'm leaving Dive Boys, Burr. Now. This evening. I've moved out of Marvistsa and I'll drive to Miami tonight."

"What are you talking about?" Burr grabbed her arm and forced her to face him.

"Just what I said. I'm leaving. Tonight."

"You can't."

"Just watch me." She pulled free of his grip.

"What about the two-week-notice rule? You have to give me two weeks' notice."

"Why should I make us both miserable for two more weeks?" Lee scowled. "I'm going. Right now."

"Are you going with Julio?"

"No."

"Lee! You'll give me a chance to talk to you...or else. I think I deserve that much consideration."

To Lee's surprise there was no smoldering fire in Burr's eyes, no white line around his mouth. He was still issuing orders, but he was right. Surely he deserved a final word with her if that's what he wanted.

"All right, Burr. We can talk for a few minutes, but that's all. And nothing you can say will change my mind about leaving. Where shall we go?"

"Someplace private. Someplace where we can be alone and undisturbed."

Lee nodded in agreement. She had steeled herself for this moment of truth, and of course they had to be alone. Again she was surprised when Burr drove to Marvista.

"The beach here is about the most private place we'll find," Burr said. "Do you want to change into more comfortable shoes?" He eyed her high-heeled sandals.

"Everything's packed in my car back at the bank lot."

Burr caught his breath in a half gasp, and Lee thought he looked less sure of himself than she had ever seen him. Tonight when he had the world by its tail he was hesitant.

They walked through the house, the courtyard and to the beach. Lee felt sand gritting inside her sandals, but that discomfort was mild compared to the discomfort of the thoughts gritting in her mind. Burr took her arm and she felt as if it were melting, but she kept walking. He led her to a sea-grape tree and pulled her down onto the sand beside himself.

"I love you, Lee."

"Oh, everyone's in love these days," Lee said sarcastically, thinking of how many times Burr had said those meaningless words to her, wondering how many times he had said them to other women. Why must he keep tormenting her like this? Her heart was being wrenched apart—she wanted so much for his love to be more than an empty illusion. "I suppose you know Raul is giving Margo a ring," she finally said to break the charged silence.

"Yes, I know."

Lee looked at him sharply. "You *do*? You know and you don't care?"

"I've been trying to tell you for some time that Raul and Margo are a twosome. You never seemed to hear me, to understand me. And yes, I do care because I want them to be happy. I'm very fond of Margo. We've had some good times together, but I've never loved her. In some ways I consider Raul a real blessing in disguise. I didn't want to hurt Margo, and now that she and Raul have found each other there is no longer any danger of my hurting her."

Lee hesitated, hardly able to believe that Burr had not been in love with Margo as Margo had tried to make her think. "But Margo's not right for Raul,

Burr. She's opinionated. She's bossy. And she always has to run the whole show. I'm surprised you've put up with her as a business manager as long as you have.''

Burr chuckled. "There are some parts of my life that I prefer to have bossed, then there are other parts of my life that I prefer to control."

"Margo will make Raul miserable."

"I really don't believe so, Lee. Think about it. I know Raul's your brother and sometimes it's hard to see those you love objectively. But no matter what you prefer to think, Raul is basically a weak person. He's a follower."

"He's loving and he's kind and he's...a hard worker now, and—"

"He's those things, too, but he's also weak. Margo loves to boss any operation. She'll be perfect for Raul. She loves him and she'll give him the strong guidance in the right direction that he needs."

"Maybe. I'm not at all sure."

"I didn't bring you here to solve Raul's problems, Lee. Let's get back to the basics. I love you. What are you going to say to that?"

"I don't believe you. You're using those three words as bait. For months I've seen your name linked with names of many women. There was Margo. There is Whitney. I don't want to be a part of your...harem, Burr."

Burr pulled a slip of paper from his shirt pocket and showed it to Lee. "Twenty-thousand dollars, Lee. This is a check for twenty thousand with Whitney Deleveau's signature on the line where it counts.

That's absolutely all Whitney means to me. She's a valued investor in Dive Boys. And you helped make this check possible."

"I had nothing to do with that check. I never saw it before in my life."

"You made it possible by identifying the *Isabella* manifest. I thought I could persuade Whitney to invest in my company by showing her the treasure, by letting her be a part of the exhibit. But it wasn't until she learned that the artifacts were really from the *Isabella* that she wrote the check. Now forget Margo. Forget Whitney. Think about us. I love you and only you and I want to know what you're going to do about it."

"I'm going to leave Key West this evening, Burr. My mind's made up." Lee was surprised that her voice was so strong when she felt so weak inside. Could it be that he loved only her?

Burr pulled her to him and kissed her, and as she felt his lips warm and demanding on hers, she relented outwardly for a moment, but somewhere she found the strength to push him away.

"I can't approve of a moneygrubber, Burr, a man who sees nothing in the salvage of a galleon except an aggrandizement of his own fortune. The artifacts mean nothing but dollar signs to you. You underpay your divers and—"

Burr stopped her words with his lips, but when Lee quit struggling against him and felt her body uncontrollably melt into his, he was the one who pushed away. She was furious at herself for her display of weakness.

"That's more like it, Lee." For just a moment the sardonic smile played on his lips, then he grew serious. "There are a few things about me that you don't know."

"I'm sure that's the truth." Lee would have fled, but Burr retained a firm grip on her wrist that held her immobile.

"For starters, I want you to realize that I am paying the divers a fair wage."

"Since when?"

"Since the day I mistakenly accused Raul of stealing the gold chain, since the day Margo told me Raul had opened a savings account and was working toward a long-range goal. It's a long story, Lee. A painful story. Will you listen?"

It wasn't an order. It was a question.

"Yes, of course I'll listen."

Burr released her wrist and she sat quietly at his side. "I know you must have wondered about Zack."

"I've wondered about him ever since I saw all those pictures of him in your office. Margo hinted that he committed suicide. Of course I was curious. Of course I wondered why."

"Zack was a good boy, Lee, a fine person. He fell in love with a girl who jilted him. He learned the hard way that a person can't order love. I've never seen anyone so put down by a woman. But instead of letting his wounds heal, instead of finding another girl, Zack started running with a bad crowd. Drifters. Holdovers of the hippie days. Florida is where the land runs out and Key West is the bottom line. Drifters end up here with no place else to go."

"Florida is where the land *begins* for some people," Lee said, suddenly thinking of the thousands of Cubans who had come to Florida shores seeking a new life. But her interest was caught, and she studied the dark, well-loved features of Burr intently as he went on in his deep compelling voice.

"The drifters Zack got caught up with were heavily into drugs. One night someone gave Zack an overdose. Some of his pals said he just waded into the sea, swam off toward the horizon. Zack never returned."

Lee reached to touch Burr's hand, to cover it with her own. "I'm sorry, Burr. Truly I am."

"Zack and I had been very close," Burr said quietly. "I lost my head. I couldn't treat any drifters rationally after that."

"So you hired them at substandard wages, practically making slaves of them. You dived at them with your helicopter just for fun and games. You were out for revenge." Lee couldn't help releasing the accusations that had been pent up inside her for so long.

"It's not a pretty picture, I'll admit. I thought that by hiring drifters to dive for me they'd get so hooked on treasure hunting they'd stick with me no matter what their salary. And on what I paid I figured they couldn't afford a drug habit. In addition to that I wanted to bust any boy I caught with drugs so he couldn't hook others on the habit."

"You wanted to play God." Lee gave a bitter laugh, wishing she had the will to stand and leave.

"You don't understand, Lee. Those boys in the skiff, for instance. Do you know what they were doing?"

"Fishing. Three boys out for a fishing jaunt."

"They *weren't* fishing. Do you recall seeing any fishing tackle aboard that skiff?"

"I don't remember. I just...assumed they were fishing."

"You assumed wrong. They were hunting marijuana. Sometimes boats smuggling a load of grass up from Colombia have to jettison their cargo if the coast guard gets on their tails. And those jettisoned bales of hemp sometimes float until they catch in a tangle of mangrove roots on some uninhabited key. Kids go out hunting for the stuff. They pick up those bales, sell them to a pusher who in turn dries the stuff out and eventually sells it on the street to people like...Zack and his ill-chosen friends."

Lee sat silently for many moments thinking over what Burr had told her. "I'm sorry, Burr. I didn't realize...."

"I've changed my outlook and my ways, Lee. Please believe that. The desire for revenge is an ugly thing and I'm ashamed of the hold it had on me. But now I've seen Raul's work aboard the *Sea Deuced* change him from a drifter into a man with a goal. I misjudged him completely. I thought he was a pusher and I did everything I could do to put him down, but when Margo confessed to the theft of the chain, the thought of my accusation of Raul sickened me. It jolted me, made me take a hard look at myself. I wanted to do something to atone for my mistake. So I'm trying to turn my hate for the type of drifters who led Zack to his death into positive feelings followed by positive actions."

"So now you're going to be the benefactor of society." Again Lee let sarcasm fill her voice.

"No. I'll try to avoid that. I've merely raised the divers' wages and I've changed my attitude toward them. I saw treasure-diving alter Raul from a drifter into a man with a purpose. I know all drifters won't turn into men, of course. Some will continue to drift. But I'm going to give them a fair chance. The ones with grit will learn respect for tired muscles, respect for the sea, respect for themselves. And that respect can open a door to a new life for them."

Lee suddenly realized how hastily she had judged him without knowing all the facts. "I admire you for that, Burr, and I'm sorry I was sarcastic. I noticed the changed appearance of your office yesterday. It was no longer a. . .a shrine to Zack. I didn't understand the significance of the change then, but now. . . ."

"Now?"

She drew a deep breath. "Now I believe you're sincere in wanting to give the drifters a chance to change the direction of their lives. You make me proud of you, Burr." They sat quietly for a moment while Lee thought about what Burr had just told her.

"I'd like to see you stay with Dive Boys, Lee. I'd like to see you write and publish a monograph on the *Santa Isabella*. The treasure means more to me than you think, Lee. We've argued a lot about how those gold chains should be displayed. Have you ever wondered why I wanted them left in a heap?"

"Yes, I've wondered. Why is that?"

"Because I never want to forget that those chains

at one time may have nestled in the pocket of someone like me, that they belonged to human beings who had hopes and dreams just as I have. This treasure does speak to me across the centuries, Lee. We'll find the *Isabella*'s hull eventually. I don't intend to give up.'' He looked at her intently with his dark, fiery amber eyes. ''And I'd like you to share that triumph with me as my wife.''

His words seemed to echo in the still air. Lee could hardly believe Burr was actually asking her to marry him. Surely that was proof that he truly loved her, that he had loved her all along. All that Burr had just told her about himself was playing havoc with her emotions. She needed time to think, to sort it all out.... She hesitated so long in replying that he spoke again.

''Lee, what do you want from life? What do you really value?''

Again Burr's smoky gaze held her captive. She hesitated, then she replied. ''I value love, family life above all else, then my job.''

Burr covered her hands with his, then entwined his fingers with her own, the simple gesture stirringly intimate. ''I thought you might say that. I value those same things, too. But there is one thing you seem to have overlooked.''

''And what is that?''

''You've overlooked the fact that love must precede family life. At least it must for me.'' Now Burr put his arm around her and looked deeply into her eyes. ''I love you, Lee. I've been telling you that for days. It seems I've felt it ever since I've known you. Now will you tell me what you want me to do?''

"Will you tell me what you want me to do?" They were familiar words, words Burr had used every time he had tried to make love to her. In the past she thought he had used them to tantalize her, to arouse her passion to the point of no return. But now she heard the words for what they were, an honest question. Burr wanted to love her. The words seemed simple as she thought about them, yet they were profound. Julio had wanted to be loved by her, but Burr wanted to love her. Now for the first time she could answer the question truthfully.

"I want you to love me, Burr. That's what I want you to do," she said in a clear voice. "And I want to love you in return." Her pent-up yearning for him was suddenly released and her shining, joyful eyes met his. All uncertainties vanished.

His arms encircled her fiercely, pulling her against him, so that she was acutely aware of the pounding of his heart, his fresh male scent, his breath warm upon her neck, made all the more precious because he was the man she loved, the man she knew loved her. The absolute rightness of it all filled her.

"I hate to think of all the time we wasted being at odds with each other," she finally murmured after a beautiful eternity had passed being held close to him.

"And I was a fool to send you to Seville," he whispered into her hair in a low throaty voice that sent tingles dancing along her spine.

"Maybe not. You know the old line about absence making the heart grow fonder," she teased playfully as she snuggled more deeply into him, resting her head against his firm shoulders. As his lean, powerful frame molded itself into her own curves, she felt she was going to burst with the intensity of her soaring happiness and the knowledge that this was where she truly belonged.

"Will you ever forgive me for acting so boorishly on our picnic the other day?" Burr said at last. "I should have listened to you, to your simple words of love, but I didn't. Jealousy will do strange things to a man's reason," he added apologetically as he drew back to gaze lovingly into her eyes.

"And a woman's," Lee acknowledged, remembering her own reaction to Margo, and later, Whitney. "You realize who Raul is now, my love, but you should also know that I never felt anything like this for Julio," she said softly, as she tried to tell him so with her eyes.

"I believe you, Lee," he murmured before dipping his head toward her once more.

As moonlight turned the palms into shadow dancers flickering new poses on the sand, Burr kissed her eyelids, her cheeks. Then his lips claimed hers until there was no resistance left in her. His hands worked their magic on her body till she was totally his. And as the waves whispered sea secrets to the sky she knew she had found the greatest treasure of all.

What readers say
about SUPERROMANCE

"Bravo! Your SUPERROMANCE was super!"
R.V.,* Montgomery, Illinois

"I am impatiently awaiting
the next SUPERROMANCE."
J.D., Sandusky, Ohio

"*Love's Emerald Flame* is one
of the best novels you have published."
A.B., Oregon City, Oregon

"Delightful...great."
C.B., Fort Wayne, Indiana

SUPERROMANCE

Longer, exciting, sensual and dramatic!

Fascinating love stories that will hold
you in their magical spell till the last page
is turned!

Now's your chance to discover the earlier
books in this exciting series. Choose from
the great selection on the following page!